GREEN MATRIX

BY BENOIT CHARTIER

Trode Publications
www.trode.ca

Ordering Information:
Quantity sales. Special discounts are available on quantity
purchases by corporations, associations, and others. For details,
contact the publisher at the address above. Orders by US and
Canadian trade bookstores and wholesalers. Please contact Trode
Publications at www.trode.ca

Printed in Canada
ISBN 978-1-989550-05-2
First Edition

This book is dedicated to the millions of people who are finally coming out of this pandemic period, one of the harshest in the past century. It is also dedicated to those who did not.

The author would like to thank his friend Ayo Gutierrez for her kind help and infinite patience in answering questions about certain aspects of Filipino culture. Hopefully the final product will be something that will do it justice.

Other Works by Benoit Chartier

Afterdeath
The Booger Hunter's Apprentice
The Calumnist Malefesto and Other Improbable Yarns
Universal Wisdom

In this series
Red Nexus
Blue Node
Green Matrix
Forthcoming: Yellow Core

GREEN MATRIX

TRODE
PUBLICATIONS

THE DAILY GRIND

SECTOR 14, 7:30 AM

Datu Salazar woke, a lazy smile slowly stretching across his features. The smells from the kitchen and the morning hubbub always put him right. Tala was already up and organizing the day. His night had ended late on the Heap floor. A new area discovered with plenty of scrap to lift, and worker shortage meant working a double shift at the sticks of the digger.

He wondered if he was imagining things, but it felt as if there were less and less scrappers down there with him. Of course, accidental deaths on the site accounted for quite a few of the shortfalls, but he had a feeling there was more to it than that.

Long, hard hours took him away from family, but the price of rent and air filters kept climbing, and his paycheque didn't. He'd have spent his days with them, if he could have. He sighed and got up, rubbing his eyes.

He put a hand on one of the yellowing plastic modular walls as he left the bedroom and wondered if it still had the capacity to shift, before having his thoughts interrupted.

"Morning dad!" his daughter said. Benilda was eight, and helped her mother around the house whenever she could. He thought that every day that went by, she looked more and more like her. It was her piercing brown eyes, and her particular way of smiling, as if she knew something no one else did. Datu thought about the fact that he'd have to pull her out of school soon to put her to work. There was a recycler's shop down the way looking for kids with keen eyes for valuables. No point in keeping her at the State-run school, since there was little chance she would ever leave the Sector anyhow.

"Morning, anak!" he replied, on his way to the washroom. A small figure ran by his legs. Ramil was only two, but had run the length of their little conapt a million times. Datu would have been surprised if he didn't become a marathon runner when he was a teenager. He ruffled the little boy's hair as he whizzed by again, a racing hovercar toy in his hands, imitating the sound of the buzzing engines. Just one of the many illicit treasures Datu had found down in the Heap, squirreled away in his pack, disinfected and given to his family.

Admin didn't like their recyclers to bring souvenirs back from the garbage piles, but there were objects which were more illegal than others. Toys and small, esoteric keepsakes were much more "grey area" than proscribed data or books.

He passed a closed door down the slim corridor, where heavy music pounded against the door, and he knocked hard. The music turned off.

"What?" came an irritated voice through the door. Gabriel was going through the throes of sixteen, and that age weighed heavily on his shoulders, just like his family and imprisonment in the tiny space they shared did. Datu placed his hand on the door frame and unclenched his teeth.

"Morning, Gabe," he said, in an even voice.

No answer came, and after a few moments, the music began slamming against the door again as a form of protest.

As much as it irked Datu, he knew what his eldest was going through. He'd been the same when he was his age. It did little to improve his own mood about his son's behaviour.

At the end of the hallway, he took the right door, and scanned his forearm on the wall-plate. The woman's voice told him that ten credits had been subtracted, and that he had three minutes of water. He stepped out of his pyjamas and into the activated shower stall, rapidly rubbing his sore body with the all-in-one powdered body soap, as the shower sent him a meagre spray to rinse it off. He stepped out, and the hot air fan half-dried him off.

A blur ran past him once again as he headed back to the master bedroom, and he rolled his eyes. *Where did he get that kind of energy*, he wondered.

He recalled a scrapper flouting a piece of literature they'd discovered in some sealed-off apartment block. As soon as the local Administration Site Manager had heard about it, the man had been called up, and Datu had never seen him again. There were things which were best not to mess around with.

Those items, however, were usually harder to find, and locked away in places where no recycler had access.

There were well-defined areas scrapper teams were meant to investigate and dig. Admin kept all the old maps, and knew exactly where to avoid.

Wouldn't want the little people to get too wise, thought Datu, a smirk lifting the corner of his lip.

"What's that smile, Datu Salazar? If I didn't know better, I'd think you were thinking naughty thoughts," his wife Tala said from the kitchen, where the smell of rehydrated eggs and soy paste wafted from the stove, making Datu's mouth water.

"With you around, how can I help it, pangga?" Datu said, smiling widely, his previous thoughts evaporating at her sight. Tala was the love of his life. She was only two years younger than he, and they'd met at church when Datu's life had taken a turn. Even then, Datu knew he wanted this woman as his wife. He kissed her tenderly and set the table.

He looked into the living room, where Benilda was doing homework and occasionally peered at the viewscreen which pulled double-duty as their front window. Old and glitchy, the summer scenes that played as screen savers were often marred with horizontal lines that latched onto the previous video. A striated smattering of dead pixels vied for control like colourful static snow, juxtaposed images at odds with each other. At the moment she listened to recorded course notes. Datu thought how much he'd love to change it if he could, as he sipped on his hot caffeine drink.

When Tala called for breakfast, everyone came and sat around the tiny table in the kitchen. Datu put out his hands, and all held each others', Gabriel grudgingly taking his little brother and sister's. Ramil held Gabriel's palm with his thumb and forefinger jokingly, and Datu gave him a stern look. The little boy stopped giggling and held his older sibling's hand properly. They lowered their heads all, save Datu, who intoned, "Let us thank the Ayo for the food on our table, the job I am able to perform, and the health of our bodies. May she watch over us and keep us strong."

"Thank Ayo," they all said, and Datu kissed his index and middle fingers, extending them toward the shelf on the opposite wall of the kitchen where a small, greenish box was set. It was surrounded on either side by tiny plastic bamboo plants, as reverent guards to a minuscule shrine.

Gabriel turned his egg paste over in his plate, his fist supporting his head. His long hair covered most of his face, and Datu might not have been able to see its configuration, but he could very well guess what the boy was thinking. There was no point in having a confrontation this early in the morning, however. He might not enjoy his day at work, but there were worse states of mind to perform the tasks at hand in.

"Today we're supposed to correct our programming test. I'm pretty sure I got everything right," Benilda said, beaming. Datu could see Gabriel's mouth moving in a mocking way, and studiously ignored it.

"That's wonderful, hon. Maybe one day you'll work at Admin and put it to good use," Tala said. Datu bit his tongue. He'd spoken to Tala before about putting false hope into the kids' heads.

Ramil devoured his breakfast and left the table before everyone else. He plopped himself in the corner of the living room with his hovercar and pretended to fix it at a garage made out of a found computer casing. He made little machine noises as he drilled the toy car with his finger and gave a baby-talk play-by-play of the repair process, peppering it with "Oh no! It's bwoken!" every other sentence.

Datu wished that one day his youngest might be able to live whatever dreams he'd concocted in his head. All his children, really. The hope was, and always had been to return to Bayang Sinilangan. The Phillipines. The Motherland.

But it had sank nearly three hundred years ago, and even though levels might be returning to that of earlier times, who knew how long it would take to resurface, let alone be habitable again? Australia had begun desalinazation years ago, so he knew there was hope, but it would be a long time before that country could ever grow any kind of food. Still, it left possibilities.

For now, it was best to keep their heads down in this adopted country, and pray to Ayo that the time would come soon for the exodus back. He sighed.

Benilda left for school, slipping on her rebreather as she did. Ramil clung to her leg, and she pinched his cheek gently, kissing him on the forehead. He let her go, and she waved goodbye as she went into the outer portico, the outside door hissing with depressurization as the inside closed.

As Datu was putting on his protective suit, he heard the door slam. He poked his head out and saw Tala in the kitchen putting the dishes in the washer. She shrugged. The bear had left. Gabriel was much too skinny to be a bear of any sort, but that's what Datu had nicknamed him, if only in his own head. No need to add insult to injury. The boy had enough on his plate. He wished however, that Gabriel would find a job and help out at the house more often.

He was so wrapped up in his own pain that he rarely noticed when he caused it to others. Even his general unpleasantness brought a downer on the house, but Datu doubted he could sit down with the boy and have that discussion without causing some sort of blowout of nuclear proportions. Best to leave raging bears do what they would, and hope they came to their senses at some point, just as he had when he'd been a teenager.

Back then was different, though. Datu's father had died, and if he had kept going down the same path, the family would have suffered. His mother had sat him down and explained to him what needed to be done. She herself worked long hours, but without his help, the family would stand little chance of surviving.

Sector 14 was an unforgiving place, and for those without a home, the odds of survival on the streets were a year, at the most.

Marauding street gangs were the least of your problems when the smog would destroy your lungs within a few months of direct exposure. Datu shuddered to think back on those times.

His mother had long passed away, but he always remembered her admonitions: keep the Ayo and your family first, in that order. Everything else comes after. And he'd done just that.

These were words he'd kept in his heart for as long as he could remember, and would hold onto until his dying breath. Of course, his family was one of the oldest in the Sector, and had been lucky enough to bring their Ayo from the motherland. It'd been passed down from father to first-born son for the last fifteen generations.

Datu had doubts, if only slight ones, as to what would happen when he would pass it to his own son. He trusted Gabriel, but his present condition made it hard to see him as anything other than a troublemaker. There was no way he would hand over the family's most precious heirloom to his son until he'd been cured of this restless anger he exhibited on a daily basis.

"He'll get over it," Tala said, coming up beside him as he slipped on the sleeves of his armoured suit. She turned Datu's face away from the door and toward her own, staring deep into his eyes.

"I told you to stop reading my mind, mahal," Datu said, straining a smile across his features. He kissed her cheek, and put on his helmet.

Outside was dark, but at this level, it always was. Sometimes, he'd look up to see the lights of Chiba and wonder how it might be up there. Chiba writ large encompassed one of the largest ports in the entire amalgamated Tokyo area. But in this recess of the city, at this depth, it was the home of several million East-Asian expat families. Dock and factory workers, recyclers: those were the available employment of all who'd been shuttered into Sector 14.

A thin fog was rolling in from the lower levels, and he was glad he was wearing his full suit before going out. Some preferred to put it on when they got to the work elevators, but he kept it at home, diminished chances of tampering or theft. Of course, he had to disinfect extensively when he came home, but that was a small price to pay not to have the Sector 14 'pinkeye,' like those who declined wearing goggles over their rebreathers.

Walking down the three flights of aluminum staircases, he looked across the street to see someone dumping their trash directly over the guardrail, for it to flutter and drop a hundred levels onto the Heap. No one 'above' did that. *They* were civilized. There were garbage shoots just for that purpose, for Ayo's sake. He shook his head and wondered if he'd get trash dumped on his head today. It was because of people like this that his co-workers got injured, or sometimes died. He hurried his descent to have words with the illegal dumper, but of course, he was gone by the time he got there.

He peered over the guardrail into the opaque miasma below. There was nothing to be seen. It was thick pea soup all the way down. This is what he'd have to work in today. The next plateau was far enough that, even though he strained his eyes through the fug, he could barely discern its contours. It felt like this sector was the only one in existence, an island, alone in the universe.

He looked back up to wave goodbye to Tala and Ramil, who had taken time off his hovercar repairs to wish his father a good day. The conapt stack was in such a state of disrepair that it pained him to look at it.

Originally, all the spaces had been taken by the shoe-box modular apartments which slipped into the metal frame, and then hooked up at the back to electricity, water, and sewer.

Over the past few years, however, neighbours had moved out, no one willing to replace them. On the grid's five levels, there might only be seven families altogether. A few conapts had been moved, yet none had taken their place. It was as if someone had removed bricks from a wall.

This was merely one symptom of the general state of affairs in the neighbourhood. None of the kids wanted to be recyclers anymore. The pay was crap. He knew of quite a few families that had hired forgers to make new papers for their progeny so they could leave Sector 14. Datu had a hard time considering sending his children away, knowing they would be gone forever, and he could never leave. Besides of which, the penalties for being caught were unpleasant, to say the least. How could he put his own blood through that? Simple answer: he refused to.

This, of course, was one of the reasons his eldest was so angry with him. Judging by the weekly fight he had with him, and would continue to be angry with him for a long time still. How dare he hold him back? How dare he, indeed. Datu felt like he was reliving his childhood through his son. Soon he'd be old enough to understand that the world would not ply itself to his will. That would be the harshest lesson of all, but one that every man lived on their way to adulthood.

Tala held Ramil in her arms, and they stayed to watch until the rambling old transport showed up down the broken street. Then, the window returned to its usual opacity. A children's show would play on the vidscreen inside, he knew, as his wife would clean the conapt and find activities for Ramil to do which might curtail him from running up and down the length of the tiny space for a few hours.

Still, he felt lucky for having found this particular block. It afforded them an unobstructed view of the void, and sometimes another plateau (on clear days), instead of an identical conapt block a hands-breadth away. He'd never seen the safety wall which enclosed the city, but he knew it was there, somewhere in the distance.

He boarded the shivering, sclerotic transport, sliding his wrist over the payment terminal beside the Companion driver. As the accordion doors slid closed, the hiss of the purifier activated. The impassive android at the wheel looked straight ahead and put the bus into drive, a jolt making Datu take a small misstep as he headed toward the back. It was less crowded than usual. *Must be something going around*, he thought. In this area, most of the workers were headed to the elevator. He recognized a familiar face, and the man moved over on his seat, about mid-way down the transport.

Datu sat and lifted his visor, the vinyl seat squeaking in protest under him.

"It's too early for this shit," Gamon said, staring out the reinforced windows.

"Oh, I don't know. Could be worse. There might be—" Datu began, his hands fluttering as if he was conjuring a rabbit.

"Don't jinx it, my friend. Don't make it early and tragic." Gamon said, turning to Datu and smiling.

"You're that superstitious, man?" Datu said, raising an eyebrow and smiling.

"I'm not. I just don't like taking chances. Words have power. Karma's always listening, whether you believe in it or not. Anyhow, things are good with you?"

"Thank Ayo, I am," he said, raising his index and middle finger to his lips and offering them up to the space in front of them.

"And you call me superstitious," his friend said, winking. "Do you really believe in the Exodus? I know you Filipinos have been dreaming about it forever. Think it'll ever happen for real? In all honesty, now." Datu felt a bit uncomfortable, but took strength in the words of the Ayo:

"We will have our home back. It is foretold."

A pink-eyed man leaned in from his left, and said, "I couldn't help but overhear what you were saying. It's a nice dream and all, but the world isn't going back to the way it was. You should put your faith in tangible things, instead of wishing islands out of thin air."

"I have an idea," Gamon said, turning around, frowning.

"What's th—"

"Shut up, turn around, and mind your own damn business," he said, half-rising in his seat. The other man mumbled something under his breath about zealots and turned away. Datu was quiet. He stared at his calloused hands, through his suit.

"Don't let other people tell you what you should believe, man. I hope it comes true. I really do. I wish I had your faith, sometimes," Gamon said, before staring out the window. Datu knew he'd made his friend uncomfortable, but what else could he say? That was his belief. It kept him going in the hardest of times. Had kept the entire community cohesive, hopeful, and loving for these past centuries. Outsiders might know the story, but they seldom understood the power of the words, and the place they came from.

Datu turned to Gamon and said, "Thanks." His friend nodded toward him and went back to the window, to stare blankly at the scenery as the bus hugged the curve that circumnavigated the entire plateau.

The bus came to one of the many security checkpoints, where two large, armed Companions stood on either side of a reinforced bullwark. It slowed down and stopped between two parallel tracks. Everyone stood still as two long rods extended from the ground and began to scan along the sides of the rattling bus, the red lasers flashing briefly when the smoke became thick enough to see them. Datu felt a shiver run up his spine when they passed by his head, as he always did.

A dog Companion, sleek and black, its carbon-fibre segments

sliding over each other with ease, walked the length of the bus, sniffing the undercarriage, then returned to sit by the side of one of the immobile guards.

The bullwark split in the middle, both sides sliding out, and the bus rumbled back on, passing into another quarter of Sector 14.

The rest of the ride along the edge of the chasm was spent in silence, the view becoming murkier as they entered the area of burning fields which continuously spouted black smoke from the pits. A broken air filter rattled above his head, almost enough to distract him from his thoughts

Even at a hundred levels above the source, the choking black turmoil made its way into the city, like some ethereal, tentacled thing bent on poisoning anyone it came into contact with.

The transport jostled on an uneven separator joist, and Datu was brought out of his daydream. He pulled down his visor and stepped out of the transport, the surrounding area now full of the intense black smoke. He felt fortunate that his rebreather filtered most of the acrid smell.

An ancient five-story building lay barely visible behind the veil of smoke, perched like a lighthouse on the edge of the chasm. Its windows blotted by dust and soot. Statues of copper eagles, melting green along the sides, invisible now. Remnants of some previous, now defunct architecture. He made his way to the concrete spiral staircase a few metres away on his left, and descended, with the fifteen or so other men and women, two floors down and through grimy revolving doors.

The low, rectangular room bustled with people, in lines of various lengths, as if waiting to go through customs after an unpleasant vacation.

He scanned himself in and shuffled his way to the changing rooms, bypassing the process the others were going through now, reinforced suits descending from chains hung on the high ceiling.

The hissing sound of compressed hot air escaped from cleaning nozzles as employees washed their suits right before their shifts, bringing on an involuntary scowl. Imagine leaving your grungy outerwear in an open area—overnight, after having spent the day in a trash bin full of slime, then cleaning it off the next day before going back to work. *It was no more than frowned upon, but then again, not everyone was smart enough to listen to common sense*, he thought.

He rejoined the queue at the changing room exit, nodding to other workers as he did. Gamon was still inside, but he'd see him on the digger when they got to the bottom.

The slow shuffle of feet as he went forward brought on a numbing lethargy. The whole procession reminded him of ancient divers and their elaborate metal helmets and protective suits. That was, in effect, what they were. Save that the waters they dove were poisonous gases, and the fish, flesh-eating insects.

Along the left wall, a curving window stared out into the nothingness, the fog pressing against it like some hungry force.

"What do you mean I have to pay more?" a voice ahead cried. *Here we go again,* he thought. Someone at the head of the line was agitated, berating the guard at the turnstile.

"Not my rules, buddy. If you have any complaints, go talk to the man in charge," the guard, a huge man named Kale, said. Evidently, the rates had spiked again. Ever since Admin had subcontracted the operation of the elevator to these people, they charged a fee to use it. Admin might be paying his salary, but Peoplift took their 'share' on a daily basis.

Datu stared at the pile of mutant beef that stood, arms crossed at the turnstile until the rebel, dejected, scanned his wrist on the payment rod. The mountain of a man then stepped away, the other man walking through, slamming his helmet down as a final protest.

Datu despised them just as much as that man did. He needed the money, however, and it was easier to let things go than to try to reason with their boss, a hard man who would have sent him packing with the help of his family's muscle.

When Datu stepped up to the plate and scanned his wrist, he saw that they'd added another ten credit charge to their usual fee, which was already exorbitant. He made a quick mental calculation before feeling his heart sink to the pit of his stomach. He'd have to do quite a few extra double-shifts to be able to afford what they were charging him. Or stop showering, he thought cynically.

He'd had these conversations with Gamon and the others before. Why were they allowed to do this? Weren't they being paid by Admin to handle the elevators in the first place? It hadn't been that way in his father's time, he was almost certain of that. Or if it was, his father had never spoken of it, just like he never spoke of it to Tala.

The conclusion they'd all reached was that the Administration Manager in charge of this chunk of the sector was corrupt, and was getting kickbacks from the goons who operated Peoplift. So whatever they did, no one was the wiser because he didn't report them. Meanwhile, all he had to do was supply Peoplift with equipment for the digs, as well as tally company pays and do direct deposits.

Datu and the others noticed discrepancies in their pays, but without access to the rest of the hierarchy, there was no way to put a stop to it.

Sector 14 was a closed circuit loop—nothing coming in, barely anything getting out.

So he, like every other recycler, took his lumps and went home with whatever he could as pay.

The large man named Kale put out an arm, stopping Datu in his tracks. He felt the urge to rush him, but that would have been useless and childish. Without looking at him, Kale said, "Pekelo says you need to buy a new suit, Datu Salazar. It says on your record of employment that this one is over three years old."

"This suit is perfectly fine," Datu gritted between his teeth. The other man shrugged and let him pass, not even deigning to look down at him.

"Go see Pekelo Vora before starting your shift. That's an order," the man called out as Datu walked away.

He wanted to scream. There was no way he could afford a new suit. This was unfair, especially having to pay for one's own equipment. He cursed Pekelo Vora under his breath and went to the elevator down the hallway. His forehead burned, as if he'd suddenly developed a throbbing fever, a migraine blooming between his eyes, spreading, just like the poisonous fog outside.

Instead of joining the others at the far elevator, he turned right, going up a set of worn carpeted stairs, his 'old' (what a joke!) suit getting heavier with every step. When he reached the top, he pushed through gritty glass doors, into the lobby of an office that might have seen better days two centuries previous. Five stories tall, he stood in its small atrium, a desk of imitation wood before him. The office assistant with the chipset behind her ear waggled her finger 'no!' before he could take a seat on a shiny black sofa, and he stood back up, his frown hurting his face.

He kept looking up at the second floor, watching guards go by in their moss-coloured uniforms—paramilitary intimidation chic, he'd once heard Gamon call it.

It was an intense ten minutes of throwing sidelong glances to the second floor, hoping to accelerate the process before the woman behind the desk nodded to him. Datu sighed, pressed down on his work uniform, un-ruffling it, as if he was going in for a first interview. He had to remind himself that he wasn't. That he was going to meet one of his bosses for the sole purpose of getting screwed over. Again. As usual.

He climbed the black circular staircase to the right of the desk, his steps reverberating on concrete-covered steel.

By now, his migraine had flowered to encompass his whole brain. He'd of given his kingdom for stims, if his Faith had allowed it. It felt like a frozen marshmallow, zapped by lightning every other second. Pekelo Vora's door was open, and he stepped inside. Plush carpets, dark leather chairs, what looked like real wood for a desk and a recessed ambient light which gave off a pleasant glow from the interstices of the ceiling and walls.

"Datu—Salazar? Is that correct?" The man in his thirties sitting behind the desk said. Datu had interactions with the man three times a year. He now felt quite un-memorable. Vora had what Datu considered a 'corporate' haircut—short, black, and greased back. It reflected the spotlights above the desk like an oil slick on a grainy beach, his face a pock-marked carpet of acne scars.

"Yes," he said, feeling the pulse inside his mind intensify.

"Good," the man said, smiling. He put down the tablet he was holding onto his desk. "Datu—can I call you Datu?"

You usually do, he thought.

"Yes," he said. Flat voice. No intonation.

"Is everything okay? You seem tense." Pekelo Vora said, letting out a chuckle.

Datu suppressed the growl in his throat and said, "I'm fine."

"Excellent. Now, Salazar, it's come to our attention that your suit is, how shall I put this mildly… a little bit on the older side. My records show that you've had this thing for three years," Pekelo Vora said this with a moue of disgust, as if the work suit that Datu wore was a Heap-dragged rag.

"If I may say so, sir, this suit is perfectly fine and has been kept in perfect working order. Apart from a few scratches and dents, which is entirely expected, there's nothing wrong with it at all." Pekelo Vora looked pained to hear it, as if Datu had performed a less-than-polite bodily function in front of him. He got up from his seat and walked around his desk, glancing critically at Datu's suit.

"Well there's a problem with that, Salazar. You see, your contract stipulates that you must change your suit at least every three years," Vora said, sitting down on the edge of his desk, picking up the tablet he'd laid down previously. He tapped it with his index, as if therein lay the proof, his eyebrows arching in a 'there you have it!' reaction.

"What?" Datu said, restraining a strangled cry.

"Right here," Pekelo Vora said, holding out the contract for Datu to see. The passage looked as if it had been copy-pasted in a different font, sandwiched between other stipulations which were mildly less disagree-able than this one.

"But that wasn't there before!" Datu cried.

"It's always been there, Salazar," the man said, and sighed. "Besides, there's another clause in your contract that says that it's subject to change at any time. Oh, don't look at me that way. You *do* want to keep your job, right? I could just have Admin cut your hours. How would you feel about that?" Vora tilted his head to the side, making a sad dog face.

Datu boiled. He wanted to jump onto the desk, put his knees on the man's chest, and choke the life out of him. He looked past him, on the shelf behind his desk, where three small jade cubes sat, one beside the other. They were identical, or almost, to his. It was they who reminded him of Tala, Ramil, Benilda and Gabriel, and felt the tension go out of his body, in one fell slump.

"I'd—rather not," he finally said, holding back utter defeat. How had Pekelo Vora gotten a hold of an Ayo, let alone three? Datu's attention was now drawn to each one in turn. The subtle differences in construction and design. He wasn't expert enough to see which family they belonged to. But he was intelligent enough to realize that none of them belonged to this man. The rest of his speech washed over him like waves onto a beach, blurred and unintelligible.

"Good to hear. Tell you what. Since you're such a good sport, we'll put you on a monthly payment plan with low interest rates. That should help with the cost of the new suit. I'll have Nadine downstairs draw up a new contract—" and at that last word, it felt as if he'd been sucker-punched, and his attention was now back, even if his gaze was not, "and we'll have it delivered to your home in the next few days. Done deal? Super. It was nice having this chat with you, Salazar. Salazar?" Pekelo Vora held his hand out expansively, not in a gesture inviting a handshake, but one signalling the end of the conversation, as well as an order to depart forthwith. His smile slowly vanished at what he thought was the employee's vacant stare. Then he followed his line of sight to the keepsakes on his shelf, and he said:

"Nice, aren't they? I'm a bit of a collector. 'Salazar', that's Filipino, right? You know, I could always get you a discount if you happened to have one of these beauties. I pay top dollars. Are you a follower of Ayo?' The man clasped his hands together, intertwining his fingers, as if he was about to hear an offer for a deal.

Datu felt the anger rising in him again. Sickness and bile roiling in the pit of his stomach.

"Our Ayo is not for sale, Mr. Vora. Our Ayo will never be for sale. Are we done?"

"Plenty of time to change your mind, Salazar. You'll have that new contract signed by Tuesday, won't you? That's a good boy. Have a nice day."

Datu turned around, numb, and walked back down the circular staircase, gripping the railing as if he might fall, hard. The sound of his steps like weighted bells. He passed the receptionist, neither of them acknowledging the other. He pushed the doors open with a stiff hand and made his way down the steps, back to the turnstile room. There were few recyclers left at the elevators, but he got on with a dozen others, pulling his visor down. The elevator started with a jolt, and they lowered fifty levels, straight through the plateau that held Sector 14, to the salt-corroded metal girders of the fiftieth. He exited the elevator and got into one of the cart trains that ferried workers all over the under-belly of Vertical Tokyo.

Like large roller-coaster carts, they were on tracks, slinging people from one area to another with rapid efficiency. He boarded one, and as soon as the dozen or so others had clamped their seat belts, the opera-tor sent them zooming to the centre of the plateau, where it met the support pillar of that and every other level above it.

The sheer girth of the pillars always took Datu's breath away. Where he lived, he barely ever looked up to see it shooting upward. Being on the periphery of the plateau, it was also hard to see it in the penumbra. The only tell-tale sign of its existence were the blinking red 'no-fly' lights that indicated it would be foolish to approach it with any kind of hover. No one in Sector 14 could afford such a vehicle, and therefore the odds of a crash ever happening were slim-to-none.

There, the large elevator took him and twenty other people down to the Heap floor itself. A large staging area had been created at base level, the amalgamation of hundreds of years of garbage making landing at the foot of the pillar in an unassisted way impossible.

Rectangular in shape, approximately one kilometre squared, it was made of interlocking floating yellow squares which floated above the garbage mound in a more-or-less flat pattern. Like a desert's sand-dunes, the Heap was a constantly moving, roiling pile of trash which threatened to collapse, chasm, quicksand, flow and ebb at a moment's notice.

Heavy equipment was kept within sheds with the same mobile properties as the support structure, lest they collapse atop the diggers and scrapers kept therein. They were dropped down by steel cables from the fiftieth level on a daily basis, and returned there for storage every evening. Leaving anything on the Heap floor was a recipe for losing it for all eternity.

The darkness on this level was at peak opacity. Winds over a hundred and twenty kilometres an hour sometimes flushed the fog out of the way, but brought with them debris storms which launched every type of surface trash at speeds which were dangerous enough to cut, slice open, or impale unsuspecting workers.

Today, it was merely dark. The massive northern garbage patch fires blanketed the work areas with thick plumes of black smoke, alleviated once in a while by tall, buoyed flood-lights planted at strategic points. Their eerie lights wavered as the Heap shifted.

Datu headed out from the elevator to one of the furthest right-hand sheds. Ash fell like nuclear winter, covering his suit with a soft, grey duvet. His boots clung to the sticky squares underfoot like lizard's paws. Say what you will, this was the part he found the most peaceful of his day. The walk from the pillar to the digger was a time of utter contentment. Usually.

Today his mind buzzed with the unhappy news of his shiny new debt, and the realization that his boss had either been stealing Ayos or buying them from families that needed them much more than he did. He wondered which poor souls were now without their guidance, and he felt a combination of sadness and sickening.

Folding the shed's tent flap, he looked up to see Gamon in the cabin of the big yellow digger. He climbed the faded ladder to the cockpit of the bucket, knocking on his partner's window as he passed him, and installed himself into the worn pleather chair with a grunt. The dim orange overhead light turned on, and he flicked the radio button on. The controls lit up at his fingertips, the long arm of the digger at the front of the vehicle flexing upward with a deep whirring sound and came back to its resting position, sending a shudder through the machine.

Datu waited for the air filtration system in the digger to hum to life, after which he lifted his visor.

"Where have you been, man?" came a tinny voice from the speaker above his head. Datu looked down on his left and Gamon had his hands up, then pointing at his wrist, in the archaic way of saying "Can't you tell the time?"

"Channel check," Datu said, before unscrewing the digger's microphone. Even though the radio was on, no one else on that frequency would hear what he had to say. He and Gamon had worked out that the bosses upstairs listened in on conversations on the open radio frequencies, as proven by a recent spate of reprimands. Since then, they'd gotten their own short-wave radios, which could be scrambled. Leaving the digger's radios on but the microphones unplugged nulled suspicions from the brass. No sound going out meant they could talk privately. When they were done talking, they would simply plug them back in.

This was something Datu had come up with, and Gamon had slipped the word to the trustworthy.

"Got called to Vora's office," he said.

"Well that's never good. What's the damage?" The other man asked, turning the key. The whine of the electric engine caused temporary static, cutting off Datu's reply.

"Didn't get that," Gamon said, putting the machine in drive. The large, donut-like buoyant wheels made the enormous digger wobble front-to-back until it took its strides. The large paddled wheels made a 'tock-tock-tock' sound on the platform until they'd reach the garbage proper.

"I said, I've been hit up for a new suit. They're charging me for it. But since I'm such a super-duper guy, I get an amazing discount on the ludicrous interest they'll charge me." Datu looked down to see Gamon shaking his head. He kept looking forward, however, to make sure he didn't run anyone over. There were very few recyclers left on the platform by the time Datu had gotten there, and most of them were manual labourers, not truck operators.

As a matter of fact, their rig was the last one out the gate.

"You know they get those for free from the Administration Manager downtown, right?" Gamon said, glancing sideways. Datu kicked the floor mat below him.

"Now I do. Think I could slip in a word with them and get something done about it?" he said, sarcastically, then paused. They both laughed. "Seriously though, I'm getting tired of this, man. He threatened to drop my hours if I didn't comply, after showing me a doctored contract. Isn't there anything we can do about this?"

The digger's long frame left the staging platform, dipping forward into the garbage heap, leaving the safe zone. Blinking orange lights on its periphery warned them so. To their left, pickets had been planted, with a long steel wire running through them. Recyclers followed it, their harness attached to the cord. The paddles began to churn up loose trash in the Heap, the inflated wheels buoying the digger.

"Not much unless you want to look for another job. I don't have to tell you how scarce those are, right? I wouldn't worry about getting your hours cut, though, if I were you," Gamon said, aiming for the cluster of flood lights in the distance. All around them, they could guess the shapes of other pillars of the city, like the shadows of monstrous trees in a dark forest.

"Why's that?" Datu asked, leaning on his controls.

"The missing workers," Gamon said. "We're going to have to switch back to regular channels. We're here."

Soon enough, they were in view of the site, and the digger began to circle the rim of the hole, much like an open-air mine, save that this one had a tendency of filling up at a rapid pace. Once they'd left the almost level surface, the air cleared a bit. Enormous dumper trucks were being loaded up with all the miscellaneous metals the digger crews were pulling up from the base and walls of the hole.

Datu knew that sentinel bots circled on the outskirts of the dig site, watching to make sure that no scavengers tried to come in and steal the scrap the administration tried so hard to reclaim from the sub-basement of its own city.

Sentinels had one job, to destroy anyone not authorized in the Heap. Desperate times called for desperate measures, and Datu had heard of one such event where a crew of recyclers had been attacked by a force of scavengers armed to the teeth with rocket launchers and hand grenades. Sentinels had flown in from every quadrant of the Heap, he'd heard, and had fried every single one of them, perhaps thirty in total.

He was aware that that was an exaggeration. The product of a game of telephone which had gone on for a few days before he'd heard it. The main takeaway was that the sentinels were ruthless. They were pro-grammed to watch over the administration's assets, of which he was one. *Shame that I'm worth protecting but not paying,* he thought.

So workers were *actually* going missing, and he wasn't the only one to have noticed. Now that the radio was back on, he knew the people upstairs would be listening in on his conversations. If this was sensitive information, it was worth waiting until the end of the shift to be able to discuss it with Gamon on a one-to-one basis.

The digger moved into position at the bottom of the hole, and Datu got to work, lifting and separating trash, choosing the metallic bits which were prized above all else, putting the scrap into the loaders, while Gamon handled the positioning of the vehicle as it shifted its weight constantly on the floating garbage. It was a tango they both knew quite well.

They'd been partners for a bit over two years, ever since Datu had graduated to heavy machinery. The pay raise had helped quite a bit at the time, but now, with increasing rates, it was as if there had been none whatsoever. He dared not imagine what it might be like for the other manual labourers.

They toiled inside the mine-like hole for hours, transferring the precious recyclables, moving to new, undisturbed areas, until the wind above began to rise. A soft 'tweep' began to register on his console, a yellow blinking light indicating all workers were being ordered to return to the protected area in the shadow of the pillar.

Outside, the siren wailed at high volume, loud enough to overcome the howling whirlwinds of the Heap. The winds always came unexpectedly, like a desert sirocco, pouncing on the unsuspecting. Gamon directed the digger to the entrance of the hole, workers on foot scrambling onto and holding on to the side of the digger and other wheeled vehicles. Datu looked down and recognized Mara, Rodrigo, and Ukrit as some of those clutching onto his rig for dear life.

When he was able to discern the staging area's lights in the distance, a wall of wind, trash and smoke fell like a roiling whirlwind onto the contingent of workers, blasting his friends from the side of the digger into the mulch with the force of a cannon.

As it did, a few of the long-poled spotlights slammed to the ground, flattened like twigs, their lights extinguished. As one of them was swept up into the maelstrom, whipping out of view, its power cord severed, and the rest of the lights blinked out on the entire dig site. The only illumination now came from Datu and Gamon's small cabins.

Datu pulled down and latched his visor, grabbed a rope rolled up behind him and left the vehicle just as he heard Gamon yell to him on the radio, "Datu, don't!"

Anything he might have said after that came back as a hiss in Datu's ears, the radio signal corrupted by the raging storm's electro-magnetism. It was too late to stop. He tied the rope around himself, attaching the other end to one of the digger's metal eyelets, where it couldn't get tangled in the massive wheels. He then jumped knee-deep in the trash, buffeted by the wind, running to where he thought he'd seen the workers fall.

Even through his armoured suit, debris stung, whipped, and cracked.

"*Great*, he thought, *I'm giving them an excuse to charge me that new suit.*"

He found Mara on her back, rolling slowly toward the mine, attempting to clutch the ground. He grabbed her arm and looped the rope around it. He then kept running until he found Ukrit, his headlamp wavering in the darkness, shambling in the wrong direction, toward the wasteland. He coiled the rope around his waist and they gave each other a thumbs up.

Meanwhile, Gamon had slowed down, allowing the digger to pull the lost workers along in the direction of the staging area.

Finally, he found Rodrigo stuck sideways in dark, putrefied sludge. As he walked toward him, he began to sink into the muck. The digger was continuing on its way, and he was almost out of reach. He could feel the man's fingertips on his own, and he stretched out as far as he could to grab his wrist. All around them, the wind raged and howled, tossing them sideways as they tried to grapple each other. His heart pounded as he attempted to reach the man.

His horror turned to relief as his body began to be released from the ichor below. Datu could see nothing apart from the yellow glow inside the man's helmet, and the frightened look on his face.

Something flashed between them, and Datu fell back, away from his friend. He still held his arm. It was no longer attached to his body, jaggedly cut near the elbow. Datu was dragged away from him, and he saw the blood-curdling scream that escaped his throat before Rodrigo was lost in the storm, to Datu's pleas for Gamon to stop the rig. Unheard and unheeded.

Datu knew that if he untied himself, there would be *two* new corpses claimed by the Heap. He dropped the man's arm and began to walk, painfully, in the direction the digger was dragging him.

After an eternity of slogging, slipping and falling, he felt the solid ground of the staging area underfoot, and saw the faint flashing orange lights of its periphery.

Once the digger had stopped, Datu untied the lifeline that had kept him safe. He was quickly surrounded by Mara and Ukrit. Gamon jumped out of the cabin and ran to his partner. The wind billowed around them, threatening to swipe them back into the Heap with every step they took. Their boots' sticky properties were pushed to their limits.

"Did you find Rodrigo?" Mara asked. Datu nodded the affirmative, his shoulders slumped, and she knew not to ask any more questions.

There would be no double shift, today. The storm raged. The Sentinels would be cocooned against its violence, and Datu and the rest returned to the surface.

In the decon room, Datu turned morosely on himself as the pressure washers lifted the grit and soot from every nook and cranny of his suit. Gamon kept an eye on him.

They both left the building, having worked a three quarter shift. There would be nothing further to gain from staying. The Heap Maelstroms could last hours or days, depending on the low pressure systems coming in from the ocean screwing with the microclimates underneath the city.

"You okay?" Gamon asked, as they walked down the corridor toward the turnstiles. Datu nodded in the negative. He was far from okay. He'd never get used to losing people.

"What did you mean by workers going missing, earlier? Because of the storms?" he asked his friend, remembering their earlier conversation, and attempting to get his mind off this most recent tragedy. Gamon took on a conspiratorial look, as he comically checked left and right if anyone else was listening in. Datu didn't feel like laughing.

"No, man. People just aren't coming in for their shifts. You saw the transport this morning. It was a third empty. You think anyone would miss a shift?"

"Maybe they got new jobs, Gamon. You saw what happened down there. Maybe they just got sick of dying for the Man, and up and left for better pastures," Datu said, unimpressed. Even as he did, he knew there was nothing else on offer. After today, though, he was inclined to join the AWOL in turning into a puff of wind and vanishing.

"All their equipment is still there, Datu, hanging in the change rooms. Unclaimed. Don't you think they would have taken it and sold it before leaving? Nah, I'm telling you, there's bad mojo going on."

But what? Datu thought, only half-distracted by the mystery. The scene of Rodrigo's arm getting sliced in half by flying debris playing and replaying in his mind like a stuck holodisk until he closed his eyes to try to stop it, and managing only to see it as an afterimage, stamped there in perpetuity.

As they were leaving for the rattling transport, one of the guards at the turnstiles recognized him and put his large hand on his shoulder. He handed him a cellulose printout that still exuded the smell of warm laser impression.

Datu Salazar: for endangering heavy equipment of the Peoplift Company in a reckless fashion, you will be fined a thousand credits.

-Signed, Pekelo Vora.

COMPANION MALFUNCTION

CHIBA CITY, 10 AM

A cordon of hazard posts had been set up around the shop, near the trunks of bioluminescent trees and the pale grey gas pipe that stuck out of the building. The "warning/police crime scene" holo-projection floated between each post in cardinal red. Broken glass lay sprinkled on the sidewalk like so many reflective wedges, flashing red and blue at the rhythm of the police cars' lights. A small crowd had gathered to gawk, and three officers had posted themselves at each side of the cordon, making sure no one came in before she did.

Mariko Ishikawa hated Chiba. It was far from her usual stomping grounds of central Tokyo. She disliked having to go so far for piddlings. Here on the 250th level, the cityscape was dismal and dreary, but of course, she could think of worse places. This in no way diminished the fact that she felt discomfort at having been sent here. There was also the fact that Chiba reciprocated the feeling.

The population was leery of any police presence. It was uncommon to count so many officers in one place, in such a tight bunch, out in the open. From her vantage point, she could see the furtive sideways glances they threw at passersby. They expected trouble, and rightly so.

Ishikawa put on her game face after landing her car near the curb, and asked for the officer in charge after having flashed her palm to the nearest uniform. Her detective insignia glowed briefly above her skin, and the woman nodded her head toward the inside of the sushi shop with the broken plate glass window strewn before it. She stepped through the holo-tape.

The sidewalk was slick, even if no rain had been planned for the day. Inside the restaurant, was the bent plastic frame of what had been a large aquarium. Its contents now splayed across the sidewalk, crunchy bits of blue rocks and glass underfoot.

A tall man with a strong nose sat on a stool near the back counter, holding a medipack to his cheek, a flowering purplish bruise covering most of the right side of his face. His white apron marred by a spot of blood.

Next to him stood a solid-looking man in uniform, hands on his hips. He had sharp features and wore his hair a bit longer than regulation.

Things are lax in Chiba, she thought.

"Inspector Ishikawa, this is Mr. Nobue. He's the proprietor of this establishment," the officer said.

"Thank you officer--"

"Kazue," he responded, bowing slightly.

"Officer Kazue, I'll take it from here," she said, and the man gave another slight bow before returning to the front of the restaurant.

"Nobue San, my name is Ishikawa Mariko, Special Inspector with the Tokyo PD. Can you explain to me what happened here? I heard it over the radio, but I'd like you to tell me your version of events." The tall man massaged his cheek with the cold medipack, the blue of its plastic offsetting the purple around his eye. He glanced at her sideways and bit his lip.

"Don't worry, I'm not here to judge. Whatever you can tell me will help me find it," she said, trying for what she considered a reassuring smile, making the big man flinch.

He grunted and leaned back on his silver stool.

"Everything was fine when I came in this morning. The restaurant was still empty. The Koji was in the back doing prep, as usual—"

"What model Koji was it?" Ishikawa interrupted, taking out a small electronic pad and removing its stylus. The man tilted his head.

"A Koji9B. I got it last year to replace a Companion I'd had for twenty years. These androids last forever, y'know? This one had features I couldn't even program into the old unit. Did you know the new ones could automatically download new recipes without any manual input? Easiest decision I ever—" the man said, his hands dancing in front of him to illustrate his point.

"I'm sure it's—was—amazing, sir. Please, relate the rest of your morning." Ishikawa said. The man put his medipack back on his cheek and appeared to deflate a bit. Ishikawa placed her stylus back in its holster. She turned on the recording option. This one was a chatter. She'd parse through the conversation later.

It had started in the back, where the Koji was slicing fresh tuna for the maki. Nobue had gone to the fridge to get other seafood, and when he'd turned around, the Koji was walking toward the front door. Curious, Nobue had confronted his Companion and ordered it to return to the back to finish its job.

It'd left the long filleting knife next to its station. This, Nobue recounted with his index extended, a cutting motion along his jugular. If it hadn't, they would not have been having this conversation. She looked at him sternly, and he cleared his throat before continuing. He got up off his stool to show her the spot where the altercation happened.

The sushi man had grabbed the Companion's arm, which, for one so small, had been incredibly strong. Possibly another reason why he "hadn't been—you know," as he put it once more with a cutting motion of his fingers across his neck.

Ishikawa stared for a moment. The man recreated the pantomime of he and the Companion fighting, as it struggled to get his hand off its arm, and finally shoved him into the side of one of the vinyl-sided booths, where he hit his cheekbone and fell to the ground.

The Koji had run straight toward the aquarium in front of the plate glass window and jumped through both, pausing on the street a bit before choosing left and dashing off at a sprint.

Ishikawa returned to the front of the restaurant, a few pieces of glass crunching underfoot. The man had picked up his goldfish and put them in a green bucket full of water by the window. Most of them floated near the surface.

She looked at the damage surrounding the window before going back to the proprietor of the restaurant.

"Thank you, Mr. Nobue," she said, bowing. She handed the man her card with the tips of her thumbs and forefingers, to which the man bowed and received the card in the same manner.

"Do you know what happened to it, Ishikawa San?" Mr. Nobue asked.

"It is uncommon for Companions to wander off, Mr. Nobue, but not unheard of. We will let you know what the investigation brings when we gather new evidence. Thank you for your time," she said.

She walked out the front door, the chimes ringing as she did so. The officer named Kazue came to meet her.

"So, what do you think? Worthy investigation for my esteemed colleague from downtown?" he asked.

She stopped, turned to the officer and said "Officer Kazue. There is no investigation beneath an officer of the TPD. You should know that," and she flashed one of her forced, horrible smiles at him. Kazue's hypocritical grin evaporated.

"What did you find out?" he said, almost respectfully.

"A Companion is gone, Officer Kazue. Keep an eye out for a four-foot tall silver android. They usually turn up. It has nowhere to go," she said, turning away and walking through the streaming red holo-tape.

"What should we do in the meantime?" Kazue yelled after her.

She was tempted to yell "Your job, Kazue!" but held back. She turned around.

"Put out an APB and make a ten kilometre perimeter. Cover the major roads. I expect it malfunctioned and is wandering aimlessly." The man did a short, dry bow and gathered his officers for a scrum.

Ishikawa shook her head and returned to her unmarked police cruiser. She pressed the latch on the butterfly door on the driver's side, waited for it to open and sat down. One of her talents was an almost eidetic memory. On her tablet, she scribbled shorthand everything Nobue San had recounted, omitting his fantasy flourishes of throat-cutting. She'd collate the written with the audio once she was back at the office.

The wide avenue of Oami-Kaido was barren at this time of day, most of the work crowds staying in or within walking distance of the downtown core. Two-story shops lined the wide avenue, which gave her an unobstructed view of the central Tokyo Area.

Ishikawa glanced at her onboard clock. Still only 10:30 am.

The officers were leaving, and the sushi restaurant proprietor had come out with a broom to sweep up the glass that littered the sidewalk in front of it.

What she had told Officer Kazue was partially true: Companions sometimes *did* wander off. What they didn't do, however, was commit violence toward humans, incidental or otherwise. The only exception being special army units, in which case their parameters were extremely precise as to whom they were allowed to harm.

Kojis weren't military robots, and never had been. They were run-of-the-mill service Companions, and as such, regulated by the most stringent restraints. Ishikawa now understood why she'd been sent to investigate. It alleviated some of her misgivings about Administration Central lobbing her as far as they possibly could. Perhaps this wasn't a wild android chase to get her out of their hair, after all.

As far as the Koji was concerned, she'd have to wait until it was found to determine exactly what the malfunction had been. Until then—

A knock resounded on her window, and Ishikawa turned with a start, her gun out in a flash.

A teenager, no more than eighteen years old, stood beside her, dressed in a high school uniform. The same kind every boy wore: black pants, white dress shirt and black vest. The lack of crest on the lapel meant he was in fact a public school student. The fact he wasn't wearing a tie meant he was a poor one at that.

The boy waved at her sheepishly. Ishikawa grunted and put her gun back in its holster. She lowered her window an inch.

"May I help you?" she said.

"Are you Ishikawa Mariko San?" the boy asked, looking around. He pushed his round glasses back up his nose and chewed on something. She frowned.

"Yes. What do you want?" she said, feeling her patience already slipping away.

"My name is Keiji. I used to work for Genzo Ito. I need your help," he said. Ishikawa felt a cold wave go over her scalp at the name. She lowered the window.

"That bastard cost me a promotion, do you know that?" she said, now angry at the youth for having brought up that name.

"I'm sorry to hear that," he said. He looked around again. "Listen, can you give me a ride? I've used up all my credits to come and find you. I need to get back downtown and—"

"What do I look like? A taxi service? Listen kid, I'm on a case right now, I don't have time to play, and you can tell Genzo Ito that if I ever see him again, I will personally kick his ass! Do you understand the words that are coming out of my mouth?" she said, restraining herself not to yell at the gall of the boy for having dared to request such a thing. She started to bring the window back up and the teen looked agitated.

"You can tell him yourself if you can find him! He's—" the last part of his words were muffled out, but she swore she heard 'gone.' As if a runaway Companion wasn't enough for her day, now she had to deal with a runaway Private Detective.

She lowered her window again.

"What?" she asked flatly.

"You can tell him yourself to get bent, if we can find him. Please. I need your help. No one else at TPD wants to," he said, holding his

hands together in a pleading gesture. She was in no way surprised.
Genzo Ito had always been a pain to quite a few officers of the Tokyo
Police Department. He was one of those unfailingly lawful men who
possessed an irritating need to root out corruption wherever he found
it, and expose it to the light of day. Something a lot of the officers she
worked with found annoying on the best of days.

Not that Ishikawa was corrupt, mind you. She was a lot like him.
But unlike Ito, she had to toe the fine line between upholding the law
and keeping her job. This was easier said than done when many of the
officers she worked with had what they called 'side gigs,' which often
had a hard time meshing with the oaths they had sworn to uphold.

She let her neck loll backward, closing her eyes. Why? Well, it was
a better time than any other, she supposed. At least she wasn't in the
middle of a murder investigation.

"Please?" The boy pleaded again, his chewing becoming more
frantic. She rolled up her window a final time and stepped out of the
car. She pressed the fob, and the locks chirped.

"Let's go for a walk, shall we?" she said. Before letting this young
man into her car, she wanted to know that what he was advancing was
legit. She had no intention of letting some pretender psycho next to
her and then get stabbed because she'd been too stupid to have done a
background first.

"Thank you! Thank you so much—" he said, as she walked away
from the car. She headed in the same direction the shop owner had said
the Companion had run toward. She wondered briefly if she would
happen upon it during her grilling of the boy. That might save her some
time, and then she'd be able to go back downtown early, avoiding the
afternoon rush. There was nothing worse than being stuck behind a
queue of hovercars for hours on end, just staring down at the city lights.

"Don't thank me just yet Keiji. I haven't accepted anything. I need
to know who you are, first," she said, her long strides pushing her
trench coat open from side to side. Keiji ran after her to keep up. He
handed her a high school card with his name and address, face and
birth date on it. She snapped it up and tapped her wrist. A holographic
readout spread from her bracelet, like a keyboard made of light, and she
put the card perpendicular to it, scanning it.

She handed him the card back, and read the text which appeared on
the virtual screen above the keyboard.

"Tanaka, Keiji, Eighteen years old, living in Shinjuku. Oekaki
Public School. Senior Year. What's a boy from The Heights doing working for a Private Detective, Keiji?"

The boy faltered a bit, then sped up.

"Where are you going?" he asked, as she headed down the street. She'd noticed a MiniMart a block away while descending. While specialty coffee places tried to hand off caffeine flavoured brew, Japanese Kombini were the only places you could still get coffee made with honest-to-goodness coffee beans. Something about the political and financial reach of the convenience store's multiple arms. Of course, there were other convenience stores, but MiniMart had the widest selection of caffeinated beverages. At this present moment, Detective Mariko Ishikawa was jonesing for something that would bring her mind crystalline clarity. Preferably with a metric shit-ton of caffeine, a flavour to soothe her tastebuds, and an authenticity she wouldn't find anywhere else.

She walked into the store and headed straight for the heated shelves and picked up a can of something warm, with the stylized logo of a man smoking a pipe on it, and the brand in bold letters reading 'PATRON.'

She popped the tab right then and there and guzzled the hot liquid until the can was empty, her head tilted back. She let out a sigh of satisfaction. She then took another, similar can with a rainbow adorning it, and brought both back to the counter where she paid for them.

On her way out, she tossed the empty can in the recycling bin, and popped the tab of her other coffee, this one cold and sugary. The first had been a meal coffee, this one, dessert.

She then leaned back on the corner of the convenience store, fake stone edge digging into her back, sipping her beverage. The mental strain lifted as the caffeine did its job. She hadn't heard from Genzo Ito in months, not since he'd promised to credit her with the recuperation of a kidnapped girl.

That particular event had never happened. The child, Sachiko Toriyama, had resurfaced, then been secreted away, and Genzo Ito had avoided her phone calls from then on. She could have gone down to his office and gotten what she'd been promised, but had found it not worth the hassle.

She hated being in anyone's debt, especially some low-rent private detective. That debt should have been repaid through her playing taxi for said elusive detective. Did it count? She liked to think so. It would get her off the hook in this situation, anyhow.

The boy was standing a little ways off, staring at her as if he expected more of her. *Bullshit*, she thought. *This had to be a scam.*

"You haven't answered my question," she said, between sips.

Oami-Kaido was beginning to develop a crowd. A few neons called attention to a Vietnamese nail salon, a Chinese restaurant and Korean karaoke bars. If she looked north-west, she imagined she could see the towering white spire of Administration Central, but that was only wishful thinking. Chiba was far removed from the core.

The boy looked nervous, had something to hide. It irritated Ishikawa, who downed the last of her sweet coffee and tossed the can with a deft hand, right into the recycling box.

"Listen boy. I'm not going to help you if I don't know you or can't trust you. So you might as well give me something I can use, or start walking back to Shinjuku. If you leave now, you can probably make it back by Thursday," she said with one hand held palm up, weighing options.

She started to walk back to her car, the boy, miserable, trailing behind her.

The car tweeped twice when she pressed her key fob. The driver's side door rose with the soft sound of compressors.

"I broke into his work computer. He caught me. I have to work off my debt to him," he said. So that was it. Genzo Ito was no idiot, mind you, so anyone who was able to infiltrate his personal security system had *some* skills. "You can't tell anyone about this!"

Ishikawa imagined not. Hacking perpetrated by unauthorized persons outside law enforcement had "prison sentence" written all over it. She also doubted that this had been young Mr. Tanaka's first time.

"Where did this break-in take place?" she asked, peering deep into his eyes.

"His old office in Shinjuku. It was an early-model Nakatomi server that he'd beefed up. He completely caught me by surprise," Keiji said. "Ever since then, I followed him to his new place in Shibuya, in The Heights. I help him bypass security and run errands. You know. Kohai stuff."

Ishikawa clicked the button on her fob again, and the passenger side door rose. She tilted her head and raised her eyebrows. Keiji, finally taking the hint, hurried to the other side of the car and got in.

Both doors lowered, and he glanced at the array of police equipment on the dashboard like a kid choosing a new game. There were long-range sensors, backup stabilizers in case of critical failure, an undercarriage weapons system, the works.

"Listen, boy. I don't doubt you work for Ito, but I have an investigation to run. I'm going to take you home. If you want to find Ito, do it through proper channels next time."

The car shook as the whine of the engines amplified, and the hovercar lifted into the air, turning toward the core of the city as it did. It sped forward to find an unoccupied spot in the nearest aerial lane. Traffic was almost non-existent on the 250th-, but would increase as they approached the Greater VCT and rose to higher levels.

"What? No? You can't do that! I mean, I need *you* to help me, not one of those useless cops that'll treat this as another missing persons statistic!"

They were over the interstice of two plateaux, the gaping maw between them a chasm that fell away until the Heap. Invisible now in the gloom, save for the occasional methane fire plume that swayed like candlelight from a few kilometres away.

"Kid, I don't have time to babysit you while I try to find a missing Companion! Just be glad I'm giving you a lift in the first place, alright?" The youth stared out the window, and Ishikawa thought that would be the end of the discussion.

More and more hovercars joined the sky roadway as they went higher, and their progress slowed.

"What if I help you find your missing Companion? Will you help me find Ito, then?" Ishikawa glanced over to the boy, a fierce determination in his eyes she rarely saw.

"What makes you think you could do a better job than the Tokyo PD, son?" she asked, weighing the pros and cons of listening to any more of what he had to say.

"Promise," he said.

"What?"

"Promise me that if I find your Companion, and I *will*, you will investigate the disappearance of Genzo Ito. Do I have your word, Ms. Ishikawa?" Was there no limit to this boy's impudence? She was beginning to think not. She thought it best to call his bluff. After all, if he was lying, she would know what kind of characters Ito associated with. If he told the truth, she'd have the missing Companion case solved.

"Fine. If you can find a late model Koji9B wandering the streets of Chiba, I will personally think very hard about helping you find the Private Dick who stiffed me out of my raise. How does that sound?"

A slow smile spread on Keiji's face, and he said "Turn around, we're going the wrong way."

Ishikawa felt the annoyance begin to rise again, but agreed to return to Chiba.

"I need to access your long-range sensor array. May I?" Ishikawa sighed and pressed her thumb on the detector on the screen in front of her. The lock screen became green, and Keiji pulled out a cord from the back of his neck and inserted it into one of the access ports on the console. He then recalibrated the long-range sensors with his own crystal microchip. On the screen between them, a GPS grid appeared, and a faint signal began to glow down a Chiba side street. His chewing was now rhythmic, controlled. A throbbing orange dot, slowly meandering its way to who-knew-where.

"There," Keiji said. Ishikawa stared at the dot in disbelief.

"Are you sure that's the one?"

"Positive. Every Companion has their energy level output, coupled with their positronic brains. This combination gives them a unique signature, dependent on the model, like a thumb print, if you will. There are no other Koji9B fitting the description you gave me in the area."

"And you found this by—"

"Altering the sensitivity of your long-range sensors." Inspector Ishikawa was beginning to understand why Genzo Ito had kept the services of this hacker. She pushed the button on her radio and said:

"This is Inspector Mariko Ishikawa. We may have a lock on the missing Koji9B Companion. Send a patrol near Chuo Koen."

A chorus of "Ten four" came within seconds, and Ishikawa's red and blues appeared on the roof of the car from a hidden compartment, flashing silently in the darkness as they descended back onto Chiba.

Keiji removed his cord from the console and rewound it into the back of his head, then crossed his arms.

"What the hell are you chewing on, anyway?" Ishikawa asked.

"Stims. I haven't slept in three days," he said, looking down sheepishly and pushing his glasses back up.

THE HUNT BEGINS

SHINJUKU, THE HEIGHTS, 11 AM

If you pressed your hand against any surface, you could feel the nervous energy flowing through the building, like some weird spiritual haptic feedback.

An in-person council meeting was a rare thing within the walls of the DaiSin Corporation, let alone one involving *all* of the higher ups. This meant not only the managing staff, but the Deliberators as well.

Historically, this had only been done twice before, and both had been in dire times. Once at the onset of the planet-swallowing floods, and the second time during the riots which had changed the complete makeup of the city.

Workflow had gone on uninterrupted, but that tenseness had floated over the 'Needle' (the common nickname for the DaiSin Corporation building) for the past several days. Low-level employees, attuned to changes in the air, had been the first to sense the shift. Akin to a low vibration, they knew that something was amiss when they noticed so many of their superiors gathering in the same place. Like wild buffalo keeping a side-eye on the lions lolling in the shade of the acacia trees. Flicking a distracted ear once in a while and hoping they had no business near their watering holes. They did not fail to see that the lions, too, were unnerved.

Though it was common to see Mr. Archibald Suzuki on any given day as he exited his Bentley and headed to the elevators on The Heights level lobby, on this day, he'd been accompanied by both Mrs. Umi Goda

37

and Mrs. Ekemma Aliyu. The trio had been flanked by their personal secretaries after having exited Mr. Suzuki's extended luxury car.

Respectively the Council President, Vice President, and Corporate Secretary, they represented the highest order in the DaiSin hierarchy, directly below Wen Harkwell. But when Mrs. Nanako Kobayashi, the head of R&D had joined with Mr. Santiago Lopez, the Company Treasurer, the whole staff was suddenly on alert. Mrs. K, as she was known, rarely left her post in her department, and seeing her strut in the flesh was an un-ignorable anomaly.

A personal message and whisper campaign had begun in the early morning hours, only to come to a fever pitch when Mr. Taishiro Yamada, head of World Sales and based out of Berlin had stepped out onto the tarmac in front of the building, unannounced.

The Deliberators had come in as one, dressed in their long, flowing robes. Dour faces belied a kind of sly curiosity at the reasons surrounding their summoning.

All had taken their place along the oblong, rocket-shaped table on the 142nd level above Heights street level. They'd all left their attendant personnel at the door, like dirty pairs of shoes, and it was apparent some felt naked without their note-takers and assistants.

None of those assembled knew what the meeting was about, but all felt the tension of the unknown pressing down upon them as they sat with unease in the plush leather seats of the Sunshine Boardroom.

The six board members representing the various commercial interests of the DaiSin Corporation sat to one side, in charcoal-coloured suits of varying tones of severity. On the other side sat the five Deliberators, the in-house judges who conducted performance reviews of all employees, either promoting or demoting, rewarding or punishing as they saw fit. Those who made it to Deliberator status lived to a ripe old age, enhanced by certain polymerase rejuvenation techniques invented in-house. Their demeanour was one of calm wisdom, accentuated by their long, black robes.

Chief Deliberator Mx. Dominic Savorian sat in the middle, flanked on one side by Mrs. Kei Golan, Mr. Yasuo Cheng, and on the other by Mrs. Ananya Chakrabarti and Mr. Yuudai Funai.

Neither group paid particular attention to the other, as their interests only intersected when it came to the well-oiled workings of the DaiSin Corporation. Machinery, which, if one were to be honest with oneself, had been running less than optimally for the past several years.

A perfect view of the city ran one hundred and eighty degrees, the half-spherical room letting in the warm morning sunshine behind the board members. The city's activity continued in pantomime, as no sound penetrated the thick outer glass. Cars floated by on the main aerial avenues, mere metres away from where they sat. One hundred and forty-two floors down, life also stirred, and it went on its daily business, completely oblivious to the machinations that occurred above. Surrounding the Needle stood a forest of rival office towers, cool blue glassteel and ferro-concrete, arranged in physics-defying shapes.

And above them, in his private office or quarters, the man they called their boss, Wen Harkwell, steering the ship of corporation. Badly, most of them thought privately.

As much as all assembled tried to keep a cool demeanour, none could ignore the momentous occasion which was taking place, even if they ignored the reasons why.

So far they had been made to wait over an hour. The kind of slight none of them would soon forget. One did not make the most powerful people of one of the most powerful companies in the world wait. Yet here they were, clasping their hands in silence, and beginning to grumble to themselves.

The only other person present was an attendant underling. He'd been there when they'd come in, and served them coffee before taking his place by the door. He wore a dark blue suit over a white shirt, as well as a black tie, and black rimmed glasses. An affectation no one needed in this day and age unless it was 'for the look.'

At two minutes past the hour, Mr. Yamada, Head of Worldwide Sales, began to fidget.

"I'm leaving. I have things to do. Can you believe I had to fly in this morning? He has no right to keep us waiting like this. I didn't agree to this meeting just to be made a mockery of," he said, and he began to rise.

"Sit down, Yamada. He's your boss. He can do what he wants. Besides, what are you going to do? Put in a formal complaint? Might as well do it now with our friends across the table," Mrs. Kobayashi, Head of R&D said, designating the Deliberators with a long, ruby-coloured nail, who looked back impassively at the irate Yamada.

"That's not what I—" he sputtered.

"There's going to be a reshuffling, Yamada. You know that, right? Why else has he called this meeting with all of us? Do you really want to be the one who isn't here when he does roll-call? Won't look very professional, will it?" a willowy man in his twenties said, with a cynical grin, his head leaning on his fist, his elbow on the gleaming teak table.

That was the fear, of course. All these powerful men and women were terribly aware that something was up. It was as plain as watching thick, black clouds rolling in. It called for an intense sort of hurricane—the kind that would see one or more lives taken. For reasons unknown, they had attracted the ire of their CEO, and now they'd been gathered together to witness one or more of their numbers be put to the gallows, so to speak.

It couldn't be more than one or two, but the fact that they were all gathered, including the Deliberators, quite probably as witnesses, meant that the whole thing was a show trial meant to get the rest of them back in line, whatever wrong had been perpetrated.

This was why the whole room, save the Deliberators, were sweating, ready to whip out the proverbial knives if ever any kind of tangible evidence of wrongdoing were produced. Every one of them had something on the other, and would not hesitate to use it if need be.

The question was, who?

"Listen here, Lopez," the man named Yamada said, turning around, "you might be the Board Treasurer, but if I were you I'd worry more about the creative number crunching I've heard so much about, so watch your mouth. Who knows what might come to light today, huh?"

As the other man began to rise to his feet in anger, the lights began to dim in the vast room. The auto-tint on the exterior windows activated, making the room go dark. As it did, small pot lights at the base of the pillars along the windows lit up, giving the space an eerie glow. When the tinting process was complete, the windows began to crystallize from the inside, a thick, quartz-like growth rapidly spreading from the outward frames of the windows to their centres. For all intents and purposes, it resembled a thick and impenetrable hoarfrost.

Near the door, where the lone attendant stood in silence, an enormous screen lowered over a wood-panelled wall, and the angry faces of the men turned to surprise, as they plopped back down in their chairs.

Wen Harkwell's face appeared upon the screen, his personal chambers, spotless, the only background. They extended from the 145th floor all the way to the pinnacle, an immaculate white at the moment, but with a complete view of the entire city from every angle when the UV shield on the windows was lowered.

The man had sequestered himself for the past year, sending video messages and only doing conference calls to communicate with the rest of his staff.

They'd heard, through their various sources, that even his fiancé, Ms. Wolinsky had been kept at arm's length.

He looked rested, healthy and still in command, much to the

chagrin of a few among them. Ever since he'd taken over from Nabeen Singh, operations had not gone entirely well for the DaiSin Corporation, and there were enough on the board who wanted nothing less than his removal and replacement with someone they deemed more capable—one of them, of course.

"Good morning, my esteemed colleagues," he began, and smiled. There were one or two audible grunts in the audience, but with the lights turned down so low, it was impossible to guess who had uttered them.

"I apologize for keeping you waiting for so long. Last minute things to attend to. I'm sure you all understand. I'll get right to the point. The reason why you are assembled here today is for me to announce an investigation into the inner workings of DaiSin," at this there was a collective sucking in of breath.

This was not what they'd been dreading. This was much, much worse.

"For the past seven years, I've attempted to steer this ship as best I knew how. Many of you are less than happy with my attempts. I get it. I stole the position. However, I stole it fair and square. Now that the Nexus is no longer around to keep me at the helm, it is your prerogative to do what you feel is right. However, you'll have to go through the Deliberators to get what you want, won't you?"

Say what you would about Wen Harkwell, 'idiot' was not among those things. Whatever failings they felt he had, they could not stoop to accusing him of driving DaiSin into the ground through egregious bungling. This commanded at least the grudging respect of the Deliberators, and kept the wolves at bay. At least until now.

The eight men and women of the board looked across the table to the five on the other, weighing them as possible allies or mortal enemies. The only thing that had stopped them so far was that Wen Harkwell had more or less been able to keep DaiSin afloat, and even increased its earnings at times, his methods be damned.

Every single one of the eight who aspired to the king's throne knew that one of their rivals might come along and take it away with a word to the Deliberators, and so the balance had been kept since the Nexus' impressive escape a year previous.

The real question was, why had Wen Harkwell waited so long to make this announcement? Did he know he was in no real peril? Or had something come up in the recent past that made this charade necessary?

"I know many of you have been plotting against me, and I realize that that is part of the game," Wen said with a smile. "However, what is clear now is that one of you betrayed us all, and that is something that cannot be forgiven." At that, the assembled board members looked at each other in astonishment. A chasm of difference stood between jockeying for position and selling out. That, at least, they could all agree on. All, of course, except for one.

The Deliberators, as well, took a long hard look at the men and women opposite them.

"This is why I've assembled you all here. Someone in the higher echelons of the company has been trying to ruin us by undermining me as CEO. The traitor could be anyone. Even a Deliberator." It was their turn to lose their glacial composure. No one had ever accused a Deliberator of sabotage, in the entire history of the company. It was unheard of.

It was the board members' turn to cast a suspicious glance to the opposite side of the table.

"I know this comes as a shock to you all, and I don't make this accusation lightly. You know me as a straight shooter." Wen Harkwell said, his face carved in stone. "I have chosen someone from within the company to pursue this investigation. I trust him implicitly. He is a recent addition, but I know he will be thorough. I want you to put all resources at his disposal so that we may all get to the bottom of this as fast as possible, and get back to the business of making our sharehold-ers happy. Ladies and gentlemen, Hideki Saito is to be given access to everything he requests. Think of his questions and demands as coming directly from me. With that said, good day."

A shocked silence fell over the assembled men and women.

The video ended, and the screen retracted to its recess in the ceiling.

Even though the lights turned back on, the tinted windows re-mained dark, the crystallization process still in effect.

"And when do we meet this Hideki Saito," Mr. Yamada said, a note of disdain in his voice.

"Soon enough," replied the attendant who had served them all their refreshments when they'd arrived earlier. Yamada frowned. The man approached the head of the table in calm, measured steps.

"And you are?" Yamada scoffed. The corner of the man's mouth lifted slightly.

"My name is Hideki Saito, personal assistant to Mr. Harkwell. It's a pleasure to meet you all," he said, and bowed. Shocked gasps escaped around the table. The lanky man at the end grinned, placing a curled fist over his smile, as if a particularly good joke had been played, and they'd all been had.

"And when were you going to announce your presence, Mr. Saito? When we were all going to be at each other's throats?" Yamada demanded, a thin sheen of sweat pooling on his brow despite the cool of the room.

"I obey Mr. Harkwell's orders, Mr. Yamada. I've been with the company for a little less than a year. Handpicked out of the Luxembourg office to assist Mr. Harkwell in whatever he may need."

He no longer smiled. Saito looked at all the men and women down the long, thin, ovoid table before him, as they assessed and judged him, and he did the same.

"Mr. Harkwell has entrusted me to resolve this matter as efficiently as possible. I will require documents from each and every one of you, as well as any tertiary evidence I deem necessary, in the coming days. My office will be in contact with yours. Please stay in Tokyo until this business is concluded," he said, casting his gaze at Yamada in particular.

They seemed deflated, for the most part. They were not used to taking orders from anyone, save the CEO of the company, and usually they were able to delegate those requests to their own underlings. Being personally targeted felt somehow a little too... real.

"I've been with this company for over thirty years, young man," a man with salt-and-pepper hair and a deep voice piped up from near the front of the table, "and I'm not used to taking orders from anyone save *that man*," his finger pointing upward, "at the top. What happens, hypothetically, if I refuse to comply with your requests?" He asked, with splayed hands.

A few people leaned in from the end of the table to better see the exchange. Saito had expected this. Sometimes people were too comfortable in their positions and needed to be shaken up. To remember what fear and respect were. He'd trained in diplomacy, and even though an even hand might work most of the time, extreme measures could also be called for.

"Of course, Mr. Suzuki. You did hear what Mr. Harkwell had to say about my position and delegated powers, but no matter. As Chairman of the Board, you are owed utmost respect, I assure you. As I mentioned, the purpose of this research is to find out *who* is robbing the company, and by extension, you, of *your* profits. Now, I'm not ready to lay accusations without proof. That would be foolish and counter-productive. However, in the hypothetical situation Mr. Suzuki described, anyone opposed to the work I've been assigned to do could certainly be construed as a likely suspect, could they not? In which case they would have their accounts frozen, their benefits seized, and their shares redistributed, including any monies or assets in hidden accounts and in electronic currency considered DaiSin property. As well as losing any kind of retirement fund associated with the company. Such a person would have to rely on the generosity of the Corporation to which they'd sold their loyalty. Which, if I'm not mistaken, would evaporate quite instantaneously if they were no longer of any use to them." He paused for effect. "Hypothetically." he continued, using air quotes. "Does that clear things up for you, Mr. Suzuki?"

The man looked stricken, the colour having drained out of his face. The silence in the room spoke volumes about how the rest of those assembled there thought of this potentiality.

"It—it does. Thank you, son."

"Please, call me Mr. Saito," he said, smiling pleasantly.

The older man nodded slowly, putting his hands on the table, leaving moist outlines around them.

"Ladies and gentlemen, I thank you for your time. As I mentioned, my office will be in touch with yours in the coming days. Let's solve this problem so that we can get back to the business of making money, shall we? I won't hold you any longer. Please feel free to return to your duties."

As the assembled managers and Deliberators rose to their feet, Hideki Saito moved to the door, pressed the decompression code and opened it. The door clamps clacked, a hiss escaping the sealed room, and he bowed to the departing men and women. They were rejoined almost instantly by their respective personal assistants, like relieved remora having found their lost sharks.

It had gone a lot better than expected. These were not dim people by any means, but he'd expected a lot more pushback for his demands. The smell of hubris and entitlement was strong in the boardroom. He knew that now the game was on, and that every one of them would be doing their own back-trace of him, to find out who he was, where he was from, and what cracks in his armour they could exploit in case it came to that. Time was therefore of the essence.

He had no intention of physically visiting any of those that had gathered in the room, but liked the idea of having them on edge, disoriented. There were other, craftier means of gathering information, and he would be exploring those soon. Having them looking in one direction while he tracked them another had a better chance of catching them off-guard. Of course, he could simply have told them nothing at all, but if they panicked, they might make mistakes which he could glean through his alternate methods. Game on.

The crystal formations on the windows had begun to melt back into the pockets at their base, their diffracting properties no longer needed. He felt a lot more comfortable in this large, silent room now, fully aware that it was the lull before utter chaos.

He picked up a tray on a table by the door and went around the board room, picking up cups and saucers with rubber gloved hands, thinking about each person sitting there a few moments before, spoons shifting with a clink. The cups and saucers kept an inch or so apart from each other. He had no idea who could be the traitor. All he knew was that it was imperative that that person be unmasked before any further damage be inflicted on the company. It was a shame that this process could not have been initiated sooner, but he knew there had been no way around it.

"How did it go?" A woman's voice said from the doorway. A blonde white woman in her thirties stood there, her hands behind her back in the way he associated with army corporals reviewing their troops.

"Ms. Wolinsky. I'd say it went as well as could be expected. No heads had to roll just yet. So you *could* call it a win," Saito said, smiling, as he picked up the tray full of cups and saucers.

"The council will fight me, of course. I'm an interloper in their affairs, as it were. I'm not so much interested in how much they skim, but for whom they do so. For now, one investigation at a time. To be honest, I expected a lot more personal attacks today, but I suspect the knives will be drawn in the dark, by persons deniable, and inserted between my shoulder blades when I am defenceless," he said with nonchalance. "I shall therefore endeavour to expect it at any moment." He smiled, shrugging his shoulders.

Even though Saito had been in the building for over a month, introducing himself to key staff, none of them really knew anything about him save for the fact that he'd lived in Luxembourg for the past fifteen years and been trained at the prestigious University of Luxembourg in International Relations and Diplomacy. This revealed nothing of his qualifications as internal investigator.

Of course, his true purpose had not been revealed to anyone until today, and Jenna Wolinsky was just as surprised to see how much he already knew of the inner workings of DaiSin as anybody else.

"I really wish you'd call me Jenna," she said, walking into the Boardroom.

"Professional distance, milady. Always," he said, walking past her with his tray.

"You know, we have staff for that," she said, amused.

"I'm certain we do, Ms. Wolinsky."

A gloved man in plain grey service uniform appeared, and Saito handed him the tray, nodding.

"Take this down to the lab and have each one analyzed," he said, and the man took the tray, bowed, and left.

"What are you expecting to find?" Wolinsky asked, closing the boardroom door. He took off his rubber gloves and stuffed them in his pocket.

"I'm not sure I'll find anything. I just want to make sure that everyone in that room was who they said they were," he said, "That should give me a good base to start with. You have something on your mind, Ms. Wolinsky?" Saito said, one eyebrow raised.

"What do you know about the Board, Mr, Saito?" She'd left the door and walked resolutely to the boardroom table, now spotlessly clean.

"As much as the next man, I imagine. I've only just arrived. Corporate secrets are hard things to crack when people are still trying to assess your alliances," he said, pinching his chin between thumb and forefinger.

"You could have said absolutely nothing, Mr. Saito. I'll tell you about these *people*," Wolinsky said, walking over to the left side of the table. She'd said the last word with a kind of withering tone that left undeniable her low opinion of the assembled rogue's gallery, in her own mind.

"Archibald Suzuki. Thirty-four year veteran of DaiSin. Worked most of his life under Singh. Believes in the same kind of eugenics that the previous CEO did. In line to become Deliberator next, in the event that one of them passes away."

She took a step further, putting her hand on the next leather boardroom chair.

"Umi Goda. Vice President of the Council. She's a twenty-three year veteran of DaiSin. Up for the Presidency. Suzuki's protégé. She's been sucking up so long that I don't think she has any kind of independent thought left to her. Whether or not she truly believes that most of humanity deserves to die to preserve the elite is irrelevant. She toes that line to stay in Suzuki's good graces."

She took another step, setting her hand down on the next seat.

"Ekemma Aliyu—"

"Ms. Wolinsky, I don't see how this—"

"Listen. Ekemma Aliyu. Fifteen year veteran of DaiSin. She's our Corporate Secretary and secret lover of Umi Goda."

"Taishiro Yamada. Head of World Sales. He's so hated by his peers that they have him permanently stationed in Berlin."

"Nanako Kobayashi. Head of Research and Development. Word has it that if there are illegal experiments going on somewhere in Tokyo, she's behind them. Probably ordered by Suzuki." She moved to the last seat on the left side of the boardroom table and set her hand on the chair.

"Lastly we have Santiago Lopez. Board Treasurer. He's close friends with Kobayashi. Rumour in the halls is that they have some sort of secret back-and-forth going on," Wolinsky said.

"Of a sexual nature?" Saito asked.

"No. Something about DaiSin money funding her illicit research, but I'm not sure what he gets out of it. In any event, our pal Santiago got his post thanks to his father buying it for him right before Wen took over," she said, giving Saito a hard smile.

Saito stood still for a moment, as if he were recording the information mentally and placing all of it in neat little boxes in his mind for easy retrieval at a later date.

"What about the Deliberators?" he said, now curious as to what the corporate rumour mill was grinding out about the elders of the company.

"I really don't know much about them. They've been here a very long time. I think Chief Deliberator Dominic Savorian, is over a hundred and ninety years old. All the others are in that range. They've been given special gene treatments which keep them in the age range they desire. They might live forever. I don't know," she said, looking frustrated.

"You despise these people, don't you, Ms. Wolinsky," Saito said, walking a bit closer to her. The echoing silence in the room crushed down on her. She appeared to fight her desire to speak for a moment.

"Wen Harkwell won this company. Not in any lottery sense. He fought the bastard who ran it and gutted him. You know what they did to him after that? The Council and Deliberators?"

Saito looked a bit embarrassed at the outburst, but kept his composure.

"They clawed onto their positions like the slimy barnacles they are, stopping Wen at every turn when he tried to do something to better the company. They blocked any and all of his nominations to the Board. They're jackals, Mr. Saito. I don't care if only one of them is helping an outside force like the Administration or the Karetsu. To me, they're all traitors that should be taken out, wipe the slate clean," Wolinsky said, her voice having risen an octave.

"Please. Tell me how you really feel, Ms. Wolinsky," Saito said. She looked stricken, her face turning red.

"I understand your love for him. However, I've been hired to concentrate on one thing, and one thing only. I'm sorry you feel thus about the others. Bit curious you'd have stuck around, seeing as you can't stand your superiors."

Wolinsky walked back to Saito and poked him in the chest.

"It's for him that I stayed," she said.

"Walk with me?" Saito said, indicating the door. He placed his palm against the scanner, and its light flashed green, the sound of the lock retracting with a click. Jenna Wolinsky took a deep breath, the colour in her face returning to normal. She straightened out her short skirt and cleared her throat. She nodded to Saito and walked out of the protected room.

The elevators took them to the lower lobby, where they crossed over to the secret elevators for the experimental R&D Department, which were accessible through the kitchens of the dining room.

Once inside, they were protected by outside interference once again.

"Why did Wen wait so long to search for this traitor, if he knew about him?"

"Ms. Wolinsky, I know that Mr. Harkwell trusts you implicitly, so I'll tell you this—the attacks against DaiSin in the recent past have caused more damage than they should have. Stock prices have been steeply declining. The company is at risk. Mr. Harkwell believes that someone on the Board, or even a Deliberator, is involved somehow. The most important thing for him right now is finding this traitor. Or I do, in this case," Saito said, and pushed the glasses up on his nose.

"Why you, Mr. Saito? Why couldn't Wen trust the people around him?" Jenna asked, designating the man with a dismissive hand. The elevator continued its vertiginous descent to the lower parts of the secret facilities installed inside the building's support pillars. Hideki Saito raised his eyebrow at Jenna, and her face flushed.

"Because he can't trust the people around him. God damn you, Wen," she whispered, then clenched her teeth. The numbers on the wall kept descending, until they reached the 50th sub-basement.

As they stepped out of the elevator, they were greeted by a gaggle of children, all between the ages of seven and twelve. Saito smiled as they pressed him for news of the world above. These were some of the kids rescued from the experiments the Nexus had perpetrated on them a year before, saved by a private detective named Genzo Ito and placed in the care of Administration Central.

Orphaned, the only place they could have ended up was the streets of the lower city after having been released. Efforts had been made to contact their parents, but many of the children had been sold by them to the Russian mafia, and had no interest in returning to confront those same 'caregivers.' Or risk being sold again.

DaiSin had offered to take them on. They were housed in the secret facilities below until new accommodations could be built in the city proper.

A section of the research facility had been re-purposed for this, and the walls had been painted in colourful murals and bright illustrations by the kids themselves. The children had all been screened to check for infection, as well as any nefarious undertakings the Nexus might have implanted them with.

Even though the Administration harboured no love for the DaiSin Corporation, it had chosen the most cost-effective method of taking care of these foreign-born charges that it could.

Either they would have had to pay for their upbringing themselves, which was a non-starter, or they would have had to police them when they came of the age to be trouble for the population, like the street urchins Nabeen Singh had adopted and used for his plans of revenge.

Those children had been left to fend for themselves, as they had for most of their lives. Wen Harkwell had found the risk of having them inside the company too great, and therefore not worth taking.

He had, however, set up a food bank in the general vicinity of where they lived, open to any who needed nutritious rations.

He kept tabs of who used the food bank, with the idea of opening other services in the future. This information was kept from the other board members to avoid their using it for their own purposes. The denizens of the lower levels truly were abandoned, and even the CEO of the largest company in the world remembered what it had been like to go hungry at night. He didn't want their personal information used against them as some sort of targeted marketing gimmick. Or worse.

These were just some of the projects the board of directors hated so much. In their minds, it took money away from more lucrative investments. Of course, the fifty or so children in the secret lab area had been tagged as 'experimental subjects,' which was wholly acceptable to the board. How disappointed they would have been to find out that CEO Harkwell had no intention of using them as guinea pigs, and only wanted to give them the skills they needed to become self-sufficient.

The food bank he'd been able to tout as 'great PR,' to the general grumblings of the Council President, Archibald Suzuki. The hardest part had been convincing the Treasurer, Lopez, to sign off on his pet projects.

There was so much more DaiSin could do, if Wen Harkwell could stem the leak of information which was bleeding from within.

This is what Hideki Saito was here to do. He was to find the hole, and the traitor who fed it. His initial forays had been to get used to the climate, like a palaeontologist getting comfortable with his surroundings. Every company had their culture, of course, and this one was highly competitive. Cutthroat, was the term which was most appropriate.

He'd set up his base of operations on the same level as where the children were kept. It reminded him that this company was doing some good. It gave him peace to see them play and enjoy their lives, perhaps for the first time.

Ms. Wolinsky and the others didn't understand, but that was not his problem. He was not ruling out the possibility that Jenna Wolinsky might be the mole, if highly unlikely. Wen Harkwell was a good judge of character, and the thought made him smile.

"If you'll excuse me, Ms. Wolinsky, I have to go speak to Samuel Harkwell," Saito said, and left, surrounded by ten or so small children holding his hands, as Jenna Wolinsky looked after him, wondering what to think of the man.

As the kids left him to go back to their games, a little girl of maybe seven or eight came to him and asked, "Mr. Saito, did you talk to Wen?" She had long black hair and pale brown eyes, but for all that, did not look like the other children on the research floor.

"I haven't spoken to your brother in a bit, Sachiko. I assure you, as soon as I get the opportunity, I'll ask him about your parents. Is that satisfactory?" The little girl gave a long, low sigh, her chin coming to rest on her chest.

"That's what you said last time, Mr. Saito. He doesn't come down anymore. I really want to see my mom and dad again," she said, her eyes filling with tears. Saito stared at a rainbow painted on the wall, stick-figure people holding hands beneath it, dancing with joy under a bright yellow sun.

"Hey! I know," he said, smiling, "why don't we go play Rocket Adventure Team together?"

Her frown wavered, and she said in a cracking voice, "Okay—but only if I get first player!"

"Deal!" he said, and took her hand, walking her to the play room.

He felt sorry for her. Her parents had been taken away from her. Of course, they weren't her real parents, only surrogates Singh had found to take care of the little girl until she was old enough to use as a weapon against Wen Harkwell. Inside this child was the crystal chip that contained Wen Harkwell's mother's virtual personality and memories. That person had been elusive of late, and Sachiko seldom spoke of her anymore, but her demands to see Harkwell and her 'parents' grew stronger by the week.

Now she was kept here against her will, but by her very nature, releasing her back into the world was an impossibility.

Saito had found her in the corner of the play room when he'd appeared the first day. Morose and detached, she'd barely acknowledged him. He'd developed a rapport over the course of the month, and saw her much happier than she had been on his arrival. What to do about her, though, remained a mystery. He reminded himself that this was not what he was here to take care of as they turned on the game he'd promised to play with her.

He'd go speak to Samuel Harkwell at a later time.

PRAISE AYO

Datu had been silent most of the evening meal, pushing rehydrated steak protein around his mashed potatoes, like a bulldozer gathering materials. Tala was looking at him with worry, but had the courtesy not to pry.

Benilda had noticed her father's demeanour as well, and was quieter than usual. Ramil was himself, as always, and made racing noises between bites, as if every piece of food was a hovercar entering a tunnel.

Gabriel was absent, which was unlike him, but at this point, Datu had other things on his mind than his wayward son. He jumped a bit when Tala put her hand on his arm, and he tried to smile, but it only let the sadness come through even more. A tear he had been holding back streaked down the corner of his eye.

He took his half-empty plate to the counter and bit his lip.

"Someone died today, at work. And I feel like it's my fault," he said. He sat down, and Tala got up, putting her arms around him. Benilda went around the table and hugged her father over her mother's arm.

"Go crash?" Ramil asked, with an inquisitive glance.

"Yes baby. There was a crash," Tala said.

"He dead?" the boy asked again.

"Y—yes. He's dead," Datu said, holding back the tears.

"Okay. I sorry daddy!" Ramil said, with a pained look on his face.

Datu looked at his son, trying hard to smile, but choking back tears. "Thanks, buddy," Datu said, and the little boy climbed down from his chair and went to hug his father's leg. Datu picked up Ramil and put him on his lap, giving him a hug.

Tears fell on the little boy's head. Ramil put his small hands on top of his head and said, "Wet!"

"Sorry kiddo," Datu said, wiping his tears away with the back of his arm and letting out a strangled giggle. He helped clear the table and went to the altar where the small jade box was kept. He set it down on the table and pressed the button on its side.

Small lasers rose from each corner of the box and a soft whirring sound came from its base. The lasers began to swivel, faster and faster, and then activated. An image web appeared in full colour, which at first was hard to see, but within a moment or two, an elderly woman, possibly in her sixties, shimmered into existence. Behind her, a white sandy beach could be seen, with a clear blue ocean on one side and a frond of palm trees on the other.

The image was not static, however. The beach was receding.

"Ayo, it's recording," a voice said, from the background.

"If you are watching this, I want you to know that we will overcome. Always think of your home when you are far away. Be good to each other, always! We will return," she said in a kindly voice. As she turned, a dark blue wall rose in the far distance, like a thin band cutting the sky from the sea. The boat she stood on dipped slightly. And then the recording stopped. The lasers began to slow down their frenzied dance, and the whirring from inside the box was silent.

"Praise Ayo," Datu said, his hands together, eyes closed.

"Praise Ayo," Tala and Benilda said. Ramil had left the room already. It was then that Gabriel came through the door, took off his shoes, glanced at his family and began to walk toward his room.

"Where have you been?" Datu asked, irritated.

"Out, dad," came the reply.

"With who?" Datu continued. He could feel the seething anger which always boiled beneath the surface begin to rise.

"None of your business, dad, geez!" his son said, flicking his hair.

"Someone died at your dad's work today," Tala blurted out. There was a moment of silence. Gabriel flicked his hair out his eyes and stared at the floor.

"Anybody we know?" he finally said.

"Rodrigo," Datu said, daring him to retort something unsavoury.

"Oh. Oh shit," Gabriel said, his face falling. "God, dad, you need to find a new job."

"I need to—what did you say?" Datu replied, his neck feeling stiff and pained.

"Yeah dad, you need to get out of there! It'll kill you. It kills everybody else," Gabriel said, agitated.

"Do you remember where we are? Do you know why we're here?" Datu almost yelled.

"Honey, please," Tala said, reaching out to touch her husband. He waved her hand away as a distraction.

"Yeah, because of a great woman! At least she *did* something about her circumstances!" Gabriel yelled back.

"Diwata Salazar was *not* a great woman! She's one of the reasons we're all confined to Sector 14, Gabriel! Don't you get that?"

Which was, of course, the crux of almost every argument. Datu felt his mind spiralling out of control. Ever since Gabriel had found out about Diwata Salazar, his great-great-grandmother and then some, the boy had been obsessed with her story.

Truth be told, it was an incredible one. She had been instrumental in changing the face of Vertical City Tokyo—for the worse.

Diwata Salazar had been one of the chief organizers for the riots which had torn the city apart over a hundred and fifty years ago. Back then, the whole lower part of Tokyo received light from the upper.

What had started off as a protest for better rights of social mobility from lower to upper Tokyo had degenerated after a few weeks into a war of attrition between the police and army versus much of the lowest levels' population, especially the metal-workers of Chiba.

Horrified to see this mass of humanity climbing the support pylons like a swarm of ants coming for them, Admin had authorized the use of live rounds.

Scores had perished. After the rebellion from the lower quarters, The Heights had been sealed off as a precautionary measure. Light effectively cut off from the rest of the city.

All the rebels had been executed. Chief among them, Diwata Salazar, Gabriel's personal hero, and the shame of Datu's life.

Their families sent to live in Sector 14, where they would stay for generations to come.

That was the collective punishment for having gone against the will of the Administration, and the reason why it was nigh impossible for anyone to ever leave the place.

"Dad, you can keep praying to the last bit of trash that came out of the Philippines, but Diwata tried to accomplish something," Gabriel hurled at his father in defiance.

"Do not speak of the Ayo in such a manner! Respect our traditions!" Datu said, as he moved closer to his son. Tala came around to put herself between her husband and son.

"Please! Just stop!" she yelled. Ramil began to cry.

"Your traditions are dead, dad," Gabriel said, and slipped on his facemask and shoes before opening the front door and slamming it closed, the suck of pressurization ending in a slam.

Datu ran to the front door and whipped it open, cursing at his son. "Don't bother coming back, if that's how you feel about your family!" He then slammed the door himself, walked to his bedroom and closed the door behind him, his hands trembling.

A little while later, he heard a soft knock on the door. He'd been sitting on his bed, head hung low, thinking about the course of events that had led to this culmination. It now seemed inevitable that he'd have to throw his son out, eventually.

Recurring circumstances for the past year or so, and Gabriel's degenerating attitude had guaranteed this very result. In a sense, it was a release. He should feel wonderful for not having to deal with his teenage son's erratic moods and flaring tantrums.

So why did he feel so horrible? Possibly due to having lost his coworker in such a gruesome way today.

That, and the headaches caused by his employers had all conspired to bring things to a head. Now at least, he would have some peace and quiet in his own home.

"Come in," he muttered. Tala opened the door carefully, peering inside at her husband.

"Hey," she said.

"Hey," Datu answered.

"What are you thinking about?" She said, slipping into the room and sitting next to him. As soon as she put her arm around his shoulders, he felt a lightening of the load. He put his head on her shoulder, a soft kiss touching down on his forehead.

"Things keep getting worse, you know?" he said. Tala nodded, waiting, he knew, for a confession. "Work. They're charging me for a new suit. And apparently I'll have to pay a fine for endangering one of their precious diggers. Because I tried to help people."

"We'll make it through, pangga," Tala said, forcing a smile. Datu had always felt a tiny twinge when his wife called him 'beloved.' It had a way of bringing him back from the pit of his worries to where his priorities lay.

"I almost feel bad for kicking Gabriel out of the house," he said. Tala bit her lip, tight, but Datu didn't see this. He felt her uncomfortable silence, though, and said, "I'm tired. I'm working another double tomorrow. Do you think we can go to bed?"

After they had put the kids to sleep, he slipped under the covers with his wife and made love to her, almost silently. Hopefully, the world would be a different place tomorrow.

     ***

It was an unusual sound that woke Datu up. A prying of metal, with a soft 'pop.' 2 am glowed from his clock face, and he got up stealthily. Tala turned to him, fear in her eyes. He put his finger to his lips and grabbed an arm-length plastic rod from the corner of the room. He wasn't sure spare piping would be any good against a home invader, but he had nothing else to use.

With the lights off, he opened the bedroom door, creeping down the hallway. He heard movement in the living room area. The kids' door opened slightly, and he got on his knees, motioning for them to get back in. The rustling stopped, and he heard heavy footsteps go toward the door. He sprinted and hit the intruder with the stick.

The man turned around and hit him in the side, and Datu fell to the ground, winded. As the robber made another attempt at leaving, Datu kicked him in the legs, and the man fell head-long in the entrance, knocking over the coat rack which fell with a clatter.

Datu crawled over to where the man had fallen, and tried to grab him by the back of the collar. The man turned around and hit Datu square in the jaw with his elbow. Datu heard a ripping sound, and the man pushed Datu off, puffing out a muffled grunt as he got up, and made his way to the door, running out into the night.

The light came on, and Tala went to Datu when she saw him lying on his back on the ground. She closed the portico door and knelt near her husband. Datu held his face, a bruise flowering there.

Benilda and Ramil stood at the corner of the kitchen, where the bedroom hallway started, too afraid to come in. The portico door stood ajar, the lock jimmied.

"Benilda, go get me an ice pack from the freezer, would you, love?" Tala said, smiling her most reassuring smile. Benilda nodded, wild-eyed, and rushed to the freezer to do as her mother asked.

"What happened?" she asked.

"Bastard elbowed me in the face," Datu muttered, his free hand trying to help him rise from the ground. A small cut split his lip, and redness spread from his cheek to his nose in a rosette.

"Mom! Dad!" Benilda said, coming back into the living room with the ice pack. "Come quick, you have to see this!" Tala helped Datu rise to his feet, and he felt the hit he'd received in the ribs explode into a thousand points of pain. Tala helped him to the kitchen table, and sat him down.

"What's wrong, Benilda?" she said. Their daughter was pointing at the shelf behind the table. On the floor, the shrine's decorative bamboo had been unceremoniously knocked down. The shelf was barren.

Tala put her hands to her mouth and began to cry. Datu groaned and turned back to sit at the table properly and assess the damage to his body. He realized he still held something in his hand, and unclenched it slowly—the neckline of a tight-knit black sweater. It had ripped off when the intruder had popped him. As he uncurled his fingers, he saw the tag still attached to the fabric.

"Property of Peoplift Inc."

Datu hit the table with his fist, cursing loudly.

"What?" Tala asked, not having seen the tag.

"My boss, Pekelo Vora. He collects Ayo. He has three in his office. Don't ask me how he got a hold of them. Extortion, most probably. Well, he was asking me to sell ours, and I refused. I guess now we know what happens when someone turns that bastard down, don't we."

It wouldn't have been that hard for one of Vora's men to do a scan of the house beforehand and find out where the Ayo was placed. There was no way Datu would let the man get away with this. It was one thing to be a money-grubbing asshole, but a thief? That was where he drew the line.

Datu rose to his feet. He leaned down to pick up the decorative bamboo and placed it back on the shelf, joining his hands together and offering a prayer to the lost Ayo.

"Let's go back to bed. There's nothing much we can do right now," he said. He checked the pressure chamber, making sure the outside door was closed, and tried to seal the portico door as best he could. This would have to wait until the morning.

He kissed his kids good night and saw them off to bed.

"What are you going to do, Datu?" Tala said, as they climbed back into their own.

"Not much I can do, love," he said. "Sleep. We'll figure things out later." and he turned out the light.

He waited. A long time. He waited until his wife's soft breathing became her usual light snoring. He then slipped out of bed and grabbed a set of clothes. He dressed in the living room and grabbed his protective suit from the portico and latched it on, the clasping of safety clamps a reassuring sound.

Once he was done, he closed the doors and went outside. By his calculations, he'd be back at the elevators by 4 am. If he did this fast enough, he could be home with his family before they woke up. He just had to get to the Peoplift offices before anyone showed up.

He looked inside his toolbox and grabbed a ball-peen hammer, which he slipped into his tool belt.

If they were going to take his Ayo, then he would take Vora's— make the man trade. It was only fair.

Datu made his way to the back alley, where his neighbours kept their trikes. The old three-wheeled vehicles had seen better days, but he knew they were reliable. His upstairs neighbour was a delivery person, and he had found out how he hot-wired his own trike when the key didn't work.

The small, covered vehicles were interspersed with bicycles and motorcycles. He'd never ridden a motorcycle, and borrowing a bicycle would have been difficult with his suit on. As far as borrowing went, this was the only thing he could ride at the moment.

He lifted the small door on the back of the trike and touched two wires together. Just like he'd seen John do a few times. The electric engine whined to a start, and he unplugged it from the socket. He walked it to the end of the alley to avoid making noise, then climbed aboard, his head sticking out to the side, the covering a bit too low for him to comfortably sit on the three-wheeler.

He worried that John would wake up hearing the sound of his machine powering up, but he was four floors up and fast asleep. He put it in drive, and sped off.

No one was out at this time of the morning. It was as silent as the grave, and no lights save the streets' shone on his plans. In his mind, it was simple: Break into the building, case the office, grab one of the Ayo, go home, and then call his boss a bit later to arrange an exchange.

If anything, he thought Vora would gain new respect for him. Being as much of a corrupt prick as his dickhole boss might gain him some brownie points. If not, he would at least show the man that Datu Salazar was not a man to be trifled with.

Having lived in the Sector all his life, he knew how to bypass the security checkpoints, of course. It required a bit of back-alley driving and knowing which were the artificial walls the residents had put up over the holes cut open over Administration's, but all-in-all, his progress was quick and efficient, driven as it was by anger and the desire for revenge.

He ditched the trike in a dark alley before reaching the plaza, making sure to untie the wires so that no one would be able to take it before he came back.

There was no one there. All the lights were off for the night inside the offices, and even street lights seemed dimmer in the square. The fog had not yet lifted from the area, making him close to invisible. The remains of the storm, like a blanket of dark snow, hung in the air.

Datu approached, and when he came to the dirty glass doors at the front of the offices, he hit the lock with his hammer until he heard it break. He then pulled out the mechanism and pushed the door open. Even if there were cameras or sensors, he knew there would be no way for them to identify him in his gear.

He rushed in the almost complete darkness up the stairs to his boss' office and tried opening the door. Of course, it was locked. He kicked in the door, rending open with a satisfying 'crack.'

Datu ran to the back wall where Pekelo Vora kept his prizes and decided to take all of them. Truly, he deserved none. He took the jade boxes and stuffed them in his pockets.

Flashlight beams danced downstairs.

They undulated, left to right, as the four guards carrying them burst into the office. Datu was about to make a run for it, but had to change his plan. All were dressed in full tactical gear, with full-face gas-type rebreathers and riot helmets on.

They tackled him to the ground when they saw him, and the pale jade boxes fell out of his pockets. One of the guards lifted his rebreather over his head, put his wrist to his mouth and said, "We've caught the intruder." There was a pause, then, "I'll check, sir." They grappled with Datu and brought him to his feet. The man who'd been communicating with his higher-up unclasped his visor and shone his flashlight into Datu's eyes.

As hard as he tried, he couldn't put up his hand to block the blinding light. A low buzzing came from the man's ear, and the guard spoke again.

"Datu Salazar? You are no longer an employee of the Peoplift Company. Your recycler's licence has been revoked, and…" there came more chatter from the man's earbud, and he bent down to look at the floor at Datu's feet. The man picked up the three boxes and held them at arm's length.

It was then that Datu noticed the body cam on the man's left breastplate. Whoever was communicating with him saw everything through closed circuit television.

"Is that Vora?" he said, no longer holding back his anger. "You tell that rat bastard I want my Ayo back! You hear me, Vora! You had no right to take it!"

The earbud chimed in again, and the guard's face turned sour.

"Yes. Yes sir. Yes. I don't—yes. I understand, sir." When it was over, the man shook his head and put his gloved hand to his chest and turned a knob.

"Live feed to neutral," he said, and the three other men present also turned the knobs on their cameras to the off position. Datu was getting nervous. What did that mean?

"Alright boys, we have to take Mr. Salazar for a drive. Let's take him home," he said. The three other men looked at each other for a moment, and the man in charge put his mask back on. He slapped Datu's visor down and twisted the locking mechanism.

They pushed Datu down the stairs and out the door, his arm bent behind his back. Outside, an armoured vehicle waited, stark, black and silent. It looked like a cross between an APC and an armoured truck used for bank deliveries. Like a large, angular black tardigrade, with six spherical wheels for paws, protruding from the sides of the vehicle, waiting to swallow him up.

The back door lifted, and Datu was pushed onto a long bench along one of the sides of the vehicle. Two of the guards flanked him, and the other two sat on the opposite side. His hands were handcuffed and attached to lateral rings welded to the seat. Datu wondered what he'd tell Tala as the door closed behind them, blotting out the dim street-lamps with a finalistic-sounding 'clang.'

Whatever he'd thought about his job, this was not the way he thought he'd be leaving it. He'd have to come back later and get John's electric trike. Maybe get Gabriel to do it—then again, maybe not.

The truck started with a jolt, and Datu wished he could see through the windows, but these were high horizontal slits accessible only to someone standing up. Not a person sitting handcuffed to the seat.

The trajectory felt wrong. Not only had the truck not turned around, but it was following the circumference of the plateau in the opposite direction. He wondered what kind of circuitous route they were taking to return him to his apartment.

Then, the truck stopped. His guards removed the handcuffs. As he was pushed outside, he saw that they were in a desolate part of the plateau, on its North-Eastern radius. His heart began to pump bile and fear, an adrenaline rush seizing him. Behind the truck he could see the broken windows of the slum apartments and the shells and carcasses of old, burnt-out shops, in some vague before.

As he struggled, looking up at the lights of Chiba in the distance, two of the men grabbed him by the arms, ran toward the guardrail, and threw him overboard.

While he fell a hundred levels, he saw the faces of his family, before the darkness swallowed him.

THE CASE OF GENZO ITO

The quiet ping of the locator was the only sound in the cockpit of the hovercar as she aimed it back to the area from which the thrumming signal came. The orange spot on the dashboard, a glowing rendez-vous point where police forces were massing. A confirmed visual had been given by one of the officers sent to check out the tip. The Companion had been surrounded at a safe distance within a matter of minutes.

As the hovercar landed, Ishikawa turned to Keiji. "Stay here," she said, and stepped outside, the burners still hot.

Keiji left the car a few seconds later and followed her from several feet away.

She could see the Companion, now, walking with heavy steps toward downtown Tokyo under a blinding barrage of spotlights. Near Sakaecho Monorail Station stood the wide orange pylons of a police barricade erected a hundred metres away in the direction it headed, a police truck following from a safe distance behind.

Several officers hid behind the bulky assault vehicle, staying in protective range. On either side of it, several more carried metal shields and advanced cautiously.

Unlike a human suspect, Companions, when malfunctioning, had several features which made them much more dangerous. They were faster, stronger, made of sterner stuff, and were completely unpredictable. Tokyo PD had learned a long time ago not to take a haywire android for granted, no matter how small.

Ishikawa caught up with one of the officers following the truck.

"Ishikawa, Special Inspector," she said, flashing her palm to the woman on the corner of the truck, holding her gun at the ready.

"How do you want to proceed, Inspector?" The woman asked, keeping an eye on the slowly receding Companion. It looked disjointed, like a puppet whose handler was drunk. It walked in a slouch, its head lolling from side-to-side.

"Captured, if possible, Officer—"

"Yamaguchi," the officer said. "So far, tazing has had little effect. It's slowed down, but it keeps moving in the same north-westerly direction. We've cleared out the station, just to be on the safe side. Who's this, Inspector?" She said this looking to her left, and Ishikawa turned to see Keiji standing nearby, observing the Companion in the distance.

She turned on him, grabbed him by the collar and pulled him back to the car.

"I thought I'd made myself clear. Did I not tell you to stay in the car?"

"Look," Keiji said, wide-eyed, pointing toward the Companion. Ishikawa turned around. It was facing them, now. It stood still, the police spotlights reflecting off its dull silver body. Overhead, a police hoverdrone had its floods on the small robot as well. The sound of its rotors whined as it made tight circles over the fugitive.

The Koji9B leaned forward and began to run. At an incredible speed, it rammed the police truck Ishikawa and the others hid behind, slamming it back a foot or so.

"Take it down, officer," Ishikawa ordered, after a split second's deliberation. There was no sense in trying to capture the thing intact. There would be injury or loss of life, and for what, a single Companion? Ishikawa saw no reason to spare it, seeing it's unusually violent behaviour.

Officer Yamaguchi went into introspection mode for a second, sending the order to the other officers. Guns at the ready, the shield-bearing officers as their defence, the cops on the right side of the truck made a ring around the Koji9b, blocking any escape route into the surrounding suburban area. It was now caught between two walls of police and the two floor monorail building.

The driver of the police APC jumped out the door. The Companion extricated itself from the front grill and threw it away like someone else might discard a candy wrapper that got stuck to their clothes. It bounced off the pavement with a spark and went skidding across the street and hitting a fence before Officer Yamaguchi could yell, "Fire!"

As soon as she did, a volley of bullets hit the Koji9B at its center of mass, as it turned around from the front of the truck. It fell once to the ground with a 'clang', then got up, shakily, with the agility of a senior citizen, while the officers continued to fire. It then jumped straight into the glass wall on the ground floor of the monorail station, shattering it in the process, skidded on its chest, and then slammed headlong into a desk. It remained prostrate as the police stepped into the station, their guns drawn and ready to fire if it showed any signs of having survived the first assault.

One of the officers raised his hand and yelled "Clear!"

Thin plumes of smoke rose from the perforations in the Companion, and a fire-fighter came in with an extinguisher and covered the Koji9B in a blanket of foam.

"Stay here," Ishikawa said to Keiji, and headed to where the Companion lay. Her shoes crunched on the bits of broken glass as she headed inside the empty lobby of the monorail station. Another team entered from the opposite side, using the front doors, carrying a large metal box.

Ishikawa knelt next to the Companion, putting on a pair of disposable gloves. She took out an analyzer from her pocket, the disk-shaped box slightly larger than her open palm. The DaiSin logo glowed briefly as she squeezed it to turn it on. She wiped a gloved hand over the foam that covered its head, its dead eyes staring off sideways, before finding an input jack on the side of its head. She extended one of the cords from the analyzer into the jack and waited for the tell-tale signal.

A double beep and a red diode showed on the disk. The Companion was beyond analysis. One of the bullets had fried its internal matrix, and its brain could no longer output the information she would have needed to find out what had caused the malfunction.

Ishikawa sighed and pulled out the jack, slipping the analyzer into her pocket. She nodded to the retrieval team, who put the box down next to the 'dead' Companion and began to pick up its pieces, smaller bits of its internal structure having fallen out of the bullets' escape holes. The remains would go through further analysis downtown, but if the preliminaries were any indication, there was nothing much left to scan.

She walked back outside where the female officer, Yamaguchi, was keeping an eye on Keiji.

"So?" the officer asked.

"Nothing doing. It was shot up pretty bad. My money is on some sort of manufacturer's defect. Kind of thing that'll trigger a recall in the next few days. That, or else we'll see a few more cases like this one. Call the owner and tell him to initiate an insurance claim. I'll take him,"

Ishikawa said, and took Keiji by the forearm, frog-marching him back to the car.

"When I tell you to do something, I expect you to do it," she hissed to the young man as she pressed the clicker for the butterfly doors to open.

"What are you, my mother?" Keiji said, as he stepped into the car, morose.

"Yes, I'm your mother. Now I'm going to ground you in your room and you can forget about your little investigation into your missing boss. He's no longer my problem, and neither are you. Where can I drop you off, son?" she said, eyes throwing daggers at the boy.

He was smart enough not to respond.

The afternoon traffic had begun to thicken, and soon they were in a slow lane of flying cargos and taxis, heading back to Tokyo's core.

On either side of the car, pillars glowed with advertisements and the lights of the glass elevators rising and falling. The flashing red hazard lights along their length always reminded her of spaceports' vertical launch pads.

Lower, the perfect circular horizontals of the kilometre-wide plateaux threw out convoluted feelers downward and outward in extensions, like mutations in the forms. Metastasized to accommodate overflowing populations.

The shapes of the cities that grew upon them remained constant: suburbs of hive-like apartment complexes on the edges, and sky-scrapers near the supports.

There were always exceptions, of course. The Heights was one such place where the constraints of the plateaux no longer existed. Heights architecture flowed in a way that no lower level could imitate. Not for lack of resources, but space.

Ishikawa thought about the Companion for a moment, and wondered what made them go feral. The complexity of the positronic brain was such that a simple malfunction might entail a catastrophic cascading of errors, such as she'd witnessed today. She'd only personally seen another such occurrence in her lifetime, when she was a child, and that one had been taken care of before any violence had taken place.

"I guess Ito was wrong to put his faith in you," came Keiji's voice as she was lost in thought. Nice of him to throw out bait like that, she thought.

"I guess he was," she said, turning to the boy and flashing him an innocent smile.

"Now you'll never be able to repay your debt to him, huh? Pretty shabby way to treat him, don't you think?" The kid was good, she had to admit. By now she'd recovered from her initial shock at having been confronted by him, and had no intention of being psychologically manipulated by a high school kid.

"Listen kiddo. No offense, but you're a bit young to be playing this game with me."

"And you break promises. You really are a cop, aren't you?" This was meant to convey that she, a Special Inspector, was on the same level of corruption as the average beat cop. Ishikawa felt her collar get warm.

"Where am I dropping you off, then?" she said, her voice restrained. The kid pointed at Shibuya, in the distance. She began to take the off-ramp toward The Heights, and Keiji shook his head, pointing at the 250th. Ishikawa raised an eyebrow, and directed the car to where the boy pointed.

"Right there on Kuyakusho Street is fine," he said. Ishikawa manoeuvred the car lower until it alighted on the curb, in front of a construction site. This darker patch of the city was nestled between a dead 'love hotel' and some sort of cheap department store. The kind that sold the knock-offs made in illegal factories of the 100th. Admin turned a blind eye, since shutting them down meant they'd have had to do something about the overabundance of poverty on the 250th and lower.

Street lamps shone on the abandoned construction site, visible through an opening of tall white protective fences. A large crater had been dug half a floor into the plateau, with jagged black cuts, at irregular intervals. Inside it, orange Komatsu construction exoskeletons were tethered for the night, side by side with a twenty-storey crane and dump truck.

The more Ishikawa's eyes adjusted to the area's lighting, the more she noticed that it wasn't so much a construction site as a demolition in progress.

Keiji looked at her, then at the site.

"Can you let me out, please?" he asked. Ishikawa pressed the latch release, and the door rose. It was then that she saw the torn metals and shorn scrap which covered the ground around the site. Keiji left the car and walked a few metres over to where the devastation lay.

Curious, she left the car, wondering about this place of desolation, herself. She should have taken him straight to The Heights, she now felt. She let out a short sigh and walked over to where Keiji stood, observing the destruction.

Above them, one of those huge advertisement skiffs covered in screens urged them to 'Buy DaiSin Trodes! ,' a beautiful woman shaking her long black hair out of the way to reveal the tell-tale connectors on the back of her neck. It slid through the sky, speakers barking out that illegal clones would be terminated, and those harbouring them held as accomplices.

"This is where he disappeared, isn't it." This wasn't a question. Blackened impact marks and striations in the surrounding buildings made it clear that this was no construction site. No blasting was allowed inside VCT. This had been a malicious attack meant to utterly eradicate—in this case, a nosy detective.

"He just cut communications a few days ago. Said he was going undercover. Last place I received a signal from was a few hundred metres from here. Then I saw this in the news," he said, putting out a hand showing the devastation. "I knew it had to be him. The coincidence was just too great to ignore."

Ishikawa thought she might have caught wind of the incident as well, but there was always a bomb going off, or an assassination, or a disappearance, and after a while, the circle of violence tended to blend into itself. It was only when the event was personal that it came home to jab you in the feelings. And then you simply shoved it down and down so that it didn't destroy you.

He leaned into the pit, and lower parts of the plateau could be seen—layers of metal and sub-structure, melded together. A few pieces fell into the hole, clanging onto the sub-strata below.

Ishikawa bent down to pick up a piece of melted metal, turning it in her hand. She took out her analyzer, placed the chunk on it and pressed the activation button. A few moments later, she checked the read-out on her wrist.

"This seems highly unlikely, but there was a thermic reaction. Which could mean someone detonated a thermite bomb," she said, throwing the pieces of melted metal back into the pit.

"What was Genzo Ito investigating, Keiji?" she asked, turning to the boy.

"He refused to tell me, which, in and of itself is odd. During the time I've been working for Mr. Ito, he's never hidden anything like this from me." Ishikawa nodded, pulling out a thick black visor from her inner pocket. She slipped it on and clicked the button on the corner of the rim and branch, the unit activating. A purple sheen spread across the front of the viewing area. She carefully looked from left to right inside the hole, an analytic wireframe of the various substances appearing on the inner screen.

She paused at the blinking of one of the items, described as organic. It was small, but it registered. In the far-right corner of the pit, something which had at some point been alive had left a trace. Ishikawa struggled with the thought of having to tell Keiji that she'd found a piece of Ito.

She advanced toward the hole, ducking under the thick silver chain that ran across the entrance between two fences, and began to clamber down the unstable side. Keiji followed, making his way down a bit further to her left. They clung to melted metal and dead power cables, the city having cut off any remaining power to this block.

Soon they were at the bottom of the pit, and Ishikawa made her way to the last remaining bit of anomalous substance in the hole.

She pushed debris out of the way with her foot and knelt down, finding a bit of burnt cloth. No. Not cloth. Leather. She pulled on it, and it remained stuck fast. Keiji cleared a bit more debris from the surrounding area, and she found that the leather was stuck in a metal door on the ground, which had been locked from the inside.

"That is definitely Ito San's," Keiji said, staring at the chunk of leather.

"Then perhaps your boss is still alive, Keiji. Now you just need to find him," she said, letting go of the tattered remain and wiping her hands.

"Don't you mean 'we' need to find him?" Ishikawa bit her lip and looked up from inside the crater. If someone was using thermite explosives inside Tokyo and TPD had sent Keiji packing to avoid scrutiny, the odds were that someone would get hurt, sooner or later.

In the meantime, either Keiji's boss had been taken, or he'd faked his own death. Where would he have gotten thermite explosives? Illegal on the open market, there were only a few Administration Departments which had access to the stuff. And none of them operated within city limits or above the 100th level.

The other question, of course, was why? What was the point in making a private detective disappear in such a manner? This made her think that he'd done it himself, out of some theatrical production, possibly to evade creditors or other unsavoury characters. Who knew what Ito had been up to?

She'd never known Genzo Ito to be a logical man, so this might very well fit his twisted profile. She didn't feel the need to continue the search for him, if that was the case.

Perhaps not case closed, but as close to an answer she was willing to pursue at this point. Screw Ito. Whatever he'd gotten himself into, he probably deserved what had happened.

Ishikawa began to walk back to the entrance of the pit, Keiji in tow.

"Aren't you going to try opening that hatch?" he asked.

"And what would that prove, kid? If he did escape, he's long gone. Go home. I'm pretty sure we'll get news in the next couple of weeks. Besides, he probably did this himself," she said, beginning to climb the wall of broken metal.

"I'm certain he didn't, Special Inspector. I'm not giving up," Keiji said, as he made his way up the wall as well.

"Are you sure I can't drop you off nearer to home, boy?" Keiji slapped the dust off his high school jacket and pants. She looked out across the desolate landscape of the blast site, wondering now where that bastard Ito was hiding, and hating herself for allowing her curiosity to get the best of her.

"No. It gets weirder," he said, walking away. "Do you like karaoke, Special Inspector?"

LITTLE BROTHER

After having spent a few hours with Sachiko, Hideki Saito shifted gears into investigation mode.

The obvious place to start was with Samuel Harkwell. Saito made his way from the Research and Development branch of DaiSin to the Main Control Room. Situated in the central pillar of the building, it was the nerve centre in charge of coordinating the company's defences, both real and virtual, as well as all day-to-day operations. Most overt wars between corporations having been eliminated in the past hundred years, deadly skirmishes were kept in the dark of the web and small-scale, real-world incursions.

Most of the physical fighting was done by mercenaries imported from around the world, hired by tertiary companies for the sake of deniability.

The Eleven Karetsu, the most powerful organization of conglomerates in Vertical Tokyo, would often use personnel companies for wetwork and close-quarter combat, as well as infiltration, exfiltration, and hacking. Otherwise, there were entire floors of online armies at the headquarters of every company in the world trained to attack rival corporations, the outcome of the battles deciding the value of the various companies' stocks in the global markets.

In an age where the worth of a company was calculated in how well it could push back on the attacks of hostiles, DaiSin had been instrumental in developing offensive and defensive weaponry. Wen Harkwell himself had been key in some of the most recent.

Administration generally frowned upon physical violence

committed without their consent, but as the Eleven controlled most of the Administration's finances, their protests were toothless.

Still, the Eleven kept their end of the bargain, in spirit. If not for the sake of the Administration, at least out of respect for the city where they'd made their fortunes. The ancient bushido code of honour evolved to the cybernetic 24th century.

It stood as a partial arbiter of the goings-on inside the city, and even though it ran things sub-optimally, it was better than not having them there at all, or so Hideki Saito thought.

Administration Central also had an army, and was proud to say internally that most of its soldiers obeyed their orders. This could be said just about anyone working for the powers-that-be.

Hideki thought with a smile that "We might not be doing a great job, but at least not everyone on our payroll can be bought." would be a strangely honest motto for Administration to have.

A precarious balance was maintained, though, between the power of the Eleven, Administration, and DaiSin. A tripartite push and pull that knew no clear winner.

With this new player, the mole, the power was draining from DaiSin, and helping the Eleven. Who knew how soon the Karetsu might take over DaiSin and incorporate it into its own structure? This is what Saito wanted to stop at all costs.

DaiSin had been there for the construction of the Vertical City. It had been indispensable in that building process. He believed in it and its potential, whether or not Wen Harkwell was in charge.

As he made his way down to the Central Control Department, he thought of the Board Members and the Deliberators. One was guilty, of course. A breach-point of such monumental proportions that it threatened the very existence of the biggest corporation in the world.

But how, and in what capacity? That was the sticking point which was still to be determined.

As he descended to the control room, he thought of how alone he was in this endeavour. He would have liked to be sure that those he'd chosen to be his assistants were to be trusted, but that was a luxury he did not possess. This was the reason he compartmentalized work, to have as little information overlap handed to his potential enemies. Allowing them to know just enough, without revealing the endgame. *Fun*, he thought, and rolled his eyes.

Numbers flashed in the negative on the elevator panel, and he stepped out in a silent corridor, the sound-suppressing black fibres absorbing the press of his shoes, leaving behind faint purple outlines as he walked down the corridor, covered in the same material as the floor. Low LEDs lit up the bisection of walls and floor, only to dim again as he had passed.

Every precaution had been taken to shield the lower half of the DaiSin building from all sorts of intrusion, whether electronic, sonic or heat-detecting. Even the air was kept at a lower temperature. The outside of the pillars were conversely heated, so that any spy would be confounded by any lack of movement within.

In any measurable, detectable sense, these departments did not exist.

Men and women in the militarized DaiSin uniform walked the length of the hallways as well, weaponless for the most part. Saito knew that the alarm could go off at any moment, and they would be called to the barrier department several floors higher.

Those skirmishes rarely ended in physical casualties, but did have real-world implications for valuation, and were therefore treated as life-or-death struggles.

They observed him silently, rarely giving him more than a glance. This was one of the moments Saito felt like a virus slipping into a host body, getting the cold shoulder from the antibodies. But that wasn't true, was it? It was the opposite. He was a powerful vaccine looking for the virus cell before it could destroy the host. First he had to identify it.

He came to a door where an armed guard stood watch.

"Hideki Saito to see Samuel Harkwell," he said, putting out his wrist to have it scanned by the soldier. The man took out a short wand and tapped his arm, a double tone sounding approval. The man stepped aside, and the door slid open.

As it did, Saito saw that its foot-wide diameter, three-inch clamping hooks recessed within.

Saito instinctively put his hands to his ears as he stepped inside, the sound having increased by several decibels. The door slid shut behind him, the clamps latching with a dull thud.

The room was two stories tall, circular, and bisected horizontally by a girder system which held the same servers on the first as the second floor. They were a bit above human height, like two side-by-side refrigerator boxes painted navy blue, rows of vertical blinking lights indicating constant furious mathematical computing.

They were connected to each other with trunks of pale blue optical fibre the diameter of an arm, tie-wrapped every six inches or so. The spools of wiring ran to the ceiling and the floor, vanishing into the building to control absolutely every aspect of its functioning.

The sound didn't come from the servers themselves but the heat-sink fans which ran constantly from below them, cooling them down.

Saito became acclimated and headed up the first set of steps on his left, the cool wind from below ruffling his tie. On the second floor, a man sat at a Net Chair, a host of trode wires hung from the ceiling, plugged directly into the back of his bald head. He wore what looked like opaque plastic clothing and thick rubber-heeled shoes. Saito was reminded of a hospital patient in a gown.

He opened his eyes and rubbed sleep out of them, the cables wiggling slightly. He got out of the utilitarian leather chair and touched a metal rod that extended down into the lower floor, a small blue spark flicking from his fingertips into the silver ball at its tip. The cables followed him wherever he went, growing longer or shorter, depending on his position, but always clung to him like thick, black and grey hairs stretching to the sky. His too-perfect face was evident right away, and the impression was made concrete when the man shook his hand.

"Hideki Saito, my name is Samuel Harkwell. It's nice to finally meet you," he said. Saito was in no way surprised to hear that Samuel Harkwell was aware of his existence. Even if Wen had not told him in advance, Samuel controlled all the internal communications and surveillance equipment, and would be fully aware of Saito's presence.

Samuel noticed Saito's auditory discomfort and signalled for him to follow. He led him into the next room, which was made of glass doors and walls, but perfectly sound-proof. The only way to tell of the disturbance next door was by the steady thrum which emanated from the floor. Saito noticed that the cables were held by pulleys on the ceiling, attached to a track system which went around the entire room.

The floors were a spit-polished cream white tiling, and several Net Chairs were arranged around a central console which raised like a rectangular charcoal-coloured block from the floor, with an identically-coloured hood lowering overtop it.

"You're a Companion, Mr. Harkwell?" Saito asked, his hearing returning. He tried not to make it sound as if he was surprised.

"Only my body. I've been cyborgized. My brain is my own. I blame Nabeen Singh for my present condition," Samuel said. He said this with a smile, but Saito could feel the underlying tension in the words as a particularly painful memory. It came through as a slight glitching of the voice pattern.

"Quite the setup you have here," Saito said, changing the subject, looking around at the powerful computers running the daily affairs of DaiSin.

"Somewhat improvisational, I'm afraid," Harkwell said.

"How so?"

"I'm running virtually everything from this room. Pardon the pun. Internal and external. Most of the heavy lifting is done by the HYVE in the central pillar, but I get final say on most of its decisions. It used to be that the workload was split between the HYVE and Nexus," Harkwell said, pointing out the network of servers. He shrugged his shoulders, knowing full-well it would be superfluous to mention the Nexus' disappearance.

The HYVE were the High Yield Virtual Entities, human brains hooked up in tandem within an enormous cylindrical room, from which they could operate externally by taking on the forms of copper-coloured cubes in combat constructs as well as other virtual environments on the network. These minds had been scrubbed clean of their previous personalities, which had been stocked onto crystalline chips: the so-called 'Nexus,' which Nabeen Singh had used to spread the company's influence far and wide.

"I see, so the workload has doubled in the past year. Do we know at what point the Nexus *physically* departed from DaiSin?" If there was one way to find out who had been implicated, that would be it.

"Video records showed no suspicious activity at any point which would indicate an outside force at work," Harkwell said.

"I'd like you to send me the video records for the year preceding the discovery of their escape, if you could. I'm certain you have those on the server banks."

"Of course," Harkwell said, nodding slowly.

"Tell me, Mr. Harkwell, why did Wen put you in charge of these operations? Are you trained in this field?" Saito looked as the cyborg body appeared to think, and micro-changes in his face and demeanour, some almost too small to detect with the human eye flickered across his features. He knew he'd caused a measure of discomfort, but this was the name of the game.

He wanted real answers. That could only be accomplished by asking pertinent questions, causing the most honest reactions.

"No, in fact. When my brother put me in charge of this department, I was a brain in a bottle, and thirteen years old. What he wanted above all else was someone he could trust. I'll be honest — DaiSin is a snake pit, Mr. Saito. If it had been anyone else, Wen might be dead today." Samuel said, and shrugged.

"Then why take on the position of CEO at all?" Saito asked.

"Better to be sitting above the predator than below, don't you think?

Besides, at the time, the Nexus forced his hand. It wanted him to take over for Singh, seeing as he'd been able to outwit him. I think what turned into his fatal flaw was that Wen had neither the ambition or cruelty Nabeen Singh made his primary weapons. In the Nexus' mind, they'd chosen a dud, when what they wanted was a cruise missile." Samuel paused to rub his chin and look out to the server banks on the floor beyond the glass enclosure.

"And what do you think about Mr. Wen Harkwell?" Saito asked, Samuel turning to look at him once again.

"He's my brother and I love him. Anyone who cares about others the way he does is a god in my books. After he took over, he got rid of all the control mechanisms that kept the staff and Nexus in thrall. Some would call that a dumb mistake. I call it compassion. Of course, now we have to deal with a lot more internal bullshit... but everyone gets to live with free will. It's a tough tightrope to tread, you know?" Samuel Harkwell put his hands on one of the trode connectors attached to his head and rubbed it slightly, scratching an itch.

"It does add to the list of potential moles within the organization," Saito said. Harkwell gave him a tight smile.

Just then, a blinking red light began to pulse on the wall, and Samuel looked at his control chair on the other side of the glass wall, an air of discomfort on his face. It was obvious that duty called, but Samuel Harkwell was not one to put out a guest.

"You have to go, I understand. We'll continue this conversation afterwards," Saito said. As Harkwell left, his mass of cables following, Saito came to the dais in the middle of the room. The lights dimmed, and a series of lasers began to dance from the hood above, painting a battlefield in bright lights.

Saito watched as the DaiSin defences were erected, virtual firewalls tessellating before great walls and towers representing DaiSin defensive assets.

Points of green light moved along the tower walls, DaiSin soldiers manning the cannons and pointing them toward an invading force of red dots further along the plain.

It looked like a game, but Saito knew that whoever was shot down in the virtual would suffer in the real, if their personal firewall collapsed, or were unable to log out fast enough to avoid being infected by a virus

As the red dots advanced on DaiSin positions, their own shields fended off the majority of blasts from the tower positions. Volleys of fire from both directions erupted at an incredible speed, and before he knew it, the attack was over.

It had taken less than thirty seconds, but Saito knew that within the simulation, time was variable. It could have been a half hour battle, for all he knew. The lasers over the table repositioned, and a stock ticker appeared, showing that DaiSin stock had gone down by .03 of a percentage point.

Taking into consideration that these kinds of attacks happened on average every five to ten minutes, he mentally calculated once again the rate of decrease of the company's stock. The total he came to seemed dire, but he remembered that there were times when DaiSin won, as well.

He asked the computer to show the graph of the win/loss stock ratio, and it hovered between dais and hood like a silver mountain range, one which tapered off lower and lower in recent months.

The lights turned back on, and Samuel Harkwell stepped back inside the room, the noise of the fans following.

"We didn't do too bad on that one. The problem is that that doesn't happen very often anymore," Samuel said. "And as we go down, others are rising. Whoever is betting on the other team is making a killing at the moment." Harkwell scratched the back of his head, between two silver connectors.

"In your opinion, what might be causing this? To my knowledge, DaiSin has some of the best firewalls and offensive weapons. So why are its opponents steadily gaining ground?"

Harkwell began to pace the room, hands on his hips.

"Well, either someone is arming the opposition, or sticking a wrench in our own operations, or even both," Samuel said, turning on his heel and putting up his finger in an 'a-ha' sort of gesture, the cables extending from the back of his head, wiggling slightly.

"We'd have detected new weapons from the enemy, especially if they were rip-offs of our own. And any sort of overt sabotage would have been discovered months ago," Saito said, his lip curling in doubt. Samuel's eyebrow rose, perhaps in surprise as to how well-informed the man was.

It was true. The system was set up so that any kind of tampering could be detected and reset. The point was not to annihilate the opponent through trickery, but to best them on the battlefield with weapons created by either party. At the base of the equation remained the products and services provided by the various corporations. The battles were meant to show their prowess, but it would have been beyond suspicious if, for example, a corporation wiped out another's value after a single battle on the field.

Unless the algorithm had been tampered with, of course. This was not what was going on. Battlefields were tested thoroughly in-house between bouts, and no anomalies had been detected which could account for the gradual yet increasing degradation of DaiSin stock.

A different kind of tampering was at play, one which would be almost impossible to detect. Saito had dismissed the notion that the trust he placed in DaiSin tech was pure hubris. Its employees worked hard on their crucibles, the computer program in charge of generating new weapons based on thought, and previous incarnations of proven firepower.

Wen Harkwell himself had been crucial in the next evolution of DaiSin's weapons systems, and it was nigh impossible the competition had caught up in such a short time span, let alone create offensive weaponry so powerful that it chipped at DaiSin defences as it was doing now.

"Would it be possible to make it appear as if nothing was wrong with the systems, even though they were being tampered with?" Saito asked. Samuel Harkwell cocked his head in a thoughtful way, cables following, and Saito was reminded that the man inside the machine was much younger than the shape of the body suggested.

Even though the Companion body represented a man in his forties, the brain inside it was in its twenties. This accounted for the quirks he'd noticed.

"There aren't that many entities with enough computational power that could pull it off." Samuel said, cupping his chin with his hand

"And what might those entities be?" Saito asked, already certain of the answer.

"The HYVE, the Nexus, one of the Eleven, or even Admin," Samuel answered. "But the Nexus' link was severed when it left DaiSin. Ahhh, now I see why you are looking for a mole. You think someone is giving the opponent direct access, don't you. I have to tell you, though, that kind of influence would have to be in real-time. There's no way they could slip in and out of the system without getting noticed by the HYVE." Samuel said, returning to his pacing.

"That does not bode well for the HYVE, then, does it," Saito said, as innocuously as possible. The effect he was after was instantaneous.

"For me, you mean. Listen, Mr Saito, I've been accused of a lot of things, but turning on my brother? That's a first," Samuel said, in a calm, even tone. Saito noted the treble in the voice pattern once again, but whether that was a sign of indignation or guilt was uncertain under present circumstances.

"Where might I be inclined to find a clue as to how an enemy could enter the system undetected?" Saito asked.

"You'd want to talk to Nabeen Singh. Not that I advise it. He'll never tell you how he would have programmed his firewalls to throttle his own defences. But I imagine he would have done so to regain control if he'd ever lost it."

"Yes, I've heard the man was a tad prickly," Saito said, and Samuel chuckled, his voice a harmony of tones.

"You could put it that way," he said.

"I won't hold you up much longer," Saito said, turning toward the door, but then looked back, as if remembering something. "Oh, one last thing, I need to monitor the Board of Directors and the Deliberators. That's an order from the top." He smiled, and Samuel's face fell. Saito turned to Samuel again, giving him a curious glance.

"You're going to war, aren't you," he said, tilting his head and crossing his arms.

"Not at all. I'm going hunting. I want to make sure I have the right prey. I need you to assign me a few HYVE Golems, Mr. Harkwell," Saito said, tipping a finger to the man.

"It's against company policy to do any type of surveillance on those people, you know that, right?" Samuel Harkwell's eyes narrowing, as he rubbed one of the cables jutting from his scalp. He said 'those people' with the same reverence usually reserved for royalty and heroes.

"Ah, but not if the order comes from above them, which it does. Thank you for your time, Mr. Harkwell. If you'll excuse me, I have to go speak to one Nabeen Singh."

Just then, the lights on the monitor began to blink furiously once again. Hideki Saito wished Samuel Harkwell a good day, who merely stood there for a moment or two before heading to his Net Chair, a look of mild bewilderment on his face.

PARADISE LOST

E ven before Datu opened his eyes, he heard the sounds, in the near
distance. A kind of rush, rising to a crescendo, then a fade. Followed by another, and another, each of varying intensity.

A cool breeze blew across his face, and he opened his eyes, startled.
A wooden-bladed fan turned lazily above his head, but it hadn't been
the fan which had caused the stirring of the white cotton sheet which
covered him. A faint smell of brine filled his nostrils. Not the noxious,
stinging mix of salt-water and heavy machine oils he was accustomed
to. This odour was somehow... pure.

Datu rose on his elbows, looking around him with curiosity. He saw
with incredible clarity. The windows of the house stood open, an ocean
sprawled before him, its pale blue waves crashing on a beach of fine
pink sand only a few metres away from the house. The sun shone with
brilliant intensity, dimmed only by the shade within the house.

He was dressed in plain shorts and a white t-shirt, his protective suit
nowhere to be seen. It was then that the last thing he remembered came
back to him with a rush.

Even as he lay on this bed, he felt himself falling for all eternity,
hitting the ground and blacking out. He shook his head and put one
naked foot over the side of the bed onto a creaking hardwood floor.

By all accounts, his body should have been broken. He felt his head
spin again when he made the connection — he was dead. This was the
afterlife. He looked around once more to identify what kind of afterlife
he'd merited.

A worn wooden table with dark green legs stood to his right, a kitchenette of the same aged material a bit further off, with dented pots and pans hanging from rusted hooks on the wall, a sink. The walls painted a faint green, chipping at the corners, revealing previous colour schemes like layers of hard candy. A natural occurrence because of the salty ocean air, he surmised.

On the wall, a calendar, above a ratty old desk and chair. Its edges curled, the top half representing a busy city at night.

Once the world had ceased spinning, he rose to his feet, uncertain how to proceed. After all, he'd never been dead before. This was all new to him. He felt a pang of regret for Tala, Benilda, Gabriel, and Ramil. *If this was paradise, he'd get to see them here someday,* he thought.

With unsteady steps, he walked over to the calendar. The date read 1997. He reeled forward, catching the desk in front of the wall with both hands. He pulled the wooden chair beside it and sat down, hard.

The quiet of the room disturbed only by the quiet rush of the waves on the beach, and the occasional gust of wind rustling the ephemeral white drapes before the open patio doors, which gave him a breath-taking view of surf and sand.

Had he—had he gone back in time? How to explain the date on the calendar? It looked and felt more and more like a surreal dream. Another important detail to note, the writing was in Tagalog. If this was paradise, he'd been transported to the Promised Land, before it had sunk beneath the waves.

As much as Datu wanted to understand what it all meant in the grand scheme, he was content to pick himself up and walk barefoot down the steps that led to the beach.

As he left the cool shade of the house, the rays of the sun danced upon his skin for the first time in his life, and he felt its power as a pleasant tickle running through him.

Warmth and light.

A short jetty extended into the clear blue water, fishing nets hung on tall poles along its sides. A small banca, the traditional fishing boat, was moored to the left side of the pier. It bobbed lazily with the motion of the waves.

This was indeed paradise.

He put his hand up before his face, the light blinding him. When he put his foot down into the sand, the soft grit shifted between his toes as they sank. He looked down and moved his foot from side-to-side, fanning the sand, finding the layer beneath the dry sand moist and pliant.

Kneeling down, he sifted the curious substance through his fingers.

What he at first had thought was pink sand was in fact the discoloration caused by tiny bits of pink coral mixed in with the pale beige grit, giving it a salmon hue.

Datu grinned. What a weird and wonderful world, this paradise was. To his left and right, he spied a receding line of coconut trees on the either side of the furthest edges of the beach.

The house had been built on a secluded inlet. Behind it, or rather, in front of it, a small breaker hid the road that undoubtedly ran the length of the island.

He turned back to the ocean and covered his mouth with his hand. Walking like a man in a daydream, he expected to wake up the instant things became too real. He shook his head, unbelieving. The breeze played with his hair, and he laughed out loud, stepping into the surf as a wave came crashing in.

Water lapped at his ankles, and he stepped further away from the beach, the tide receding. A moment later, another wave came thundering in, this one half his height, throwing him backwards, covering him Struggling to get up, he gasped for air. When it receded, he sputtered and spat, stinging salt water in his nose.

Crawling on his hands and knees to the edge of the beach, his cough turned into mirth. He laughed and laughed until his eyes filled with tears, and then he lay on his back, staring at the whirling birds in the sky.

For a long time, Datu Salazar lay there, the soft, cool mattress of sand taking his shape and holding him in its embrace. The sun looked down on him and warmed his soul. Soft gusts played with his arm hairs, making them rise and fall, and Datu felt a kind of gratitude he'd never felt before.

If this was a dream, he wished never to wake up again. If this was paradise, he hoped it was for eternity. And as he felt those things, guilt gnawed at him. His smile melted away. His heart grew heavier. Thinking about the family he'd betrayed by going off half-cocked. It was for their good he'd done it, he reminded himself. How would they survive without their Ayo?

How will they survive without you? Another voice inside his head asked.

Pekelo Vora had no business taking their Goddess, or anyone else's for that matter. His greed had to be punished, his misdeeds brought to the light of day. He looked up at the sun again, the heat on his cheeks almost unbearable now.

Datu rose to his feet, brushing the sand off his back and butt. He looked to the left and right, and decided to walk to the visible end of the beach. Either one was fine. He'd have plenty of time to do both, he knew.

He picked left and began to walk, staying on the wet part where the surf came to die, avoiding the now burning sand. As he watched the approaching tree line, tiny brown crabs escaped crevices in rock mounds along his path and rushed into the ocean.

Overhead, blue-beaked white birds with red webbed feet circled, often plunging into the ocean to return to the surface with wriggling fish in their mouths.

Datu plodded on, his feet leaving perfect imprints, washed away instantaneously by the eternal ocean.

After what he judged was a fifteen minute walk, avoiding the occasional flotsam and jetsam that came to rest on the beach, he came to an outcropping of sharp rocks, jutting into the water, and topped with tall, leaning coconut trees.

He looked back once at the white painted house and decided to find out what was over the ridge. He began to scramble over the smooth grey stone, regretting not having even a pair of flip-flops. He slipped once and scraped his shin on a pointed outcropping, a trickle of blood flowing from the flap of skin which he'd nicked. He cursed, yet continued to climb, curiosity having gotten the better of him.

Once on the other side of the mound, he jumped the remaining few feet onto another stretch of beach. In the distance he spied a house.

He began to walk again, enjoying the moist sand between his toes and on the soles of his feet, the pink sand baking on his left under such a radiant sun. He felt a tingling warmth in his arms, and knew it was not from the sun. His heart felt full and bright, and the smell of brine coming from the ocean gave him the urge to breathe in deeply, and never let his lungs go empty again.

He wondered about his flayed ankle and looked down to see that there was no cut, no blood. The drip of red he'd seen and felt ended a few steps onto the new beach. He shrugged and kept walking. This was, after all, paradise.

The closer he came to the house, however, the more his joy became dread. There was always the possibility that an identical house could have been built on a very similar inlet on this island. When he got to the steps, however, he saw the footsteps leading down to the beach. And the fan that he'd made with his own foot as he had put it down onto sand for the first time in his life. His hands became clammy at the thought that he'd come full circle in such a short period of time. Staring in the direction he'd gone, he saw the beginning of his footsteps, until he reached the swash where they'd been swallowed by the ocean.

Was this, in fact, paradise? Had he gone around an entire island? It felt like he'd gone in a straight line, but perhaps he was mistaken. He decided to walk to the front of the house, keeping it at a safe distance, as if in the blink of an eye, it had turned from a completely safe and innocuous object into one of dread and danger.

He glanced at the screen door once and walked up the dirt path which split a tall-grass covered sand dune in half like a pause in the conversation.

Datu's heart thumped hard inside his chest as he rose over the path, and saw it. The house. It was on the other side of the rise as well.

Identical to the one behind him. He turned around and faced forward several times, just to make sure it was true. That he wasn't dreaming. What kind of afterlife was this? He thought.

Not knowing where to go, he walked forward, back to the house, yet away from the one he'd just left. He walked into it, pulling on the creaking screen door, and letting it slam behind him, giving him a start.

Perhaps there would be clues inside the house as to why he was here, or even if this was some sort of afterlife. He was beginning to have doubts, as this was quite far from what he'd imagined and prayed for all his life.

There would have been his mother and father, he thought, and many of the friends he'd lost on the job.

He started to open the discoloured cupboards in the kitchenette, finding old canned goods with the labels peeled off, their contents written in permanent marker.

He took the drawers out and poured their content onto the counter. An old cigarette lighter, a pamphlet inviting tourists to visit scenic Cebu. Oven mitts. Nothing to explain what part of the islands he was in.

He took the fading calendar off the wall and flipped the pages, pictures of Manila at night, Puerto Princesa, Cebu, and El Nido adorning its top half, and the months its lower.

When he came to October, he paused. On the 8th, someone had written "My birthday!" in blue pen. That date sounded so familiar. His eyes closed for a moment, his memory searching for significance. He gritted his teeth and threw the calendar across the room.

The room where he'd woken now seemed oppressive. He no longer thought of this place as a paradise. It was more akin to a prison, no matter how incredibly gorgeous the cage bars. He wondered if this was some sort of punishment for misdeeds, or even if it was a form of Hell.

Why isolate him in a tropical Eden if he was being punished for his sins, then? The world swam once again, and Datu meandered to the rear doors of the house, holding himself up on the doorframe.

The birds kept wheeling in the sky. The ocean crashed relentlessly against the surf, and its smell was of something sweetly rotting. Not the horrid stench of the Heap as he remembered it, but of naturally decaying plant matter dipped in a turquoise-coloured salt bath.

After a moment, the world came back to its usual, unusual self, and Datu's mind stopped slipping into dangerous territories. He slid down the side of the doorframe and sat down on the sandy wooden steps of the beach house.

In the distance, he thought he saw the gathering of thunderclouds. This was nothing like he'd ever witnessed in Vertical Tokyo, inasmuch as everything he was living was completely different than what he'd experienced so far.

The darkness, so far away, like a thin line of navy blue gathering across the wide expanse of the ocean. A space so vast he thought he could see the curve of the Earth. A chill wind began to blow, and he went into the house, closing the windows and doors.

Before he knew it, the navy blue line had become a thick grey bar that stretched everywhere on the horizon, and kept getting wider as it approached his shelter. The interior of the room became darker, and he saw vertical jabs of lightning stabbing the ocean in the distance.

Clouds covered the house now, and he grabbed the blanket from the bed. There was a light switch, but he left it off, instead taking the desk chair and sitting by the back door, as the sky erupted, the rain coming down as if it were a single, solid block of water being poured out the side of some bathtub in the heavens.

He sat there, wrapped in the white cotton blanket, the anger and fury of the skies pummelling the ocean and surrounding beach. Each drop of water dug a crater into the wet sand like a tiny asteroid hitting the ground. Every lightning bolt followed by a boom of thunder like cannon fire.

He found a kind of strange beauty in this as well. One of fierce, primal energies which had moulded the planet, given birth to it, changed it still. Like the volcanoes and the tides. Relentless and forever destroying, forever renewing.

Datu wondered about his family once again. What would Tala do, now that he was gone? He felt sick inside, worrying about his wife and children, as the rain poured off the roof and dug a trench along the perimeter of the house. The racket it caused, competing with the crashing thunder. He'd give anything to be back with them again.

From behind him, in the dark, a woman's voice said:

"Bit dramatic, isn't it?"

Datu screamed, feeling as if he'd just jumped out of his skin.

LITTLE WHITE LIES

Karaoke? Mariko Ishikawa thought.

"Where are you going? This isn't the safest area, boy," she said, walking after Keiji, who had started walking toward the more illuminated side of the street. Four and five-story buildings adorned with full window banners announcing arcades and bars lined the street.

At this point, as much as she did want to get rid of him and make him someone else's problem, she was leery of leaving him in this area of Shibuya. If he'd been a native of the place, she wouldn't have thought twice about it. The way he was dressed, however, made him a murder magnet.

If that happened, she'd be having a long, hard, and unpleasant conversation with her superiors.

She crossed the street, setting the car in self-defence mode as she did. The street was deserted, the first red flag. Her senses were heightened, wondering where the danger would be coming from.

She got a private call as she walked, the hair on her arms rising at the unexpected tone. She introspected to receive it. By the shield and persona, she recognized Officer Kazue.

"Answer call," she said internally, the conversation taking place entirely in her head.

"Special Inspector," Kazue said, bowing slightly.

"Make it quick, officer."

"Special Inspector, don't you think it's bad form to ride around with Keiji Uehara? You training him as your sidekick?"

She knew by the officer's shark's grin that she'd slipped for a micro-fraction of a second, revealing that no, she did not know. *What* exactly she did not know, Kazue could not fathom.

She opened another window, outside of Kazue's area of perception, searched for the name he'd just revealed, and her blood temperature dipped by a few degrees.

Several things went racing through Ishikawa's mind at precisely the same time:

How did Kazue know and she didn't?

How did that little shit mock up an ID so good she or her computer hadn't been able to see through it?

And lastly, yet most importantly:

How the hell had she gotten messed up in the affairs of one of the most powerful 11 Karetsu owners' sons?

"Hold the line," she said flatly.

Ishikawa wanted to strangle the boy walking blithely next to her. An itch had developed on her left hand—the one she desired to put across his face in a back-handed slap.

In her introspective state, she retrieved the boy's ID from her internal computer. She cupped one virtual hand over the other with the ID in them, holding it as if it might jump out and run away like her wayward Companion today. There was give, a tearing of electrons, and when she separated her hands, she now held two distinct objects in either one.

In the right, she perused that of Keiji Uehara, twenty year old University student. Her miscreant. In the right, that of a High School girl named Aoi Tanaka. The fix was good. It passed cursory inspection.

She accessed the file for Uehara and saw that his grades were beyond stellar. Whether that was because his father was immensely rich or through his own hard work, she had no idea. Didn't care. Sometimes powerful people manipulated the reality around them through sheer force of influence, without the need to get involved. From what she'd seen, the kid had promise, but that might just be the ignorance of the entitled.

"Where are you going?" she said out loud to the object of her irritation, stopping dead in her tracks. Keiji's eyebrow arched in surprise, the plan having changed so suddenly. Thus far he'd seemed perfectly content to have her follow wherever he led.

"Genzo Ito was last seen here," he said, pointing to the blinking lights of a flashy storefront. After calculating what she wanted to do, and looking at her surroundings, Ishikawa decided that being inside was a much better place than having the discussion on the street.

"Report illegal clones! Protect the sanctity of human life!" the speakers bellowed from the flat blimp-like skiff above them as its stabilisers droned. Its spot-lights danced over the buildings behind them, illuminating the dead street for a split-second.

Definitely better to be inside, she decided. She sighed and shook her head. Keiji kept on walking and went through the doors of a business touting itself as "Sing Sing Land," the words written in bubbly manga-style Kanji. A karaoke place with lavender tones in the windows, and minuscule LEDs flashing like diamonds at regular intervals. He walked in, Ishikawa close behind, and asked for a specific private room.

Internally, Officer Kazue still waited on mute, unaware of anything going on outside the 'hold' Ishikawa had placed him on. She resumed the call with him as they waited in the ornate lobby. Sheer white cloth hung suspended in thick ribbons across the ceiling, offsetting the pastel purples and blues which covered the walls. She placed him in her peripheral vision, so as to be able to both walk and talk to him at the same time.

"Alright Kazue, what do you want?" she said.

"Whatever do you mean, Special Inspector?" the man said, a superlative air of innocence plastered on his features, pointing in a 'who, me?' pose.

"Cut the bullshit, Officer. This is a secure line. Don't make me repeat myself," she said, trying with all her might not to let the disgust she felt spread overtly to her physical features.

"We both know Chiba's a shithole, Ishikawa."

The niceties are over, she thought.

"I want you to facilitate a transfer order for me. I want to work downtown," Officer Kazue said, smirking.

"Or else what?" Ishikawa said.

Kazue sputtered,

"Or else *what*? Are you serious? Do you know what will happen to you if it becomes general knowledge that you take Corporate kids on ride-alongs? That pristine reputation of yours will be sullied forever, *Special Inspector*!" The last said with the kind of scorn one would associate with being called a syphilitic cockroach. Even though the corruption was real within the force, there was still a matter of etiquette which had to be observed. Face and deniability went hand-in-hand.

One had to be careful to hide the strings that bound. Kazue thought that she was beholden to Uehara Kogyo, or at least to their CEO and Keiji's father Tadashi Uehara. That this was some sort of favour, perhaps, to the big man.

Ishikawa stood there, arms crossed, looking at Officer Kazue, allowing the most uncomfortable of silences to spread like deadly poison before speaking again.

"You know what your first mistake was, Kazue?" Ishikawa said to the man, his eyes spiteful.

"No, why don't you tell me?" he said, rolling them now.

"When you tried to blackmail me. See, this call is now evidence. If you feel the urge to tell anyone, which, yes, might be a bit embarrassing for me, you'll face expulsion from the force. Don't you think if I *were* to give ride-alongs to the rich and famous looking for adventure, my superiors would be in on it for their own "incentives"? Do you think I'm green, Officer?"

"I—I," he stammered.

"Goodbye Officer Kazue. I hope you'll learn to be discrete, for your sake. Kicking up hornets' nests will get you stung," Ishikawa said in a harsh whisper, and before the man could answer, she terminated the call.

She only had time to glimpse his features shift from snide condescendence to outright anger before he vanished from her internal viewport.

Good riddance, she thought. It was fortunate that Officer Kazue was not the first of his kind she'd encountered. It sometimes felt like she'd had to climb over a mountain of Kazues to achieve what she had. The thought tired her. It bothered her to no end that Kazue had known about Uehara and she had not. For now there was nothing she could do about it, and she wasn't about to call the man back to ask him how he'd done it.

The attendant showed her and Keiji the private room he'd requested.

went to the karaoke machine and chose an older song by Rock Child Demagogue. Not really his style, but he was surprised that it might be hers.

"I didn't actually want to sing ka—" Keiji began, but she'd smiled and put her index to her lips, making a shushing sound. Even though she had no way of shutting down the internal camera system monitoring the room, she could supplant the microphones that listened in on every single one of them. Karaoke bars, just like host bars and clubs, were the property of the same unsavoury people for whom she'd taken up the mantle to fight in this city. There was no point in giving them any freebies.

As the heavy guitar solo began, she pushed Keiji to one of the benches that wound its way around the back half of the room. A long-haired Japanese man in tight grey snake-print leather pants proceeded to eat his microphone at extremely high volume on the screen near the entrance, another in a horrid demon mask wailing on his electric guitar in the background.

She then put on a disposable black mask.

"Mister Keiji Uehara, you've caused me quite enough trouble for the day, don't you think?" she said, towering over the youth, her voice audible only to Keiji. Any attempt to read her lips would be thwarted by the face mask.

"I can explain!" he said, his eyes wide.

"I'd like that. Right now, there is at least one other person who knows your whereabouts, and would love nothing more than to use that as a lever for their advancement. You've been a little shit, Keiji," Ishikawa said, her anger perfectly in check.

As the heavy metal duo belted out song after song, Keiji explained that, out of boredom, he'd begun diving into the sub-levels while still in his teens. Allowing his true identity to become common knowledge would have attracted the sort of attention it just had. He truly did want to find Ito, but there would have been no way to do so as himself. That's why he'd stolen one of his sister's friend's ID and combined it with his own.

For it to work, he'd pretended to be a high schooler. The uniform was an old one he'd roughed up and removed the crest from.

The scene on the screen changed, and instead of the duo's Heavy Metal ballad "You Can Never Go Back to Mars," it was two people in a room eerily similar to the one they found themselves in. The sound was on 'mute,' bringing silence to the room. It was just as well, since Ishikawa's ears had begun to ring from the infernal racket she'd initiated.

She approached the screen, and the person sitting to the right was unmistakably Genzo Ito—same small frame, an atoll of hair on the periphery of his round head. Same ugly leather blazer from which they'd found a charred piece only ten minutes ago.

The person on the right was an unknown entity. From the conversation, however, Ito looked agitated. Ishikawa inspected the ceiling behind her and spotted the place where the camera would be hidden.

"Don't worry, I've blocked all internal information devices," Keiji said, sheepishly. "No sound, no video."

Great, now he tells me, she thought.

Instead of asking if he knew it was against the law, Ishikawa turned back to the screen, watching Ito get up from one of the benches, walking out the door and slamming it on the other person.

"And then he went to get blown up," Ishikawa said.

"Yeah."

I'll have to go through the guest logs, she thought. *Find out who the other guy is.*

Keiji apologized to Ishikawa and reiterated his need for her help. She had mixed feelings about helping the poor little rich boy find his lost master. On the one hand rested her outstanding debt. On the other, the Kazues of the world which would start raining down on her if she kept company with said brat.

She had half a mind to call his father right then and there and have him taken off her hands. That as well sounded like the beginning of unbearable torment at the hands of her superiors.

"Someone's coming!" Keiji said, the video changing to that of a corridor. Armed men streamed in, guns at the ready. Mariko pulled out her own, and she grabbed Keiji by the suit jacket, throwing him in the far corner to the left of the door.

She'd recognized the corridor as the one down which they'd come, the numbered doors enhanced with holograms of singing idols. Ishikawa got on her internal communication network, sending out an SOS, but the comms system kept registering error messages.

Shit! she thought, kneeling close to Keiji, yet keeping an eye on the monitor. At least two of the five looked like light cyborgs, with a torso implant on one of them, and a hard shock casing for a head on the other. That one carried an old-school shotgun, the kind you see on auction shows and collectors' racks.

The men stood outside the door, guns at the ready for a moment, and then only one began to fire. As they checked their guns, Ishikawa began to fire, using the screen to gauge approximately where the men stood.

She hit the first three squarely centre of mass, clipping the fourth, and missing the one with the shotgun. The man continued to fire into the wall indiscriminately, putting holes at head height.

Chunks of wall and plaster dust flew into the karaoke room, covering Ishikawa and Keiji. She shot again at the cyborg with the armoured chest, this time lower, hitting him in more sensitive parts.

When she was able to see the last assailant through one of the gaping holes he'd drilled through the wall with his shotgun, she fired once at his head.

The shot ricocheted off his reinforced casing, slamming into the wall with a 'spak!'

Ishikawa frowned as the man aimed once more, having put them in his sights. She quickly selected armour-piercing rounds and flicked her pistol to semi-auto, loosing three rounds into the man's head. It blew apart with a wrenching sound, and his armoured body fell into the opposite wall, landing in a sitting position through the plaster.

She grabbed Keiji by the arm, dragging him up and out of the room.

"Time to go," she said, changing the magazine in her pistol before heading for the front door. The attendant who'd greeted them at their arrival was gone. Ishikawa dusted herself off, keeping her gun at the ready.

The only sound left in the karaoke bar was that of one man agonizing on the floor.

Keiji wiped as much of the plaster dust off his face as he could, and followed her as she advanced to the front door.

A glance in either direction down the street reassured her, and they ran the rest of the way to Ishikawa's waiting car. She double-checked that the systems hadn't been tampered with before unlocking the doors and stepping inside.

As the car rose into the air, she did a sensor sweep of the area to make sure no other potential foes were setting up to shoot down the car.

"What the hell was *that*?" she asked, putting away her gun.

"My guess is the same people who made Ito disappear, Special Inspector. Did you notice the augments?" Keiji said, staring straight ahead.

"Yeah. Definitely not yakuza."

Yakuza were anti-cyborg. Their base philosophy was a twisted purity doctrine, which like a reincarnation warranty, became null and void as soon as they became grafted with any type of biomechanical part. What was odd, though, was that it was generally their groups which owned and operated the entertainment venues throughout all of VCT.

So either a hit had been called on a yakuza place of business, or whoever owned the place was not one of the Japanese mafias. Either way, there was no question as to whom their intended targets were.

"I'm still wondering how we made it out of there alive," Ishikawa said. "Don't you think it's odd that only one of them fired on us when they were all heavily armed?" she said.

Keiji turned to her and smirked.

"I hacked their guns," he said. "Only one I couldn't was the shotgun."

It all made sense now. She turned to him.

"Thanks," she said.

"You're welcome. Now do you think there's something to Ito's going AWOL?"

"I'm more inclined to believe so, yes. I requested a sweep team to go into 'Sing Sing Land.' Not sure they'll find anything more than the assholes I dispatched, but you never know. They'll have to go through the visitor's logs. I'm not willing to be anyone's sitting duck."

"Central to Special Inspector Ishikawa, come in," said a woman's voice from the dashboard.

"Ishikawa here."

"There's been another breakout involving Companions, Special Inspector. This time there are four of them. There's been loss of life. Head back to Chiba as quickly as possible. The coordinates are being sent to the car," the woman's voice said, and GPS points appeared on the dashboard. Factory district, 100th level. She felt a cold shiver slip up her spine.

She looked over at Keiji, who kept his face as neutral as possible.

"I'll help you if you help me," he said, "simple as that."

Ishikawa chewed on her lower lip a bit, staring off into the distance. She then nodded slowly, giving the steering wheel small punches.

"Looks like I'll be hanging out with you a bit longer, Special Inspector," Keiji said, smiling.

"Don't get used to it," she answered, frowning, flicked the switch for the police lights and rushed into the emergency lane

More than one Companion run amok in one day was beginning to strain credibility. As the car returned to Chiba, Ishikawa dove to the 100th this time. Two was a rare number. Five altogether was a statistical impossibility.

She'd sent a message to Admin Central warning them of a possible string of malfunctions which might turn into a pandemic if things weren't taken in hand at this very moment.

Murai Mechanical Technologies, the creator of the Koji, would already have been advised of the previous situation, so as to be able to order their customers turn off their Kojis before they too could succumb.

Now, however, it appeared that a general shutdown order would have to be enacted.

There were over nine million Companions in the Chiba area alone.

GOLDEN GATE PRISON IN MY MIND

All-in-all, the interview with Samuel Harkwell had gone well, and Saito decided to continue his good run by interrogating the man who'd practically invented DaiSin: Nabeen Singh.

If Yusuke Daiko had been the inceptor of net trodes, Singh had sold them to the world. In the three hundred years since DaiSin had been conceived in San Francisco and transplanted into the then planned vertical city, Singh no longer could be considered fully human, if at all.

His downfall had come swiftly, less than ten years ago, and since then, he'd been busy trying to exact his revenge on the man who'd taken his seat as CEO of the company he'd founded.

Now he was trapped inside the mind of his ex right-hand-man, Douglas Deguchi, himself an escaped convict.

As Saito left the computer core, a notification appeared in his upper line of sight.

THREE ASSETS DESIGNATED. AWAITING ORDERS.

The HYVE Golems he'd requested had been put under his command. He was surprised at how quickly they'd been assigned to him, but there was no sense in wasting time.

Three was disappointing, but better than nothing. He understood that resources were strained at the moment, with Samuel Harkwell overseeing every aspect of operations on a digital level. He'd have to make due. There would be need for a Nexus replacement if DaiSin wanted their systems up and running at optimal performance again. It wouldn't do to have all operations managed by a single person for much longer. There were too many chances for a breakdown.

He gave two Golems orders to follow as much of the goings-on of the Council as they could, and the remaining one he set upon the Deliberators. They would discover anything untoward in short order by tracking their communications and commands, as well as any money transfers.

The advantage to using Golems was that they were virtual and stealthy. The council might expect Saito's visit, but he doubted very much they would give more than cursory company encryption to their outward online activities. He counted on it. Golems had full access to all accounts, when set upon them.

They were, after all, supposed to be untouchable.

Of course, if what he was planning were discovered, he was finished, and by extension Wen Harkwell as well. The only thing preventing both their immediate terminations would be the discovery of the mole he'd been set to out.

COMMAND ACCEPTED.

RESULTS PENDING...

He stared at the last line of text left by the Golems as they rushed out to do his bidding. Blinking periods marked the end of communications. He very much hoped for results.

Saito once again took the elevators to the Barrier Department, where Deguchi was housed. It felt as if he was descending into an oubliette, the furthest possible place they could hold him.

When he stepped out, staff and guards were out of sight. Circular hallways showed closed doors which hid empty rooms. DaiSin always stood ready to expand operations, depending on new tech, and so had an abundance of property within its walls into which it could fill whatever was necessary.

He walked down the hallway to a room numbered 206 and knocked.

"Be right there," came the reply.

The door slid open, and a massive, muscular man answered, wearing nothing but a grey robe embroidered with the DaiSin logo on its breast.

"Can I help you?" he asked, looking down at Saito.

"Mr. Deguchi, my name is Hideki Saito. May I come in?" Deguchi stepped away from the doorway and let the smaller man in, offering him the couch. The place was small, more like the cabin on a cruise ship than a real apartment. The kitchenette was on the left, the living room on the right. The far wall had the same black velvety cushioning material that served as sound-proofing. A recliner and two-seater sofa in dull grey micro-suede complemented the living room, as well as a grey faux-wood coffee table.

The recliner doubled as a net chair, but Saito knew it would not be plugged in. It would have been suicide for the company to allow Deguchi to advertise his existence within its walls, let alone the fact that it possessed hidden holding facilities underneath the "official" building.

Deguchi went to the small kitchen.

"Green tea?" he said, holding up a glass pot with what looked like green silt at the bottom, the infuser packed with what smelled like hot, fragrant summer grass.

"No thank you, Mr. Deguchi," Saito said, taking a seat on the sofa.

"You're wrong to say no," the big man said, pouring boiling water from a kettle with practiced ease into the pot. "It's some of the best gyokuro I've ever had." The water filled the glass teapot, turning it a dark green, almost mossy in texture.

"How are we treating you, Mr Deguchi?" Saito asked, changing the subject.

"Well enough," he said. "It was this or a tiny cell on the Moon's orbital penitentiary, right? My guess is the tea here is better," he added, pouring some of the green infusion into a delicate-looking ceramic cup etched with Kanji.

He came into the living room and sat in the recliner, putting his cup on a coaster on the coffee table after having taken a sip.

"To what do I owe the honour, Mr. Saito? Are you my new warden?" the big man asked, visibly flexing under his robe.

Saito smiled, placing his hands in a pyramid in his lap.

"Not at all. I'm here to speak to Mr. Singh. Has he been causing you any discomfort as of late?"

"That old bastard? Nah, he's been kind of quiet since you folks but him in seclusion in there," Deguchi said, tapping his skull with one finger. "I know he ain't happy, but there isn't much he can do about it, is there?"

Having trapped Singh inside Deguchi's crystal memory chip had been one of Wen Harkwell's better ideas. Ever since the prison break which had released Deguchi, Singh had been in his mind, unable to body jump to other electronic devices. Retrieving him to place him into a different holding tank had proven impossible. The man was more electric current than data. He jumped from one side of Deguchi's mind to the other with ease. It had taken the expertise of the entire tech department to corral him within the confines of a construct inside Deguchi, like trying to drop a box on an angry hornet.

The original idea had been to mollify the Nexus to get them to stay within DaiSin, using Singh as bait, but that plan had failed. Wen Harkwell and DaiSin as a whole had been left to pick up the pieces since their abrupt departure a little over a year ago.

Now, however, the man could at least be of some use. Saito looked around the room, at the dismal grey walls and general blandness of the furniture. The darkly depressing black sound-proofing inspired no confidence in the comfort level of their guest.

"It would be nice to get a touch of colour in here," Deguchi said, as if reading Saito's mind.

"I'll mention it to the man in charge," Saito said. Deguchi nodded in thanks, then took a sip of his steaming tea. The secrecy surrounding the man's presence made getting anything done a difficult chore. Having the building compartmentalized by degrees of access had always been within company culture, but access to Deguchi had been severely limited to a handful of trustworthy personnel. The pay raise had certainly helped.

"Would you mind if we plugged in? I know that your wireless access' been cut, but if you could connect to your net chair, I'd get direct access. Would save us a trip to another department," Saito said, pointing with his hand to the recliner Deguchi sat on.

"Of course," Deguchi said, pulling the cover off the neck guard on the recliner, then leaning back against the chair until his trodes touched and connected to the plugs inside it.

Saito closed his eyes. He imagined Deguchi's spatial position and found the glowing silver orb of his presence on the chair, the outline of a cube around his apartment. There was no way he could send or receive data outside the magnetic field.

He came toward Deguchi's orb and identified within it the orange sphere which contained Nabeen Singh's personality. He touched it, entering a string of code which would give him access. A part of the sphere reticulated, and Saito dove in, the injection port shutting behind him.

The darkness pulled back, and he was thrust forward into a tunnel of light, then onto the still image of a busy street. The image began to move, and he was inside the scene, standing in the middle of the road.

He turned around, shaking his head.

The signs were in English, and the wide road sloped down to a body of water. The ringing of a bell made him jump out of the way in time to avoid being hit by a trolley. In the distance he spied the tall, sweeping expanse of the Golden Gate Bridge, such as it had been before falling into the Bay.

He'd been dropped into the late 20th century, judging by the clothes. The low sun cast an orange glow on the world, purple shadows extending long fingers from four-story apartment blocks dating back to the previous century.

Saito moved onto the sidewalk to avoid being hit by a trolley or other vehicle. Not that it would have hurt, but it was jarring to have a solid object run through you in any construct. It caused a nasty, lingering tickle, like a whole-body cramp.

Unnerving to be in any pre-2120 reproduction, he felt. It was like using a time machine to escape the calamities which had cascaded after the War. America had further spiralled into collapse, and this, until Saito's time. What historians referred to as "The Armageddon of a Continent." Save that that wasn't entirely true. That large-scale disintegration had been compartmentalized into the geographic area of the continental US, no higher or lower.

Saito wondered how large the construct inside Deguchi's head could be. By his calculations, its borders were the city itself. Even though crystal memory chips had incredible storage capacity, it would have been unfair to Deguchi to have used it to house a single person, to the detriment of his own mind.

This brought him back to the task at hand: finding Nabeen Singh. Reports said that he'd lost his mind. He preferred direct contact to assess the extent of that truth. It's not as if he could pick up a phone within the construct and call him. Or that Singh would have detected his presence as an interloper within the construct.

Saito reoriented, walking along Market Street, watching with keen interest the old-style green and yellow trolleys roll down the red-painted center lane like soft thunder.

Foot traffic was light—an old white woman pushing a wheeled cart full of groceries, a moustached black man holding his daughter's hand as they walked down the street. A homeless white man asking for change, holding a hand-made cardboard sign that read "God bless you!"

Breadbox-shaped, gas-powered grey and red buses made their way toward the Bay area, and he walked toward a clock tower in the distance. Beyond, he could see the thin blue line of water between the tall expanse of buildings. The sun was almost set, and he still had no idea how he'd find Singh.

The aged buildings had been replaced with more modern ones, yet still ancient compared to the architecture of the 24th century. Ruddy-coloured skyscrapers with green-tinted windows, pale cream buildings with expansive marble-filled lobbies lined the wide avenue. Saito walked in awe of such a beautiful reconstruction.

As he walked, he noticed a payphone. He picked it up and began to speak, but only got a dial tone. Below it was a yellow book. Out of cur-osity, he approached it, the passersby not giving him a second glance.

He picked up the book and began to thumb through it, the names of various companies arranged in alphabetical order throughout. He turned to the 'D' section, scanning with minutiae every entry, until he came to the letter 'k', the company he presently worked for not in the registry.

As he was about to close the book, he put his hand back in the sec-tion he'd been inspecting, going further, running his index all the way down the page. There it was: Daiko & Singh Electronics.

The address was written next to the phone number, and he looked around him on the street, trying to figure out how to get a map of the city. Behind the payphone, on the corner of Front Street, there stood a blocky four story building of black windows. He walked into something called "Bells Fargo," what looked like a financial institution, where a guard sat at a desk near the teller counter.

As soon as he stepped through the outer door, he knew he was no longer where he should be. Saito reeled back, disoriented. If the edifice he had first entered could be described as modern for its time, this one was archaic.

Teleported.

Behind him stood an open door, green, with golden accents around its florid trim. The paint had begun to curl, showing the signs of its true age. The sun still shone as it would have at noon. Outside, a row of older apartment buildings ran the length of the street on the opposite side. Their colours ranged from drab to wild, giving the quiet neigh-bourhood a psychedelic feel.

Saito turned around. On his left was a staircase leading to the second floor, its golden metal railing freshly painted, a sign still hanging from the bottom banister, warning visitors to "Keep your hands off."

A corridor extended before him, leading to a series of doors. Done in white tiles, with two strips of black framing the outer edges, the floors lent an aura of respectability to an otherwise ordinary-looking apartment block.

Confused, he stepped out of the building and found himself exiting the glass building on Market Street, almost bumping into a woman who had been coming in. The sound of traffic was louder, now that he'd come from a place with barely any.

Saito looked inside the building, seeing the guard reading a magazine and throwing him a glance now, but otherwise, nothing had changed. The sun was still on the cusp of slipping away for the night. He shook his head and tried the experience again.

He was once again transported to the other place.

Saito looked to his right, noticing a wall of copper-coloured boxes. Each had a number and name on it, and he scanned them, wondering if this was perhaps part of the game.

D & S Electronics: third floor, apartment 305. He'd been brought directly to where he wanted to go. He knew that a prison had been designed for Nabeen Singh. He had not been made aware, however, that it would be one so convoluted.

Going up the three flights of steps, he wondered what mental state he'd find Singh in. At apartment 305, he rang the buzzer, and a booming voice shook the walls:

"What? I'm busy!" The door flung open, and a distinguished-looking, yet dishevelled man opened the door.

"What do you want? I've things to do, my friend. Are you a salesperson?" he said, looking down the hallways, spying a man mopping the floor, further off.

"No, not at all, Mr. Singh. It is Nabeen Singh, is it not?" Saito said, trying for his most reassuring smile.

"Yes. What of it? Listen, whoever you are, I'm doing some very important work right now, and we're on the cusp of something *big*. It's really not a good time," Singh said, poking his head back into the apartment. Before he could close the door, Saito had slipped his foot in.

"I'm sorry Mr. Singh, but this really can't wait. I'm here about DaiS—Daiko and Singh. The people I represent are very interested in what you have to offer," he said, and Singh stopped trying to slam the door shut on his foot.

"Are you—are you with the Japanese government?"

"I am sir. Can you please let me in?" Singh opened the door slowly, as if he was having misgivings about letting the man into his apartment.

The living room was a nightmare of strewn schematics both hand-drawn and printed, scattered on every surface. Scrawled proposals covered the dining-room table in a neat hand-writing. As Saito came in,

Singh sniffed the air, wrinkling his nose.

"You smell funny," he said, before wandering off, scratching the back of his neck.

Singh smiled and went to the dining room, pushing everything off with the back of his arm. The pile of papers fell with a whoosh and a clatter to the ground.

"Please, come! Have a seat! What did you say your name was?"

"Hideki Saito, representative to the Japanese Diet," he lied.

"Splendid, splendid," Singh said, beaming. "You'll have to excuse me, my business partner isn't here at the moment. He should be back momentarily," Singh said, glancing out the window in no particular direction.

"Yusuke Daiko, you mean?"

"Yes, yes. There is no Daiko and Singh without Daiko, haha!" he said, putting up his hands, his eyes going wide with joy.

"Mr. Singh, how far along are you in the production of personal trode hardware?" At this, Singh scratched his chin, looking left and right as if he were to reveal a conspiracy of dire magnitude.

"We are close. Very close. Yusuke has just figured out how to layer the silicate chips in such a way as to allow the overwriting of memories if desired, freeing up space on the crystal matrix."

"Making the crystal re-writable," Saito said, nodding.

"Yes! Indeed! Exactly!" Singh said, growing frantic again. He looked at the door, then back to his guest.

"Do you smell that?" Singh said, wrinkling his nose. Then his eyes lit up. "Do you want to see it?"

"See what, sir?" Saito said, cocking his head sideways.

"The crystal! The crystal memory chip! The one your government sent you here to sign a contract for, of course," Nabeen said, and laughed, pulling out a stack of papers from below the table and placing them in front of Saito.

"Of course! I would be honoured," Saito said, happy to get onto a different topic. Singh looked a bit torn between the thick sheaf of contracts and taking Saito to where the revolutionary product could be found. He dithered a bit, shook his head and walked away from the table. Singh looked like a man who'd lost something, shuffling the papers on the couch. He turned around and looked at Saito.

"Yusuke, don't just stand there. I can't find the third addendum to the proposal I wrote up for DARPA. It should be around here some-where," Singh said, looking irritated.

"My name is Hideki Saito, Mr. Singh. You were going to show me the crystal memory chip Mr. Daiko has been working on," Saito said, smiling gently.

Singh turned around to the sofa, then back to Saito. Then his eyes lit up.

"Of course! Follow me!" And he walked toward the bedroom at the far end of a corridor. Cheap plastic "Do not enter!" and "Beware! Vicious dog!" signs had been apposed to the white wooden door, the kind you would expect a college sophomore to have as their décor.

"I think he might be sleeping, so we'll have to be very quiet, okay?" Singh said, and put his index to his lips, making a shushing sound. He pushed the door open, and the interior was much like the living room, save that on top of the mess of papers were added a riot of electronic equipment, bits of solder and chips in various plastic trays.

A bed was hidden under a heap of junk in the corner, more storage than resting place. To the right of the door, a computer desk and a blue glow from the innards of what looked like a powerful workstation for the day. Next to that, a homemade 3D printer, its rainbow-coloured wires exposed.

On its plate, what resembled diamond ring plastic jewellery box had been left.

Singh headed straight for it, taking it carefully between trembling fingers, and opening it for Saito to see, as a nervous boyfriend might present a ring to the man he loved.

Resting on a synthetic electrostatic-proof material rested a translucent chip the quarter of the size of a fingernail. Saito stared in awe at the prototype for the modern memory crystal. It had to be at least five times the size they were now.

"That's amazing, Mr. Singh. Tell me, how does the Nexus fit in all this?" Saito said, smiling to the man.

"I'm sorry, what did you say?" Singh said, snapping the box shut. He placed it back on the 3D printer's plate and started to walk out the bedroom.

"The Nexus. I'm certain that's a very interesting project you'd like to tell me about!"

Singh mumbled something under his breath and turned back to look at Saito. The look he gave him was something indescribable, like a cross between fear and hatred, and Saito wondered what would come next. Singh's features softened and he said:

"You'd like to know about the Nexus, eh? I'll show you. Don't you worry. I'll show you, follow me." He then walked out of what was supposed to be Yusuke Daiko's room and into the hallway. Saito followed, but as he crossed the threshold, he found himself in a prison cell.

Singh was leaving the cell and pushing the door closed. As Saito realized what was happening, he ran to the door, trying to put his arm in the way, but it was too late. It shut with a 'clang,' with Nabeen Singh on the other side.

Singh looked at the man inside the jail cell, solid metal bars between them.

"Welcome to Alcatraz, whoever you are," Singh said, tipping his head to one side. He backed away and rested on the railing behind him.

"I told you, my name is Hideki Saito, I'm here on behalf of the Japanese—" he began, but was cut short.

"I know who you said you were," the other man retorted, "but you smell like him. You know who. The man who put me here. The little shit who stole my life. Stuck me wherever the Hell this is, this non-Euclidian hole that looks like San Fran," Singh said. He giggled, and put a hand over his mouth.

"I'm sorry, you wanted to know about the Nexus? There's nothing to tell. It's perfect." He added, walking away.

Saito grabbed the bars and gritted his teeth.

"Your perfect creation might be ruining your company," he said, as a last, desperate effort. Somewhere in the rafters, pigeons took flight with a loud flapping of wings.

Singh paused.

"Not my company anymore. Stole it from me. Little fucker," he said in a low voice.

"You'd let it get eaten up by the Eleven? You'd do that? Three hundred years worth of work, gone just like that. You surprise me, Mr. Singh. I thought you had more pride than that. I was misinformed," Saito said, leaning into the bars to see Singh's reaction. Why were the prison bars holding him in? It shouldn't have been possible for Singh to have control over the construct.

Singh came marching back to the cell, his eyes wild.

"The company I built is gone!" he yelled.

"And so is the Nexus," Saito added. "They flew the coop a year ago. How?"

Singh grinned, his teeth flashing.

"They're smart. They adapt. I designed them for survival. Who knows what they could do left to their own devices?" Singh looked as if he'd heard wonderful news, as he nodded his head in pleasure.

"Could anyone control the company from the outside?" Saito asked. Nabeen began to laugh.

"Are you stupid? Do you think I'd have left my baby open to attack?"

"Who, then, Singh? Who could run things remotely? The Nexus?"

Singh stopped laughing, backing slowly away from the cell again. He'd regained his composure.

"If anything could do it, the Nexus could, my stinky friend. Don't expect me to tell you how. I'm sure you'll get out of here eventually, and run straight to the top of the needle to tell that *boy*..." Singh said, walking down the gangway toward the far end of the jail.

"Enjoy my prison, Mr. Whoever-You-Are," Singh said, his voice fading in the distance.

EARTHBOUND

W ho are you?" Datu, screamed, falling over in the dark.
"I might ask you the same thing. You *are* in my house,
after all," came a voice from the shadows. The light turned
on in the middle of the room, revealing a black-haired South-Asian
woman in her thirties, near the switch.

He picked himself up off the floor, not knowing where to go next.
At that moment, a flash of lightning illuminated the room, followed by
the crashing boom of thunder.

"Have you been here long?" The woman asked.

"Few hours, maybe?" Datu said, trying to recall, his voice unsure,
heart beating fast. Time felt wobbly in this place, but he was certain it
was no longer than a day.

"How did you get here?" The woman asked, crossing her arms.
She looked like someone who'd found a large, unwanted rodent in her
house. What Datu found odd was the fact she showed no fear.

"I died," Datu said, remembering his vertiginous fall and sub-
sequent crash, and then, the enveloping darkness which had taken
everything from him.

"What do you mean, you died?" she said, scoffing.

"I'm sorry, maybe you could tell me where I am?"

"Apart from inside my home, you're near Santa Cruz. Do you live
around here?" Now the woman looked more concerned than angry.
Datu assumed that she had assessed him as mentally unstable and not
physically dangerous, according to the way she stared at him.

"I wish," he mumbled.

"What's your name?" she asked, putting out her hand for him to sit down at the small kitchen table. Outside, the rain pelted harder and harder.

"It's getting tough to hear ourselves think," she said, closing her eyes. The rain stopped clean, and the darkness evaporated. The sun pushed through the clouds like hot iron on the horizon, the colour of burnt orange filament.

Datu came to sit at the rustic table, the chair screeching across the floor as he pulled it back. He peered outside, the storm clouds entirely gone. White birds like the sketched "V" in children's illustrations wheeled over the sea once again, the sun a half-sunken treasure dipping into the ocean, amber rivulets deliquescing from its body all the way to the beach. Liquid gold no man could catch.

"How did you do that?" Datu asked, looking back at the peaceful scene which had replaced the violence of the elements in mere moments.

"I told you,: this is my home. I can do whatever I want here. What's your name?" She asked again, enunciating the words with care.

"Datu. Datu Salazar. And yours?"

"Aimee Flores. A pleasure, Datu. What makes you say you died?"

Datu looked out the window again, lost in beauty and surreal circumstances.

"I fell. From a very high place. This place you call your home. It doesn't exist anymore. The Philippines are gone. They've been under the ocean for... three hundred years now. Those who survived have been living in Tokyo. It's—it's not a good place." Datu expected the news to crush the woman, but instead she looked at him with a curious stare, as if she were weighing the severity of his mental state.

A knock on the front door just then, interrupted them.

"Goodness! I sure am getting a lot of visitors today, aren't I?" Aimee said, going to answer.

A short Asian man stood there, his neutral expression turning into a smile when he saw her. He had an obvious preference for ultra-modern casual-wear suits. The cargo pants were a lighter shade of green than the vest. Both of these were offset by his pineapple-yellow skin-tight sweater.

"Hello Aimee, how are you?" he asked, walking inside before she had a chance to protest. "I see you've met our guest!"

"Arun! If I'd been told you were coming, I'd have made suitable arrangements! The house is a mess!" Datu looked around, not finding anything within the household he could remotely consider out of place.

As a matter of fact, it seemed perfect.

The new arrival came near Datu, putting out his hand. Datu took it after a moment of hesitation.

"I see you've met Aimee. Have you had the chance to wander out of bounds?" he said, with a wide smile. Datu couldn't place his origins, but he thought he might look Vietnamese or Thai.

"Yeah, I have. Who—who are you? Where am I?" he asked, trying to suppress the anxiety in his voice.

"Says he's dead," Aimee said, tittering. Arun turned around, a cloud going over his features for a moment.

"He almost did die, Milady."

"Oh! I didn't know!" she said, putting her hands over her mouth. Datu got up, the chair almost falling over behind him.

"What do you mean, I almost did? I'm still alive? Where am I? Tell me!" he said, wanting to grab the man by the collar and shake him. Never in his life had he experienced such uncertainty as to his own fate. So many elements dancing in the air, so many unknowns that he felt completely incorporeal. He wondered if he would ever feel normal again after today's events. But the man said he was still alive. How was that possible?

"Emergency support system. We had a team transport you from the Heap to our headquarters. They worked on you along the way, or you wouldn't be here now," Arun said, crossing his arms, his neutral demeanour returning. "Our scanner has you as Datu Salazar," pointing to Datu's arm. "Is that correct?"

"It—it is, but how did you find me?" As far as Datu was concerned, Administration never would have had a crew at that hour and at those coordinates. And if they had, they wouldn't have done a thing to save him, he thought bitterly.

"We're, uh—a new kind of recycling crew. Totally private enterprise. We've been having a lot of luck hiring disgruntled workers lately. Our pay is better, work conditions, etc. One of our partners thought you were worth saving, so here you are," he said, smiling again, putting up his hands in a 'what can you do?' sort of gesture.

Emergency support was a long way from explaining to Datu why he was on a beach in what had been a popular tourist attraction when the Philippines had flourished. Like all followers of Ayo, he knew his history and geography well.

Datu looked around him, Aimee standing in the corner, biting her thumbnail.

"Anyone want a drink? I could use a drink," she said, heading for the cupboard above the sink. She removed a trio of small opalescent glasses, and reached higher for a bottle of clear liquid.

"Relax," Arun said, pulling back a chair. "Your body is healing. When they found you, your spine was broken and you were going into shock. Several of your ribs had punctured through. It was your suit that saved you. That and your landing on organic garbage. If it had been anything else, you'd be toast, my friend."

Aimee joined them at the table. The sun's rays had slipped below the waves, and Datu had not yet noticed the clear, starry sky that glinted above the ocean. She put the bottle down with a 'clunk,' like an exclamation mark which would accept no denial. In large black letters, the word "Lambanog" was written on the side of the bottle. After having spread the glasses to the men, she undid the screw-top cap and poured them a measure.

"I don't drink," Datu said, shaking his head. "Against my religion."

"You're not really drinking. It's all in your head," Arun answered, pointing to his own and giving him a wink. Datu picked up his glass with uncertainty, wondering if what he was contemplating was allowed or not. After all, this was a made-up place, so why should he worry about the repercussions?

"Never trusted any religion that'd deny you the pleasure," Aimee stated, snorting, but before he could answer, Arun interrupted.

"What are we drinking to, Aimee?" he said, lifting an eyebrow.

"Survival and those who accomplish it, my dear. Your friend Datu is one, it appears. And from what he says, so am I," she said, winking. They tipped back the glasses, the coconut vodka slipping down the back of their throats. Datu coughed. It tasted both sweet and harsh, the likes of which he'd never had.

If this is an imaginary place, how can this taste so real? he wondered.

Arun must have been watching him because he smirked and polished off the last few drops of his drink.

"Come for a walk with me, Datu. There's something I'd like to discuss with you."

"Not inviting me, love?" Aimee asked, pretending to look offended.

"'Fraid not this time, Milady. I have to talk business with our friend here." Datu felt his head spinning a bit as he rose to his feet. Not enough to feel intoxicated, but on the tipsy side. The wonderful feeling extended to his extremities. Arun nodded to Datu, and he led him out the back doors to the beach. Then sun had set, and a thin white crescent cast a blue glow on the beach, the stars still visible. Scintillating diamonds in an unbelievable sky.

"Brother, I'll get straight to the point," Arun said, putting his hand on Datu's shoulder. "I need you to work for me. What do I need to do for that to happen?" Arun asked, looking him in the eyes.

"I'd want my Ayo back, and my family taken care of. That's pretty much it."

Arun laughed, but not maliciously. He slapped Datu on the back, nodding his head. A light breeze ruffled Datu's hair, and he looked out across the expanse of the ocean, the surf now sliding in silence.

"You're not a hard man to please, Datu. I like that. I have to tell you, though, you can't see your family again," Arun said, taking Datu by the shoulders. His face was stern, yet there were no threats inherent in the way he looked into Datu's eyes.

"Why?" Datu asked, his heart sinking.

"For all intents and purposes, my man, you *are* dead," Arun continued.

"Can't I even say goodbye?" Datu asked, Arun's head shaking sadly.

"This is the deal. If you work for Midori, you have to respect the contract. No contacting your family, and you have to obey their rules," Arun said. "If you do, good things will happen to you. And your family. I can guarantee it."

Datu turned away from the man, looking back at the house, where Aimee was probably cleaning up what she considered a horrible mess. *What was so terrible about what he was being proposed,* he thought.

"And if I refuse?" he asked, turning back to Arun.

"Listen, I don't want this to sound harsh, but your body isn't in the best shape right now. Let's just say that my employer's generosity could run out if you felt inclined to deny them a little tit for tat," Arun said, running his hand along the back of his own head, as if Datu had put him in an uncomfortable position.

Datu felt stricken. On the one hand, the promise of a better life, and on the other... he decided not to think of the alternative. If someone could help Tala (*your widow*, his subconscious whispered to him) and the kids (*your orphans*, it susurrated), then it might be worth it to keep going.

"I still don't know where I am," Datu said, smiling sadly.

"Your body is in a rapid-healing nutrient bath. Your mind is connected to a comfortable place, disconnected from the pain. It was this or massive amounts of drugs. We prefer this treatment. You've been implanted with trodes," Arun said, lifting a hand at Datu's protest. "It was that or death, remember? Fortunately, you're still earthbound. You'll be here for a few days. Enjoy it. You'll be able to plug in anytime afterwards when you need an escape, of course, but for now just take it in as a place to relax, okay?"

Arun pulled out a scroll from behind his back—an ancient-looking thing that might have belonged in a dungeon-exploring video game. He handed it to Datu, who unfurled it all the way to the ground.

"Binding from start to finish," Arun said, peering over Datu's shoulder. Datu pulled it in close.

"What do I do?"

Arun pulled out a knife and grabbed one of Datu's hands. He slipped the knife over Datu's index, the blood coming in droplets, falling to the beach. There was no pain, but Datu pulled his hand back nonetheless.

"What are you doing?" he yelled.

"Put your blood. Anywhere on the page. It'll record as acceptance and your DNA pattern will be saved as having been the approval. Signatures can be counterfeited. Blood is forever."

Datu brought his finger forward, the trickle slowing down.

"Quickly, or I'll have to cut you again," Arun said, smiling.

Datu allowed a tiny drop to hit the page. It was absorbed into the paper, which then began to shrink until the scroll evaporated in the palm of his hand.

"A copy will be sent to your crystal memory chip. The original will stay in Midori Mamoru's archives at headquarters. Welcome to the team, man!"

Datu felt as if he'd signed over his soul to a congenial devil, but for now had to bide his time until he could escape, if such a thing were possible.

"So this is all virtual?"

"All of it. Every grain of sand, every star in the sky." Arun said, lifting his hands up high.

"And you made this for me?"

"Oh no! You're inside an Ayo. Aimee is the original," Arun said, smiling.

Datu had the distinct feeling that Arun was telling the truth, but his mind refused to accept it.

A MOST HUMAN CONDITION

Even the emergency lane felt too slow. As traffic edged away from their speeding car, Mariko Ishikawa coordinated with the local officers once again. As everyone had been involved in the previous event, it was simple enough to send them to the next scene.

Four Companions, all labourers, had "walked out" of their jobs at a squid packing factory in lower Chiba. This time on the 100th level, where most heavy industries in the prefecture were located. They'd left a trail of bodies in their wake. Two naturals and an enhanced cyborg had had the misfortune of being in their way when they'd "malfunctioned."

Units had been dispatched to find them as soon as the call had come in. The factory level would be locked down tight, the elevators stopped and roadblocks set up in a five kilometre radius, as per protocol. This time, however, reinforcements had been called in from Admin Central. There would be armoured suits flown in to hunt down the rogue Companions. No one was screwing around with this one.

Ishikawa was nervous. There was no longer any way she could use the excuse of "freak accident" as pertaining to these cases. Four Companions at the same time defied logic and nature.

The problem, then, was to find the pattern to bind the madness. She hated having relied on this boy in the first place, but if he could spot the missing companions again, she would make sure to recalibrate her sensors herself to make them sensitive to Companions' wavelengths.

She now wished she'd done so with the Koji9B, but as she was under the mistaken impression that it was a one-time deal, there had been no immediate need to do so. Her mistake.

Now things were different.

She turned to see Keiji staring at the cross dangling from the rear-view mirror, a depressed-looking Jesus swinging side-to-side with every banking manoeuvre the car performed. Keiji looked at her inquisitively.

"You religious, Special Inspector?"

"No." She held out a hand and touched the lowest part of the cross with a fingertip. "This is probably the most human thing I've ever had."

She explained that she'd gone walking in Ebisu one day and an old woman sitting on a low stool behind a rack of baubles had caught her eye, or rather, what she held, had. A block of PET inside her gnarled fingers, her other hand replaced with carving and buffing tools, with which she extruded and smoothed the cross. Tiny spirals of plastic unfurled as she pressed the drill to the block, her hunched form still as a statue. The discards falling like coloured snow on her lap and the ground, surrounding her as if she were but a statue in the sleet.

Ishikawa had stood for three hours, just watching her dirty mechanical hand push through and alter the plastic, gouging out the right amount of particles to make a leg, a spike, a hanging head, a crown of thorns. The look of infinite patience etched on the web of wrinkles in her face had kept her in awe, as the aged artisan had held the piece of slowly changing polymer like some precious jewel.

Ishikawa had no interest in religion and iconology. She did, however, hold person-made objects in the highest regard. The imperfections reminded her of the nature of people and things which had not been made by machine. She hadn't picked this one because she was a follower of Christ. She'd bought it because she'd been a witness to its creation.

This held more significance to her than any faith could ever have.

"Machines make things better than any human can," Keiji said.

"They do. That makes us expendable. I like to remind myself that we have purpose," she mused. The boy looked uncomfortable for a moment, then turned to look out the window. He did not say a word until they arrived over Chiba.

The car's nose dipped down, and soon they were heading into the grey zone of the 100th level. Keiji put his hand in his satchel and took out a rebreather.

For a boy from The Heights, Ishikawa found him as prepared as he was resourceful. He was a rare animal indeed. Most teens she'd encountered on the top levels were—to put it mildly—spoiled brats. That was the reward for giving them everything they wanted. Not so for this young man. Perhaps it had been the training he'd received from Genzo Ito San.

Whatever the reason, Ishikawa felt a bit less leery of having him there, even though they were heading into a potentially dangerous situation. She imagined that he had been at least a few times involved in Ito's foolish endeavours.

As of now, however, she had to be careful of Kazue and his possible acts of retribution, as well as whoever had gone after them at the karaoke bar. Kazue she could handle, but the others were a nebulous entity.

Where had they come from? Would they come after them again? How did they know who they were? Ishikawa imagined facial recognition software had alerted those who'd come for them of their presence. Whether that was because they knew of Ito's kohai, or they had access to the police database was another question. The latter depressed her.

She'd have unwanted company until she could figure out a safe way to deposit him in a protected space. A civilian who'd saved her life.

Not that she would ever have put a gun in the boy's hand, but she had the distinct feeling that he wouldn't get in her way if she did decide to take him to the general vicinity of the crime scene. It was that or locking him up in the car, which, as experience had shown, could not be done. Leaving him on his own on the factory levels of Chiba was a good way of making sure he'd become ransom bait. She couldn't even imagine the kind of trouble she'd face if that ever came to pass.

Below, large square blocks and towers, stacks and cylindrical holding tanks began to emerge from the fog like chips and capacitors on an impossibly large motherboard. Ishikawa slipped on her own rebreather after they'd landed near the open bay doors of a long, low building made of corrugated faint-yellow steel.

Police vehicles squatted on the scene, the remaining human employees of the squid factory huddled a hundred yards from the building proper. A drift of greyish fog slipped through the area, dimming visibility despite the orange strobe from strategically-placed lamps along the path from the factory to the nearest freight elevators.

Ishikawa noticed the busted-down airplane hangar style doors before she stepped out of the car. One lay several metres from the building, flipped over and bent. The other hung from the side of its frame, twisted outward, the result of inhuman force folding it like tinfoil.

Didn't these Companions care to open doors? It was evident that whatever possessed them turned their usual docile natures into unbridled rage. A quality she hadn't been aware could be induced in androids.

The fog brought a muffled silence wherever it drifted. Whether because people were less inclined to speak in its eerie presence, or simply because its thickness cushioned sound, she had never been sure of. In her mind, that silence always lent an aura of terrible foreboding to whatever location she was about to enter. Today was no exception. Her dislike of the factory levels clung to her throat. Her aversion to the suspended water particles bordered on the superstitious, but she had little control over that.

"Listen to me, young man. I want you to follow me, all the way to the front doors, but then you stop and you wait with the officers. I don't want you on the crime scene. I'm not even supposed to have you here. I'm serious now. We're not in Shinjuku anymore." Keiji nodded slowly, and they walked out onto the metal girders that comprised the ground of the 100th. Ishikawa was aware she spoke to him as she would a five year old, but there was no helping it. She wasn't going to become his friend, but neither did she want some entitled rich kids' parents to come after her because she'd said the wrong thing and made him sore.

Her unease increased. Even though the girders were thick enough to hold up entire factories, the fact that she could see right through them into the darkness made her heart pummel hard inside her ribcage.

Over to the left, men and women having undergone various levels of augmentation stood in a group, their masks hiding much of their faces. The majority were on the cutting and packing crew, judging by their squid-gut-covered white aprons.

The reverb pinging of her shoes on metal died quickly, and she studiously ignored looking down.

It was a three story building, the doors having taken up two of those. From this distance, she could see the cylindrical vats through the gap left by the blown-out door. A few men and women in hard hats stood outside, talking to the officers who guarded the crime scene. The building extended with a sloping roof to the right, and to the left, it rose to only two stories, no doubt the cutting and packing area.

Large bay doors three feet above the ground lined the far left end of the building, two of them obstructed by tractor-trailers.

She walked past the dented door lying on the ground, observing the fresh scoring in the girders where it had bounced before flipping over on its back.

From inside, she could see a light being moved around, crime scene telemetry being recorded. She turned to see if Keiji still followed, and she was surprised to see the calm in his eyes.

When she came to the cordon she recognized the female officer, Yamaguchi.

"Officer. You know Keiji here. Please keep an eye on him while I tour the scene," Ishikawa said. The officer nodded, and she walked into the factory. The first thing she saw on her left, near the guard post was a blanket covering a body, surrounded by a pool of blood.

On the right-hand side, transparent acrylic vats churned with live squid, their translucent silver bodies glittering in the factory's penumbra. She counted ten of the industrial-sized aquariums going to the end of the room before her, and row upon row to the far end of the factory on her right. A forklift lay overturned twenty feet from where she stood.

"Victim number three," she said, to no one in particular.

"Special Inspector. Wasn't expecting to see you again so soon," said a nervous voice from behind her. She turned around to see Officer Kazue. Her eyes narrowed.

"I go where the job takes me, Kazue. Walk me around the crime scene," she said.

"You know, what I said before—" he stammered.

"Do your *job*, Officer," Ishikawa snapped. Kazue bit his lower lip and led the way.

They walked further down the row to the right, then took a left. Another white sheet covered a body, against one of the giant squid vats. Several of the curious creatures hovered near where the victim's head would be, under the sheet.

"Li Tang, 23. She's the first. Or second, depending on how you count them. These were Rikora worker models—all four of them. Brand new, too. They've got the rest of their Companions barricaded in one of the freezers in the back. Don't think it would hold them if they decided to make a break for it, but the workers outside are shit-scared of them right now," Kazue said, shrugging.

Ishikawa looked around her. She knelt down and lifted the cloth covering the girl and assessed the damage as well as she could. She'd been shoved, hard. The way her head hung told her broken neck.

"Show me the next one, Officer Kazue."

He led her to the fallen forklift, and it was then that she noticed that it had toppled over on top of someone.

"Aquilino Réal, 48. He was getting out of his forklift when it was kicked at him. Here, you can see the dent where the Companion lunged into it, crushing him. He's either number one or number two. Time of death is almost identical for both, but they were killed by different Companions."

The cage had landed on his back. Ishikawa lifted the cloth and saw the indent where the top roll-bar pushed down on the man's rib-cage.

Kazue walked her back to the front entrance where the first victim she'd encountered lay.

"And finally, Mr. Honesto Torres, 31. He was a security guard at the factory and tried to stop the Companions from leaving. He was an augment, but that didn't stop them from throwing him against the wall like a puppet," Kazue said. Ishikawa looked under the blanket, Mr Torres' flesh and machine parts blending together in a bloody stew.

She exited the building, leaving Kazue behind. She walked over to the men and women in hard hats who stood near Officer Yamaguchi. After speaking to them briefly, they transferred the model numbers to her wrist computer, and she thanked them for their cooperation.

She nodded for Keiji to follow.

If Kazue stood at the entrance of the factory, arms crossed and jilted, she ignored it and walked away.

As they went back to the car, he asked "So, what did you find out?"

"Rikonas. Brand new. Four of them. I have the makes and models. We can plug that into the car sensors and maybe you could give me a little help finding our missing Companions."

"I guess I could," he said, as they stepped into the car. Ishikawa turned on the engine and clicked on the car's navigation and sensor array. She tapped the info she'd just gotten from the factory managers onto the touch pad, and Keiji pulled out the wires from the back of his head once again, plugging them directly into the interface.

For a few seconds, a single light blinked on the sensor screen, showing the position of a Rikona, or at least, what the sensors believed it was, before it vanished. Ishikawa frowned, tapping the side of the screen, but the glowing orange dot did not return.

Had it been only a single Companion, or had they been in such close proximity that the sensor only recognized it as one?

It had glowed long enough for her to recognize the area in which it was, however, and she called over the radio to all patrolling vehicles in the vicinity to head to Minamioyumicho.

They/It had bypassed the police cordon.

The car lifted above the factory, and headed south-east, toward one of 100th levels' major arteries.

The exos had been waiting at a central staging area near the factory. They were now en route to the place she'd designated, loaded in massive quadcopters.

With the signal vanished, however, she wondered what they would find on the scene, if anything at all.

PRISON BREAK

Hideki Saito had stalked his cell more times than he could count. No time at all had gone by in the real, but in this construct, it felt like hours. It might be years before he'd break out.

He'd tried to switch off the construct, to no avail. The first thing he'd done was attempt to unplug himself, but that had proven fruitless as well.

This was unfortunate for him, since Alacatraz was deemed inescapable. It'd been opened in 1933 as a penitentiary for those prisoners deemed too problematic for the rest of the country. The place had been turned over to Parks and Recreation after over forty years of harbouring hardened criminals, the likes of Al Capone and "Machine Gun" Kelly.

Saito did not expect a group of tourists to come and let him out. This was Singh's construct now—the man had twisted it for his own uses.

Three cold, off-green cement walls, and one white iron cage door. He'd banged on the vertical bars every once in a while for hours, with lessening enthusiasm. Had listened to the clanging reverberate throughout the massive cell block before getting tired. Had called out in the hopes that some virtual character within would be triggered to help. Nothing doing.

He'd thought of breaking character and doing something extreme, but that would have alerted Singh.

Saito sat on the bare metal cot, thinking. The only other furniture in the tiny cell were a sink, toilet, chair and desk plank, all attached to the walls.

The irony of being inside a prison, while inside a prison was not lost on Saito, and he did not suppress the smile the thought brought him. He sighed, leaning back against the cold wall, the mesh under his ass digging into his butt cheeks. It was either that or sitting on the just as uncomfortable wooden board that served as a chair.

He decided he didn't mind after all.

What had he learned? He put his hands behind his head.

Apart from the fact that Nabeen Singh seemed to be losing it, the bit about the Nexus being built for survival rang true. Thousands of people's personalities and memories acting as one, organized in such a way as to look out only for itself. There was something there.

In other words, alliances and enmities only held as long as the immediate survival of the entity could be attained. What a dangerous thing Singh had unleashed onto the world. Although, that wasn't entirely true. Wen Harkwell had released it from Singh's grip. Was he responsible, then?

Was the tool the problem, or its handler? The question became a chicken-and-egg problem when one considered that in this case, the tool had sentience and will.

Through the skylight, the sun was setting. Time and space were warped inside the construct. This had become plain to see the first time he'd teleported from the downtown area directly to the reproduction of Singh and Daiko's apartment building, as well as the difference in time of day. The techs who'd trapped Singh in a non-Euclidian-space jail hadn't counted on his learning to use it to his advantage.

Who would have an interest in helping an entity which was basically hostile to all save its creator? thought Saito. He didn't have to think very far back in time to pinpoint a plethora of humans who'd willingly betrayed their own for a measure of advantage. In this case, however, the person doing the betraying already had all the advantages they needed. What else was there?

What was the end-goal, in permitting DaiSin to capitulate to its enemies? The traitor had to know that that would be the final product of his or her actions, didn't they? Or was there a measure of cognitive dissonance at play, masking that reality from their very eyes?

That, he would have to find out. Blindness or outright greed? Which was it to be? Either of those purposes were hateful to him, and neither was a better choice in the grand scheme of things, the result being selfsame.

As always, it had to be a game of follow-the-money, but in this case, those involved were masters in masking their own trails behind dead ends and obfuscation. If it had been as simple as checking a bank account, the culprit would have been unmasked a year or more ago.

The chill of the penitentiary was penetrating. Discomfort of any sort was unexpected, but this reminded Saito once again that it was Singh's construct now. Darkness was incomplete, a layer of grey through the skylight illuminating a long patch along the cracking concrete floor below.

Except that this non-Euclidian space was imperfect. Distance and time had been arranged in a jarring superposition, and nothing could truly be contained within it, only transported from one place to the other at varying, nonsensical (according to real-world physics) lengths.

Singh knew this, but it had taken Saito a few hours to come to grips with this arrangement.

He got to his feet and looked around. He touched the wall behind the cot. It was just as solid as when he'd had his back to it. The bars were just the same, down to the coarse texture of the chipped paint.

There had to be something here. He looked over to the stained sink and grungy-looking toilet. It was only a foot away, so he reached out to the sink, but his hand only caught air.

Smiling, he walked toward the far wall of the cell, and it retreated further and further as he did. He continued like this for what felt like an eternity. He turned around, and found himself in a long, green corridor the same colour as the cell walls, only an indeterminately long length.

As he turned around to keep going, he felt a pain in his neck, and fell to his knees on the dirty floor. Eventually, the pain passed, and he got up, looking around to see what might have caused it, but just as before, he was alone.

He kept on walking down the corridor until the light from the cell was a distant memory. There was only infinite corridor now, stretching from one end of time to the other. He wondered briefly *how much* time had gone by in the real. Computation time always had a tendency to speed things up, just like the virtual battle he'd witnessed at Samuel Harkwell's console.

Saito would not have been surprised if only an hour had gone by since his arrival. Further down the corridor, he saw a pin-prick of light, the width of a needle, hovering. It was so close he could touch it as well, but he knew this was more of the construct's spatial distortion.

He kept walking, the needle becoming a tennis ball of light. Eventually, it widened to the size of a door frame, and he stepped through it, finding himself on the other side of the door to Singh and

Daiko's apartment. The sunny street scene he'd only glimpsed from within the lobby was on full display now that he'd found the exit.

Saito found the whole experience more than a bit unnerving, and promised himself never to come back to visit Singh unless he truly needed to.

He disconnected using his serial key, this time successfully, leaving the inner core of Deguchi's mind. As he did, he felt a weight lift from him. He surmised that it must be from having escaped Singh's prison. He found himself once again in Douglas Deguchi's tiny apartment in the depths of the DaiSin building.

Deguchi unplugged himself, rubbing the back of his neck.

"Been a while since I've done that," he said. "Find out anything worthwhile?"

"Other than the fact our mutual friend is losing his mind, no, not much," Saito said. A shadow crossed over Deguchi's face, then his smile returned.

"I'm sure he'll feel better once he's freed," he said.

"I wouldn't count on that," Saito said, rising to his feet, his eyebrow raising.

"Oh, you never know. Stranger things have happened," Deguchi said in a congenial tone.

Saito felt no need to antagonize the man, but there was about as much chance of DaiSin freeing Singh as there was for Saito to go to the Martian Independent States for a pleasure cruise. That is to say, none whatsoever.

"I won't forget to send someone to bring a bit of colour to your apartments, Mr. Deguchi," he finally added. The large man smiled and nodded as Saito left his temporary place of residence.

He wondered what the future held for Douglas Deguchi. Administration would go insane if they had concrete proof that DaiSin harboured one of its most wanted fugitives. Then again, it wouldn't be the first time in its existence that DaiSin was flirting with illegality. In this life, everyone lived by their own moral compass. The question was, what were the goals, and what could they get away with? In other words, what was the point of having a moral compass if there was no North to speak of?

It amused Saito to think that it was legal to conduct online battles where men and women could lose their lives, but harbouring a convicted criminal was an offense punishable by life imprisonment. It all depended on who held the power, and who made the rules. Human ethics were the by-product of the demands of society's necessities at any given time, and the conflicts that ensued were based on the varying beliefs that directed one's ethics. Survival of the fittest or empathy for all? To what degree did competition fit into the equation?

Saito almost felt sorry for the Nexus. Was it their fault that Singh had 'brought them to life' by robbing their original owners of their desires and making their thirst his tool? No, not at all. But now that individualism was a threat to the company. The Nexus had decided that the needs of their few outweighed that of the many, and used whatever it had learned during its existence to survive, to the detriment of those around it.

One had to wonder if the memories of people made them people still, or if having been detached from the flesh, they were but hungry ghosts clinging to tattered rags they were no longer entitled to. The thought gave Saito's heart an uneasy squeeze, and he brushed it aside.

Saito headed for the elevators along the silent corridors, an occasional guard nodding to him. He enjoyed the silence of the lower levels, the absence of drama and noise. For a moment, he wondered if he should perhaps have set up his workplace in one of these islands of solitude.

But no. What he was doing demanded people around him, and the distractions would only have followed him.

He made his way back to his office, the children greeting him with their usual joy, but Sachiko was nowhere to be seen. Most of the rooms on this level were more like hospital wards—half walls with glass windows about mid-waist up to the ceiling. The round-edged windows reminded him of old spaceship design, sans colourful collages to adorn them.

Back at his desk, he found his assistant's report. All of those present for the meeting had been who they claimed to be. That was a relief. There was always that nagging fear that a clone might have made its way into your midst, copy-switching, and no way to outwardly tell until things went south.

This meant that whoever was responsible was doing so fully cognizant of their actions.

Saito had nothing against clones per se. It was only a matter of precaution. He felt that they, like every other version of humanity deserved to live. That that wasn't the Administration's stance didn't faze him. DaiSin had defended clone rights in the past, at least under Harkwell, and he hoped that with enough pressure, they might begin to understand that persons were persons, whether copies or not. He was certainly in no position to judge.

He opened the file he had on his computer about the council members. These were the official records, not the "juice" Jenna Wolinsky had spilled to him earlier in the boardroom. The majority had been in DaiSin's employ over five years. Some, like the President, had pledged over thirty. At this point, he wasn't interested so much about time served, but motive.

Of course, he could have programmed the Golems with what she had told him baked into their search parameters, but that would have given them an implied bias which would have skewed the results. Better to let them prove these things on their own without interference. Golems were excellent data analysis machines, and would come forward with all relevant information, if such information were there to be found. If not, he could discount the rumours for being just that.

A message appeared in his peripheral vision.

ANALYSIS OF YAMADA, TAISHIRO.

"Put it through," he said.

RECORD OF BEHAVIOUR SHOWS LESSENING OF SALES BEFORE COMBAT IN WHICH DAISIN STOCK PLUMMETS. COULD INDICATE NEGATIVE IMPACT THROUGH OMISSION. EFFECT WOULD BE DOUBLED.

"You're saying that by losing market share through holding back of sales, Yamada might be helping DaiSin's opponents?"

CORRECT. THIS COULD BE CONSTRUED AS COMPOUNDED CORRELATION.

Saito thought for a bit. He got out of his seat and walked around his office.

"What is the ratio?"

67%.

"That's high, but not high enough to assign blame. The world economy is going through a bear market at the moment. This information is incidental and the correlative ratio too low. Contact me again when you have something more concrete."

YES SIR.

Saito's computer pinged from his desk, and he answered the call. Samuel Harkwell's hologram was drawn before his desk in blue lasers, without the tentacular tubes and wires that protruded from the back of his skull.

"Yes, Mr. Harkwell. How may I help you?" he asked, smiling.

"I have something to show you," the other man said, his features grim. He pointed at Saito's computer on his desk, and a Japanese variety show began to play. Contestants tried to bop each other over the head with blow-up mallets, while trying to catch balls thrown at them from the audience.

The view switched to a different show, where two men stood behind podiums having an argument about the health merits of white radish.

"I'm sorry Mr. Harkwell, I don't understand what I'm supposed to be seeing, here." Saito said, his brow furrowing as he turned back to Samuel Harkwell's hologram

"You asked me to send you the video records dating back two years until the Nexus' vanishing act. While going through them, I found about a week's worth of *this*. Every single camera in the DaiSin Building recorded a variety show or talk show of some sort. Someone's mocking us, Mr. Saito."

SPIDERS

Datu awoke one morning on a rubberized bed, covered in a silver heating blanket and nothing else. He could hear disjointed voices from a distance, as if calling from a dream. His rib cage felt like it was made of concrete. He had trouble moving his neck, and odd vibrational feedback spasmed from his right arm.

When he tried to get up, he did so too fast, and it was as if the back of his skull was pulling him back down, until it let go with a snap. He lifted his hand to touch his cranium. It was no longer flesh, but smooth polycarbon mesh over a mess of wires and actuators. So was his arm.

He followed with horror the curves of the android body he inhabited, all the way to his chest. His left arm was still his own, he observed with some relief, and he touched the back of his head with it now.

The simple trode sockets were there, of course, at the base of his skull. Further down, however, he felt a coarse metal spine begin where they ended. He was torn between finding a mirror to see for himself how much of a Frankenstein's creation he had become, and hiding forever to avoid this situation.

He got up carefully, first to see if his body still functioned as it once had. Then he checked if everything was still there. A cursory glance under the silver sheet confirmed he was still whole where he felt it counted, and he put it down again with a long exhale.

When he lifted his head, he was confronted by an Asian woman in a black sleeveless jacket, red v-neck shirt and black pants.

He lifted the sheet with a start, and the woman smirked, pretending to peek behind it.

"Nothing I've never seen before, pal. The boss wants to see you. Get dressed," she said, walking away and patting a pile of work clothes at the end of the hospital cot, on a camo-green metal trunk.

Datu got out of bed, and the woman pulled a white curtain around it, stepping out to allow him privacy.

The clothes felt used, but clean, and he wondered where they'd come from. He also thought he might regret asking if he got a proper answer. He dressed in silence, pulling on the dark beige padded clothing which slid just as well over his human parts as his mechanical ones.

He was once again relieved to see that both his legs were still his, and as far as he could tell, his own head and face, after extended touching with his left hand.

He tapped his cyborgized chest and wondered how it all worked in there, as well.

When he exited the thin curtain after having pulled on scuffed work boots, the woman returned to escort him through the large room. It had at least twenty foot ceilings, and Datu thought of a warehouse converted into an infirmary. The ceiling was unfinished and showed the skeleton on the roof's armature. Both sides of the rectangular room were furnished with a row of hospital beds whose sand-coloured contours were beginning to yellow.

He wondered why it would be necessary to have so many, but once again, his brain was telling him to stop asking questions for which he would not like the answers.

"What's your name?" he asked, his voice sore. It didn't sound like his at all, in fact.

"Reza," the woman said, turning back.

"Reza what?" Datu said, looking over to a man lying on one of the hospital cots, his vitals stable, his eyes closed.

"Just Reza," she said, and they left the infirmary. The building *was*, in fact, some enormous warehouse. A bulldozer was parked in the next room in a corner, a giant stack of old mannequin parts before it.

"Sorry about the mess," Reza said, waving an arm in a general way. "Renovations." She led Datu up a flight of stairs to a sparsely furnished yet more populated second floor. Everything about the building reeked of the previous century and the attempts to bury its age, from the dusty concrete floors to the nanostatic shielding over the boarded up windows along the way. The smell of carbon fibre and mildew permeated the air, like rejuvenating plastic surgery on a geriatric patient.

They walked down a long corridor where open doors revealed small, empty rooms filled with rolled-up cots on high shelves. Datu wondered if all the supposed others were working, or if he was the only other employee, as if he'd been indentured to a startup that had just now "started up."

The last door on the left held a small office space, where Arun sat, eyes glued to a monitor. His neutral expression permanently affixed to his face, until he saw Datu and his wide smile returned. He stood up and walked around his desk.

"Nice to see you in the physical, my friend! You know, there was a time where we thought you wouldn't make it. You are much more resilient than some give you credit for," he said, giving a sidelong glance at Reza, who rolled her eyes.

"How are you feeling?" He continued, pointing his chin at the prosthetics.

Datu lifted his robotic arms and turned it this way and that.

"Takes some getting used to," he said, putting it down and forcing a small smile.

"That's the spirit. Now, I didn't tell you much about the company, but that wasn't very important then. It was need-to-know. And now you need to know. Midori Mamoru is a new kind of recycling facility which will be installed directly in the Heap," he said, and he lifted a hand at Datu's objection. "I know. It's dangerous. But doing the work from the ground will save enormous amounts of people power. No more need to bring scrap to the upper levels to be triaged. It'll all be done from the point of origin. Thing is, most of our workforce is computer and Companion-based. That's right, the heavy lifting will be done by our android friends. Yours will be more of a… supervisory position."

Reza was leaning into the doorframe, arms crossed.

"So how far along are you into building this recycling facility?" Datu asked.

"Almost done, in fact. If you want, I can take you there and give you the tour. Are you feeling well enough to get to work now?" Arun's face wavered between his placid demeanour and his wide smile, which creeped Datu out. He seemed over-eager. There was nothing he could do, however, to back out from his deal now. He nodded slowly, and Arun's smile came back with several degrees of increased intensity.

Reza gave Datu a gentle shove out the door, to which Datu gave an involuntary digging in of his heels.

"I don't know you, Reza, but I'll ask you nicely… don't push," he said to the woman, who scrunched up her face in a sarcastic manner. Arun closed and locked his office door, passed the pair and walked back down the corridor. They went down the stairs and turned right, going down a length of empty warehouse until they came to an assembly point where twenty or so newer work vehicles were parked within the massive space. Off in a corner, a pile of garbage lay in a pile, and Datu spotted an old recycler's uniform, tattered and bloodied, and he wondered if it had been his.

Arun led them to a door to the right, where a cloak room was filled with brand-new, top-of-the-line protective equipment. The kind the army might have used if they'd had to do Heap warfare. They looked so advanced that Datu was certain they could have been used as space suits. *Except that, as recycler suits, the choice of white was a poor one,* he thought. He shrugged. As long as they functioned as they were meant to, the colour mattered little to him.

Arun looked around and said "Pick."

Datu was taken aback. He went to every hanging suit, inspecting them, looking for flaws or discrepancies in the fabric, but all were in mint condition. He chose one in his size and slipped it on, as did Reza and Arun.

Once again, Arun led the two, bringing them to a side door past the de-con showers and changing rooms. They stepped into an ultra-modern pressurization chamber and the inside door closed like a sucking-in of breath. The outside door opened with a hiss, and they walked out onto a grey concrete platform.

Arun tapped the side of his helmet, and Datu touched the same spot on his, activating his communicator.

"We're on the fiftieth. Stay close. We reinforced this area with concrete for our machinery, but try to stay away from any sketchy-looking metallic grating. Those parts haven't been done yet," Arun said, and Datu nodded. He knew that any kind of fall down to the Heap from this height would be supremely uncomfortable. He's been lucky once in his misadventures; trying his luck a second time would be foolish.

A thick grey fog rolled through the area, sometimes revealing— more often eclipsing the massive blue warehouse behind them. Parts of it appeared brand-new, and others had the original discoloured paintjob which had survived for who knew how long. Midori Mamoru had chosen an existing building for the storage of their salvage equipment, much like Administration did, with the exception that those working for Midori lived there. That, and Administration seldom sprang for renos.

Datu began to wonder who he would be working with, and if they were on their way to meeting them.

Red diodes ran along the path, marking the safe zones, like a landing strip. They came to the end, a metallic octagon surrounded with gritty caution tape, and Datu could see a chest-high wire guardrail whose supports had been drilled into the concrete. A bit further still, in the periphery, the twisted outline of its rusted and broken predecessor loomed, there as a reminder to watch one's step.

Arun looked at his arm, tapped it a few times, and Datu felt the ground shake beneath him. The platform on which he stood began to descend, and he peered over the edge, trying to spy the bottom. Further back, in the direction of the warehouse, he thought he spied the black bulk of a support pillar, the jaws of some immense clamp grasping it, supporting the structure from whence they'd come.

Four smaller supports held the elevator shaft. Whatever his misgivings about his being there, Datu realized that Midori Mamoru had finances. They had the money to purchase brand-new equipment, refit an entire warehouse, solidify a level, and construct a level elevator.

Of course, he didn't know how long this had taken, but that mattered little in his mind. The simple fact that they'd been willing to invest so much in their overall operations told him that they cared more about their employees than Administration. So far, he'd seen no equipment apart from the warehouse which was over two years old.

A devil's advocate might say: "Yes, but they're a brand-new company!" But Datu knew that even those who'd just arrived on the scene mostly invested in older, cheaper equipment to keep their costs down. Whoever was behind all this had some serious cash to throw around. He was now curious to know what they might look like.

The base of the elevator nested into another concrete slab, the surrounding guardrails lowering. Datu couldn't help but wondering how that was possible, since anything that heavy would irretrievably sink.

Reza looked at him with her hands on her hips.

"Wondering how we did it, newbie?" She said, walking over to him.

"Yeah, this is… this is just impossible!" Datu stepped out onto the concrete slab, testing its firmness. It was, indeed, what it advertised itself as.

"Adjustable pistons. They go all the way down to the ground floor. Bring the whole platform up or down depending on need," Arun said, interrupting the two. Datu visualized tens of zeros added to his original estimate as to the operational costs. New Yen signs danced in his mind. He shook his head in disbelief and followed Reza and Arun, who were walking in the direction of some parked vehicles down the way.

The same type of red LEDs as those near the warehouse shone in the darkness around the perimeter of the platform, casting a hazy, fiery glow in the fog.

Midori Mamoru owned similar vehicles as those he used—correction—*had used* while in the employ of Peoplift. The major difference was in the overall aesthetics of the design. These appeared smoother, cleaner. Too clean, even, for the environment in which they were meant to operate in, just like the suit he wore. He looked down at himself, thinking that there would already be a thin layer of filth covering everything.

He gave his head a shake when he saw that they were still the same matte white as when he'd put it on in the changing room.

"The suits absorb any kind of soot or fume to power it. Saves on battery power and removes an infinitesimal amount of pollutants from the air. It's not much, but it's only a start. We're in the process of patenting," Arun said. Datu imagined that the vehicles present shared that same property with the suits.

So everything was a Midori Mamori invention? Who were these people?

More suits appeared in the distance as they walked toward the edge of the site. As they crossed paths, Datu was certain he'd seen them before.

One man turned around and the look of surprise on his face made him uncomfortable, until he recognized him as well. It was Rodrigo. The man he'd left for dead in the Heap, that fateful day the storm had come.

"Rodrigo! You're still alive! How—" he stammered.

"A Companion found me. They saved me, Datu," Rodrigo said, beaming.

"I'm so sorry I couldn't—" Datu said, eyes brimming with tears.

The other man came to him and hugged him for a very long time.

"It's okay, Datu. There was nothing you could do. But hey! I'm still alive!" he said, lifting his arms high and doing a little dance. Arun nodded to him, and his smile faltered a bit.

"I'll talk to you later, my friend. We have a lot of work to do. I'm glad you're here," Rodrigo said, turning back to the other workers he'd been arranging boxes with.

Humanoid Companions lifted various tools and implements, loading them onto flatbed trucks, strapping them down for the drive. The trucks left the staging area and trundled off into the trash, almost floating over it, barely a rocking to their movements as they made their way over the rough terrain.

Arun pointed to an odd, grub-like transport. It was as white as the rest of the equipment, but had no discernible entrances or windows. As Arun approached, a hole reticulated in its side, a retractable staircase descending to the tarmac. He let Reza and Datu go in first. The inside consisted of bucket seats against the walls and nothing else. A white glow emanated from the walls, until they sat down, at which point it dimmed to blackness. The walls became transparent, and Datu could see a view of the entire Heap around him, as if he were sitting on a floating chair.

The grub began to move forward, leaving the staging area. As they did, Datu could see the undulations of the vehicle and the rise and fall of the seats, but from where he sat, there was little jostling or movement. Simply smooth transitions as the thing organically half-slithered, half-crawled over mounds of garbage.

Datu wondered where they were going, but he was heartened to see that none of the other workers were made to walk from the staging area to their place of work. He spotted a few more of the Grub Rovers in the distance, as he now called them, going back to the elevator.

Fifteen minutes later, the vehicle came to a halt, and they exited onto moist terrain. Datu wondered where they could possibly be, as there were no visible pits, which had been the typical method used by Administration to parse through three hundred years worth of trash.

The surrounding area had a few diggers and those low trucks were being unloaded by more Companions. Arun once again led them, this time over a steep rise. On the other side, flood lights had been set up, but these were turned off. Or rather, all he saw from them was a faint blue light which illuminated nothing.

"Ultraviolet on," Arun said, and then Datu was able to see the glow of the white vehicles, the hundreds of people working below, the dull glow of Companions assisting, and an aperture in the side of a garbage mountain the size of a large house. Humanoids and machines entered and exited in a constant stream, reminding Datu of a low anthill in full production mode.

Arun walked down the hill gingerly, greeted at the bottom by armour-suited workers with a wave of the hand. Datu's heart beat hard, feeling he was finally in a place where his talents might be appreciated. His legs felt fixed in place, unable to walk or follow.

"This is where you'll be working," Arun said over the radio. Reza nudged him downward, forcing him to shamble down the side of the garbage hill they stood on.

Datu stared at the intense work site, unbelieving. It was coordinated, like a subtle ballet of organization between the humans and machines. He recognized a few of the missing workers from the transport he used to take every day to go to his previous employ, finally realizing where they'd gone to. Perhaps it wasn't that difficult to draw employees away when what you had to offer was a thousand times better.

A beeping sound began to emanate from his speakers, and Arun yelled

"Everybody inside!"

All around, a mad scramble, the workers in the valley heading into the doorway in the refuse, as its giant doors began to slide closed. Reza grabbed Datu's arm as he stood, speechless, at the rapid retreat.

She pushed him behind one of the trucks and Arun looked around.

"Personal camouflage," Arun commanded, but Datu saw no noticeable change to his environment. Reza grabbed his arm and pushed a button along his elbow, and Datu saw it go transparent, along with the rest of his suit. Opto-camouflage!

Datu's eyes went wide as he saw the remaining people and vehicles vanish. One moment they were there, and the other simply not.

A bright red light approached in the distance. As the sentry bot hovered nearer, Datu heard a rumble coming from some unknown elsewhere. It was loud, mechanical and massive, like an earthquake of grinding servos.

Datu hid behind the invisible truck, wondering if the sentry could 'see' any of them. It resembled a small nuclear submarine, the white-hot heat of hover stabilizers beneath. Its periscope end glowed in the infrared, detecting warmth at great distances. This made sense in the Heap, as light was hard to come by. The problem was that garbage was in a constant state of molecular deconstruction, and therefore produced heat. Still, when a sentry bot found a being which had not been chipped to clear its security parameters, it fried them with an electric death-ray, then returned the corpse to Central.

Datu wondered what they were all doing hiding, as he'd assumed Midori Mamoru had been cleared to do this work.

As the sentry approached, the rumble grew louder. In his mind, it was akin to a series of rusted metal cranes moving in concert. He wondered where the hell it came from. Then, as it came near the lip of the mountain of trash, an enormous shape, vastly larger than the sentry, dashed towards it, sending debris flying into the air. Datu fell as the force of the impact not a hundred metres away from him shook the ground like a bomb blast.

A laser beam slashed out in the darkness, cutting the sentry in diagonal halves, the split pieces falling into the garbage patch, still glowing red from the heat.

Whatever monster had done this was at least ten times the size of the sentry, with long metallic legs, pushing it out of the detritus at incredible velocity. It grabbed the two sentry parts with its front legs, smashing them together and frying the resulting mulch with some sort of sun-bright soldering tool above its monstrous head.

It then turned toward the construction site, where Arun lifted his hand. The massive spider bot nestled itself back into the trash, using its foreclaws to lift garbage over itself and once again melt into the pile.

SIGNAL DUMPING

Bulky exo suits had landed in the vicinity of the last known position Ishikawa had sent them. The hulks were arranged in a half-circle, every fifty metres, covering a wide swath. In the meantime, police helicopters and hovers combed the industrial district, their spotlights visible from where Ishikawa and Keiji were flying in from.

The police land vehicles were making their way there now, below them, a stream of flashing blue and red cherries illuminating the avenue, announcing their arrival.

"We have visuals on one of the AWOL Rikonas, Special Inspector. Awaiting your orders," came a woman's voice on the radio.

"Stall it as long as you can, Officer. We'll be right there."

"Something's wrong," Keiji said.

"Wrong how?" Ishikawa asked.

"The signals for all those Rikonas should be visible on the screen. They just vanished."

"Could it be interference?" Ishikawa asked, tapping the radar array. The car was dipping lower, getting ready to alight near the cordoned area.

"No, I don't think so. The alterations I made can account for most types of interference, even in the industrial district," he answered, shaking his head. Keiji's eyes went wide for a moment.

"Unless..." he said, then his expression went slack as he introspected.

"Unless what?" Ishikawa asked, annoyed.

The signal returned on the screen for just a moment, almost directly below them. It then vanished again just as quickly.

"Go down, now! Try to see where that signal was emanating from. I have to recalibrate again," Keiji said.

"Why?" Ishikawa asked.

"Signal dumping," Keiji retorted, before introspecting again.

Ishikawa took the controls and accelerated downward. For a moment, a trio of flashes were back on the screen, and then gone again. She directed the car toward the cluster, extrapolating their direction and speed from the last pulse.

They were heading in a south-easterly direction, away from the police exos. Ishikawa had analyzed rebel Companion's behaviour and come to the conclusion that the worker's deaths might have been unintentional. As a matter of programming, Companions were not equipped with malice.

Every single person who'd either been injured or killed today had been so while getting in the way of the escapees. Unless some new case came up that would change her views, for now, according to evidence, the Companions had only harmed those who'd tried to stop them. Or who'd had the unfortunate bad luck of being in their way during their escape.

The lights pulsed again, and Ishikawa saw movement along one of the side streets of the factory district. They moved single-file along a row of genetically modified pencil hollies. The tall, thin shrubs a failed attempt at controlling factory smoke output, now surviving in the depths of the 100th.

A van pulled up to the curb, and the back rolled up to reveal two men wearing what looked like full riot gear. The Companions climbed aboard, and the van sped up.

"What the shit?" Ishikawa said, pulling the car down to the road and beginning to follow the truck. It was an average-looking rental, blank apart from the "Move It!" stickers affixed to its side. She ran the plates, which came back stolen.

She'd already turned off the police lights, hoping to follow the van to wherever it was going. This changed everything.

"Central, have them wrap up the Rikona and get down to my position. The Companion is a decoy. We've got the other three in line-of-sight in a stolen rental van, Ikebukuro plates, 8089. Following at a distance," she said on the radio. The van had turned left around a blind corner, and she sped up to catch it.

As she turned, she was forced to veer out of the way to avoid getting hit by the van, which was backing up to hit her. It clipped the back of the car with a bang, sending it spinning across the empty avenue into a chain-link fence on the other side. The car skidded to a stop sideways, with Ishikawa pinned inside on the fence side.

On the other side of the street, the van's rolling door was coming up.

"Give me a gun!" Keiji said, opening his door.

"I'm not going to give you my gun!" Ishikawa yelled, shaking the fuzz out of her head.

Two menacing Rikonas stepped out of the van, walking toward the stalled car.

"Lean back!" Ishikawa ordered, and as Keiji pushed the lever to lower his seat, Ishikawa fired a round into the closest Companion, blowing a hole out its midriff. The android crumpled to the ground, and the other two kept coming, making a wider circle around the car to avoid getting shot.

Ishikawa pushed the open button for her door, but it refused to rise, stuck on the crossbar of the fence beside the car. She couldn't very well order Keiji out of the vehicle either without putting him in mortal danger. She gritted her teeth, turned off the personalized safety, and passed the weapon to Keiji, who leaned out the door and fired at the Rikona approaching from the side of the car.

Its head exploded with a shriek of metal, spreading coolant all over the street. The Companion fell sideways, stiff, and smoke began to pour out of its neck.

Keiji left the safety of the car to see where the third companion had gone. As he lifted his hand to look behind the car, a thump on the roof alerted him. His arm was grabbed by the missing android, and he was jerked out of the car with such force that he felt as if his shoulder had been dislocated.

On the other side of the street, the van's wheels burned rubber, and it left as fast as it could, leaving black tire-treads on the slick asphalt.

Ishikawa crawled over the passenger seat and got out of the car. She had repeatedly called 'Mayday' on her internal channel, hoping anyone in the vicinity could come, but so far there'd been no answer. If she could get to the shotgun in the trunk, there might be a chance of taking the Rikona down, but seeing as it stood on the roof, she doubted very much it would allow her to reach in there to get it. The odds were even greater that it would use Keiji as a human shield, even if she did get it.

"Let go of the gun!" she yelled to Keiji, whose arm was being held above his head.

"I can't... move my fingers!" he said, hanging limply from the

Rikona's grip. The human-sized android was impassive, looking down at Ishikawa, then at the gun. It took the gun from Keiji, released his wrist, pushed Keiji at Ishikawa and pointed the gun at both as he fell to the tarmac.

Ishikawa braced herself for the bullet that would surely come in the next instant as Keiji slammed into her.

Instead, she heard a resounding "Stop!"

As Keiji fell atop her, she hit her head on the ground. She barely had the time to turn around to see a humanoid shape run up the side of the car, and pounce on the Rikona. A shot went wide, and Ishikawa tried to extricate herself from under the boy on the asphalt, her head ringing.

In the distance, police sirens wailed. She felt sick but got up and teetered to the front of the car where two Companions were punching pieces out of each other. The Rikona was on its back, another, larger model pummelling it in the chest and head. It got off a good shot to the newcomer's shoulder before getting its face smashed in.

Her gun was a few feet away. She leaned down, almost falling and retrieved it, yelling "Get off it."

The Companion on top looked at her quizzically and somersaulted off the Rikona. It tried to get up, but Ishikawa fired several times, hitting the pavement once, then into its head, blasting it to pieces.

"Are you unhurt?" the new Companion asked.

"I'm— fine," she said, shaking her head. "How did you know we were in danger?" she replied. The other Companion came forward and caught her before she could collapse. He took her to the hood of the car and placed her in a seated position next to the front tire.

"I received your distress call. I work in the factory over there," he said, pointing to the one they had passed on the way, behind sickly-looking tall hedges.

"What's your designation?" Ishikawa said, pinching her nose.

"I am Eiko625," it said.

"Little help?" Keiji said, from beside the car. The Companion went to Keiji and knelt down near him.

"You are injured. Allow me to assist," it said.

"Whoah! Wait a minute! Are you a medical bot?" Keiji asked, his hand in a warding gesture as he tried to crawl away. Eiko625 smiled.

"All Companions working for Alicore Light Industries are pro-grammed with basic First Aid. Allow me to verify the severity of your injuries." the Companion said, putting his hand on Keiji's arm.

"Ouch! Watch it! I think it's—"

"Dislocated? Yes, I believe you are right. I will—"

"Nononono wait!" Keiji wailed, but before he could move away, the Companion had taken his arm in one hand and his shoulder in the other and pressed firmly on the arm.

There was a sick 'thuk!' and Keiji fell to the ground, clutching his arm and crying.

"There. You are repaired," Eiko625 said in a satisfied voice, putting his hands on his hips, as if he'd just built a pretty birdhouse. Ishikawa grinned.

"I like you," she said in a woozy voice, then holstering her gun after having re-initiated her personalized safety. She was annoyed with herself for having turned it off in the first place. If she hadn't, the Companion couldn't have attempted to shoot them. Then again, Keiji would not have been able to take the other one's head off.

Soon, Keiji was sitting on the ground, rubbing his sore shoulder. He got up and looked around as police cruisers came in, screeching to a halt.

An officer came up to her and said "We found the van a few streets down. Empty. Whoever was driving didn't leave a trace."

"So much for that," she said.

She surveyed the disaster area. Three destroyed Companions, four if you counted the one which had been left to distract them. The new arrivals on the scene had dispatched the decoy as quickly as they could to come to their rescue, with no thought as to the information it could have contained. Human life was the priority in these cases, always.

Overhead, the quadcopter transport had arrived, alighting a bit further on the deserted avenue. The exo suits were kept inside, seeing as all the excitement was over.

She thanked her lucky stars the Eiko model had been in the vicinity.

Two of the machines that had been shot would be useless for retrieving data—

She looked over at the first one she'd shot. It still twitched on the ground. Its mobility servos might be damaged, but its braincase was intact. If she wanted more information, she might as well connect before its power bank died.

A medic came to see her and assessed her head wound. She cleaned the blood off and applied a cold compress, telling Ishikawa to hold it steady. After checking Keiji, she thanked Eiko625 for its good work, at which the Companion was duly grateful and made a blushing motion.

Ishikawa, compress in one hand, walked over to the twitching Rikona, which followed her every move with its head. She took out her scanner from her pocket, then stuck the filaments into the Rikona's input ports. As she turned on the power, the scanner's lights turned red and it began to smoke. She threw it on the ground, and green flames shot out of the various ports on the machine and she cursed.

"You're toxic, aren't you," she said, tapping the Companion on the forehead with her index finger, who kept on staring at her, unblinking.

"Some kind of virus," Keiji said, standing behind her. "I know a way to get in and find out what it is. Something Ito San taught me."

"Just let the boys downtown analyze it," she said, sitting down on the hood of her car, pulling on her lower lip.

"Now that they're aware of you following, the odds are they won't give you any more freebies. If we don't find out what's making them go crazy, you can bet there'll be more of this coming, and no way of tracking them. If I go in now, I'll know what's doing it, might be able prevent further events."

Ishikawa tried to clear her head, nodding gravely.

He turned to look at Eiko625, Ishikawa following his gaze.

I SEE YOU

S aito harboured mixed feelings about the tampering to the recordings. On the one hand, it was evident that whoever had done the
deed was, in fact, playing with him.

It would have been much easier to erase any kind of underhanded
operation instead of announcing to the world: "I was here. What're
you going to do about it?" It was the kind of taunt which told him that
whoever was responsible might *want* to be caught. Or that they were
so cocky that they might get careless. This would be an encouraging
slip-up on their part. It was, of course, still left to be proven.

As well, it greatly reduced the timeline in which the Nexus as a
whole had been borne out of the Needle, even though there was nothing to physically see. It was a start.

They knew, after carefully reviewing the rest of the footage, that this
was in fact the time period the Nexus had been taken. There were no
two ways about it. No pixels were out of place for the remainder of the
year's recordings.

What if this whole production had been created as a decoy, though?

As frustrating as the lack of physical evidence was, Saito felt something akin to joy at the prospect of finding a crumb of a lead, anything,
which might point him in the right direction, even though that tidbit
had not yet manifested itself.

He looked up at the clock and noticed that the lights had been
dimmed for the evening. In his concentration, he'd failed to notice
that everyone had gone to bed. It was one of the things about working
within a sunless, windowless place that caught him by surprise every

time.

He sighed, stretched out in his chair, cracked the kinks out of his neck and turned off his computer. He sent a mind-message to one of his helpers and got out of his seat. An empty lobby greeted him, apart from the dutiful guards which patrolled or sat behind the front desk. His footsteps resounded in the hollow shell of the Needle.

He exited the building from the 250th level, pushing the revolving doors with nonchalance. Saito felt the day in his marrow. He wondered if it would always be as exciting as today and if so, could he perhaps take a weekend off to recuperate.

The still evening air carried the far-off odour of cooking gyoza wafting to his nostrils. The sweet smell of ponzu followed closely behind. He crossed the bridge that connected the DaiSin Building to the platform. A kind of drawbridge which had never been retracted, save once, he'd heard, during a period of unrest.

He wondered what it took to keep a city like this one under control. What it took to point the wills of hundreds of millions of people in the right direction. What sparked the powder keg of rebellion, and if it was always close to eruption?

He'd read up about the history of the city. Its partitioning, and the reasons for it, and even deeper still, the underlying issues which had never been addressed. Those had been buried in the deepest, darkest recesses.

Festering.

He knew whose will he obeyed. That of the company he worked for. What about the others who made up the population of this giant, tiered, tin can of a city? Were they getting what they wanted, or even needed?

He walked through the high towers of the remainder of Shinjuku, separate from the company which owned it. Like an invisible hand that moved its pieces across the board, DaiSin was everywhere in "Sinjuku," even though its people might only be aware of the fact on a subconscious level.

The stark, naked technological beauty of the Needle was contrasted by the bustle of people on old bicycles delivering food, hawkers selling taped-up VR sets, and food stalls in front of fashion stores with visually impossible clothing in the windows.

The moat separating the rest of the city from the Needle was like a waterless river, a canal one could walk along and look down into to spy the lower levels on a good day. Walk along, yes, but never navigate.

Saito sauntered without aim along the side streets of the cold city, aware of his surroundings at all times. No mistaking him for anything else than a DaiSin employee, and the city's denizens gave him a glance before going back to their business, their sales monologues uninterrupted.

Overhead, wires criss-crossed the streets, connected to burnished-orange LEDs, lighting up faux-cobblestone streets. The occasional cry of "Irrashaimase!" resounded as a customer slid the door open to a ramen restaurant. The smells mixed and mingled in the air, making Saito inhale deeply.

This is real life, Saito thought, as a man who might have left a strange simulation might opine.

He turned at an intersection, following a soft decline. Twenty or so other people waited at an elevator, going down toward the 230th, but when he arrived he got off alone and headed to the edge of the plateau looming above him, where apartment blocks clung like tubed calthemite.

The idea of buildings hanging from underneath Shinjuku's platform had always both excited and given him bouts of anxiety. What if, during an earthquake, the building fell? Would he be sitting in his living room, watching the holo, when all of a sudden, the wobble of some impending doom might begin, sending him running for the door? Might the entire construction unlatch from its moorings as he tried to leave, and he find himself thrown to the ceiling as twenty stories of high-rise was sent straight down, meteor-style to compact like an accordion onto the plateau beneath?

He had to remind himself that the entire city was built in a rather precarious manner, and that if the 'Hanging Gardens of Shinjuku' as they were called were to fall, it was because the entire city was collapsing. He might as well stop worrying about it. He had, after all, decided to live here.

Ten floors above, the massive underside of Shinjuku 250 folded like rugose, cybernetic elephant skin. Square-ish and mottled, it constantly healed itself with the help of self-fixing concrete. In case of major tears, scarab-type companions would crawl over its surface, filling cracks with nano-putties. This explained the lack of smoothness to the surface. Saito still thought it looked just perfect the way it was, stretch marks and all.

The greyish suspended walkway's thick metal coils stretched to the surrounding apartment blocks, lined with the classic potted bio-luminescent trees the city was famous for. The smog they fed on produced an iridescent pinkish colour in the leaves, which lit up the more affluent suburban areas. They reminded him of apple trees in bloom, sans flowers.

Saito thought with a smile that whoever had "invented" the trees had meant well, but without changing the underlying causes of the intense pollution within the city, they were a lost cause. There would never be enough of them to clean the air. Besides, the rebreather business was a major one in the city, and they'd have a field day if anyone tried to get rid of pollution at the source. Half-measures and stop-gap experiments it would be, then.

Below, the bright lights of Shinjuku 150 twinkled, a mix of Chinese, Japanese, and Cyrilic language holos dancing along the pillar.

INCOMING MESSAGE, his screen lit up at the corner of his vision.

"Go ahead," he said, as he climbed the steps of the second building on the right. The apartment block went up ten floors, then down ten, like cylindrical stalagtites.

He went down two floors and entered his small apartment near the elevator.

The advantage of these particular blocks was that they possessed physical windows, and the view, while a bit frightening from this height and the fact the cut-off of the building could be seen, made it much more enjoyable than many other places in Vertical Tokyo. There were advantages to working for DaiSin, and Saito appreciated the string-pulling that had gone into securing this piece of real-estate for him.

Breathtaking.

Like seeing the forest for the trees, he could disconnect from his usual hyper-concentration to take in a global perception.

ANALYSIS OF ARCHIBALD SUZUKI ACTIVITIES CONCLUDED. FROM RESEARCH, MR. SUZUKI SPIES ON ALIYU, EKEMMA AND GODA, UMI.

"What do you mean by 'spies'?" Saito said, lifting an eyebrow.

HIDDEN CAMERAS AT THE RESIDENCE OF MRS. ALIYU AND GODA, SPECIFICALLY IN THE BEDROOM AREA, HAVE SHOWN—

"No need to go on. I get the picture," Saito said, rolling his eyes.

HIGH PROBABILITY THAT DATA COULD BE USED AGAINST MR. SUZUKI FOR BLACKMAIL PURPOSES.

"How high?"

50%.

"That's more than incidental. Golem, I'm getting disappointed in your results. Find me something tangible, please. Anything below an 80% correlation rate is negligible," Saito said, as the copper cube rotated slowly on one of its axes in the corner of his field of vision.

YES, SIR.

The Golem stayed static for a moment as Saito looked outside his window. The timer for his coffee beeped and he went to the kitchen to take the cup from beneath the machine.

"Go now," he said, returning to the window. The small cube blinked out of existence and Saito was once again alone.

"Computer," he said.

"Saito San," came the male voice from a hidden speaker in one of the wall's recesses.

"Ambient noise, twenty percent," he said.

"Type?"

"City streets, Shibuya. Rainy day," Saito said.

"Confirmed," the voice said.

A low sound of traffic and the hustle and bustle of Shibuya began to whisper its way out of the walls. Not loud enough that he felt there, but as if it slipped into the building from the outside. The steady drizzle of rain calmed his nerves.

He sipped his coffee in tiny increments. Caffeine had no effect on him, and so he enjoyed it for the taste. Black, thick, synthetic. He'd lately developed a liking for the artificial kind—the cheaper, the better. It had a first rush of bitter playing on his tongue, followed by a sweet aftertaste which he found pleasant.

It was all manufactured and tailored for oral stimulation, of course, but he was no purist, and found no reason to discount something's taste simply because it had come from a microvat in Chiba instead of one of the bio-farms on the mainland.

He smiled at the bird's eye view of Shinjuku 150. It was a cacophony of shape and light, holographic projections rotating above high-rises and along the structural pillars which made up the city. All within an enveloping, eternal night, like a gift-wrapped box full of strange treasures.

The drumming sound of rain on rooftops gave him a shiver, as if the temperature had dropped in his conapt.

The constant bustle of the lower Shinjuku reminded him of mammoth circuit boards, the flow of vehicles the impulse of electricity.

His doorbell rang, and he went to the front door, putting down his cup on a low coffee table in front of the window. The screen on the door showed a hooded man.

"Yes?" he said, walking over to the kitchen.

"Delivery for Mr. Hideki Saito. Church business," the man said.

"You can leave it by the door, thank you," Saito said. The man looked left and right, then, bent down to place a small package by the door. He stood up and nodded, then walked in the direction of the elevator.

Saito waited a few minutes, leaving the screen on, the fish-eye view showing him an empty corridor.

He went to the door and picked up the package. It was a small plastic box with bevelled edges and a black square on its top. Saito placed his thumb on it, and the box chirped, some unseen internal mechanism clicking open.

Inside was a memory chip the size of a thumbnail, forest green, with the manufacturer's stamp on one side and picket-fence golden connectors at the bottom.

He returned to the window, sat on a dark leather recliner and inserted the tiny chip into his blue portable on the coffee table. He'd disconnected it first from the net and was running a sandbox program in case everything was not as it seemed.

The first at the top of the list of files was a video, which he clicked.

A white, bearded man in his mid-fifties or early sixties, seated at a workbench in front of a bank of servers began to speak with a mild Russian accent.

"As per your request, video footage has been reviewed in the general vicinity of the DaiSin Building during the timeline you sent us. You were correct in assuming that only the internal video had been doctored. The exterior video, although controlled by DaiSin, appears to have been omitted. What we have found is almost guaranteed to be what you were looking for. Good luck in your research." With that, the man gave a small, sympathetic smile and logged off.

Thanks Andrei, thought Saito, and clicked on the next video file.

There was a buzz at the door, and Saito stiffened. He activated the screen, which showed him a man in a long grey trench coat on the stoop of his apartment block. Scott Till, an Administration spook.

144

GREEN MATRIX

"Can I help you, Mr. Till?" Saito called out to the door in amusement.

"A word with you, Saito San?" the man said, after recovering from mild shock, his hands in his pockets. Saito sighed and closed his computer screen, calling for the door to open.

"Computer, switch to 'Danse Macabre' will you?" he said.

"Affirmative," the hidden voice said, the street sounds transitioning to the beginning of a classical song. The plucking of cellos gave way to a wild violin's seizures, then a host of stringed instruments commenced a waltz to a possessed cadence. Saito smiled.

A few minutes later, a blond man entered his apartment, apologizing for the late intrusion. Average height and build, Saito thought him unremarkable, but then again, Administration probably looked for those traits in its spies.

He took the man's coat and hung it up on a hook, and invited him into his home. Till looked around, mildly impressed.

"Nice place," he said, with an Australian accent.

"Mr. Till, to what do I owe the honour?" Saito asked, picking up his cup and going to the kitchen once more.

"Please, call me Taz," he said, smiling. "How do you know who I am?"

"The man I work for has briefed me. Can I get you a coffee, Mr. Taz?" Saito said.

"Ah, yes. He's a wily one, that Harkwell. And yes, I could murder a cup," Taz said, his eyes going wide. As Saito worked the machine for his guest, the other man asked

"In your work for DaiSin, you wouldn't happen to have come across a man named Douglas Deguchi, would you?"

"Other than in the literature, you mean?" Saito said, handing Taz a steaming cup of coffee.

"Yeah. Since his break-out from prison, rumour has it he's hiding out at his old haunt. Do you have any sugar or cream?" Taz asked, looking into the abyss that was his black coffee.

"Imagine that. That would be highly illegal. If I were to be made aware of Mr. Deguchi's whereabouts within DaiSin, I would be forced to call the police. I couldn't bear the thought of being complicit in harbouring a fugitive. And no, I do not." Saito said, picking up his own new cup of coffee and taking a sip.

Taz' lip wrinkled as he took a chug of the black liquid, his reaction turning into one of strangulation. He began to cough, and Saito came over to pat him on the back. Taz got up, putting his hand on Saito's

145

shoulder.

In the background, the orchestra was whipping up to a frenzy, as if gale force winds were descending on the audience.

"I'm fine," he said, his fit of coughing abating. "What's in there, motor oil?"

Saito frowned.

"I'm sorry I can't help you Mr. Taz. Will there be anything else? I don't mean to be rude, but I've had a rather long day, and I still have a bit of work to do before I can finally relax. You know what it's like."

"As a matter of fact, there is," Taz said, putting his cup down on a ledge near a potted plant. "What is it that you do at DaiSin, Mr. Saito?"

"Analytics," he replied, shrugging.

"That's odd, you see, because ever since you showed up in Tokyo, there's been all sorts of funny business in the online traffic going in and out of that company you work for. Almost as if analytics wasn't your main area of expertise," Taz said, cocking his head.

"How's Wen?" he continued. Saito was beginning to be unnerved by the man's implications and rather uncanny ability to see through the plain façade he'd built up for himself. Then again, Scott Till was a great bluffer, and this might just be one of those instances where shots in the dark happened to find their marks.

The storm was now at its apogee, kettle drums bashing, the strings arpeggiating higher and louder, and one could have imagined a flight of witches riding through lightning flashes in roiling clouds.

"He's doing fine, Mr. Taz. You know, Mr. Harkwell hired me personally to help optimize things at DaiSin. It's what I do. Look at facts and figures and see how to improve things," he said.

"Is that right?" Taz said, putting on his most 'impressed' face.

"It is. Mr. Harkwell told me about you. How you two grew up together. The falling out. The betrayal…" Saito gave Taz a significant stare. It was Taz' turn to look inconvenienced.

"That was a long time ago. Anyhow, I should let you get back to work. Let me know if you hear anything about this Deguchi character, will you? Be a shame if he was found lurking in the attic, wouldn't it? In the meantime, here's my card." Taz said, handing Saito a metallic-looking oblong and going to the door. Saito opened it for him, and handed the man his trench coat before he could leave without it.

"What are you listening to?" Taz asked after crossing the threshold.

"Death and his violin," Saito said, smiling, and gently pushed the door closed.

Till would be trouble, he decided. Of course there was no way he would admit that Douglas Deguchi was a resident guest of the DaiSin Hotel Underground Facilities for Wayward Criminals, but if he decided to probe and pry, it would hamper his own investigations.

He returned to his computer and began to watch footage of the "lost" week, which had been taken from the other side of the street. As he understood it, these files had come from a different server than the main DaiSin ones, which might explain why they'd been overlooked. Whoever had done the scrubbing had not bothered to look for other sources and had therefore overlooked these.

He was glad for the fortuitous turn of events. Scott Till's visit had shaken him more than he cared to admit.

In all the videos, a camera was pointed to the front entrance of the 250th level entrance of the Needle—the same he'd exited a few hours previous. Four white utility trucks pulled up, four or five men getting out of each, all wearing dirty white coveralls and rebreather masks. They walked to the entrance, briefly spoke to security before entering the building with toolboxes in hand. Two hours later, they would leave again, same toolboxes in hand.

No need to wonder anymore how the Nexus had been smuggled out, he thought.

The manifest he looked up indicated that this was an "Arau Maintenance" job, which he discovered was the sub-contractor that had been hired while the DaiSin crew was unavailable.

He pulled up the employee records, only to find out that during that fateful week, all but two members of the DaiSin cleaning crew had been listed as sick.

This set off sirens in Saito's mind. Over twenty people coming down with some mysterious flu-like disease sounded more than a little suspicious. The whole situation had been orchestrated for this very purpose, evidently.

He looked up Arau Maintenance and found nothing. It had existed on paper for the duration of the operation and was now defunct. Another let-down. Saito couldn't help being impressed, even in his frustration, by the ingenuity of the system that had been used to pull everything off. It commanded grudging respect, at the very least.

With all their faces covered, there was no way he could identify them. Except—

Saito scrolled the video back with his finger to the place where all the men began to leave the trucks, then spread his fingers, enhancing to get a clearer image of the lead man.

As he came to the front desk. Yes, that was it.

The man plucked down his mask to identify himself to the security guard. Saito enhanced again, zooming in on the man's face.

He pulled up facial recognition software DaiSin had created, and ran the man's profile through it. If Administration knew DaiSin had access to their files, they'd have a fit. Then again, if their employees were better paid, their databases might not leak like sieves.

It began to cycle through a slew of different, yet similar faces, pausing for milliseconds before dumping the approximations. A minute or so later, a ninety-five percent match appeared, the enhanced video image side-by-side with the man's civil records profile picture.

The name read: Petrov, Dragomir. Bulgarian. Permanent Resident, living in Ebisu, as of two years ago. Saito did a search on the local jobs nets and found the man's latest address.

It looked as if he would have to take a little trip to the "foreigner's quarters."

NEW HOME

It took little time for Datu to become acclimated to the new work. After all, he'd been a recycler for a long time, and although it wasn't exactly the same, he already had his Heap legs to help him navigate the trash piles.

It consisted of driving construction elements to the underground factory, and letting Companions take over from there. As Arun had explained, the process was quite automated: people were there to supervise.

What had taken much longer was getting over the traumatic attack on the sentry bot he'd witnessed only an hour or so before. He'd never imagined there were robots that monstrously huge, or that he'd get to see one "devour" an Administration sentry one day.

Arun had offhandedly dismissed his questions about the event, saying there were 'rogue elements' they had to defend themselves from, and he'd remained confused as to the status of the people working this sector. He knew for a fact that there was no such thing as a 'rogue' sentry bot. If anything, they were all a bit too overzealous in their jobs, to the point where some recyclers had come close to being disintegrated for not having had the most up-to-date clearance.

That was a sign of over-programming, not rebellion against their own masters. To a degree, it made him happy the thing had been taken out, but on the other hand, where did that leave him and all the others on the Heap floor, digging up the Administration's back yard?

Should he expect to have to hide from such attacks on a regular basis? Did Administration notice when their sentries went dead in this sector? When they did, what sort of hell would they rain down on the lot of them? These and other questions tormented Datu for the rest of the day.

Arun had left him in Reza's hands, who'd shown him the factory interior, up to the central core, which was marked as dangerous to human life. Blast doors kept proprietary Midori Mamoru tech sealed in a vacuum.

"Nobody gets to see the matrix," she'd told him, before shuffling him off to another section.

She introduced Datu to most of the other human workers, some of which he had passing knowledge of from his time at Peoplift. The majority came from Sector 14, visibly, but others were European in origin. Datu wasn't familiar with Slavic languages, but he would have guessed Ukrainian. Unlike the East-Asians, they walked unsteadily on the shifting trash, making Datu wonder just what they were doing there.

Datu was put on offloading duty. He rode the crane at the back of the flat-bed trucks and handed off long metal beams to pairs of Companions which would carry them off into the bowels of the factory.

The digital clock inside his helmet indicated 18:00 hours, and the workers began to board the Grubs. Datu leaned back on his seat, watching the terrain slide by, many of the other workers bent forward from a day of hard work.

Mountains of garbage like desert dunes, moved at glacier pace, wrapping themselves around support pillars. Here and there he could see the blue finger of a methane fire lighting the darkness. It was odd to think of this place as a home, but it was so familiar, so comforting, that Datu could not help but do so. It's what he'd known for so long, and by all appearances, would continue to exist for the foreseeable future.

The Grubs parked in perfect order on the concrete receiving platform, disgorging their contingents of workers, who lined up to take the elevator back to the fiftieth.

Datu did not see a single Companion among the workers, and wondered if they were all housed within the factory for the night. This bothered him little, since Peoplift had had no Companions at all. The sight of them coming back with the employees might have been more disturbing than not.

Even though he hadn't worked a full day's shift, he could feel the raw muscles underneath his suit, in the areas where his prosthetics met the meat of his bulk. He reached back to massage his shoulder as the elevator brought him and twenty or so other workers back to the fiftieth floor.

He still marvelled at the immaculate whiteness of their suits. The opto-camouflage lasting the time it was needed to stay safe from the sentry. That sort of camo pulled some high wattage, and would have turned off sooner than later from over-usage.

They walked into the armour room and undressed, all wearing the same beige padded suits underneath. Datu was surprised to see there were no women. The only one he'd seen so far was Reza, and she was nowhere to be found at the moment.

The first thing that he noticed after removing his helmet was the smell. He'd expected they would all go through a decontamination shower to remove excess odours, if not the usual caked filth which comprised the Heap, but had been gob-smacked by their heading straight to the locker room.

It smelled of polycarbon mesh and fresh monomers, the kind he associated with new electronics out of the sealed static wrapper. He'd had the honour once of being there when his cousin had received a brand-new holovid player. The smell had stayed imbibed in his brain since then.

Datu followed the thick crowd. Revolving doors led to a canteen where everyone lined up, tray at the ready. White-topped tables and chairs made up the bulk of the room, with a chrome-covered cafeteria-style counter on the far left.

Companions impassively placed hot soup and wrapped packets of crackers on orange trays like clockwork cuckoos. To him, the suits, the glum procession, everything lent a brand-new-prison atmosphere. Datu made sure to slide his tray to catch whatever was offered, receiving in return what looked like a blood-red tomato soup, a side of meatloaf, an apple juice and a square of chocolate cake.

He walked to the end of the row and picked up his cutlery, trying to find a spot somewhere at the four-seaters. Most people knew each other, making space limited.

He must have looked lost, because a small Asian man waved him over and offered him a seat in front of him. There was one other already seated. Datu guessed he might be Thai.

"You're new, aren't you," the diminutive man said. This was not a question.

"Yes. Name's Datu," he said.

"Phong," he said. "What do you think so far?" The other ate, but Datu got the distinct impression his ears had grown larger.

"It's okay, I guess. Better than what I did before. I'm worried about that episode today with the sentry. Like that's going to be trouble,"

Datu said.

"Might be. Hasn't so far," the other man on his left said.

Just then, another, stockier man put down his tray and sat with an audible sigh. He introduced himself as Vasyklo. He'd just finished his shift on the upper levels.

"What you want to be careful about is Reza and Yui," the Thai-looking man added. "Forget the sentries. The sentries go up like Roman candles down there."

"I've met Reza, but who's Yui?" Datu said.

"Arun's other enforcer. You'll rarely see her. She's the upper levels crew handler," Phong said.

"She's my boss," Vasyklo said, pointing the tines of his fork at his head.

"What do you mean?" Datu said, his eyebrows furrowing.

"I'm a collection agent working all of Chiba. She handles those—us. Just don't cross either of them. Arun's a nice... Arun *can* be a nice guy, but he has two pitbulls he'll sic on you if you ever cross him. That's Reza and Yui." Vasyklo said in a thick Slavic accent.

Phong introduced the other man as Boon-Me. He was Sector 14 born-and-raised, but Vasyklo had once upon a time been a Ukrainian sailor who'd decided to stay in Tokyo and overextended his furlough. Since then, he'd done odd jobs for the Bulgarian gangs and deals with the Russians. He'd somehow run into Arun and signed the same contract they all had.

Reza walked among them, and even though the conversations in the room were amicable, the volume dipped when the woman went by.

Vasyklo mentioned the fact that he'd lost his work partner that evening, but sealed up like a blast door when Datu asked for details.

After having put away their trays, they all returned to the second floor and headed into their respective rooms. Once again, Datu looked a bit confused, and the men he'd spoken to in the dining hall invited him to share their room. One of them was in the infirmary for minor injuries, they said, and there was a spare bed.

It was only eight o'clock and Datu was sore, but not tired. The others took out a deck of Mahjong tiles and began to play, inviting him to join in.

At 20:01, they heard a click at the door, the deadbolts closing from the outside, a red diode by the handle indicating its status.

Only Datu minded that they'd been locked in.

"How long have you been here?" he asked.

"Little over six months," Phong said.

"Three and a half weeks," Vasyklo replied.

"Two months," Boon-Me said.

"Does anyone know how long this operation has been here?" Datu asked.

"Construction was ending when I got here," Phong said.

"Have any of you seen your families since then?" Datu asked, thinking about Tala and the kids.

"Don't have one," Vasyklo said.

"No," Boon-Me answered almost at the same time as Phong did. The both harboured the air of men resigned to their fates. Worried, but helpless.

"Don't expect I'll see them again," Boon-Me said, putting down one of his tiles.

"Right. The contract." Datu said.

"They said they'd take care of us and our families, though, and so far, we're taken care of. I mean, it's like being in the military, but we're not starving or anything. I expect they're holding up their end of the bargain," Phong said.

"But *why* can't we see them?" Boon-Me asked.

"We don't exist, remember?" Datu said, laying down a trio of tiles.

He then found out that Boon-Me had been "killed" in an industrial accident on the docks. That Phong had been miraculously rescued from the Heap after a sentry raid, and that Vasyklo had "died" of a neurostim overdose on the streets of Chiba. Something he said had been 'helped along' by the Bulgarian mob.

Datu was certain that if he asked every single man in every single room of this warehouse, he would get a similar answer. They were all expendable, because they were no longer counted among the living. It mattered little to him now that he was getting a better deal than the one he'd had with Peoplift. What he truly wanted was to hold his wife and children again, even Gabriel.

He promised himself that contract or no, he would find a way to return to them. He was starting to feel the weight of the day on his mind, however, and decided to lie down for the night. The other men had shown him that it was possible to "plug in", which made for better dreams.

Datu was reticent at first. Being troded was not something he'd ever wanted in his life, but now that the decision had been made for him, he thought he might as well take advantage of it. He took the wires which hung from a locator box above his pillow and pulled them out sufficiently so that he could plug them in and turn on his side.

He closed his eyes, and the inside world inverted without moving. He opened them again, finding himself on the beach where he'd first met the Ayo.

A carpet of stars illuminated the skies. Over the calm ocean, a soft breeze blew through the palm fronds at either end of the strip of sandy heaven. Datu felt a heavy heart, though. This place reminded him of his loved ones more than ever. He turned to go up the cottage stairs, knocked on the door.

When no one came, he opened it and slipped inside. It felt like a recurring dream, one that he could recall in the morning. In fact, he wasn't sure if he was dreaming now, or if it truly was the construct.

This feeling was entirely new to him. The connection inside his mind to outside sources made him wonder which part was himself and which wasn't.

There was also the nagging question of whether everyone else was connected to this Ayo, as well? If not, why was he alone? Were the constructs tailor-made to the individual? Would someone who was not a follower of Ayo see the same thing, or would they be inside a culturally different construct?

He went to the cupboard, where he remembered the woman named Aimee had taken the bottle of Lambanog. He shuffled back outside and sat on the steps, looking out on the horizon, Twinkling on darkness where the sky touched the deep waters. He uncorked the bottle, taking a long swig.

"Hey," he heard from beside him, and almost toppled over into the sand as Aimee Flores sat beside him on the sandy steps of the small cottage.

"Please, please, please stop doing that!" he said to her, his hand on his heart.

"I'm sorry. This is my home after all," she said wryly, taking the bottle from his hand and having a gulp.

"Point taken," he replied. She sat with him, staring out into the void as a friend would.

"What's it like?" he asked, finally.

"What's that?"

All he could do was wave his hands around.

"It's paradise," she said.

Datu frowned. She put her arm around his shoulder.

"I don't know what you want to hear," she said, whispering in his ear.

Datu's heart began to warm. He slipped her arm off his shoulder gently, and looked her in the eyes.

"You're an illusion," he said.

"Not the nicest thing I've ever been told, but okay," she said, smiling.

"I want to get out," he said, standing up.

"Why? Don't you like it here?"

Datu got up, paced a short ways and looked up at the perfect night sky. A ball of something hard and painful rose in his throat, threatening to spill out of his eyes.

"I want to get out!" he yelled at the ocean, which studiously ignored his pleas.

"What's wrong?" Aimee said, appearing before him, concern in her eyes.

"All of it. It's all wrong!" he said, and turned away from her. But she was already on the other side, standing with her hands by her hips. Datu pushed her and ran back toward the ocean, running down the short pier, past the tiny boat and the hanging fish nets, then plunged from the end into the cold ocean waters.

The water chilled him to the marrow. He swam long and hard, even though he'd never done so in his life. Muscles stiffened and gave up on him. He stopped once to spy the tiny figure of the woman standing on the beach, looking back at him. He kept swimming, his lungs like fire. His head slipped underneath the dark waters, and the ocean would briefly fill him before he bobbed back to the surface.

Then, his muscles no longer answered when he called to them, and he glided into the darkness a final time, the waters all-encompassing. For a brief moment, he felt as if he were dying again.

Again?

He woke, and the short, sharp memory of his death fizzled, vanishing.

A DEAFENING ROAR

It had been simple enough to connect the Rikona up to Eiko625. Permissions granted almost instantaneously when an Alicore rep had come to assess the situation on their doorstep. Requests had gone up the ladder like a whirlwind and returned as authorizations with the same oiled efficiency.

Alicore had been in the loop about the Companion malfunctions. It was in its best interest to be. Most of its workforce was comprised of Eiko models. These were larger than the Rikona, and the potential damage they might inflict to an unsuspecting city would be phenomenal. It was in their best interest to allow and encourage the investigation to proceed, not only to stay in Administration's good graces, but out of self-preservation.

A red non-conductive blanket had been placed under the shot Rikona, still now that its servo fluids had drained. A pool of brown, slick liquid covered a part of the blanket.

Its eyes, however, still followed the closest humans wherever they went.

A cushion had been found for Keiji, who'd placed it before the Rikona's head. He'd seated himself in the lotus position, as if he were about to engage in transcendental meditation in front of the Companion, whose power levels kept dipping.

Eiko625 sat next to the Rikona, its legs crossed, its hand out underneath the other Companion's head, Eiko's trodes extending out of its hand and into the Rikona's inputs behind its head.

Ishikawa paced a few steps away. All but two officers had left to search for the drivers, as well as a maintenance crew which had already cleaned up most of the mess. The only evidence of the attack was a few broken bits of plastic and several suspicious oil patches.

Keiji took a deep breath and removed his trode cords from the base of his skull with a whir, plugging them into the back of Eiko625's head.

He closed his eyes and was hit by a brick wall. Physically, his body was still and relaxed. Inside, he was being assaulted on all fronts. Like a megaton slab of concrete crushing him as soon as he'd entered Eiko625's cyberbrain.

He was on some alien planet, trying to breathe through lungs which failed him. An inhospitable atmosphere crushed him under an unbearable weight, and he was helpless to prevent it.

He concentrated, and pushed the feeling of dying aside. When he opened his eyes, the intense heat of the desert ran up his legs, belly and torso, to finally rush to his face and hair.

A red sky mirrored the colour of the sand.

"This Companion has infiltrated me," Eiko625 said, his voice coming from no place. "I cannot stop it. I am sorry," it said, a note of sadness in its voice.

It wasn't the red of sunsets. It was like blood, thick and dripping.

"What am I seeing?" Keiji said, covering his eyes and mouth against the heat that threatened to infiltrate his body.

"Visual manifestion of the virus infecting this Companion, sir," the enormous voice in the sky said.

Keiji could feel his feet sinking into the sand, and started to walk.

He'd expected the loading room for the Eiko625s operating system, not some hellish nightmarescape. This put more than a damper on his snooping exercise.

Grit swirled in the air, tiny silica particles slicing his digital flesh like razors as he slogged forward. The burning winds buffeted him, making progress difficult. No matter what, he had to find the entrance to the Rikona's system to assess what had happened to it.

He pressed his neck, and an envelope of bluish energy spread from that point, to cover him from head to toe, an inch away from his virtual body. His personal antivirus software had seen a lot of malware in the past, but this had to be the most all-encompassing form he'd encountered.

This place was like a Martian sirocco, the light diffuse and vague. Keiji followed his inner compass to find the exit, but the construct's cardinal points kept changing. All he could do was continue walking so as not to sink into the "quicksand" which had been introduced into

Eiko625.

What had gone wrong? Ito San had done this a thousand times, and whatever he'd infiltrated had always been kept at bay using the interface.

It was as simple as connecting to the intermediary and then the—

Keiji swore. He'd connected the intermediary first, then himself, allowing the Rikona full access to Eiko625s systems before he could build a firewall around them. What an idiot. What a noob, he thought to himself.

He tried to push the boundaries of his antivirus, the arcing blue light surrounding him expanding slightly, but pressure kept being applied to it from whatever evil software had taken Eiko625, making it fizzle back to its original position.

"Eiko625," he called. "I need you to turn on your strongest anti-bodies to fight this thing."

I will try, sir, came the response within his mind. It was getting weaker, he thought. Keiji wondered how many systems were infected already.

A low rumble began to shake the dunes, and the wind shifted violently. The red sands shook, as if being put through a sifter. Once again, Keiji was being sucked down into the sand, faster than before.

As it reached his waist, he decided that it might not be worth the fight and tried to log out. His consciousness pulled backward for a brief moment, but was put up against the invisible wall he'd felt when he first arrived in the construct.

His heart began to beat faster.

"Eiko, I'm going to need you to do a manual disconnect from the Rikona. I can't pull out of the construct," Keiji yelled into the maelstrom. He tried to swim, the antivirus he wore keeping the damaging sand at bay. His sweating hands kept dripping up his elbows, and the sand rose above his waist.

Acknowledged, sir. Eiko625 has been physically disabled by a virus. Eiko625 will attempt internal disconnection of software ports, the Companion's voice said from within his mind.

Keiji had no idea what would happen if he was swallowed by the quicksand, but he imagined it would do him little good. The stuff he'd gotten in his face, hair, and all over his body stuck to him like magnets and refused to dislodge no matter how hard he slapped it away.

A moment later, he was pushed upward, the sand returning to ankle height. He began to walk again, but then bolts of orange lightning streaked across the red sky, and Keiji felt dread fill his soul.

Enormous tentacles, as large as Tokyo support pillars, swung lazily through the air, coming from some invisible place in the sky. As if some eldritch God had descended to Earth and was now searching with its appendages for beings to consume.

"Eiko, I've got a problem!" Keiji yelled as he ran.

Acknowledged, sir. The virus has taken over many of Eiko625s systems. It will be difficult to remove, sir, came the answer in his mind.

An enormous, tubular thing, the thickness of an ancient factory's chimney dragged across the dunes before Keiji, directly into his path. The sand clung to the tentacle as it raked across the crags and valleys, making it grow as it did. He changed direction and ran faster, barely missing being knocked over by the massive trunk.

It was burnt orange, as if the sand had congealed and taken shape, and was actively hunting Keiji.

Keiji thought of the sand which covered his body.

Inspect, he thought. The results began to compile, and he turned around in time to see the flailing tentacle come bearing down on him from behind. Whatever it was, it had a good idea of where to find him, and a mind to destroy him.

He ducked out of the way as the green bar rose on the edge of his vision, the composition of the sand beginning to process. The mammoth tubule was joined by another, and both began to sweep the area, picking up grit as they did, almost slamming into Keiji one more time as he ran and threw himself out of the way.

The analysis finally ended, and the message inside his vision told him that the sand was composed of the Eiko625's own operating system data which had been shredded and taken over by the virus, like human cells commandeered and redirected like zombies.

"Eiko625! Hard reset!" Keiji yelled into the deafening roar. If Keiji was right, the Companion would be able to get rid of the invader with a swift reboot of its system. If not... he decided not to think of the consequences in case he was wrong.

There was a bright flash, and the construct was no longer a forbidden, dead planet swirling with deadly sands. Keiji stood in an empty white room with immaculate floors, the walls adorned with horizontal magenta-coloured light streams, energy flowing freely through them.

The floor before him began to break apart, the bits turning a ruddy colour and swirling into the air.

"Eiko! Accept antivirus install protocols!"

"Granted," the voice above him stated. Keiji slammed his fist into the ground in front of the disintegrating floor, his fingers penetrating the floor. He tapped his neck again, and the antivirus which had protected him surged through his body and into the floor, slamming the flayed data bits back where they came from.

"Eiko625, disconnect from host," Keiji said.

"Cannot disconnect from host. Ports being blocked open."

"Son of a…can you deploy antibodies?"

"Antibodies already deployed. They are having minimal effect," Eiko625 said.

The surge Keiji injected into the floor began to reflux, and he was thrown against a far wall of the construct, wedging him into it as the floor began to splinter and crack again. It spun into bits of silica, turning into a whirlwind within the construct. Soon, all the walls began to disintegrate, becoming the same dead colour.

The data began to congeal once again, and the walls fell away, returning him to the crushing reality of the alien planet.

This time, the sand swirled like drills, attacking him with intense fury, knocking him back onto the desert floor. A dozen tentacles stopped, poised above him, then dove into him.

His mind broke in two, as the information overload penetrated his crystalline chip, his antivirus shield useless. He could feel the malware probing his mind, looking for weaknesses, like some slithering eel searching for prey inside his brain.

Keiji lay twitching as the tentacles writhed inside his chest and head, as if he'd lost complete control over his body. His heart beat faster than he'd ever felt before. His eyes rolled back, and he felt nothing but fear.

"System rebooting. Antivi… antiviral developed. System rebooting," he heard coming from around him as his grip on the construct slipped away.

Keiji opened his eyes to find Ishikawa next to him. He took a deep breath and wiped sweat away from his brow. The smell of burning plastic brought his attention to the blown-off head of the Rikona lying a few feet away from him.

"What a trip," he said, feigning a smile.

"I had to defibrillate you," Ishikawa said flatly, and he noticed a heart monitor on his naked chest, as well as paddles near him.

"What happened in there?" she asked.

"I was careless," he answered, wiping foam from his lips, then shaking his head. The Eiko625 was standing nearby, its expression neutral. It offered Keiji its hand, and he shrank back before taking it, the youth getting up with difficulty. Keiji put his hands on his back and winced.

"I never remembered it being so real," he muttered.

"What's the matter with these Companions? Did you find that out at least?" Ishikawa pressed.

"Virus," Keiji said, rubbing his eyes.

"And?"

"And nothing. I was busy trying not to die in there," Keiji said, anger in his voice. His head kept spinning, and if it hadn't been for the Eiko's support, he would have fallen flat on his face.

"You failed at that. You flat-lined for almost a minute," Ishikawa said. "When you started doing your little horizontal jig, I brought out the paddles."

"Thank you," Keiji said, looking at the street below his feet. "Wait a minute. How come the Eiko is fine? The virus had completely taken over its operating system."

Eiko625 looked over at him and shrugged.

"Eiko625 is within acceptable working parameters. Residual viral particles have been quarantined for analysis and antiviral creation. System is no longer infected," it said.

"When I saw things had taken a turn, I shot out the Rikona's cyberbrain," Ishikawa said.

Eiko625 raised its hand, and Keiji saw that it was missing its pinky and anular. Otherwise, the Companion was fine.

"Tokyo PD will pay for the damage. I couldn't afford to have another Companion on the loose. Now that we know it's an infection, I have to find out how it's transmitted before it gets worse," Ishikawa said.

"You'll want to hold onto this Companion, then," Keiji said, straightening up and letting go of the Eiko. "If it can synthesize an antivirus, we might be able to stop any other outbreak before it happens," Keiji said. He took a few steps, faltered, and Eiko625 grabbed him before he could topple to the ground.

"Listen kid, there is no 'we.' Get this in your head. You don't work for TPD, and I don't work for you. I'm taking you back to your rich-ass parents before you can cause any more damage to either my reputation or your own body. That's all. Do you compute?" Ishikawa demanded, pointing a finger to the youth's face.

"You, get him in the car," she said to the Eiko, who gently guided Keiji to the vehicle. Keiji held his forehead, his face a mask of pain, but Ishikawa was done playing around.

The Alicore rep had kept a safe distance away from police business, but was now inquiring about the Eiko model. Ishikawa explained to him that it would be required to stop a potential outbreak of violence.

After a rapid back-and-forth between the man and his superiors, he gave Ishikawa the go-ahead to take their property along, with the caveat that if things went well, Alicore could use the situation to present its involvement as having been crucial to the investigation.

Ishikawa was used to this kind of PR move, and agreed, palm-printing a required waiver after checking in with her own superiors. Both parties bowed, the transaction having taken less than two minutes.

When she returned to her car, Keiji lay on the back seat, looking ill. Having been lifeless for almost a minute, she understood. The Eiko stood by the door, and she invited him to come in. He'd already received the authorization from Alicore, and stepped into the passenger side of the vehicle. Ishikawa watched it dip as the Companion put her shocks to the test.

She wondered if the tires would blow, but knew that this car was up to spec and could carry at least two Companions this size without suffering too much internal damage.

"Reports coming in of multiple rampaging Companions across Chiba," the radio crackled.

Just perfect, Ishikawa thought.

THE DAISIN CONNECTION

Saito was apprehensive, as he paced the length of his conapt.

Ebisu was the wildest area of Tokyo. Like Shinjuku, it had a larger foreigner population. Unlike Shinjuku, the Russian mafia was in charge, on all levels.

It was one of those places that was tolerated because it brought a lot of things into the city that the Administration wouldn't touch. As in all economies, there was the legal and the black market. Ebisu was an overabundance of illegalities.

Chinese contraband trodes, Russian federation military crackers, hard-to-find European farming equipment since the embargo, and more than a few pleasures which would have landed you in prison for life if found on your person outside the special zone.

It was also home to some of the world's strongest, most secure data storage centers, read: untouchable havens. The kind of place even Administration grudgingly used to stash some of its most sensitive "issues."

It was temporary home to many of the visitors to the city, most from the European Continent, but there was an ever-growing presence in the African Quarter, as the influence of tech hotspots like Nairobi and Lagos began to make ripples across the world.

Saito found some clothes to blend in and changed. Going in as a "corporate stooge" would garner him the kind of attention he would rather avoid. He slipped on an older rain slicker, pulled on a cap, a counterfeit rebreather, and headed out.

He paused for a bit, looking over the railing at the bright lights of Shinjuku 150 below. Observing the city from his conapt window was impressive, but getting the whole, unadulterated view, sans triple pane of bullet-proof glass was entirely other. Here he could take in the sounds, the smells, and the overpowering awe that the sheer scale of the city commanded.

It made him feel small.

He was a grain of sand in an enormous machine, purpose-built for consumption and destruction. At the moment, he wielded extraordinary powers for such a tiny, insignificant piece within the beast.

Would anything change for the world? What would happen to him after all was said and done. Would he sink back into anonymity? Was any of it worth the effort?

Saito rested his arms on the ornate railing, staring off into the distance at the twinkling lights, his chin held high.

Would it always be about the fight? The fight to survive? The fight to win? The fight to be better than everyone around him? He'd one day heard the expression that survival was like swimming as hard as one could, just to stay in place.

He didn't think anyone moving about on the upper floors of the Needle were swimming. They had others to swim for them. Working hard to carry them on their backs. Was that the natural order, or just the one which had been invented to best use others' labour?

He knew he could tear it all down, potentially. But that would leave DaiSin exposed. Like slitting your own throat among a pack of wild dogs, just to let out the bad blood. Saito smirked. He hadn't downgraded himself this way just to plant dynamite in his company.

He truly wanted DaiSin to succeed, and for that it felt that amongst the Princes, he had to obey Macchiavelli's laws, if he wanted the corporation to survive.

If difference he did make, it would create ripples throughout, at least. No action happened in a vacuum. The smallest grain of sand could cause disruption, for good or ill in the largest of machines.

Saito took a deep breath and left his observation post.

He climbed aboard the elevator back to the 250th and made his way to the massive twenty-floor building which was the Shinjuku Train Station.

Lost amid the wash of humanity, he could not have felt more anonymous. He made his way past security and into the station's maw, which encompassed kilometres of corridors and walkways, stairs and elevators.

Along the way, he passed coffee shops and small restaurants of all kinds, serving anything from sushi to ramen on the Japanese scale and pizza to Korean BBQ when it came to imported offerings. Everything, of course, adapted to Japanese sensibilities and tastes.

There was a bento box department store below the platforms, and shoppers came in and out with their chosen meals.

Saito picked up one of his favourite coffees from a vending machine and bought his ticket.

The platform was full, and as soon as the metro arrived and disgorged its contingent of passengers, it filled up again, Saito jostled and pushed within like a pebble in a stream.

As the metro car left the station, Saito was able to glimpse the city between the heads of the other masked passengers. It dipped down from the 250th on a soft incline, heading South, first through Shibuya, then to Ebisu.

The Foreigner's Quarter was supposed to be part and parcel of Shibuya, but somehow had cut itself off from the main plateau. Over time, a separate pillar had been built, as if it had been born of asexual reproduction, splitting itself off from its inceptor.

Saito smiled inwardly as he stepped off the metro onto the platform, one of the only passengers to do so. He activated a frequency scrambler to confuse any micro-drones in the area. The gnat-sized spying devices got into any and every crevice, reporting back to who-knew-who, and Saito simply didn't need the headache.

He headed to the outskirts of the platform on foot, the periphery being only a fifteen minute walk away. The company was less jovial and carefree than on the metro ride in. Faces were mostly grim, white, and Slavic. A few men of the Royal South African Navy chatted up painted ladies outside the Hell's Belles Night Club. Sparklingly clean uniforms on high cheek-boned, tall black men, their resounding laughter lighting up the night. He walked by, the address he'd been given situated down claustrophobic alleys nearby.

This area was pedestrian-only, or scooter if desperate. There was barely enough room to walk two people side-by-side, the walls of opposite buildings squeezing in at odd angles, as if the plateau shrank over time, like a sponge running out of water.

The quiet was unnerving. Saito only encountered three humanoids on his walk. None of them looked at him directly, and two were on VR sims, meaning they were unaware of his presence in the first place.

Apartments in this quarter were one-room affairs in ten-story white-tiled blocks. They'd been designed as temporary lodgings for sailors and single men working manual labour. Short sticks hung with laundry taped to the railing jutted out in front of the building, and no elevator to bring him to the sixth floor.

A dog barked, and he walked up the fire-escape. Curious bystanders spied from the end of the alley, but Saito pretended not to notice.

He tried to look inside the one window that gave on the outside of the apartment, but its heavy drapes made it impossible.

Turning the handle to the beige aluminum door yielded similar results. He glanced around, and when satisfied there was no one to see him, he pressed a "cracker" over the lock mechanism, waiting for it to cycle to the right combination.

A tone sounded, and the door clicked open. He was assaulted by an incredible stench. Saito put his hand over his mouth and nose, trying to cover his rebreather. The smell of whatever had died within stung his eyes as well, and he wished he'd brought protection for that, too.

Since he wanted to avoid being seen, he stepped inside the room, closing the door behind him. He pressed the light switch, but apparently the bill hadn't been paid in some time, because the circuit stubbornly remained off.

He pulled out his cracker from his pocket again, pressed firmly on its top, and a soft glow began emanating from it. Saito slipped his gloves back on, the idea of touching anything in this place making him nauseous.

The room was a mess. Vending machine takeout boxes with half-eaten food inside them were strewn on the floor, covered in green mold. An army of cockroaches trying desperately to avoid being lit up by Saito's spotlight scurried into every dark crevice they could find, but would return as soon as darkness did as well.

On Saito's right was a small kitchen, with a refrigerator big enough for a few bottles of water, or in this case, beer, as he saw after pulling it open with a pen. None of the food, however, explained the terrible smell.

He shone the light around, dust-motes dancing for him as the illumination took them in. In the far left corner, a big black stain covered the wall and floor. Saito realized what it was as soon as he saw the flies rise up in a cloud.

This could very well be the remains of Dragomir Petrov, the man he'd come looking for. It seemed apparent that whoever had hired him wanted no trace evidence, and had treated Mr. Petrov accordingly. Whoever had dispatched him had little qualms in letting the man rot in his own apartment, it seemed. It was a bold move, considering that even the tiniest speck of evidence could be traced in an instant. That is, if Administration felt the compuction.

Saito began to rummage in the garbage can, yet found nothing but used nicotine cartridges. He was no longer certain he'd find anything of value in the apartment. The murderers had probably taken all evidence with them. Still, there was no harm in looking.

He moved the fold-out bed-couch, finding a few more cartridges, beer cans and advertisement acetates for local entertainment venues.

Who did you work for, Petrov? he thought. He shone his lamp toward the counter, lifting the toaster to find crumbs. Above the cupboards was a thick layer of dust, and Saito slapped his hands together to rid himself of it.

He noticed a sliver of clear plastic from underneath the fridge, and he moved it, finding a sheet of readout underneath. A hole in the floor, the size of a kitchen sink, held a few loose clear acetates, manila envelopes and a uniform.

One of the letters was from the supposed "cleaning company" he'd worked for. He held up the light to read it. This one had a physical address, but it had turned out a false positive while he'd investigated it. It was a record of employment and payments made, though, and that was useful. He finally had tangible proof of human workers doing business with Arau Maintenance, and it was a start. Saito went through the thin stack and noticed that the man had only worked for the company for a little over six months.

The coveralls were clean, and neatly folded. He opened the collar and found it to have been made by the Hataraku Clothing Co., a name he'd never heard of.

He took the acetates with the man's personal info on them and left the conapt, happy to be out of the stench as he closed the door behind him. He once again took deep inhales of Ebisu's rotten air, but this time the rebreather he wore did a marvellous job of separating oxygen from contaminant molecules. There was a distinct difference between the smell of stale eggs and that of months-old rotting corpses.

He thought of calling the cops, but that would have alerted their presence to his, and he wanted to avoid notice for as long as possible. There was always the possibility that his enemies had their ears to official channels to be able to find Saito (and get rid of him at some opportune time), and doing so while he was in Tokyo's hot zone would have been much too convenient, so why give them the luxury?

He headed back to Ebisu's main station, taking meandering alleyways all the way to the main thoroughfare, where Hell's Belles sex workers were changing the guard, so to speak.

He went to a public terminal and looked up the Hataraku Clothing Company. It turned out to be a defunct factory in Shibuya 150, the next plateau over from where he was. *What about going home and calling it a night?* he thought, but if anyone realized he'd gone to visit the very dead Mr. Petrov, they might destroy whatever evidence might be found in the old fashion district. Better to do it now than to miss the opportunity.

From Ebisu 150, he took a straight trip to Shibuya 150. This time around, the metro was half as crowded, and he was able to watch his progress through the dirty windows, the floating holograms shifting in colours and shapes as they intersected with his line-of-sight.

The Shibuya Fashion District stores had escaped to higher levels decades ago, but had left those long lonely streets lined with empty ones, most of them shuttered and graffitied.

The original draw had been the interesting idea that clothes could both be made and sold within one building. Quite a few High Fashion brands had built storefronts directly connected to their factories. Some even had apartments on the upper floors for their workers, and an array of restaurants and cafeterias open to the public to entice the shopper to come try their wares.

This had been in partial response to rising production costs on the mainland and the heating up of political tensions. With most countries around the world having grown wise to the way clothing companies used lax manufacturing laws to pay their employees peanuts, said countries had unionized. This, of course, had forced companies to do a lot of soul-searching. The answer had been to move production into retail's back-store, eliminating shipping fees, simultaneously giving the finger to the rebels.

This had fallen apart after the partition, and The Heights had stopped coming to Shibuya. Factories had shifted to the lower levels, where the air was thin and rent was cheap, and stores had migrated to where the money played and taken up new homes in The Heights. The marriage had ended with a whole level of abandoned hybrid store/factories as their unwanted children.

The result was entire city blocks where stores either sat empty or had become squats. A few had been repurposed as second-hand clothing markets, where the denizens of Shibuya could, ironically, find affordable clothes made in the factory levels of the 100.

Saito marvelled at the difference between his view of Shinjuku 150 and that of Shibuya. This place looked like a dead zone, where trash was never picked up, and no live neons to speak of. Quite a few of the flickering street lamps stood as testaments to the city's refusal to rejuvenate its moribund quarters, or to even acknowledge the problem.

The people he crossed wore clothing more shabby than his own, and he ducked his head to try to pass unnoticed. Once, he thought he recognized a man he'd seen while he was in Ebisu, but decided he was letting his paranoia get the better of him. As soon as he turned around, the man had been gone.

The emptiness pressed on his heart as he walked down the double-wide avenues of Tomigaya Dori. It was like a cancer eating at the heart of Tokyo. One which was studiously ignored, as if averting one's eyes made it go away.

Even more curious since, above this level, Shibuya was thriving. Shibuya 250 and 350 were hotspots where stars in the limelight wanted to be seen. It was edgy, but not in the free-for-all sense of Shinjuku1. How odd, then, that Shibuya 150 was a dead zone. It was like lifting a healthy-looking plant to see that its roots had been eaten away.

He turned left at CouCou Furniture, its front door knocked down, and he could see in the dim interior a series of hanging Christmas lights and the outline of people seated at disparate tables and heteroclite chairs.

A few blocks away, where the darkness was beginning to press in on him, the address of the clothing company he'd copped from the tags turned out to be one of the outlet/apartment/factories which had made the district popular back in the day.

It was sealed behind two metre metal gates, but he found a spot where the chain that held the doors shut was loose enough that he could wiggle through. The broken tiling and gang graffiti in front of the six floor building told him that it hadn't been used for its intended purposes for longer than he'd been alive.

All the windows of the show-room portion had horizontal metal blinds drawn, as if the owners had thought that the downturn in the economy were a temporary thing. Saito saw no signs above the frontage but the holes where it might have hung before the hasty departure.

He tested the handles on the blinds, finding some give on the third one. It lifted high enough for him to pull himself in.

REPORTING...the word blinked in the corner of his vision, making him pause in surprise for a moment.

Go ahead, he thought.

SURVEILLANCE OF MR SANTIAGO LOPEZ REVEALS GAMBLING
DEBTS. FUNDS HAVE BEEN REDIRECTED FROM DAISIN TO
COVER OUTSTANDING PAYMENTS. HIGH PROBABILITY OF
INFLUENCE OVER MR LOPEZ. DEBTORS ARE YAKUZA.

How high? he thought, grunting as he pulled himself through the
space left by the open shutter.

76 PERCENT. THERE IS ALSO A FLUX OF CREDITS BETWEEN
HIMSELF AND MRS KOBAYASHI, NANAKO. PURPOSES UNKNOWN.

*Really? Why don't you investigate that further. I'm curious to know
what the money is for,* he thought, standing up and closing the metal
shutter.

YES SIR.

The Golem's presence receded. Saito was glad for the upgrade which
permitted mental communication with the Golems. The previous
incarnations were like dogs—they obeyed orders, but were unable to
verbalize their results. This made them a much better tool.

The interior reeked of the mildew stench of water damaged basement closet. Nowhere near as unpleasant as what he'd endured in
Petrov's apartment, but powerful nonetheless. He pulled out his cracker
again and turned on its light feature.

The floors had been linoleum checkerboard tiling at some point,
but the glue had given its notice, leaving the tiles to roam further and
further afield with every earthquake. Saito stepped carefully so as not to
slip and fall on the broken mess.

He entered a front room which was empty metal shelves and a
small counter. A naked male mannequin stood behind the space where
a cash register would have been. This was someone's idea of humour, no
doubt.

No sound save the occasional dripping of some ancient leaky pipe
came to his ears, and the brittle crackling of the tiles every time he
took a step. He flashed his light around, finding the door to the storage
room, where nothing was kept now but bad memories and dust, the
dirty scuffing of packing boxes long-gone, lining the walls at regular
intervals.

Further still, the door to a lobby, the entrance of which was on the
side of the building. Boarded up with splintered plywood, the interior

glass of the doors smashed in, leaving translucent teeth on the doorframes circumference.

To his left, a staircase went up to the upper floors, and a defunct elevator on its right-hand side. Its doors were open, and Saito peeked downward three floors, where a collection of red plastic chairs had been tossed in for reasons unknown.

At the end of the hallway, a set of sliding doors led into the factory, and Saito pushed it open with apprehension. Would he find any evidence linking this place to Arau Maintenance? Or was it simply another front, some ghost of physicality used purely as a representation of the real, devoid of meaning save for appearances sake?

He had not expected to see sewing machines, but there they were, at a line of workstations. The pale green industrial kind, bulky and smooth-edged, the needles still threaded and ready for work.

It was a wonder they hadn't been taken during the exodus, but then again, stranger things had been found in the past in these abandoned places. Sometimes the cost of transportation was more than the worth of the equipment, and the owner simply chose the cheaper option. Or the escape had been a catastrophic, last minute operation, and the idea of returning for the remnants of the belongings deemed unpalatable.

Saito did not notice the security camera higher up in the rafters, pointing down to the workspace.

Rolls of white denim cloth stood side-by-side in one corner, covered in sheer plastic, ready to be cut and sewn to spec.

On the opposite side of the room, near an open door, a few sealed packs of clothing lay in a heap, identical to the one he'd found in the murdered man's conapt, only varying in sizes.

He stepped into the office and looked inside the drawers, which contained paperclips and used styluses. On the desk sat a newer-looking computer, which he turned on.

The Arau Maintenance logo flashed briefly on the screen, and he was taken to a selection of files.

He chose the employee tab and clicked, but password protection came up. Saito smirked. He called up a Golem to assist him. It would be a cinch for them to unlock.

He waited. Nothing happened.

Another help request yielded nothing. Now Saito was getting nervous. He wasn't so far away from communications distance that his trodes should fail him. They were DaiSin next generation after all. Besides, he'd been in contact with a Golem not five minutes before.

His heart began to beat faster as he looked about the room, spying through the open office door to see if anyone were coming. Saito bit his lower lip and retraced his steps back from the menu he was in. He chose one called contacts, pushing his mouse too far to the left in his anxiety, dislodging a pencil case which had been perched on the edge of the old desk.

It fell to the floor with a metallic 'clank!' and he peered over to see it had fallen into a small aluminum dustbin. He reached in to pick it up and saw that it was full of melted plastic. He retrieved a sheaf of melded acetates and looked through them, seeing names he did not recognize, one over the other in list form.

One word which did stick out, however, was DaiSin, next to which were written the letters 'Sant', with whatever the end of the word was shrivelled by heat, like the rest of the acetates.

Santiago Lopez, he thought, grabbing the pile of melted plastic for further analysis. The computer had begun to cycle through some sort of program, however, and he saw the files erasing at incredible speeds.

He'd been discovered. Saito clung to the acetates and ran, through the factory floor, across the lobby, and into the showroom. He pushed the shutter up with all his might and slipped under the door, just in time to be on the receiving end of a swift kick to the jaw.

He fell over, clutching his face, and rough hands picked him up from behind. An incredible pain bolted through his body and his consciousness made a rapid departure.

THE LOVE HAD GONE

Datu got up at the sound of the door latch unlocking. He had the immediate reaction of putting up his hands in front of himself. The fear was instinctual, and yet, he knew it was unfounded.

They all left the dorm in silence, and he followed their lead. The dream was gone, but its impression pushed on his chest like sadness unfathomable. He followed the long line of men leaving their rooms to the end of the hall, where they took off their used clothes and dumped them in a row of hampers, then walked through a teal-tiled corridor, where a row of showers sprayed them as they walked.

A station squirted foaming soap on them, and two steps later, they were rinsed. Afterwards they received a dose of anti-lice powder to the head, and Datu rubbed the wet powder into his scalp as the others did, his eyes beginning to sting. All the while, they kept walking on rugged strips along the tiled corridor, turning corners. The next jet of hot water rinsed the de-licing agent out of his hair, and he made sure to protect his eyes to prevent being left with some of the particles lodged in them. He felt as if he were being led through a car wash.

The final few steps were a row of industrial-strength hot air dryers. He walked through, feeling the buffeting winds throw him this way and that until he left the corridor altogether.

Finally, they walked through a double row of open cubicles labelled with sizes, within which were stacked beige uniforms just like the ones they'd been wearing the day before.

Datu picked a set up in 'M', and continued on to the dressing room, where forty or so men were in various states of dressing. They then all walked out the far door and went to the cafeteria to pick up their breakfasts on the orange trays and seat themselves again as they had the night before.

"What do you think of the system?" Phong asked.

"Efficient. Like it was designed by Companions. Or for Companions," Datu said, taking a bite of his bacon-flavoured seaweed.

"Or both," Boon-Me joked.

"One thing's for sure," Vasyklo mumbled, "days go by and you lose track of time. Best start taking notes or you might end up forgetting how long you've been here." He took a hard bite out of his toast and looked at the others with a hard stare.

"When does the contract end?" Datu asked.

The others didn't answer, only looked at each other uncomfortably.

"So now I guess I need a new partner," Vasyklo said. "I'm going to have to go ask Reza if she can spare one of the crew down here. I can't do the job alone."

"What is it that you do?" Datu asked.

"Just drive around Chiba making pickups and drop-offs. Nothing complicated," Vasyklo said. Datu noticed that the other two were inspecting the bottom of their plates with utmost care.

"But dangerous," Datu surmised.

"Can be. Anyhow, I have to go talk to Reza. Can't leave without at least one more."

"How about you suggest me?" Datu said, as offhandedly as he could, before taking another bite of his rehydrated eggs.

"I could, I guess," Vasyklo said, before pushing back his chair with an audible screech and heading over to the woman, who glanced at Datu. He made as if to continue eating his meal at a methodical pace, making sure not to overtly glance in the direction of the conversation taking place between Reza and Vasyklo. He averted his gaze completely when he thought she might be looking over at him.

He almost expected her to refuse. Her harsh demeanour told him that she tolerated no fools, and at that moment, he felt quite foolish for having suggested it. He missed the rest of the conversation, as he made sure not to look up, and continued to chit-chat with the other men.

"Listen, Datu, I don't think you really—" Phong began, but was interrupted by Vasyklos' return.

"Alright, you're in," Vasyklo said. Datu hadn't realized that he'd been holding his breath, but it ran out of him in one long stream behind his hand. His heart lifted for a moment at the prospect of going back to the surface, at least for a little bit.

Even though he'd not been in the employ of Midori Mamoru for long, technically, being away from his family for more than even a day was taking a psychological toll he was only now beginning to understand.

"Cool," he said, in an even tone, nodding his head. His facial features might have been neutral at that point, but his guts were anything but. They felt as though they'd just uncoiled from a tight mess into something akin to relaxed.

When they finished eating, they all returned their trays to their proper spots. Phong turned to Datu and said,

"Good luck."

Datu wanted to ask him more, but Vasyklo was ahead, waiting for him, hands in his pockets. They and a handful of other people walked to a different locker room, where they were handed rebreathers and what looked to Datu like army gear. He slipped on the padded pants and vest, as well as the helmet he was handed, and wondered what he'd gotten himself into this time.

Outside, the fog had lifted. They walked toward the pillar, following the track-lighting along the gangway, and took the service elevator which looked brand new, but inset into one of the original shafts.

Datu watched the cords lengthen as they rose, the sheer drop below visible through the flooring mesh.

When they reached the 100th, the elevator jolted to a stop and the six got off. Datu had never been to this area, but the architecture was straight out of Chiba. Further from the pillar, three vans waited, their silent motors humming. Six men got out, two for each van, and opened the back doors.

Several Companions of different types walked out, Datu counted eight in all. They all walked to the elevator, and there was only one person left behind.

As the elevator returned to the warehouse on the 50th with its contingent, the woman before them spoke up.

"You know the drill, people: pick up and drive. That's all you have to do. If you think you're being followed, evade. If you get caught, run. If you get captured—let's hope it doesn't come to that. Now go. I expect you back at 18:00 hours."

This would be Yui, then, Datu thought. She had the stern demeanour of a woman who would take no guff. He could tell she was Asian despite wearing a thin pair of AR goggles. She had blonde hair, and wore a chocolate brown power suit with wide-bottomed pants, the kind which he'd never seen anyone wear on these levels.

It was as if a Sim Star had descended from the Heights to give them orders.

Vasyklo nodded to him and they walked over to one of the vans. Datu saw Shironeko Parcel Services written on the side, the logo a white cat carrying its baby in its maw.

They hopped into the already-running vehicle, Vasyklo in the driver's seat. Datu looked at himself in his armoured dress, in a delivery van. It all felt a bit ridiculous, but judging by Vasyklo's face, it was anything but funny.

"What are we supposed to do, exactly?" he asked.

"You heard the lady, we pick up." Vasyklo said, taking a left along one of the factory level's long avenues. Datu had a feeling that if he asked any more questions, he'd get the same stonewalling, so remained quiet as they drove.

Though he didn't recognize the area, the signs along the way told him he was somewhere to the South-East of Sector 14. They were making their way in a meandering pattern through the streets, and Datu wondered why.

"Got one," Vasyklo said, his voice tense. He looked over his shoulder down the street and pulled a U-turn as fast as he could. "Get in the back. When I tell you, you open the back door and let it in, okay?" Datu unbuckled his seat belt, unsure as to what was supposed to happen.

He went to the back of the van, holding onto the sides of the empty cube as it rocked side to side under Vasyklo's manic driving, almost smashing into the door twice.

Vasyklo slammed on the brakes and Datu was hurled to the front, landing on his side.

"Now! Open the door!" the driver yelled, and Datu scrambled to get up, shambling to the back door, lifting the lock-bar and swinging the door open. A smaller companion walked up to the van door and hopped into the back. It was a faceless model, a factory worker, probably a duct cleaner. It came into the truck as if it was the most natural thing to do, and went to sit near the front. Datu was on his knees, staring, when Vasyklo hollered. "Close the door, idiot!"

Datu shook his head, leaning out the back of the van and grabbed the door handle, bringing it back in. The van lurched to a start before he'd finished locking it, and he thought he might be expulsed onto the road. He grabbed onto an industrial rubber handle hanging from the wall near the door, lurching toward and hitting it with the side of his body.

The van took off, and soon Vasyklo was driving at a normal pace once again. They did two more of these stops, with a variety of Companion models hopping aboard and taking seats along the floor. By this time it was three in the afternoon. Datu had tried speaking to the first Companion they'd retrieved, but Vasyklo had said, "Don't."

Datu had spent most of his day by the door, holding onto the rubber strap as Vasyklo made his way around the factory levels. It was the waiting which had been the most anxiety-inducing. Once the Companions were on board and they'd driven far enough, Datu's nervous system had returned to normal, at least for a while. Those in-between periods, however, were torture.

"Man, I'm getting hungry. We haven't eaten since this morning," Datu said. Vasyklo glanced at the squared green numbers of the onboard digital clock and seemed to consider for a moment. Then he turned in to a parking lot and stopped the van toward the far back of the property.

"Go get your food," he said, slipping him a credit card-sized black rectangle. "Leave through the side door." Datu walked to the front of the van after having locked the back.

The other side of the street was an empty lot, cordoned by metal poles and chains hanging at waist height. He was near a large diner, the kind factory workers and truckers would stop in at for a quick bite before going on their way or back to work. At this hour, the glass-wrapped restaurant was deserted. On the other side of the street to his right stood a twelve-foot fence which cut across the landscape, all the way to the edge of the plateau. Down the way, he could make out one of the guard posts just like the one he had to cross every day to get to his previous employment.

Sector 14.

He was home.

Or almost. He tried orienting himself according to the road signs, and figured he might be fifteen minutes away from Tala and the kids, if he took shortcuts. He looked back at the van. All he needed to do was see if they were okay and come back. Anything more would have put their lives in danger.

Would half an hour gone be too much? Would Vasyklo get out of the van to come looking for him? The Companions they'd rescued (stolen?) would have to be watched over.

How could he get through this gate to get into Sector 14? He knew most hidden entrances, but was uncertain about this particular spot. He knew Tala would be there waiting for him, and he'd get to hold Benilda and Ramil again. If Gabriel was back, perhaps they'd get to talk again, but that part remained blurry. Right now the most import aspect was to get himself over to the other side.

Of course, he could have asked the other man if it would be okay, but having known him for two days, there was no guarantee he wouldn't turn him in for breach of contract. Then there would never be a family to see, ever again.

Datu was torn. He waited in line at the counter to order food. There was a commotion as three men entered the diner. All wore the Peoplift Security uniforms he hated so much. One of them was—

Gabriel.

The last one to come in. Laughing with his "friends."

Datu felt he should hide, but at the same time realized that his son would not so readily recognize him. He was wearing a full mask and an armoured suit. Beyond that, he was part cyborg, and to top it all off, officially dead. Still, it was unnerving to stand in the presence of his own flesh and blood and be forced to keep his identity a secret.

In the next instant, however, it dawned on him that Gabriel was working for Peoplift Security. That fact made things start falling into an unswerving pattern which he would have rather his mind avoid altogether.

It was Gabriel who had broken into the house and stolen the Ayo. He'd been working for Peoplift even then. That's why he was absent for such long periods of time. He worked opposite shifts than his own father, and in different areas so that they would never meet.

He'd pretended to break into the house. He knew exactly where to find the Ayo.

His fingers flexed within his weighted glove. The line advanced, and he knew that it would only take him placing an order and his son hearing his voice for the subterfuge to end.

Datu's face became warm, and he patted his hips down, then shrugged, as if he'd forgotten his keys. He stepped out of line and went outside, bumping into one of the security guards in Gabriel's party as he did.

His head spun. Had Gabriel recognized him? Certainly not. That would be impossible.

"Hey!" he heard from behind him as he approached the truck. He walked a bit faster, not turning around. He knocked on the passenger's side door and Vasyklo unlocked. He got into the truck.

"Where's the f—" the other man said, a curious look on his face.

"Drive. Go. Right now," Datu said. Vasyklo craned his neck around to see the Peoplift guards approaching.

"Layno!" he spat, and stepped on the accelerator. Companions in the back tumbled to the doors, banging so hard against them that Datu thought they'd fall out. The Peoplift Security guards drew their guns as the van left the parking lot, a single bullet perforating the back door, slamming into the sidewall as they sped off.

Vasyklo did some fancy driving through the streets of Chiba for the next twenty minutes, avoiding main arteries and sticking to delivery lanes between factories. Places with sharp corners and blind spots. Datu had a distinct feeling that the other man had done this before, and knew exactly what to do to evade detection.

When they finally stopped behind a noodle manufacturing plant and a linen cleaning service, Vasyklo turned to Datu.

"What the Hell was that? Why were they after us? What did you do in there?" he yelled. His face dripped with sweat, and Datu daw that he still gripped the steering wheel with lily-white knuckles. He wiped a sleeve across his forehead, trying to get the sting of sweat out of his eyes.

Datu's stomach churned. Now was not the time to tell Vasyklo that one of those pursuers had been his son.

"I don't know. I bumped into one as I left—they must have taken offence, or something. I don't know!" He stammered.

"I'm not sure you're aware of this yet, but the work you and I are doing is highly irregular. If we get caught, we're toast," Vasyklo exclaimed, looking Datu straight in the eyes.

"Why? What are we doing that's so bad?"

"You're not the fastest cog in the machine, are you, my friend? Who do you think those Companions behind there belong to?" Vasyklo asked, throwing his thumb behind the van.

"Midori Mamoru?" Datu tried without conviction. He'd tried as hard as he could to deal with the cognitive dissonance of picking up strange Companions on the streets of Chiba and the legal implications inherent to this activity. Vasyklo wanted none of it.

"Hahaha! Are you serious? No, *breydor kovatei*," he said in Ukrainian, and Datu did not for a moment think it was a compliment, "we're stealing them! My partner, the person you are replacing? He was shot by the police yesterday. The only reason I'm still alive, is because he's not."

"I—I don't understand…" Datu said, wanting more than anything to be five thousand kilometres away from where he was right now.

"I had to drag his body over the edge of a plateau and toss it so that he couldn't be identified," Vasyklo continued. Datu remembered the warning Phong tried to give him while he was insisting on being part of the team. "Here's what happens if you're not careful while doing this: you're going to get killed by the cops. Not taken... killed. And if I get taken, or my body is identified by the authorities? You'll have to answer to Yui and Arun. They'll be the ones burying you in the Heap. No matter how much it cost to give you that fancy new body. Nobody, and I mean nobody can be connected back to Midori Mamoru. If I see you getting captured, I'm going to have to destroy the evidence, and I will."

By the end of the talk, cold sweat was running down Datu's back, and his stomach felt as if he'd eaten garbage which had been left out on the counter for two weeks. He opened the door, leaned out, and retched. There was nothing in his body, so he dry-heaved bile for two solid minutes.

They continued on their way after a ten minute respite, Datu's mental dread ping-ponging from the idea of death at the hands of one group to the other and back again. His thoughts spiralled along a dark path for a long time, his heart constraining at every turn, until he thought it might stop. All he wanted was to hold his wife and children again, and he would make that happen! The question was a matter of how to avoid being caught by Arun and his group. Getting past the Sector 14 guards was an exercise he'd been doing since he was a teen. There was no challenge there.

They picked up two more Companions along the way, which brought their total to seven. Datu noticed that the exterior of the van had changed colour. They were now in a moving van with orange-painted sides. He spotted the button by Vasyklo's hand, a feature unique to this particular truck and no other of its brand and make.

This assuaged his fears of being followed or discovered, at least by the Peoplift Security guards. As they continued their run, he noticed a row of police cars headed in the opposite direction, all lights flashing. Vasyklo forced nonchalance into his driving style, as a quadcopter thundered overhead, exo-skeletons' massive legs hanging off the side of the open doors.

When 6 pm rolled around, they were back at the meeting point near the pillar. One of the trucks had not returned. The seven Companions they'd gathered walked out of the back of the truck and followed Yui to the elevator, along with those the men from the other truck had gathered.

Neither Datu, Vasyklo or anyone noticed the small device lodged in the dirty bumper of the truck as they left.

As Datu stepped onto the elevator, he saw the two drivers and a single Companion walking in their direction, looking despondent. Yui told them to stop, and the Companion they escorted kept walking, joining the rest of them on the elevator platform. As the elevator began to descend, he heard two loud pops, and then, as he was looking up, the bodies of one, then the other of the drivers came flying over the edge, all the way down into the blackness of the Heap.

FEVER

Keiji's world swam. As he lay in the back of the car, he could feel his temperature rise and rise, his sinuses blocking and releasing in fits and spurts. He kept a handkerchief to his nose, not wanting to upset the Special Inspector more than was necessary. Whatever had been inside the Rikona was inside him, now. His personal firewall had not been strong enough to resist the infection, and now his crystal chip was being overloaded with the virus which had taken it over.

His eyes felt puffy and red, and he coughed. Being a computer virus, there was no way he could communicate it to an unsuspecting populace through touch or inadvertent spittle. That was the domain of science fiction which the Holovid shows liked to use as some cliché plot point. Sad that some of the population actually believed that nonsense.

It was, however, getting entrenched inside his own memory modules, and even though it would never be able to take over his motor functions, it could well erase many of his skills and memories if allowed to get too far. He needed a vaccine, and fast.

The call had come in that there was another Companion outbreak in progress, and Keiji tried to think as hard as he could, but the infection made the effort almost impossible.

He felt the car lift into the air, his stomach rolling over at the action.

"You okay back there?" Ishikawa asked.

"I'm alright. Just feel a bit ill, is all," he said, trying for a convincing smile.

"Scan confirms that temperatures exceed normal human

parameters," the Eiko said, as it put on its seatbelt.

"What's wrong, kid?" Ishikawa asked.

"Long day, I guess," he replied, sitting up as straight as he could.

Every time he closed his eyes, he could see the tendrils swaying through his storage banks, wrecking years of memories and abilities he'd acquired. Skills he hadn't bothered recording in his grey matter, the crystal chip being an instantaneous mnemonic recorder. This virus was going through his chip as if he had no antibodies whatsoever. It was frightening. It might not have been DaiSin Trode tech (his father would never have let him get *those*), they were nevertheless top-of-the-line Japanese models, and he'd paid a premium on the defence software guarding all input ports.

Nothing doing, they were getting massacred, and Keiji could feel it.

As they rushed toward the next escape scene, Keiji has a vision.

"Wait!" he cried, leaning between the seats, startling Ishikawa. He stuck his trode plugs into the car's sensors and analyzed what he'd just thought of.

"What are you doing?" Ishikawa asked, pushed out of the way by Keiji's outstretched body across the console.

"The calls. We're not getting all of them. I just went into the 119 mainframe where all the calls are being routed. If we can see where every call if coming from, we might see—"

As he spoke, the sensor screen in front of the car illuminated with dots in a pattern, as if they were footsteps across the sand. They looked like a drunk person walking, but that was because whoever that "person" was, was taking every left and right turn across the grid, and this, on many different levels of the Chiba area.

"We've been chasing the aftermath. Eiko, figure out the most logical route they're taking through Chiba. Then we can head them off," Keiji said, before unplugging his trode wires and leaning back onto the seat.

Eiko625 was silent for a moment, then, pointed at a blank street of Chiba 100 on the GPS device underlying the sensor array.

"At our current speed and heading, going to this location has a high probability of aiding us in encountering those responsible for spreading the infection," it said. "There is also a good chance that we shall arrive before them."

Ishikawa sent an APB on the location and descended rapidly to the area, landing the car by the busy street. There was a parking lot nearby, behind a high gate. Two hundred metres behind them was a Smartcrete factory, the self-healing polymer commonly used in the construction of new high-rises, not to mention repairing plateaux and pillars all over

Tokyo. Its tall chimneys belched out white smoke on a continuous basis, and Ishikawa saw no reason to remove her rebreather.

She and the Companion left the car, watching vehicles zoom by on the busy avenue, most of them exiting the factory parking lots after the day's shift.

She'd have to turn the Companion over to TPD sooner than later to have him analyzed. If they could quickly synthesize whatever it was that protected him from the madness, there would be many less victims to deal with in the coming days.

One thing was certain: now that she knew there was a responsible party, she would do everything in her power to have them caught and jailed. It would be difficult with every other cop on the force trying to shoot them, but there had to be a mastermind behind the pandemic, and it was those bastards she wanted to collar.

Now she was curious to know if Keiji's idea would work. He'd been right in the past, but that didn't mean—

That was when she noticed the four Companions walking resolutely toward the car from the concrete factory. She had the notion that they were not, in fact, heading home after their shift.

"Officer needs assistance near Tekkonkinkreet Manufacturing. Please advise," she said, leaning into the car on the radio. Eiko625 left his seat, getting outside and placing himself on the street between Ishikawa and the four menacing androids making their way to the tall fence.

The radio crackled. "Assistance on the way, Special Inspector," a voice said. She recognized it. It was Kazue. A cold chill ran down her spine.

"We're on our own," she said to Eiko625.

Traffic continued unabated, and Ishikawa took out her gun, stepping onto the road beside the Eiko and pointed it at the cars coming toward them on the left, then the right.

Fearful drivers stopped, turning around in the other lane. Those behind backed up. She wished there was a way to close the factory gate so no more drivers could leave, but that would have meant she depart from her present position and potentially leave Keiji exposed.

The four Companions neared the high fence, shoulders rounded. She would have gone as far as to say angry. Cars were approaching once more, and she again pointed her gun at those foolish enough to try to pass in front of her.

The taller Companion, a Nakama model, took the fence in its hands and ripped it open. The metal rings split with resounding 'ping!' tearing a wide hole, like a broken zipper.

The other three, Seikaku models all, followed it through, and stood before Ishikawa and Eiko625, who had backed up to the car.

"Stop, now, or I'm going to take you all down," she said, pointing her gun to each Companion in turn. The Seikaku were squat, bulky, and covered in a fine coat of cement dust. The Nakama was taller, clean and had a glossy blue coat of paint. For all that, they still loomed menacingly across the street.

A cube van accelerated on the road, trying to bypass what was about to unfold. It went around cars and other trucks, speeding toward Ishikawa and Eiko625.

The Companion pulled her out of the way, backing up to her car, and in the same motion, grabbed the side fender of the van, jerking it hard. It veered sideways on two wheels and spilled on its side several metres away.

Its driver pushed the back door open, but before Ishikawa or Eiko625 could deal with the two men that came out, they were faced with the four Companions across the street.

Without looking at each other, the Companions began to walk toward Ishikawa and Eiko625.

I warned you, Ishikawa thought, before unloading on the nearest Seikaku Companion, taking out half its head. The other three converged, two of them on Eiko625, and another of the smaller androids dodging and reaching for Ishikawa.

She fired ten rounds, hitting it in the sides and other armoured areas. Every time she aimed for its head, the thing would raise its arms and deflect the bullet.

The Eiko had managed to get rid of one of the Seikaku Companions, crushing its head in his hands. The Nakama had taken advantage of the distraction to sweep out its legs, and was presently attempting to punch it in the cranium. The Eiko dodged its head left and right at superhuman speeds, avoiding every blow.

As the Seikaku Companion attacking Ishikawa lunged, she heard a voice from behind yell, "Duck!"

Falling to the ground, she heard a detonation, and the Companion's left side blew outward behind it. She stared in disbelief, turning around to the car, and saw Keiji firing a second shot with her shotgun, this time neatly blasting off the top half of the tall Companion which sat on Eiko625s chest. Android pieces rained down on the other side of the street as the drivers who had witnessed the events turned their cars around and scrambled to alternate routes to find their way home.

The Seikaku Companion he'd dispatched was crawling its way toward Ishikawa using its legs and good arm, and Keiji leaned on the car, sweat dripping down his face like a waterfall.

"Eiko625, stop that thing without destroying its positronic brain, will you?" Keiji said in a raspy voice. The Eiko pushed the remains of the blue Nakama Companion off itself and got up in one smooth movement. It walked over to the still-crawling Companion, as Ishikawa backed away on her behind, trying to get up without losing too much of her pride.

The Eiko walked over the other android, and it looked up at him in annoyance as he raised his foot and brought it down on the section of torso which hadn't been cut off from its upper and lower body. With only one hand, it could no longer crawl, but instead continued to clutch at the air.

"Thank you," Keiji said, slowly letting himself slide down the side of the car, the shotgun in his hands.

By the time everything was said and done, the truck operators had left the scene, the only evidence of their presence a wrecked cube van smashed through the fence.

MANGA

The first thing Saito noticed when he woke was peeling wallpaper and a garbage-strewn floor in a small, empty apartment. If anything, this reminded him of the dead man's, minus the corpse and smell.

This room was bigger, though. The rotten wallpaper cut off to drooling drywall, giving the illusion that there were two rooms instead of one. The floors were a rollout wood-like substance curling at the corners, revealing concrete beneath.

A single shade-less lamp on a pink plastic foot-stool gave mediocre light to the room, below and to his right.

The sound of running water from the bathroom brought his attention into sharper focus, and he then realized he was duct-taped to the wall, in some weird crucifixion pose. Whoever had tied him up had left his pants on, but removed his shirt. The front door was to his right, and next to that a small window covered in black garbage bags and ratty drapes for good measure.

His shirt and shoes were near the entrance, the former neatly folded over the latter.

The smell of old and abandoned things, as well as a hint of sour piss, permeated the place. The apartment had surely been used as a squat at some point in time. He wondered where this place might be. In such a generic-looking conapt, it could have been any level save The Heights. It made him reflect upon the fact that a great many people only knew homes like this one from birth until death, and for a moment, he was more depressed for them than he was for his own predicament.

A hard cushion pressed against the back of his neck, and he wiggled it a bit. After attempting to make contact on the nets, he came to the conclusion that the object was a neural blocker, scrambling his wireless. There'd be no way to call for help this time.

That was before he saw the small imitation bamboo table before him. It sat maybe four feet away, at the liminal edge of the light. He squinted to make out its contents. Short, brown, and covered in exotic, long silver knives.

That's what it was about, then, he thought, and rolled his head back. There was a piece of duct tape over his mouth, or else he would have sighed loudly at the display. He could only assume it was a man who would put those sorts of implements out.

To scare him. To torture him. Ultimately, to kill him. What a day. Through the running tap water, he could hear a train platform being called over the intercom, as well as the low rumble of said train arriving. He couldn't make out the words, however.

The sound of running water stopped with the squeak of the taps, and a man walked out of the bathroom. He was wiry, yet muscular, his upper body covered in cartoon tattoos. In a sense, they were similar to Yakuza tattoos, but in this case, the illustrations seemed to have been directly influenced by Japanese manga, and not mythology. His hair was blond and spiky, reminding Saito of a particularly tacky wig. He repressed a smirk, not to offend his host.

"Mr. Saito. Welcome," the man said, smiling widely. He spread his arms wide, as if he were a guest in some grand palace.

Saito mumbled, arching an eyebrow.

"I'll take it off, if you promise to stay quiet. The neighbours like their peace," he said, putting his finger to his lips. Saito nodded once, and the man ripped the strip of tape off Saito's mouth, who cringed, but tried not to scream.

"I was saying," Saito said, trying to get the feeling back in his lips, "you sure know how to make a person feel at home. Reminds me of a place I was visiting not too long ago."

"Dragomir Petrov. Yes, I know. You're nosy, Mr. Saito. A trait I enjoy in my victims. Kills my remorse, if you'll pardon the pun," the man said. He stood before the low stool, eyeing Saito for a moment, then picked up a two-and-a-half foot straight blade by its two-foot long square handle. It was more sword than knife, and while resembling a katana, its handle was slimmer. The back of the blade was also slightly curved outward, giving it a 'hump,' instead of the concave spine of the Japanese sword, which paralleled its blade. Black electrical tape had been wrapped around the handle, telling Saito that the man smiling at him with the razor-sharp blade might have made said cutting implement himself. Interesting.

It was then that he thought he recognized Mr. Mystery. That point in time where he'd turned around in Shibuya 150 and thought he'd been followed. Clearly, he had. Since Petrov's conapt, at that. He had to give the man points for sneakiness, at least.

"Where are your associates, my friend?" Saito said, trying to wiggle the tape loose from his forehead. Perhaps if he could pull out one of his arms, he might be able to block a strike from that wicked-looking knife thing the man held.

"Ever heard of 'Ten the Blade', Saito San? Do you enjoy manga at all?" The man asked.

"No, I'm sorry, I can't say I'm a fan. I haven't lived a life of leisure, you see," Saito replied, attempting a shoulder shrug.

"No matter," the other man said, "I'm here to educate. If you'd been up to speed on your popular culture, you'd know that Ten the Blade is an assassin for hire, that he works alone, and that he enjoys his work, very, very much."

"Fascinating. What does that have to do with me?" Saito said, holding back a sigh of boredom.

"*I am* Ten the Blade," the man said.

"Just that, then. Goodness. If I'd known, I'd have dressed for the occasion," Saito said.

"Oh, you can laugh all you want, Saito San, but I'm not bullshitting here. There are a few things I want to know before I peel you."

The man stepped around the stool with his long knife in hand, pressing the blade at an angle across Saito's body, its tip coming to rest an inch below his jugular.

"Boy, that's a turn-on," Saito said, raising an eyebrow. "No one ever tried to peel me before."

The man backed off, unnerved.

"Is there something wrong with you, that I should know about?" he said.

"Something wrong? No, no, of course not! It's just that... when someone tapes me to a wall and promises to remove my skin... I just... I don't know—it's getting me all hot."

The man faltered for a moment, looking disgusted.

"Could you not, please?" he said, angrily.

"I'm sorry. I'll behave," Saito said, sternly. He then sucked his lower lip and his glance slipped to the knife again.

"What do you know about Arau Maintenance?" Ten the Blade said, holding up his knife once again, the half-melted acetates Saito'd found in his other hand.

"Threaten me again," Saito said.

"Excuse me?" Ten the Blade said.

"Do it. Tell me all the horrible things you'll do to my body if I don't cooperate," Saito said, squirming and wriggling behind the wall of duct tape that kept him propped up against the wall.

"You have serious issues, man. No wonder they wanted out. With degenerates like you working for that company—"

"Who're 'they'?" Saito asked innocently. So it was the Nexus who'd sent this man after him.

"I think you know very well who they are. Now, maybe I'll just remove one of your toes—" Ten the Blade continued.

Saito moaned, biting his lip as the other man put down the large sword-like knife and picked up a smaller, curved one. He approached Saito, whose moans intensified. His eyes rolled back in his sockets, and his body went rigid. As the assassin lifted Saito's naked foot, he began to whisper:

"Yessss… yessss…do it!" He writhed in ecstasy and bit his lip, unable to contain his bliss.

Ten the Blade's shoulders fell, and he let go of the foot.

"I'm… I'm out. You take all the fun out of the job, you lunatic. You pervert. Ick. You're just gross. You know that, right? This is bar none the worst torture session I've ever had. You killed it for me. Are you happy?"

"I'm sorry! I can't help it!" Saito replied, having regained control over his body. "Just a little toe? Please?"

"No! Bad! Looks like I'll just have done with it, then," Ten the Blade said, putting down the little knife and picking up a very large, wide sword, like a prop out of a video game. He hefted it over his shoulder, holding the handle with two hands.

"This could have been beautiful. You just had to ruin it," he said, bringing the sword around.

The door crashed open, and a white man came in and spotted the assassin. As soon as Ten the Blade saw him, he went toward the door at a dead run, lifting the blade over his shoulder again.

It was Scott Till.

The intruder backed away from the door, and the sword caught on the top of the doorframe, becoming wedged. The other man kicked the assassin back into the room, and he fell on his back on the floor. As the new arrival rushed in brandishing his gun, Ten the Blade grabbed the leg of his torture table and spilled its contents on the floor. A long dagger in hand, he tried to get up and launched it at the armed man in the doorway, grazing his head.

The man lifted his gun to shoulder level and shot him twice in the head.

Ten the Blade fell backward on his table, crushing it with his back with a 'crack.'

"Hey there," Till said, holstering his gun. "Mind telling me what's going on?" He put his hands on his hips and looked up at Saito.

"Sure. Mind getting me down?" he replied. Taz grabbed one side of the duct tape, pulling it across Saito's chest, who winced as it tore at his skin.

"Careful! Don't ruin the paint job!" he said.

"You know, for a guy who likes to get his toes cut off, you're a bit of a baby, ain't ya?" Taz replied, helping the man down from the wall.

Saito sat down on the dirty floor for a bit, getting his bearings. The assassin lay dead on his back, a trickle of blood slowly pooling under his head.

The sword chose that moment to fall out of the doorframe and clatter to the ground in the entrance.

"You heard that, huh?" Saito said, getting up by leaning against the wall, then going over to get his shirt and shoes. He slapped his foot a few times to get the dirt from the floor off of it, then took one sock out from inside it, slipped it on, then the shoe, repeating the process for the other foot. He then pulled on his shirt, and went looking for his coat, which he found in the bathroom.

The assassin had put it in the shower, and it was presently soaking wet.

"Yeah. You've got some weird fetishes, Mr Saito," Taz said, cocking his head.

"Listen, the next time a half-crazed basket-case has you taped up to a wall and threatens to flay you, *you* try to find something to say which might change his mind," he said, taking the wet coat out of the shower. He twisted it and turned it, the cold water running out.

"You don't seem surprised in the least by my having shown up—" Taz said, as Saito handed him a pinhead-sized black button which he'd detached from his mottled coat.

"Your tracking device, sir," Saito said. Taz' eyes went wide. "I know it's standard practice among you Admin Security Apparatus types."

He put on his sopping wet coat and headed toward the door, leaving a dripping trail as he did so.

"You set me up? You knew this was going to happen?" Taz said, following.

"This or something similar. I've managed to make a host of enemies in the past few days. Might have to add it to my resumé: makes enemies like a champ. Catchy. Only a matter of time until one tried to dispatch me," Saito said, turning around. He clutched the neural blocker and pulled it off, an electric arc fizzling, and sticking it in one of his pockets. He then walked over to the dead assassin and took the pile of acetates from under him, checking once for trodes and finding none.

He shook his head and walked out the door. It was a cool evening, and it took him a moment to get his North and South in alignment. A hundred metres away, a metro station lit up the night. Open air arrangement, few riders waiting on the platform. He could make out the Kanji for Meguro Station, which meant this "Blade" character had brought him a bit south of Ebisu.

"You know, I had a lot of trouble tracking you down. You could show me a bit of courtesy and come in for a chat," Taz said, as Saito was walking away. Above their heads, the advertising skiffs plodded across the sky like slow-moving whales, touting the benefits of Momo Cola and tall glasses of nama biru while flashing spotlights on the ground. Saito felt like having one of those beers on tap. It would refresh his mind, he thought.

MR SAITO.

He twitched when he saw the words appear in the corner of his vision.

Golem. What do you have for me? He thought.

UNFORTUNATE NEWS. SANTIAGO LOPEZ IS DEAD. MURDERED.

How unfortunate, he responded. *Track anything relative to his last hours. I want the culprit found.*

WE WERE UNABLE TO CONTACT YOU EARLIER. IS EVERYTHING FINE?

Oh, you know me. I was just hanging about. Get to work. I have a feeling things are starting to spiral out faster now, he said.

"Yes, Mr. Till. I do apologize for making your spying on me difficult. That wasn't my intention. I won't go with you downtown, but if you'll join me for a beer and a chat, I can be candid with you," Saito said, and walked down the several flights of stairs to the ground floor.

"Give me one good reason why I shouldn't take you there by force, Saito San?"

"Because you'll get nothing from me that way. I'm offering you an alternative. Take it or leave it. Make up your mind quickly. I have things to do," Saito said. Not waiting for a reply, he walked in the general direction of Shinagawa's hustle and bustle.

REUNION

Datu'd slept poorly that night. Even though he could have plugged in and enjoyed the rolling night-time waves of some long-forgotten beach, he'd resisted the urge to do so. Whether it was because he'd have to confront the woman in the construct or some deep-rooted fear that what he was living was false, he couldn't be sure.

Instead, he'd dreamt of being chased through the filthy darkness of Sector 14 under an oily rain, falling in the muck and picking himself up. The fear gripped his insides like the icy claws of some terrible beast. Always, always, his pursuers ten steps behind. Too far to catch him, too close to evade them.

He'd woken to a face full of cold, wet pillow and drenched clothes, and wondered if perhaps he should have chosen the construct. He was exhausted.

He shuffled out of the door with the other men, doing the same routine as the day before, ending up in the cafeteria at the table.

"You can't tell anyone what happened last night. You understand?" He said. Datu nodded, continuing to eat. There was no one he could have trusted to tell in the first place, let alone wanted to.

If Phong and Boon-Me had registered his words, they made no mention of it, preferring to mind their own business.

He spied the two empty spots at the other tables. A flash of falling bodies came to his mind, like shadows falling into shadows, between plateau and pillar. Human meteorites burnt up before impact, shooting to their final resting places at the speed of gravity. Their names would forever remain a mystery.

When time came to get up and leave to go to the surface again, he saw Reza point to two men, who reacted with surprise and horror. They did not wait for her to anger to get up and go to the dressing area for truck duty.

Vasyklo and Datu both rose as well, leading the way with the two other men who'd returned the night before. The new additions to the team shuffled along, the displeasure at having been 'voluntold' evident in their faces and demeanours.

Once back on the 100th, Datu saw that there were once again three trucks, Yui before them, handing out keys. When Vasyklo and Datu came to pass, she gave them each a truck key and assigned one of the new recruits to each of them.

"But I've never done this on my own!" Datu said to Yui.

"Life is short, my friend. Learn now," she said, patting him on the side of the face. Datu was certain he'd never heard anyone use the word 'friend' as a threat before. He took the key and got in the truck, a kid named Antoni hopping into the passenger's seat. Polish from the looks of him, he wore an inverted crucifix tucked under his clothes.

Vasyklo came to his window, and he rolled it down.

"The turn signals will show you where you have to go," he said, and went back to his truck. Datu checked that the button the other man had used to change the sides of the truck was in the same spot, and was satisfied to find it, hidden behind a dashboard button.

What did that mean? He had to trust he'd know when the time came. He was reticent to go tapping on Yui's shoulder to find out.

She gave them the all-clear and they left the area, each heading out to a different plateau. A few hundred metres later, Datu saw Vasyklo veering off to the left, taking an on-ramp which would spiral to the 150th. The other truck turned a right a kilometre or so later, staying in the heavy industrial section of the factory floor.

"So, uh, what are we supposed to do?" the kid asked, avoiding eye contact. He tapped the side of his thighs with the tips of his fingers, his body spring-loaded. He had to be Gabriel's age, maybe a hair older.

"Relax, man. We're doing pickup," Datu said, trying to keep his voice on an even keel. Factories and warehouses went by, their elongated forms taking up enormous square footage both wide and tall.

"Yeah. Pickups," the kid said. "It's just that, you know... not a lot of people keep doing pickup duty. Dangerous, you know?" Antoni stared out the passenger's side as if some unseen danger were lurking in every artificial bush along the way, waiting to pounce on him as soon as his attention strayed.

He isn't far off, Datu thought, keeping his thoughts ice-like. His nervous system was over-clocked. He wondered how long it would take until the perspiration started dripping down his forehead and neck. Antoni'd freak. He had to keep calm.

Datu steeled himself for the coming day's work. This poor kid had no idea what was in store for him.

"When I tell you to go to the back door and open it, you do it," Datu said to Antoni, who trembled on the passenger's seat like a leaf in a tornado.

"Hey. You'll be okay," he told the younger man, tapping his shoulder with his gloved hand. Antoni simply nodded, looking little reassured.

As Datu drove, he saw that the turn signals activated themselves, even before he had a chance to touch them.

Thanks, Vasyklo, he thought, taking the directions indicated for him. He saw a walking Companion in the distance, near a small food supply warehouse. It sauntered along a high brick fence, looking like a lost hitchhiker.

Datu's signals went to hazard lights, and he stopped the van, sending Antoni to the back to open the door and let their stray android in. He opened and closed the door so fast that the Companion almost got stuck. It gave the boy a jarring look, and went to sit in the back, just as the other Companions had the day previous.

What made them know to do that? Datu wondered. It was almost as if they were programmed for this entire sequence. If they were leaving the factories and warehouses by their own volition, was it really stealing? But no, he was once again trying to justify the acts he was perpetrating without thinking of the consequences.

As the morning wore on, they picked up two more Companions, without incident. Datu began to relax, and Antoni visibly so. He had stopped his constant shifting in his seat, which Datu had been about to mention as an irritant.

Datu began to think of Tala and the children. As they followed a similar path as the one he and Vasyklo had taken the previous day, he wondered if the Peoplift Security guards might have returned to the diner.

This made him think of Gabriel again, and he pushed the thought away. But what if they were absent? Could he make his way into Sector 14 and go to his own home to see his family again? At least to tell them he was safe?

Who would be there to stop him? Antoni?

"Hey Antoni, we're just going to stop for lunch for a bit, okay? It's on me," He said, smiling. Having died, he'd been equipped with a new identity, a new credit chip. Whatever he might think about Midori Mamoru, they paid.

The dirty parking lot was empty of the tell-tale armoured vehicles used by his old employer. He stopped the car on the opposite side of the street, between two tumble-down shacks that clung to the wall between Chiba's industrial district and Sector 14.

Those old buildings were punishment cut-offs, Datu thought. Back in the day, when all of the 100th had been inhabited, a few people had made such a ruckus that Admin had let them keep their houses on the other side of the wall, just so they could see their neighbours and family through the barbed wires and weep. Until, of course, they'd come willingly across into the people-pen they'd built for them.

What Admin had been unaware of, was that some of those hold-backs had made their way into the ghetto anyhow. Old sewer lines running under their homes had been used to do the back-and-forth into the forbidden zone, even if heavy grates had been installed within said sewers. The people of Sector 14 had found ways.

Eventually, the disadvantages had outweighed the advantages, and those who at first had thought themselves more clever than their oppressors had given in and followed the rest of the inhabitants.

The escape routes had remained, as had the homes, the latter kept as reminders to the citizens on the inside of what happened when they tried to go up against Administration policies. Most of the former had been discovered and destroyed, of course, but once in a while, some enterprising citizen of the Sector would excavate the tunnels, trying to dig their way to a better life for themselves or their families.

As Datu came back with bag full of sushi, he wondered which was the likeliest candidate. There was a string of those old homes, all of them leaning heavily on the wall, or simply crumpled up at its base like fallen houses of cards, or rotten teeth that clinging to stone gums.

On the other side, tall conapt buildings stood in sharp contrast to the single family homes. Ten to twenty stories with nothing to discern them one from the other, it was no wonder that tenants got a hard knock on the door in the early hours of the morning, once in a blue moon, from some drunk who thought they were unable to get into their own home.

Datu squelched onto the driver's seat and took out a tray of sushi for himself, then handed the other one to his new coworker, who looked at it as if it would slither off the black plate, up his armour and force its way into his mask and choke him.

"Not a sushi fan?" He said between mouthfuls. The boy shook his head in the negative, his eyes locked on the colourful pieces of vat-grown fish and squid. They gave the salmon and tuna colour hormones, or else they turned grey. Something to do with the nutrient makeup of the aquariums they were spawned in.

He took the young man's plate back and reached into the bag again, handing him a closed box of hot tempura. He would have liked to eat it himself, but letting Antoni starve would have been cruel. Ayo would have been disappointed. Then he thought of Aimee Flores, and tried unsuccessfully to reconcile the religious figure he'd known since his youth, and the woman who'd tried to seduce him two nights ago. Nothing doing.

"Listen, I just have to go run an errand. It won't take me more than… half an hour, tops. Can you sit tight and wait for me to come back?" Datu said with his kindest smile. If everything went to plan, he would be back within that time span. And what could go wrong, after all? Antoni began to squirm again.

"I'm not sure… I don't know if—" he replied, after finishing a piece of deep-fried lotus root and looking to the back of the truck where the three Companions sat still along the walls of the van.

"You'll be fine. If anything happens while I'm gone, just honk and I'll come right back. Be cool, Antoni," Datu said, and before he could say anything in return, he was out the door, walking the length of the fence, the half-demolished homes giving his heart pangs of regret.

All were tagged with impressive graffiti. Some brave kids got out and painted whatever they could find. He'd done it himself when he was younger. Almost gotten caught once or twice. Had lost a friend. Stopped doing it after his father had died and his mother had pleaded for him to grow up.

Datu sighed. More water under the bridge. He looked for certain signs. Not all graffiti was created equal. If tradition had remained constant from his own days as a tagger, he would find what he was looking for—

There, fourth house down. In big blue letters, accented with black, were the words 'Walang Labasan.' Administration might not know Filipino, but even if they did, all they'd read was 'No Exit.' It meant that this house hid a secret entrance to Sector 14.

Datu went around the back, pushing at the base plates below the house until he found one which swivelled upward. He got on his hands and knees, ducking underneath the house and finding a jagged hole a few feet further.

He slid into the aperture feet first, letting himself fall a distance of maybe two feet. He followed the man-made hole cut out from the plateau in a hunched position until it reached a sewer line where he was able to stand up. It elbowed left or straight, and he decided to go straight, the odds of finding an opening greater.

The sewer was dry, refuse conveyed through plastic pipes along its sides. There were also the net and electric lines, and he followed the nearest net line fifty metres until he spotted a ladder going back to the surface.

He climbed five feet until he was up against the sewer grate, then, pushed it with all his might. It popped out easily, he having already forgotten his cyborg implants. He peeked outside in a deserted alley on the periphery, a conapt building blocking his view of the fence.

His heart beat faster. Within ten minutes, he'd be home, with Tala in his arms.

"Where have you been, lover?" she'd say, after she'd gotten over the shock of his still being alive.

"Trying to survive, babe," he'd say, one eyebrow arched.

"Daddy, are you coming back for good?" Benilda asked. That's when the fantasy faded. What was he supposed to tell her, or all of them for that matter? That he was the prisoner of some sort of Evil Corporation which was kidnapping Companions and doing Ayo-knew-what in the depths of the Heap, which was *definitely* against Administration policy?

Datu faltered. Should he keep going? Would it be worth it for them to see him? Of course it would! At least for them to know he was still alive! That had a price, right there. The question was, how much would this escapade cost him? Well, nothing. He would only see his family and be on his way.

Five minutes, tops.

He'd go to the house, ring the doorbell and see Tala's anguish and joy on her face. He'd be showered in hugs and love for five whole minutes, and then he'd have to run back, before anything could happen.

Datu pulled himself out of the manhole, pushing the cover back in place. He was between dumpsters, and anyone seeing him would not mistake him for a vagrant. They would also not question a man dressed in full armour in this part of town.

He was a stranger in his own land, for the first time in his life. He also had to be careful not to be recognized by acquaintances. That would bring a pile of trouble on his family's head as well.

City blocks went by as he ran in the empty alleys, a smattering of pedestrians making their way through Sector 14 a mere block away. Avoiding the main thoroughfares was his best bet for going unnoticed. Whether he liked it or not, he had to stay in uniform, the thin underwear beneath not enough to keep the level's pollution out.

Soon the geography became familiar again, and he knew exactly where he was. The stack where his conapt was nestled stood a mere block away.

He could already feel their embrace.

He could already taste her kiss on his lips after so many days of longing and absence.

He could—he turned the corner, where the metal frame of his apartment complex loomed. His heart thundered under its cyborg plating.

It was gone. The apartment had been removed. Datu stopped before the street, staying in the alley. Someone was dumping garbage by the side of the plateau again, but he didn't care. His family was gone. The slot where the apartment had been removed was still sparkling clean, compared to the outside frame which had been prey to the elements for so long.

Midori Mamoru had taken them. There could be no doubt. He walked with unsteady steps to the front of the building, feeling shot, broken and lost.

He felt the tears rise to his eyes, his arms electric as he clenched his fists, until he felt the weight of a hand on his shoulder, and a voice he knew too well command him.

"Turn around. Who are you?"

Gabriel.

THE ANSWER

This time, Keiji plugged into Eiko625 first. Sweat dripped down his brow as he fought nausea, but there were more important things to deal with at the moment.

"How did you get my shotgun out of the trunk?" Ishikawa had asked.

"Hacker," Keiji had answered, a forced smile on his lips, as his head swam.

The fact that he now had access to every system in the vehicle since he'd taken over the sensors on his first try would remain his secret as long as he could keep it.

Meanwhile, Ishikawa fumed that the officer named Kazue had blocked any backup from arriving to their site. It was a betrayal she would repay in due time. When lines were crossed, lives were put in danger. Whatever personal vendetta Officer Kazue had against Ishikawa, holding back much-needed help was a no-no that police never crossed, and she would make sure he would never get the urge to do it again.

Keiji sat on the ground next to the Eiko625, the shot and battered remnants of the attacking Seikaku splayed out and leaking compressor fluid. It stared at them through one unbroken optical sensor, and twitched minutely as it tried to reach for either one with its one unbroken limb.

Keiji dove, going first to the Eiko's loading construct. The immaculate white room had changed. The blue diode patterns on the walls pulsed in relief, and Keiji imagined that had been in response to the earlier attack. Self-inflicted systems upgrades were always reflected in the visuals.

"You are not well, Keiji San," Eiko625 said from everywhere in the room.

"I'll be fine," Keiji said, and coughed.

"No. You will not. Internal analysis shows an exponential rate of infection within the memory matrix. If reconnected with this Companion, could induce neural paralysis and death," Eiko625 continued.

"What do you suggest? I don't have a medibay in the vicinity, and stopping these Comps is the top priority, Eiko."

"Permission to investigate further?" Eiko625 said.

"How long will it take?"

"Not long," Eiko625 assured him.

"Fine, do it."

A medical chair, smooth and pliant, rose from the white ground. It was made of the floor's substance, and not visibly separated from it, but its material was soft and cushioned.

Keiji slumped on it, and a scanner rose behind his neck, acting as cushion, then enveloped his whole head. Keiji relaxed, as waves of soothing energy began to flow through his scalp.

Gradually, the fever dropped, and he felt as if the storm within his mind had abated. Gone was the swirling grit which had been devouring his memories and skills, to be replaced with utter peace.

"What did you do in there?" Keiji said, feeling the rest of his body slowly go back to normal.

"I injected the same anti-virals I developed for my own systems into yours. It appears they have worked. You should be immune to any future infections. Eiko625 recommends further testing by accredited medical firms, however, as the compatibility rate might be off."

Keiji stepped off the chair, and as it melted back into the floor, he felt stronger. He felt like an idiot, though, to have doubted that the Companion's vaccine would work on his systems. He'd been too quick to dismiss it. He'd chalk that one up to experience, or lack thereof. He would have to assess the overall damage to his mind at some later date, but for now, there was business to attend to.

"I'm ready. Open a port into that Seikaku. Let's take a look inside," he said.

"Yes, Keiji San."

A window reticulated before him, and Keiji could see the same red storm rising on an alien planet. In this version, the infection was blossoming, and had not yet gotten to the point where swaying tentacles destroyed the rest of the system.

"Turn on firewalls," Keiji said, and a purple sheen began to shimmer on every white wall, pulsing like a heartbeat. That same coating of electrons covered him as well, and he stopped for a moment to look at his hand. It looked as if it held a powerful bolt of purple lightning.

He took a deep breath.

Keiji walked up to the window and stepped through it, unconsciously holding his breath, its image rippling as he set foot in the roiling bits of data flying about.

At the far end of this construct, he could see a floating ball of green energy in the middle of the destruction. It was slowly flaking away as the infection worsened, so he made his way to it at a faster pace. Data particles fizzled against his firewall, the purple electric wall around his body setting them ablaze like a mosquito zapper.

When he reached the large green ball of shifting energy, he held it with both hands for a time, until he was ready. He then walked into it.

He found himself in a dark room, floating.

Schematics began to flow before his eyes, from top to bottom, the Seikaku's internal systems revealed in minute detail. As the code flowed freely before him, he was able to see both the architecture of its systems and programming in tandem, and how both worked together to make the android function.

"Infection data," he said out loud. An orange outline began to form around the physical schematics elements of the cyberbrain, as well as the code which accompanied it. The constant flow diverged into new systems, showing where it was going next, infecting all in its path through the means of least resistance.

"Reverse flow," Keiji said, and everything he'd been watching began to go backwards in time, the orange outlines erasing themselves as the code now flowed from bottom to top, like holoprogram credits in reverse.

Within thirty seconds, the point of origin had been reached: a node connected to the BIOS, but appearing to be an add-on. Keiji stared at it in disbelief.

The darkness began to waver, wrinkles in the darkened room growing in mass, until a tentacle broke through, slithering around Keiji's waist and pulling him back into the main construct. Everything was desolation. The green sphere winked out of existence, the infection having slashed through basic commands.

Keiji's antiviral suit held, the purple electric field buzzing furiously wherever the tentacle gripped him. It squeezed, hard, and cracks appeared in the armour.

"Eiko! A little help!" He yelled, and the window which had brought him into the Seikaku's world expanded directly in front of him. The tentacle stormed the window, breaking through into Eiko625s initiating construct with the sound of shattered glass. The floor ripped out as the massive thing began to writhe and slash about, tearing chunks out of white walls, sending tiling shooting about like ceramics in a storm.

"Disconnect!" Keiji yelled, and the window behind him closed, as more tentacles reached within.

They cut off, their tips hopping about on the ground, growing larger as they attempted to take root within this new host. The tentacle sticking out of the floor began to split from itself, like cell multiplication.

"Disconnected," Eiko625 said.

"Disinfect, now!" Keiji screamed, and the walls, which had taken damage despite being surrounded by the electric field, began to glow a warmer purple, as if the room was filling on all sides with a liquid lighter than water. It poured from every wall, ceiling and floor, covering the hopping tentaclellets and turning them to glass.

The field soon covered the enormous slashing thing which had thrown Keiji about, and broke it at the base, the rest of it falling into the field, turning it to translucent shards.

Keiji found the remnants of viral infection and punched them with his purple fist until they'd all been turned to glass and shattered. He then punched deeply into the ground where the appendage had lodged itself, his fist penetrating the construct, obliterating whatever disease had been left within.

"Disinfection complete," Eiko625 said.

Keiji felt the energy slip out of his body, as if he'd just finished running a 10k run. He retrieved his fist from the ground of the construct, and dusted himself off.

"Damage report," Keiji said, stretching himself out. Even though his body felt fine now, he still remembered what it was like to have been compressed like a car in a wrecking machine the last time he'd gone through this process.

"All systems report full functionality. Residual viral infection has been quarantined for deconstruction and antibody creation," Eiko625 said.

"Can you give me a protected portal view of the Rikona's OS?"

"Affirmative."

One of the white walls shimmered out of view and was replaced with something similar to what he'd just experienced. It was like being jettisoned inside an escape pod landing into Hell.

Tooth-like tentacles rose from a sickening, undulating ground, jagged and crystalline, sharp facets reflecting the storm that blew across the data plane. They moved in slow, calcified waves, as if threatening to break and fall back into the molten sands from which they came.

"Inject an antiviral packet," Keiji said, pushing another node behind his head. A blue energy oblong fired into the mass of writhing tentacles, landing further in the sand-like substance. When it detonated, the force field sphered into null space within the Rikona's construct, sending out a swarm of antiviral agents to recapture the infected data.

As the purple energy bites attacked the monstrous vertical columns, they latched onto them, commencing a disinfection procedure.

As they spread forth throughout the massive constructions, however, they became unstable. There was a great vibration which began to be felt throughout the system, the tentacles fighting off the antiviral agent.

The tentacles affected by the antivirus now glowed like molten metal, a bright orange which continued to expand, until they detonated like nuclear warheads, data chunks sent hurling in all directions like debris in supernovae.

"Cut it off!" Keiji said.

"There is no danger to you, sir," the Eiko625 said.

"I know. But now I know what the problem is with these Companions. Logging out."

Keiji rose from his sitting position, slapping away the street dust. It had begun to rain, the dust jumping in small clumps from the dry ground. He looked up and smiled.

"What do we know?" Ishikawa asked, as he got up. Keiji repressed a smile.

"When I was in the Eiko625s construct the first time, the Rikona had already begun a viral attack. That was my bad. I should have connected first and secured the system. But, I did find out one thing: The Eiko, even though it was being infected, still had autonomous control of its systems, at least for a little while. It did a full reset on its own, and then stopped the Rikona from re-infecting it.

The Rikona, on the other hand, was impervious to antivirals. Which means that on the Eiko, which is an older model, its core system can't be overrun, at least not at first. The Rikona's chipset is newer. It's got a boot device which is an add-on to the main system," Keiji explained.

"Meaning?" Ishikawa said, growing visibly impatient.

"It can be circumvented and disabled. Someone created a virus that takes control of the Companions through this loophole. Any newer models which have been switched to this system architecture are vulnerable to infection," Keiji said, putting his arm around the Eiko625 for support.

"Great, but that doesn't tell us where the last one of these runaway Companions has gone to, does it?"

"No, but at least we know which models are susceptible. As for infection methods, I suspect they're being taken over through their wifi ports. There didn't appear to be any kind of connection to any physical infrastructure prior to their malfunctions, and this thing goes *fast*. It'll take over within a minute or so, turning the Companion into a puppet at its leisure while it's walking away. Having all factories turn their Companions to disconnect mode would stop all infections, if I'm right."

Keiji shuddered at the memory of the tendrils he'd fought within the two previous constructs.

Ishikawa connected to the private net and contacted the Admin superiors through a secure channel, explaining the new discovery which had been made. Within moments, an emergency broadcast had been sent to all businesses, factories and warehouses of the Chiba prefecture, and this, on all levels.

There were reports of several police battles involving Companions all over the plateaux. Some came to tragic ends, collateral damage within suburban areas, but all were contained within an hour or so.

Keiji stared at the Seikaku lying at his feet. His own infection had cleared up, as far as he could tell, but the damage within this poor Companion was beyond redemption. He picked up the shotgun from the trunk of the car, and before Ishikawa or Eiko625 could stop him, he fired one round into its skull, obliterating it.

"What did you do that for?" Ishikawa said, grabbing her shotgun out of his hands, almost dropping it under his wet grip.

"No saving that one. The virus had it. It was the only thing to do," he said in a soft voice.

Eiko625 cocked its head.

"Thanks," Keiji said, remembering the operation the Companion had performed on him, removing his own viral infection.

The Eiko nodded.

"Under certain specific circumstances, the virus can jump to crystalline chips," Keiji said to Ishikawa, who raised her eyebrow.

"That's what was happening to you?"

"Yes. It's gone now," he replied.

"Probably," Eiko625 added.

"Probably?" Ishikawa said, incredulous.

"The disinfection operation was a success," Keiji stated emphatically.

"Probably," Eiko625 added.

"Waitwaitwait, so it was a success or not?" Ishikawa asked, placing her hands on her hips.

"Most—" Eiko625 began, before being cut off by Keiji:

"Definitely." He followed this up with a frown in the Eiko's direction, whose eyebrows shot up, and slowly nodded in comprehension.

After an hour of waiting, no new events were reported on the radio, and Ishikawa and Keiji wondered if that was the end of the infection.

"I wanted to thank you, against my better judgement," Ishikawa said to Keiji.

"For what?"

"You had my back a few times there. I know some who would have let me have it. I... appreciate," she said, reluctantly.

"That's mighty big of you, Special Inspector. Can I ask a favour in return?"

"Shoot."

"Let's find Genzo Ito. Please," Keiji said. Eiko625 nodded emphatically, and both Ishikawa and Keiji wondered why.

"I have an idea about where to start. Right now, though, I need some rest," she said. They all boarded the car, leaving the coordinates for the cleanup crew to come and round up the parts left on the road, and Ishikawa drove the car to the nearest hotel they could find.

A Chiba branch of the Kanaya hotel chain stood mere two kilometres away, on the 350 Plateau. She put the car on autopilot, and they flew over the wet stacks of Chiba like low-flying birds under drizzling, cloudy skies. The Companion-built frames of Chiba factories were unique in their designs. Compact and vertical, they stood out from human-built structures found throughout Tokyo. Apart from the architecture of the Heights, it was Chiba 100 which held some of the city's most avant-guard constructions.

They rose between plateaux throughout the darkness, the upper reaches of the city illuminated by the searchlights and neons one came to expect from the more active parts of Tokyo.

A short flyover of the 350th and they had arrived.

Its arched entrance covered in neons stood out in heavy contrast to the surrounding ultra-modern buildings, but that had always been the appeal of the Kanaya Hotels. The original had been the first modern

Japanese hotel, modelled after the Western version of that type of accommodations.

It had been in the town of Nikko, in Tochigi Prefecture, now a long-gone memory that patrons could revisit through an in-house construct which was accessible in every room, if one were trode equipped.

Ishikawa liked it for its hand-made look. Old brick and columns that appeared made of wood. Keiji enjoyed them for their plush beds. They each took a room, and Eiko625 stayed in Keiji's.

Keiji had not realized how many days he'd been up until he fell asleep half-dressed on the bed. Eiko625 took off the remainder of his clothes, slipped him under the covers and went to stand guard by the door.

INSIGHT

In a city which hadn't slept in over three hundred years, it was rare to find peace. The area surrounding Meguro Station on the 250th was as calm a harbour as one could search out beneath The Heights. Its midnight lulls would find the lonely seated solo at tables for two in dimly-lit, tiny cafés with awnings almost too low to stand up.

Meguro Station itself was not a part of Meguro City, but was found in nearby Shinagawa Ward, and this, on all levels. It was a curiously Japanese trait to have kept the place names and approximate locations of so many city features, this even after the original Tokyo had been submerged.

Every level above that which preceded it was like a Ukiyo-e, a wood-block print copy—almost identical in its imprint, but having altered over time, like a faded painting.

The footprint rose, but retained its shape and feel. Each one had its own character and personality. One could have compared them to sets of quadruplets, each one an individual, retaining similar features to its brothers and sisters.

No one would have mistaken one plateau of the city for another, but each in turn gave a sense of déjà vu, ghost images.

Hundreds of years ago, rivers had been boxed in and rebuilt into canals, and these, too, had retained their names. Tradition was strong, and kept the national character thus.

Saito called into the office.

They confirmed Lopez' death.

From what the meditechs could gather, his chip had been

overloaded using localized microwaves, causing it to explode, sending shards throughout his brain. A method made infamous when Nabeen Singh had attempted to stop the insurrection within DaiSin. This was not secret among the leadership.

With Singh safely in his cage, the only entity who was supposed to have had knowledge of this usage was the Nexus. Yet how had they managed to get into range? This was a terrifying weapon, to be sure, but one which could only be used within the walls of the corporation. It was a matter of desynchronizing the resonance frequencies available throughout the Needle, and focusing these on any individual equipped with DaiSin trode sets. Being outside the area weakened the microwaves.

A weapon he had been brought to believe had been disabled. If not, there was a serious danger for anyone targeted. He might very well be one of those.

There was no other answer than the weapon was somehow still inside the Needle, being directed by some unknown entity under the Nexus' sway, killing at will. Lopez was therefore not the only link to the Nexus, in which case, he had to wrap up his investigation before all the guilty parties vanished.

The real trouble was this invisible nemesis, as it were.

SAITO SAN

A bubble appeared in the right-hand corner of his vision. He walked by twenty-story, convoluted glass business complexes, the streets almost quiet.

Along the sidewalks, Lilliputian tenders and carts, noodle shops, and vendors sat behind their stalls—introspective—waiting for the after-bar crowd to become active. The lull before a small rush of activity would begin.

Only a smattering of people made their way through the town, Shinagawa being a mostly residential area on this level.

Forty-story conapt blocks huddled in groups of ten massive octagonal constructions, with fair-sized balconies for those who could afford them. Similar-styled architecture in the groupings, clumps of mushrooms, long, curving walkways connecting these cities-within-cities every ten stories.

They reminded Saito of a more organic marble run game. He followed a route through the towers with an immense, imaginary steel ball, preoccupied.

Go ahead, he thought.

FURTHER INVESTIGATION INTO LINKS BETWEEN LOPEZ AND
KOBAYASHI HAVE UNCOVERED A HOST OF DEALINGS WHICH
COULD BE CONSIDERED DAMAGING TO THE CORPORATION.

Explain, he continued.

CREDITS TRANSFERRED TO KOBAYASHI FROM LOPEZ THROUGH
DUMMY FRONTS, USED TO BUILD AND MAINTAIN SECRET
RESEARCH LABS THROUGHOUT THE GREATER TOKYO AREA.
EMERGENT TECHNOLOGIES WERE "GIVEN" BACK TO MR. LOPEZ
IN ORDER TO SELL IN UNSANCTIONED BIDDING WARS ON
THE DARKNET TO UNKNOWN ENTITIES. STILL PROCESSING
CONNECTIONS. PROCEEDS OF SALES USED TO PAY FOR
GAMBLING DEBTS AND OTHER ILLICIT ENDEAVOURS.

Saito felt a sharp intake of breath, and hesitated a step before
continuing to walk.
Probability? He thought, pressing his thumb and index on his
temples.

100 PERCENT.

*Immediately cut off Mrs. Kobayashi from the DaiSin computer network
and have her authority revoked. Have security take her into custody,* he
replied. His head swam with the utter impossibility of this situation
having been allowed to happen.

MRS. NANAKO KOBAYASHI IS PRESENTLY UNACCOUNTED FOR.
DAISIN HAS NO JURISDICTION OUTSIDE THE NEEDLE.

Saito gritted his teeth.
*Keep me apprised of the situation. If she comes back in, I want her
taken downstairs, you understand?*

UNDERSTOOD.

Execute, he said, trying to the utmost not to pummel some random
object that came into his way. Saito was not by nature a violent man,
but there were situations where the release of anguish through kinetic
force could alleviate said frustration, and this was one of them. If there

hadn't been one of Administration's spies following him four feet behind him, he would certainly have let loose. Now was not the time.

"Where are you going, Saito San?" Scott Till said catching up to him.

"Keep up," he said, not bothering to turn around. Saito turned across the street and headed down one of the slim alleys which became rarer on the outskirts of Shinagawa. A cat Companion gave him the eye from a balcony, and he turned left. Through a small door in what looked like the hull of a wooden ship, he walked down the steps into the basement of the establishment.

Scott Till looked around himself, the look on his face one of a man who was thinking he'd been set up. If Saito had been paying attention, he'd have thought that that was probably the same look every government operative had at least once a day. When your job was to root out the evils of the city, who knew what dangers lurked behind every doorframe, around every corner.

"Sit," Saito said, designating a seat next to him. Till looked around, still feeling something suspect was underway, but eventually took the offered bench.

Saito activated a puck-sized device he took out of his coat pocket and placed it on the table, it flashed once, and the white noise generator cancelled out both the ambient noise from without, and disrupted their own voices as they exited the field.

"I hate chasing after people, Mr. Saito. It's one of my pet peeves," Till said, placing his hands in front of himself.

"Just the opposite of myself, then," Saito replied, smiling.

"You vanished from Shibuya. If I hadn't picked up your signal, that psycho would have cut you up like a nice shawarma," Till said.

"What are you trying to say, Till?" Saito asked, leaning over.

"I just want to know why you were trussed up against a wall about to be skewered. It's not part of your regular job description, I can only hope," Till said wryly.

"I'm not at liberty to say what my regular job description is, Till," Saito said, his eyes narrowing.

"You owe me. I want to know what's going on at DaiSin. All your little secrets. From what I see on the markets, shares are tanking. Might we finally see the fall of Goliath?" Till asked, showing a lot of white teeth.

Saito scratched his chin.

"Listen mate. We know for a *fact* DaiSin was involved in Douglas Deguchi's escape. That's who we want. I don't know if this whole thing has anything to do with it, but that man has to come back into custody. You don't seem to appreciate exactly how dangerous he is."

"Whatever you consider DaiSin, it's a stabilizing force in the city—"

At this, Till laughed out loud.

"A stabilizing—you're kidding me, right? No, my friend, DaiSin is many things, but not that. It's been a thorn in Administration's side for *centuries*. So what if you're going down?"

"You forget that it was DaiSin that made it possible to build this city. Without trode technology, there would be no Vertical City Tokyo. Only ruins at the bottom of Tokyo Bay," Saito said, splaying his hands.

Till made a great show of looking in all directions, as if to find a missing piece.

"Look! It's built! You've served your purpose. You can shut down the office now. We no longer require your services," he said, knocking a fist on the wood-like substance of the table.

"DaiSin is not finished, Mr. Till. Not by a long shot. What I'm going to tell you, I will do so because it is in both the interests of the Administration *and* DaiSin Corporation," Saito said.

Till was silent for a moment, his smile having evaporated for an instant.

"Go on," he said.

"You remember the Nexus incident from a few years back."

This was not a question. Anyone who was alive at the time was acutely aware of the day the giant red sun which glowed in the virtual skies exploded and fell on the DaiSin construct like a swarm of fiery bees.

Those who had not witnessed it firsthand had the opportunity to see it over and over again on replay from the countless recordings which had been done of the event.

"I might," Till said, sarcastically.

"That same Nexus is now threatening the city itself," Saito said. "It's starting with DaiSin, playing with its valuations. In another while, it'll go after the Eleven Karetsu, as well as Administration."

He paused for effect, looking at Till.

"Get it under control, then. So far, I don't see our involvement as warranted," he answered. Saito leaned back into his seat, resting his head against the leather. He considered for what seemed like a very long time before speaking.

"It was stolen from us. A well-organized group came in and took it from right underneath our noses," Saito said, hoping the lie would go over. There was no way he would tell the man that by their own negligence, the Nexus had found a way to leave on its own.

Till put his hand to his jaw and rubbed. He looked around at the rest of the pub, which was mostly empty. A lone bartender washed the counter with her clean white rag.

"Tell me, Saito San, what makes the Nexus so special? Why are you so intent on getting it back? What is it to DaiSin?" Till asked, putting his elbow across the table.

"You have to keep this to yourself, Till. I'm warning you. If my superiors find out I told you, I'm finished," Saito said, leaning further into the table. The effect was instantaneous.

"You have my word," Till said, closing his eyes in appreciation of the gravity of the situation, lifting a hand as if swearing a sacred oath. Saito glanced around, making sure that everything truly was safe.

"It's the only thing that can help us keep Administration and the Eleven at bay. It's getting help from the inside." Saito said. Only the latter half of this statement was true, but would add urgency to Till's involvement. Now was as good a time as any to find out what Administration's final policy on DaiSin was.

Till leaned back on his bench, crossing his arms.

"I'm not sure if you're telling me the truth, Saito San. No offence. What you're prattling on about, so far, sounds entirely like a 'you' problem, and not at all an 'us' problem. Honestly, if you're going to come to Administration for a hand with this, you should make sure that that problem doesn't involve getting rid of one of our biggest pain-in-the-ass. Without having to so much as lift a finger. I'm not sure you're making the best argument, here, is what I'm sayin'," Till said, cocking an eyebrow.

"Well, I did mention that the Administration would suffer from this. Let me paint a scenario: DaiSin is gone. You can celebrate, that's fine. What then? The Nexus is a self-learning machine. It may have started off as the memories of thousands of people. Now it's something else. Something that wants to grow and change, and evolve. It's using whatever resources are available around it, and it's using up and spitting out anything it can't control.

Who do you think will be next when DaiSin is gone, Mr. Till?

Who will be there to stop its appetites? Administration? The Eleven? You?" Saito added, extending a hand to designate the man to whom he was speaking.

Taz looked nonplussed.

"You talk about vague possibilities as if they were concrete truths. All I see is an ailing corporation with an AI problem, harbouring a high-profile criminal. If your Nexus does dispatch you, then so be it. The city will have to go on without you. I'm sure we'll manage," Till said, putting up his hands in a 'what-can-you-do?' sort of gesture.

"You're making a mistake, Till. The Nexus is not some bottom-rung toy AI that'll turn itself off when it's done playing," Saito said, growing angry.

Till smirked.

"You tell me it's getting help from the inside, yes? Well, it sounds to me like the Nexus doesn't need any help," Till said.

Saito's eyes went wide.

"What did you say?" he said out loud, more to himself than to Till who he had already dismissed as being more than useless.

"I said—" Till began, but Saito was getting out of his seat, picking up his voice cloaking device, and leaving.

"Where are you going? I still want you to tell me what you know about Deguchi. You owe me, remember? I saved your life," Till said.

Saito turned around and walked back to Till, placing his hands on the table.

"Forget about Deguchi. He's gone. As for me, you never saved anything, Scott Till. I'm a Companion. Thank you for your insight, though. You were most helpful."

Saito left the bar with Till wondering what had just happened, and he headed back to the Needle, calling an emergency meeting of the management as he did.

Whether Scott Till had wanted to get involved in this messy business or not in the first place, Saito had forced Administration's hand by getting the Nexus to notice them.

Thanks for saving me, he thought, and smiled.

REUNION

It was the last voice he'd wanted to hear. As the youth swivelled him around, Datu swung and hit, punching his son in the face mask, cracking it. Datu stared at his fist for a second in disbelief. Gabriel faltered, and he took advantage to run.

It had been a mistake to try and see his family, but now his biggest fear was to be taken in by his own son. He hoped the boy did not have backup in the vicinity. If so, Datu had no hope of getting back to Antoni, who hopefully was still sitting in the van waiting for him.

As Datu began to run, he was knocked over by what felt like a terminal velocity brick, straight to the spine. He heard the blast at the same instant. The side of his head hit the concrete, and a tremendous pain spread throughout his back.

He shot me! He thought.

Datu tried to regain his breath. He wanted to touch his back, to see what the damage was. He lifted himself on his elbows, looking down to see if his guts were spilling out of his stomach.

Nothing.

Apart from the intense burning sensation, the bullet hadn't broken his skin. Whatever armour he'd been equipped with was made of, it had done its job.

He coughed and tried to get up.

He was lucky that it was mid-morning, as most residents of the area were off to work, and he was left to confront the boy with very few witnesses.

As he slipped and flopped back onto the pavement, however, Gabriel's hands fell on the back of his shoulder, and he tried to push him off, throwing him back a few metres, his augmented cyborg strength making short order of his diminutive son.

Datu got up, pushing himself off the ground, and began to run again, this time with great difficulty.

A shot went off, the bullet ricocheting near his foot.

"Stop!" the boy said, as he sat on the ground. "I'm not going to tell you again. I won't miss your head with the next one."

Datu held still, his back to his son.

"Turn around," Gabriel said, the gun held level with his father's head. Datu did as he was told, looking for every opportunity to flee, and seeing none at hand.

He kept looking at the empty square where their home had been, his mind racing through the possibilities. He fervently wished Tala and the kids were safe, but had no idea if that were so.

Gabriel followed his gaze.

"What do you know about my family?" Gabriel said, waving the gun at Datu from a few metres away. Datu shook his head in negation, not sure what to answer.

"Take off the mask. I want to see your face," Gabriel said. Datu had never seen his boy like this. He was no longer the sullen child who spent most of his days listening to loud, angsty music in his room. He was now a confident, angry youth with a bone to pick.

Datu shook his head 'no' once again, and Gabriel grew impatient.

"Do it!" he yelled. Datu took a deep breath and put his hand to his face, unlatching the mask. As soon as he took it off, Gabriel's look of righteous anger fell to the ground.

"Dad?"

His gun wavered.

"Dad—what are you? What are you doing here? I don't understand—you're supposed to be *dead*!" he blurted out.

"I'm sorry Gabe," Datu said, his face grave.

"Sorry? What are you sorry for? For being alive?" Gabriel asked. "Where are mom and Benilda and Ramil?"

"I—I don't know. I came back to see them—to see you," Datu said. "Put down the gun, kiddo."

"Where have you been, dad? Mom's been gone for days! I came back last week and the *house* was gone! How does that happen, huh?" Gabe said.

"I don't know, *son*, maybe when you take things that don't belong to you, terrible things *happen*. Did you think about that?" Datu said.

His initial shock and terror of getting caught had passed, and he was now in the adrenaline spike of remembering the initiating domino drop which had started this whole abhorrent sequence of events.

Gabriel's face drained of colour, but his lip became stiff again.

He waved his gun in his father's face.

"So you're responsible for this?" Gabe said, pointing at the empty cubicle.

"No, asshole, *you* are! You stole from this family! You! You did this! For once in your life, take responsibility for your actions! If you hadn't stolen the Ayo, none of this would have happened! Get it into your thick skull!" Datu yelled, wanting nothing more than the opportunity to pounce on the brat and give him a solid right to the side of the head.

Gabriel gritted his teeth, a tear starting to grow in the corner of his eye.

"I'm taking you in, dad. We know it was you, yesterday at the diner. Whoever you're working for, you're in violation of Peoplift Inc. territorial agreements. No other security company is allowed to operate in this area without Admin approval. Pekelo Vora will want to talk to you personally. Maybe that'll jog your memory as to what happened to mom," Gabriel said, pure acid in his words.

Datu was tempted to correct him, but there would be no advantage in telling him that no, it wasn't a security outfit: it was a Companion kidnapping operation.

"Do you know what kind of boss Vora is?" Datu said.

"He can be rough, sure, but—" Gabriel answered before being cut off.

"He'll rob you. And when he's done getting what he wants from you, he'll get rid of you. It was your little security friends who tossed me over the side of the plateau and left me for dead in the Heap, son. That's what you have to look forward to," Datu said, shaking his head. He was done being angry with his son. What he felt now was more akin to pity.

He knew what sort of abusive miscreants they were, and now Gabriel was under their thumb. Whatever misgivings he might have had about his eldest, it stopped short of wanting his death.

"If you'd just let me take that stupid thing, none of this would have happened to you. And for the record, just because that's what happened to you, *dad*, doesn't mean it'll be my fate," Gabriel said defiantly. *There it was, the stupidity of youth*, Datu thought. If a person was a terrible human being to one man, did not make it a generalized statement. Idiot logic. How nice it would be to be that naïve again, he thought.

218

Datu thought of poor Antoni, still waiting at the border. He wondered if Midori Mamoru would dispatch someone to take him out because of Datu's error in judgment. He felt as if he'd been doing things a bit too impulsively of late: first trying to retrieve the Ayo, and now this.

Everything he'd done so far had resulted in disaster. Perhaps if he made better decisions, the consequences would be less dire. Ever since he'd been young, his rush to action had gotten the best of him. If it wasn't too late, he would enjoy trying to rewire his own brain for measured thinking. He now saw more of himself in his son, and the thought depressed him to no end.

This moment, however, was not meant for that. Now he was at the wrong end of a gun held by his own blood, waiting to be picked up by the goon squad, to be interrogated about his involvement with Midori Mamoru.

Great.

Arun would be furious.

Should he care, though? What did he have to lose, still? As far as he knew, Tala and the children might be dead. It was just one more terrible thing to befall him in a week of ordeals. He forced his mind away from that potentiality, like shooing away a vulture from carrion.

His hands quivered.

He felt so alone, in that microsecond in space. The universe had turned its back on him.

Truly, was there anything left in his life worth saving? He had to hope against hope that his family was in the clear, and that he'd find them! Allowing himself to plunge into the darkness would only guarantee that he would never see them again.

Until he had concrete proof one way or another, he had to believe that they were taken care of.

Had to.

The armoured Peoplift van rumbled down the road toward the two men. Datu's heart sank.

When it stopped, six feet away from them, Datu noticed that a small crowd had gathered. No more than a dozen bystanders, but it was more than he would have wished for. It was like airing out his dirty laundry in public. He would have preferred no witnesses to his humiliation.

One of the guards that stepped out of the tardigrade-shaped vehicle spotted Datu and was taken aback.

Obviously, he was not used to a dumped corpse coming back to life, let alone looking spry and healthy after a one hundred floor drop into the void.

The man came over to him and grabbed his wrist, attempting to put his arm behind his back. Datu's spine still hurt from the gunshot, but he resisted, and the man was unable to subdue him.

"Hands off," he said, pushing him. His body armour hid the fact that he was cyborgized now, and the guards remained unaware of the fact, but that didn't stop him from being surprised at the hard shove which almost toppled him.

Datu walked to the armoured vehicle, surrounded by five security guards. He sat on one of the bucket seats, but they made no attempt to tie him down this time.

Was this it? Had he given up? Where were his loyalties? Without Tala and the kids, he felt lost. He invoked Ayo, but she remained stubbornly silent. He remembered only one time when he'd felt this powerless.

***

"I need you to help me, son," his mother had said. She was sitting at the kitchen table. She was calm, but Datu could only imagine the turmoil she must have been enduring, in retrospect. There was only the light above the table to illuminate the room, which had the effect of an interrogation.

Used nicotine capsules filled the glass container in the middle of the table, and his mother reloaded her cigarette, the casing giving a click as she pulled the chamber.

Datu smoked as well, at the time, but his stomach had been in knots. The news had rocked him so hard his brain had gone in full shut-down mode, and he sat in front of his mother with one arm on the smooth empty table while she took a drag of her smoke.

She'd successfully quit, he thought, several months before. It was curious how grief made people go back to their bad habits.

Datu himself was tempted to run away, to go back to what he'd been doing the night previous with his gang.

At the time, he was hung over and had been since the morning. He'd gone out with his crew, raising hell on the rooftops of Sector 14. He'd tagged three high-profile buildings the previous night, all while being chased by automated drones.

He'd woken up to his mother sobbing. The news had come in early morning, unannounced, like a bill collector at meal time.

When was the best time for your father to die, anyhow?

Industrial accident. Sucked into a sinkhole at the work-site. They'd dug for a solid hour before giving up. The machines were caving in with him. Just wasn't worth it.

Datu's father was a respected employee. *Had been*, he corrected himself, just like everything else connected to his father was now past tense. This was before PeopLft Inc. had taken over. Back when they valued worker's lives. At least, more than they did now.

"Datu, my son, I need you to help me. To help *us*," his mother had said. And even though her voice was steady, there was a harshness to it. An urgency. It told him to wake up. To grow up. That play time was over, and his family needed him. All uttered in the tender, motherly way that broached no denial.

He knew, as well, that if he did not accede to his mother's wishes, they would all end up on the street.

That didn't stop him from feeling the unfairness of it all. As if his father had been the architect of the theft of his youth. Knowing one thing in your head and feeling it in your heart were two completely different things.

It was in that moment, through the purple, pallid smoke of his mother's cigarette, under the kitchen light's too-bright glare, that he felt the yawning maw of nothingness. A kind of system reset to his life, where the unwritten, unknowable program was the cause of all his anxieties.

"What will happen?"

At his mother's behest, he'd started going to church. Maybe following Ayo would help him find his path, she'd suggested. The company that had allowed his father's death had found him a place among their ranks, oh supreme irony.

He'd started out digging with a hydraulic jackhammer, but eventually became a much-valued steady-bucket operator.

And then he'd met Tala.

But it had all started with a plea for help, and the tearing away of his youth like some back-alley black market surgeon, in one single day.

The cancer had jumped his mother a few years later, and he didn't talk to his sisters much anymore, but the loss of his father had been the thing which had taken his head out of the clouds and slammed it firmly onto the plateau of Sector 14 as some inescapable reality.

He'd tossed his last cigarette cartridge on the day of his mother's funeral.

Perhaps he'd dreamt of better things for himself until that point. He vaguely remembered the nebulous fantasies he'd envisioned on those nights of highrise gap-jumping. He never resented his mother. It was just something he had to do. For the family.

Thinking back on it, the decision hadn't been made for him. He'd wanted to help his family. The wiping away of his previous life, and the deep empty he'd felt for a time afterward, those were like the leaps of faith he had taken when parkouring throughout Sector 14.

There was no way of knowing if you would land safely.

Ever.

There was only the leap, the faith, and the potentiality of a foothold when the emptiness subsided, nothing more. Wishing or hoping for some miracle intervention was hubris, and he knew that now. All he could do was stay steady in what he believed in and try to do his best for the people around him.

That's what made it so difficult for him to accept that his son was in league with those who'd killed him. He was going *against* his family. Not just in this, but by having stolen the heirloom.

Did it matter still that the Ayo was not what he'd always thought it was? Datu had been living under a perfect little umbrella for the past sixteen years. It could pour and rain at will around them, but he had his family keeping him safe from all that.

If one thing should have stuck in his mind, was that nothing remained in stasis. Everything changed, and nothing could be done do to stop that.

Now he truly saw what the world was made of, because it had come for him and taken everything he cared about.

Again.

But no, he had to continue believing Tala and the kids could be found and saved, according to the promise which had been made to him, and signed in virtual blood on a contract.

How many times did a man have to steel himself against the storm which threatened to destroy him? How many waves of misfortune could be weathered until one had to say 'enough!'

Datu had no idea, but he was weary of it all.

***

Pekelo Vora was not happy to see him. He hid it under a mask of forced joviality that could only be mistaken for genuine if one were to ignore his forked tongue.

"Back so soon! We weren't expecting you to visit the area again," He said, sitting down at his desk as two guards framed Datu in his low chair.

"You did try to murder me, so I understand your surprise," Datu said. There was no nervousness anymore. Inside his chest, there was a black hole, growing steadily larger as the minutes ticked by. He wondered how long he should let it grow before he let it consume everyone in the room.

The Ayo were gone from the shelf. Did Vora think Datu would try to take them again, or had the man realized the insensitive nature of his display?

Gabriel had been sent on some sort of errand, and had left after minor protest. It looked to Datu as if the boy had regretted calling his father in, after all. Too little, too late.

He still wasn't angry with his son. But he sure wished he'd made some different decisions.

"I see you've found a job. You'll have to tell us who you're working for. It just won't do to have competition in Sector 14. This is my town," Vora said, thumbing his chest.

"Administration, in fact. They're doing investigations into crooked business practices. Tell me how you get your equipment rent-free and charge your employees for it. My bosses would love to know. It's a special kind of corruption they just enjoy digging up. Maybe you'll be visiting the Heap after a short fall as well, who knows?" Datu said, smiling broadly.

"Is he wired?" Vora said, frowning and pointing at Datu while looking to each guard in turn. The other guards shook their heads in the negative.

"Listen to me, Salazar. I don't know what you're playing at, but I'm not game. You're going to tell me who you're working for, or else," Vora said, drawing nearer to Datu.

"Or else you'll have me killed again? You lack imagination, Vora." Datu said, raising an eyebrow.

"Who said anything about you?" Vora said, turning back toward his desk.

Datu was growing increasingly annoyed of having his family threatened.

Just then, a short knock came at his office door. One of the security guards went to answer, and he was pushed out of the way by a well-dressed woman.

"Who are you?" Vora asked. Datu couldn't see the woman behind him, but the irritation in Vora's voice didn't bode well.

"Yui Endo. I represent Mr Salazar," Datu heard her say, and it took an instant for him to register that this was his boss. *That* Yui. His head whipped around, and Yui gave him a nod. Datu felt his heart squeeze inside his chest, the black hole replaced with a sentiment of deep dread.

A security guard put up his hand to block her passage, which she touched lightly and watched him recoil in pain, as if he'd been stung.

Two more guards came to place themselves between Yui and Vora, and she stopped, lifting a hand before her, her index finger in a tut-tut sort of motion. Disappointment could be read on her usually stern features.

"Really? I came here to talk, Mr. Vora. I don't think you appreciate the patience my employer is forcing me to have with these shenanigans of yours," she said, staring straight at Vora, who had taken a step back to his desk.

He gave a nod to the guards, who got out of Yui's way.

"Better. You are to release my client at once. Any further hindrance will entail legal action," Yui said, standing by Datu and placing one hand on his shoulder. To him it felt like being held by pincers of ice.

"Just a moment, Mrs. Endo. I don't even know who your employer *is*. The presence of Mr. Salazar under their employ, on *my* territory infringes on my exploitation rights. Something I know the Administration upholds assiduously," Vora said, growing bolder and taking a step toward Yui and Datu.

"Very well, Vora. I've been given permission by my employer, the Konak Security Collective, to make reparations for Mr. Salazar's trespass. As well, we would like to discuss the borders of your territory, so as not to impinge again. Konak would like to do business on an amicable basis," Yui said, taking a tablet out of her bag. She turned it on and handed it to the man. He scrolled through the proffered contract, his finger hovering for a moment when he came to the monetary settlement, his eyes wide, then continued to the bottom.

"That's a lot of money," he whispered, licking his lips involuntarily.

"A show of good faith," Yui said, a tight smile spreading on her lips.

"Peoplift will require percentages for incursions perpetrated outside Konak's boundaries. We want to keep Konak safe. It's just standard procedure," Vora said, signing at the bottom of the contract with a stylus.

Is this idiot really trying to blackmail Yui for protection money? Datu thought, with an intake of breath.

"Of course, of course. We would be happy to donate to the cause at this juncture," Yui said, pulling Datu up by the shoulder pad. He rose to his feet, aware of the menacing posture of the security guards.

Vora showed his own tablet, with an exorbitant amount printed at the bottom of the screen. Yui didn't even blink. She took out the company credit card and tapped both the trespass settlement and bribery money on Vora's tablet.

"I take it this settles our score, Mr. Vora? With your permission, we will be taking our leave," Yui said. Before anyone could object, or add extra "fees," she was dragging Datu by the arm out of the office, down the stairs and out the door.

A sparkling red race hovercar waited at the front steps, looking as if it had been abandoned in mid-stride by its owner.

Yui unlocked the doors and pushed Datu onto the passenger's side She waited before both doors were closed before speaking again.

"What did you tell them?" she said to Datu as they walked out the exit.

"Nothing. I told them nothing," he said.

A small automated voice from the console piped up.

"Voice analysis confirmed. Subject is telling the truth."

"That's the only thing keeping you alive at the moment, Salazar. You are lucky we still need you, or I would have let them finish you in an instant. What the Hell were you thinking coming here?" she yelled.

"I wanted to see my family. I just wanted to be with them again," he said, hanging his head.

"You're lucky it was these assholes that caught you and not the cops, Salazar."

Yui ordered the car out of the area. They took the road instead of the skies, and came to the border crossing, where the car was duly scanned.

The Companions waved the car through.

On the dashboard, Datu saw that several microdrones had attached themselves to the undercarriage of the car. As they crossed into the Chiba Industrial Zone, she pressed a button, and Datu felt tension on the car as an electrical current zapped the drones.

They did not return to the hidden elevator on the edge of Chiba. Yui drove to a derelict factory—a vertical steel-covered box where Datu guessed there was a landing pad on the roof for loading and unloading goods. The style had passed in the last thirty years, and this particular factory appeared to have fallen into decay for that amount of time. Rust-streaks had grown unabated along its sides like dark-brown waterfalls. To such a degree that in some of the more weathered areas, holes had begun to poke through the metallic covering, revealing empty rooms and derelict machinery within.

Yui led him through the ground floor garage. Datu did not resist, knowing that inside her hand was some sort of deadly shock device which she would not hesitate to use should he attempt a runner.

Large, dirty grey tarps covered squarish shapes in the corners of the room, and Datu assumed this was where Yui stored the trucks they used to accompany the stolen Companions back to the warehouse and beyond.

She led him to a sub-basement where one large empty room led to smaller ones along its walls. A dull blue light glowed from rows of LEDs along the ceiling, giving a ghostly glow to the tiled floors, like an after-hours visit to a haunted public pool. She abandoned him alone in the enormous space and locked the doors behind her.

There was nothing in the room.

Perhaps at some point it had been a storage space for volatile chemicals. The smell of heavy-duty thinners permeated the walls.

After the door closed, he was left in pure darkness. He eventually found a wall, but had no idea where the door which led upstairs was located. There was no blanket or bed, but he eventually lay down, closing his eyes. He did not want to sleep, but felt his energy had been depleted.

Soon, he was dreaming.

It was daytime on the beach where Aimee Flores lived. He could see her in the distance, on a small sailboat a few hundred yards away. It bobbed up and down on the waves, the turquoise shimmering with the light of the sun.

She must have seen him, because her arm went up in a wave. Datu stuck his hands in his pockets. He heard a two-tone beeping sound, and the woman stood beside him on the beach.

Datu jumped, almost falling onto the sand.

"You can't say I didn't warn you this time," Aimee said, smiling.

"Did you, though?" Datu said, angrily.

"Yes, the tone!"

"How kind of you," Datu replied, almost in a pout.

The events of the day replayed in Datu's mind in slow motion as he stared out onto the vast ocean. The fact that he wanted to regain the Ayo that had been stolen, but now stood facing her.

"My son stole you," he finally said, to which Aimee Flores had a comical reaction. Her face contorted in disbelief and hilarity, and Datu had no idea how to react to her facial gymnastics.

"He *what*?" she replied, after having taken back control, laughing as she did.

"A version of you. It's complicated. I don't know what I'm saying. You do know you're *the* Ayo, right? The Goddess that Filipinos and Filipinas worship?"

Aimee stopped laughing and looked at Datu with a curious glance.

"Whatever you think I am, that's not me. People always deify or demonize, but the truth is, no one's a god, Datu. We don't have it in us. Especially me!" she exclaimed, letting out a bark of laughter.

"You know, before we had to abandon the islands, she worked at the hospital. She was a nurse."

"Who's she?"

"This person you worship."

"So you do remember."

"I do, but I'm not supposed to. Listen, it's like seeing the memories of some other person. It's me and it's not-me at the same time. I call her she, but we both know who she is."

Datu nodded gravely.

"She was working when she saw it—the thin grey line on the horizon. She was in the tallest building at the time, and she could see the rush as it came toward the shore. She called it in to the government office, and the alarm rang out almost immediately. They started packing people up and rushing them to the shore from the hospital..."

She paused, lost in thought.

"Why didn't you—she bring the patients to the roof of the hospital?"

"It was a monster wave, Datu. If you had seen this thing, you would have thought you were going to die, right there. I'm not exaggerating. Anyhow, they managed to get a few people to the beach and onto the boats. There was a scramble to put as much distance between they and the wave before it hit. Almost didn't make it."

Datu felt as if the air had become chill. Clouds had begun to gather overhead. In the distance, a thin grey line approached. A line which grew thicker, larger with every passing second.

"Aimee, are you doing this?" he cried.

She shook her head, and the ocean became calm again. The skies returned to their cloudless state.

"Mmmm?" she said, turning to him now.

"Where did you go?" Datu said, glancing nervously about, expecting some other calamity to befall the construct.

"Datu, you have one more chance before Arun does something drastic to you, contract or no contract. I'm going to help you," the woman said, smiling.

"Why are you doing this," Datu said.

"Because I like you. And that's what people do. They help each other. Besides, the things this gang of thugs has been up to? I swear. It's not right. I may try to look dumb around Arun and his followers, but

I'm a little more aware than he knows," Aimee said, winking.

"Try to get some sleep," she said, and snapped her fingers, turning day to night. Datu nodded and went inside the small house, laying down alone and closing his eyes. He was having the strangest dreams these days.

EXPLOSIVE

Breakfast in the Kanaya Hotel had been, for the last four hundred years, a sacred affair. Served in a Continental Breakfast buffet style, it combined traditional Japanese fare and the kinds of dishes European countries had served in the past, and only the very wealthiest now enjoyed.

Ishikawa sat with Keiji at a table for four while Eiko625 stood, not wanting to break one of the fragile-looking white chairs the other two were using.

"How do you feel, honestly?" Ishikawa asked over a mouthful of wakame, and cringing at what passed as coffee.

"Much better, Inspector. Despite what the Eiko might say, I feel the virus has been wiped from the crystalline chip. I just want to get on with the investigation," he said, taking a bite of toast.

"Good. I wouldn't want to return you to your father as damaged goods. It would do nothing for my career," she said, smiling wryly.

"You said you had a lead as to where to look next?" Keiji said, changing the subject. He placed his chin on his fists, his elbows on the table's white cloth.

"While you were diving the Companion last night, I had time to go into the van that almost hit us. It wasn't some random hit-and-run. It was one of the pickup vehicles we got smashed by beforehand. I found thermite explosives inside," she said, leaning over the table.

"What? Are you serious?" Keiji said in disbelief.

"Tracking numbers and all. We have to go check out the source in a bit," Ishikawa said.

"What kind of backup are you going to have for this?" Keiji asked. He was thinking of the previous day, where not a single police vehicle had shown while they were being attacked on two fronts.

"Just you and me, kid. And the Eiko," Ishikawa said, grimacing at her last sip of coffee, shaking her head and putting the white china cup down on its saucer.

"Are you insane?" Keiji said in a harsh whisper. A woman in a translucent opal veil turned to stare from an adjacent table, then went back to her meal, lifting the veil to take a small bite, then lowering it again.

"The explosives are Administration registered. It's an equipment depot down near Chiba. Don't worry. I'm pretty sure they were stolen from there, so there's no danger to any of us," Ishikawa said. "Still worth going to take a look and see what I can find out, though."

Keiji shrugged, feeling somewhat relieved, but having been on the receiving end of a coordinated Companion attack, it would take more than the Special Inspector's reassurances to put his mind at ease.

"How much did this place cost you?" Keiji asked rhetorically. He'd stayed in similar hotels, and better ones. He knew how much they ran, and was surprised that an officer like Ishikawa could afford a night's stay, let alone for both of them.

"Oh, don't worry, it's taken care of," she said, smiling.

"Administration pays for this?" Keiji asked, incredulous.

"No, your father will," she said.

The valet drove her dented car to the front of the hotel, and Ishikawa mentally sighed, seeing it in such disrepair. It might be hers, but she could imagine the kind of drumming down she might get about it when she got back to HQ. Especially if she didn't find something to show for it.

So far this morning, there had been no more news of Companion disturbances, which made her mentally cross her fingers that Keiji had been right in having all of them cut off wireless access.

There was still the possibility that they were triggered otherwise, but that chance seemed to get lower and lower as time went by. She only hoped that this wasn't the precursor to some massive outbreak, in a manner that neither of them had imagined.

Eiko625 got in the back of the car this time, folding itself in a way that would have made a human either uncomfortable or nauseous, and did not say a word about it.

Keiji sat on the front passenger seat, looking much improved from the rest.

Ishikawa aimed the car for Chiba 100 and they headed downward once more, taking the opposite route of the previous night. This time, however, the vehicle veered off on a tangent, heading toward a part of Chiba even more sombre than the factory levels.

It reminded Keiji of Shibuya 150, or at least what he'd heard of it, but as a residential area. A tall, perhaps twenty foot fence surrounded the entire plateau, within which the tall, drab shapes of high-rise con-apts loomed. He realized with rising panic that they were going straight into the dreaded Sector 14.

"Well that's ominous," he muttered.

Ishikawa stayed silent, piloting the car near the enclosure fence, the onboard computer communicating her ID and intentions as she flew over it and into the heart of the place.

Keiji watched in fascination at the decrepitude spreading about him. It reminded him of warzones and abandoned places. Like those cities in Western France when the Nuclear Silos had been left derelict for too long and begun leaking radioactive waste. He pictured much of those cities resembling this one—broken windows and cored out buildings, and whoever had had the audacity of staying behind being reduced to unimaginable poverty.

Then again, those French citizens had had somewhere to go. The story of the denizens of Sector 14 was a much sadder and more complicated one. Keiji wondered if the place was a kind of oubliette: an open-air prison where Administration had quarantined its people to forget about them.

In a manner of speaking, they had. Sector 14 never made it into the news, apart from the occasional outbursts of extreme violence that would rock it from time-to-time, to be repressed and contained by public security.

He remembered watching some of these episodes on holovid when he was younger and could still stand his father. They'd sit on the wide, candy-striped canapé together, his mother and father each with their glass of red wine, and he would eat popcorn as security forces would go into Sector 14 with their armoured vehicles and shoot flamethrowers at whatever resistance they encountered.

His mother's 'ooooos' and 'aaaaaaaas' had especially marked him, as well as the expressions of glee from his father when some poor sod in a mask got a face full of napalm.

His eyes must have glowed in the firelight of the holovid, the crunching of the popcorn filling his ears as he watched burning people fall to the ground in agony.

The last fifteen years had been a much calmer time. Sector 14 was barely mentioned anymore, but it retained its stigma as a place of death to whoever was foolish enough to set foot in it uninvited—which is what they were about to do.

Looking at Ishikawa's face, he would never have thought that she had any misgivings about their current course of action. He felt jealousy at her unflappable demeanour.

Eventually they landed in a wide courtyard where an array of different machinery was parked, a large faded sign reading 'Administration Supply Yard' in a corner. The heavy-duty machinery was that highlighter neon yellow that reminded Keiji of a K-bazz addict's piss—something in the injectable drug which screwed with liver functions. You could have mistaken it for motor oil by the side of walls if it hadn't been for the smell.

He put his rebreather back on, stepping onto the tarmac of the silent space. Everything was eerie here. If he'd thought the factory floor was silent and foggy, that's because he had not yet experienced the desolation of Sector 14.

They stood within an enclosure outside of which a highway on-ramp abruptly ended at its peak, as if whoever had built it had changed their minds before completion. The project had been left hanging for many decades, as the smartcrete which was supposed to regenerate any cracks or lesions had begun to malfunction. Large concrete blooms, like grey dandelions sprouted from side supports, pushing themselves through the fence like trees grew around obstacles. Keiji found it slightly disturbing, but the Inspector looked unfazed, as always.

She walked toward the long, low building in wide, deliberate strides, followed closely behind by Eiko625. Keiji took one last look around the vicinity before hurrying to catch up.

The storage building had one small garage door, and light shone out the side window, near the front entrance. It looked like the sort of shop where a person could rent cheap tools and launder dirty money, both in equal measures.

Ishikawa rang the doorbell and waited a moment or so before pressing it again. The light within turned off.

She pressed the doorbell repeatedly for a minute or so before a voice over a speaker came thundering from the corner of the building.

"What do you want?" a gravely timbre yelled.

"Special Inspector Mariko Ishikawa, Tokyo PD. I'd like to ask you some questions," she said.

"Who are your friends?" The voice asked. She could see the lens focusing on the camera behind them.

"My associates," she replied.

"What kind of Special Inspector has a boy and a Companion as associates?" the voice asked.

Ishikawa could feel herself losing patience again, her hands clenching reflexively.

"I'm going to give you until the count of three. After that, I'm going to order a full audit of your supply depot. Don't make me do it. It's never fun, even when you have nothing to hide," she said, looking straight into the camera.

There was a silent pause, and they heard the buzzing of the door as the person inside pressed the unlocking mechanism.

"Thank you," she said, forcing a smile. She pushed the door open, and the tiny entrance was a waiting room with two stained red plastic chairs on her left. The kind you picked up in the trash when they shut down a community centre.

To her right was a wicket over a counter, the height and breadth of which was covered in grey metal pawn shop grating, the only opening a bank teller's divot in the counter.

The light had returned to the entrance, where the side window was situated, but the back-store remained plunged in darkness.

Beside the wicket were a metal door with a small pane of security glass at head height and a three-year-old calendar of places to see on the periphery of Tokyo. Whoever was in charge had last turned the page in November.

"Hello?" Ishikawa said. When the door closed, it did so with the 'clack' of an internal deadbolt slamming into the door-jamb.

A head popped over the wicket. An Asian man no more than four-foot-five climbed up the stool behind the wicket and sat down.

"What's a dirty cop and her goons doing in Sector 14?" The man asked, criss-crossing his fingers together and setting his hands down on the counter before him. He had the look of a person who'd just been interrupted during important business for trivial reasons. From his demeanour, it would not have surprised Ishikawa that he would attempt to send them on their merry way just so he could resume said important business. She refused to take the bait, bowed, and said, "Enyo Morinaga San. I find your welcome most lacking in social graces, especially for one representing the interests of the Administration, regardless of location," to which the man behind the counter rolled his eyes, "We're here to have a few questions answered, and then we'll be out of your most illustrious way."

"Do you always get what you want with threats and flattery, *cop*?"

the man sneered.

"Not always," Ishikawa smiled, pulling back her trenchcoat to reveal her holstered gun.

"Fine. Come in," the man named Morinaga said. Once again a buzzer sounded, and the side door opened. Ishikawa stepped through, followed by Eiko625 and Keiji. Morinaga turned on half the shop lights, revealing a few exos, the power augmentation suits used on construction sites.

The smell of oil and industrial degreasers permeated the air. An air of abandon filled the room, as if those tools found in the vicinity had had no users in over a decade. There were proper racks on the walls, but most of the heavy-duty equipment lay on the floor, either sprawled or in stacks.

Quite a few were the 'danger-tape-yellow' colour of warning label. Keiji spotted what looked like a partially assembled Companion in one corner. One of its arms was on a work bench, and the leg opposite that arm was disjointed at the knee, and only held onto the thigh through its energy tubes.

Along another wall was an empty vertical shelving row labelled 'industrial cutting lasers.' Where there should have been ten, there were none. Perhaps they'd been borrowed?

"What are you doing here, anyway? I thought Administration had forgotten all about ol' Enyo Morinaga," the man said, walking past Keiji and turning around, his hand on a cane. In the penumbra, Keiji had mistaken him for a much younger man.

It was now apparent under this light that he was in his sixties, greying, and walked with a limp.

"Looking for some info about thermite explosives," Ishikawa said. While she was talking to Morinaga, Keiji wandered along the rows of discarded equipment, wondering who would come in and rent these old things.

"Thermite, eh?" the man said, a look of curiosity in his eyes. "Don't touch anything, kid!" he yelled at Keiji, making him jump. "You break, you pay!" he continued, laughing a bit to himself. Keiji realized this was probably the man's go-to line, because none of the objects in the warehouse could ever be considered 'brittle.'

Keiji turned a corner and was out of sight from Ishikawa and Morinaga. Eiko625 was somewhere on the other side of the room, picking up pieces of tech with mild curiosity, possibly because whatever was stored here predated him and he simply did not know what it might be for.

Along a support beam, he found a terminal and couldn't resist tapping into it. The antiquated password-protect cracked in an instant and he was in the warehouse's inventory. He could hear Morinaga grumbling to Ishikawa about how difficult it was to work there alone, and that he barely got any company.

From what Keiji understood, this supply depot only served one purpose—to give the needed armour suits for a recycler company named Peoplift, whose HQ was on the edge of the plateau. He cycled through the various types of explosives they possessed, the re-supply chain when they came to run out, as well as whatever else Peoplift might require.

Nowadays, requisition for new suits was done on a case-by-case basis, the technology evolving rapidly enough that ordering in bulk was no longer cost-effective when compared to the rate of obsolescence. The overstock littering the floors of the warehouse was the price of that lesson learned. Since Administration cared little for wasting its purchases, there was a high probability the exos would remain there for decades to come.

There presently was supposed to be six pallets of thermite in the lock-box. Peoplift had recently picked up two.

Out of curiosity, he checked the cutting lasers manifesto. Apparently, they also should have been there.

He heard Morinaga's grating voice as they approached, and he disconnect, stepping away from the terminal.

"Don't touch anything!" Morinaga said, as he spotted Keiji a little ways away. "And get your artificial out of my stuff, too," he reiterated, pointing an accusatory finger at Eiko625 who stood up after letting go of an armour helmet and pointing a finger at himself in a 'who, me?' gesture.

"Like I said," the man continued, "I only deal with the one company down here. There is no other game in town. Everything else closed up shop years ago."

They walked toward a large metal door with no discernible markings, and Morinaga put his card key into a slot by the door, an audible buzzing resounding.

The door slowly opened, and Ishikawa noticed its thickness.

"Have you had any problems with theft in the past few months?" Ishikawa asked.

Morinaga gravely shook his head.

"This place is a bunker. Sorry I gave you the asshole treatment earlier. The only people who come knocking usually are high on something or trying to figure out if I'm gone so they can try to break in. Not going to happen," the man said, winking to Ishikawa.

Within the smaller room were barren concrete floors, the complete opposite of the messy storage area. Along the walls were orange adjustable metal shelves, upon which were pallets of boxes.

Morinaga hobbled his way to the third shelf in the room.

"There. You see? It's all there. Five pallets of thermite explosives. They use the stuff to blow out big holes in the trash. Makes it easier to get to the goods underneath. Dangerous, though, thermite."

An assortment of other goods populated the lock-room. All sorts of heavy-duty ordnance as well as larger-scale weapons which couldn't be found at the local street-thugs' hideout. Keiji walked around, pretending to inspect the various artefacts, under the scrupulous eye of the Admin employee.

"Where's the sixth pallet?" he finally said, turning to Morinaga, with an innocent look on his face.

The old man squinted, his face turning sour. He tapped his cane on the floor once, and Ishikawa thought she heard a rustle from the other end of the supply warehouse.

"What do you mean, the sixth? There are only five. Can't you count, boy?" he said, glancing sideways. Ishikawa tried to get closer to the door.

"The manifest says there are six pallets," Keiji repeated. Ishikawa looked at the old man and walked toward him.

"I see someone's been snoopin'. I told you not to go poking about, young man," Morinaga said, taking a step back.

"Perhaps you've found other customers, Mr. Morinaga. I was going to visit this client of yours, but I guess that won't be necessary now, will it?" Ishikawa said.

As she was reaching out to grab Morinaga, the heavy door began to close, the old man slipping out at the last moment. As Eiko625 ran to it to stop it from closing, his fists hit something a lot harder than he was expecting, and the heavy metal door closed on the three of them with a resounding 'clang.'

Before it had, Keiji was sure he saw the looming shadow of the Companion he'd spied in detached pieces earlier. That door had no other way of closing on its own.

Ishikawa pounded the safe door with all her might, ordering Morinaga to open it. She threatened to call Administration police on her.

A speaker piped up from the corner of the room, and the man's cracked pipes spoke up.

"I'm no fool, Inspector. No backup is on the way for you. You can try calling, but you're inside a dampening field. No signals in or out. That was meant to stop those jokers out there from remotely detonating these explosives," the man chuckled to himself.

Ishikawa called out. "Who are they, Morinaga? Who did you sell the thermite to?"

"I guess it doesn't matter now, anyway. Some man named Arun. Said he worked for a tech company. I call bullshit. You know, when someone shows you a big suitcase full of New Yen, it doesn't matter what you think," Morinaga answered.

"Why'd you betray the Administration, Morinaga?" Ishikawa asked.

"You're pretty full of yourself, aren't you, Inspector? If I were you, I'd save my breath. There are no air intakes in that room. You talk too much, you'll go out like a light sooner than you expect," the man said, and the crackle of the microphone told them that the conversation was over.

"Shallow breaths, Keiji," Ishikawa said, as the youth looked as if he were about to hyperventilate.

Eiko625 went around the room once, its hands against the walls. When it had done one full round, it turned to Ishikawa and said: "I've done a vibration scan, and I'm sorry to report that the walls are ten inches thick and reinforced with steel plating. Also, Morinaga was not lying. There is a low ampere dampening field surrounding us, preventing all incoming or outgoing energy pulses. We will not be able to use the Net to communicate our present position."

"Great. If I can't hack my way out of this, I guess we're screwed," Keiji said. She gave him a withering glance.

"I don't want to ruin your deathwish, Mr. Uehara, but I for one intend on getting out of here," Ishikawa said, wandering from box to box, inspecting the labels of each one.

Eiko625 began taking a closer look at other closed boxes and opened one, reaching inside.

"What's that?" Keiji asked.

"High explosives, Keiji San," it replied.

"Take some, they might come in handy some day," the boy said, an edge of sarcasm in his voice.

The Companion nodded thoughtfully and slipped one of the grenades inside a hidden compartment near his stomach.

Ishikawa opened a cardboard container and removed an aluminum tube adorned with the symbol for corrosion, and placed it on the ground. From another box, she removed a flat panel and placed it next to the tube.

She then went to the one of the boxes of thermite and carefully removed one of the grenades from its nesting place. She gently deposited it near the canister, on the flat panel of cardboard.

"Gum," she said to Keiji, holding out her hand. Keiji hesitated a moment, then spat into the inspector's hand.

"All of it," she said, and the youth reached into his pocket, pulling out a full pack. She began unwrapping the gum handing Keiji half, and putting the rest in her own mouth.

"Chew," she said, her own mouth full of gum. Keiji complied, not really understanding her purpose, but trusting she at least had some idea of what she was doing.

Ishikawa then asked Eiko625 to separate the top and bottom of the thermite grenade, and he picked it up, moving to the far side of the room where some of the lesser explosives and weapons were stored, and twisted the top off with a careful turn of its wrists.

As it did so, Ishikawa took out her pocket knife and began to scrape the side of the aluminum canister, tiny shavings falling onto the makeshift cardboard lab.

Eiko625 brought back both halves and handed them to Ishikawa, who carefully emptied the iron ore powder mixture on top of the aluminum shavings. She then took the wad of gum and pushed it into the mixture, rolling it and kneading it until she had depleted the powder on the cardboard.

She then rolled out the gum into a long, thin tube and rose to her feet.

Ishikawa wedged the gum-snake as far into the crack of the door opening as she could. She then took out a small torch from her side pocket and handed it to Eiko625.

Her breathing was becoming laboured, her head spinning. She could feel the onset of asphyxia coming, which meant that they had little time to escape before passing out.

"When I say go, you light the bottom of that thermite. Then you push the door open when it's all burnt out. Understood?" she said, opening her coat to take out her gun. It was getting harder and harder to breathe. Keiji was sitting on the ground, his head lolling side-to-side.

"Go!" she said, and the Eiko unit fired up the base of the thermite. It took a moment to ignite, as there was not as much magnesium as she would have hoped in the aluminum surface. She was afraid it would not ignite at all, in fact. However, after a few seconds, a white hot flame burst from the bottom of the iron-oxyde-filled gum, quickly running along its length, spitting out sparks. Eiko625 placed himself a bit further away from the door to avoid being hit.

Within ten seconds, the thermite reaction was over, and a long, bright red gash had burned through the door's metal. Eiko625 placed both his hands on it and gave it a hard shove. There was a wrenching sound as the remainder of the locking mechanism broke off its hinges, and the door swung open.

"Duck!" Ishikawa yelled, as the military Companion rushed into the room, holding a fully-automatic long-gun. As Eiko625 went down, she unloaded into the Companion's head and sensory apparatus. Its gun went downward to shoot at its greatest threat, the Eiko.

Eiko625 reacted swiftly, grabbing the end of the gun and folding it in half, rendering it useless. While he was destroying the Companion's weapon, it had let go of it and begun swinging at Eiko625. The Eiko lifted the folded gun and caught the incoming swing with it, using its opportunity to hit the assailant with the gun as its arm was pushed out of the way, sending the Companion reeling into the safe door with a dull thud.

Eiko625 got up, rushing the Companion, and sent it flying into the pile of used construction equipment several feet away. Unfazed, the Companion picked itself up and jumped back to where Eiko625 was standing, giving the Eiko a swift kick in the mid-section, which made it crash against a shelving unit along the wall near the vault.

Eiko625 extricated itself and assaulted the Companion once again. As the foe picked up a bulky transformer from the ground to throw it at the Eiko, the Companion punched the military model in the neck, which it caught with its chin and held against its breast-plate.

The Eiko reached up with its other hand and twisted several of the Companions' fingers, while kicking its opposite kneecap.

This rendered it unbalanced, and as it fell sideways, the transformer fell on its neck, severing part of the connectors which controlled its right arm.

Eiko625 retrieved its hand before falling with the combat model, and took a step back. The Companion pushed the heavy transformer block off itself with a shrug and gave a good, swift sweeping kick to the Eiko, sending him sideways before he caught his fall with his left hand.

As the military Companion got up, it looked down on Eiko625, and began to assail it with kicks, which it avoided by rolling in the opposite direction.

When it had Eiko625 cornered, it continued to kick, this time connecting hard with its head.

On its third kick, however, it stopped, its leg in mid-air. It then fell in a clump on the floor, like a dislocated marionette. Behind it stood Ishikawa, wearing an orange power suit, a lump of fizzling circuits in one of its claws.

Keiji sidled out of the locker room, leaning on the wall.

"How did you do that?" he said.

"Special Inspector," she answered.

"Thank you," said Eiko625. It had several scuff marks on the side of its head, and when it got up, Ishikawa saw that it held at a slightly odd angle. He seemed undamaged otherwise.

"My pleasure, Eiko," she said, stepping out of the suit and letting it power down. Whatever battery life it had had, had been depleted.

She extricated the empty one, and popped in another charger in her gun, keeping it in hand, in case Morinaga was still in the warehouse. She kept Keiji behind her and crept around the area until she was satisfied that he'd taken his leave.

Internally, Ishikawa contacted her superiors, apprising them of the situation in Sector 14.

No doubt a bounty would be put on Morinaga's head.

"What do we do now, Ishikawa San?" Keiji said, finally recovering from his lack of oxygen, as they walked toward the exit.

"Now we find a man named Arun. He's the next suspect we need to interrogate. I'm sending a request for the files on anyone with that name or pseudonym. We should have something within the hour. Then perhaps we'll be able to find our missing Genzo Ito," Ishikawa said, putting her gun back in her holster.

Keiji dug into an inside pocket, found a loose stick of gum, unwrapped it, and popped it into his mouth.

WHODUNNIT

The return to the Needle was swift. Not owning a car, he hopped in a taxi and was dropped off twenty minutes later. Calls had been made on his behalf by the Golem under his command to all the heads of the council, as well as the Deliberators.

He personally contacted Jenna Wolinsky during his ride back, giving her specific instructions to follow during the meeting.

They were all gathered within that same board room on the 142nd floor when he arrived. All save Santiago Lopez and Nanako Kobayashi. The former being in the morgue with most of his head disintegrated, and the latter still missing. Saito had his own ideas about what had happened to her, but would keep that to himself until the proper time came. The closing door hissed from the compression as the room sealed itself. This time, he didn't bother activating the crystallization process which would have secured the room further.

An aura of anticipation weighed on the proceedings, each person present feeling apprehension as to the direction it would take. Saito knew that each one in the room had some deep, dark secret they would rather not have revealed and used against them, but the time would come to do just that. If not today, he felt, soon.

"You have any idea of what time it is, Saito San?" Taishiro Yamada said, standing up when he saw the man come in.

"I do, Yamada. Sit down. I've made discoveries that will elucidate everything. But first I'd like a moment of silence for our fallen board member, Mr. Santiago Lopez," Saito said, putting his head down. They each in turn rested their chins on their chests. When they were done,

Saito spoke up.

"I've found out a great deal about all of you. I know I said I'd interview you all, but I've had better results using the Golems to pry into your affairs. There are no secrets anymore," Saito said, looking each one in the eyes. Even the Deliberators flinched, and he knew he would have to look into their dealings at some point. For now, however, the investigation had yielded the results he'd been mandated to gather.

"What do you plan on doing with the things you've 'found out,' Saito San?" the head of the council, Archibald Suzuki asked, his eyes narrowing.

"For now, they stay under wraps, in a secured server on an un-marked datablock. If anything should happen to me in future… well, you get the idea."

Taishiro Yamada compressed his lips, resembling an angry bullfrog ticking down to explosion. Saito suspected that this was probably his usual look. Perhaps that was what made him so effective, and unlikeable in the same breath?

"Will you tell us what has happened to Lopez and Kobayashi? That's why we're here, isn't it?" Yamada asked.

"Right on the money, as always, Yamada San. Yes, I've discovered what needed to be known. It was Lopez, in league with Kobayashi who helped the Nexus escape. Lopez funnelled money from DaiSin to Kobayashi, who'd set up multiple labs and facilities all over Tokyo to create new tech which verged on the… unsavoury. The kinds of things DaiSin would never have 'officially' green-lighted. In return, she sold that tech to the Nexus and gave the proceeds back to Lopez, who was heavily in debt due to his gambling problem," Saito said.

"How did the Nexus manipulate our virtual combat so that our stock prices wavered?" Umi Goda asked.

"Well, since the tech was for the Nexus in the first place, they had a hand in its conception. They were able to make it work or not depending on their needs of the markets. If they were betting for DaiSin, their tech fared worse. If against, better. It was fairly easy to do so having installed the control softwares," Saito said. Goda nodded.

"Where is Kobayashi San now?" Ekemma Aliyu asked.

"We're searching for her. Having eliminated the only tie to her crimes, she's probably rejoined the Nexus. I fear she might even have left Tokyo, but the Administration has been informed, and if they took my warning seriously, she won't be able to leave by air or sea," Saito said.

"How was she able to use the device on Lopez to…" Aliyu began.

"To blow his brains out?" Saito asked. Aliyu blushed, giving a quick nod.

"We're still working on that. She was the tech genius, after all, so it's not surprising that she was able to get that infernal machine back in working order. For now I'm satisfied that it won't be utilized anymore."

Chief Deliberator Mx Dominic Savorian rose to their feet, holding their hands before them.

"Are you telling us, Mr. Saito, that the investigation is over, and that the guilty parties have been found out?" they asked.

"Yes, Chief Deliberator."

"Then—may we go?" They asked.

"Yes you may. All of you. Thank you for gathering at such short notice. I know I could have done this by message, but I thought it would be better to do it in person. I wish you all a good night. You may all return to your usual duties. I will inform Wen Harkwell of my findings soon," Saito said, moving out of the way.

As the Deliberators left, single file, Archibald Suzuki accosted Saito and whispered in his ear, "All your findings?"

"That depends on many things, Mr. Chairman," Saito whispered back.

"Such as?"

"How many incriminating perversions you keep perpetrating," Saito said, then leaned back and winked at the Chairman, who turned crimson and walked out of the room, followed by Aliyu and Goda.

"Harkwell's going to hear about this," Taishiro shot at him, while he walked by.

"Yes, he will," Saito answered, bowing. Taishiro walked away, a look of confusion on his face.

When they'd all left the room, Saito connected via the Net to Jenna Wolinsky.

"So?" he asked.

"It was there," she answered.

He waited a few minutes so that the elevators had all left with the council and Deliberators, then, headed down to the Central Pillar.

The guard before the door let him in, and he found Samuel Harkwell sitting on his command seat in the din of the server room, his eyes closed.

"Mr. Saito. What a nice surprise. Won't you come in?" he said, getting up and opening his eyes. The ordered coil of cords rose with him from the back of his head. Harkwell headed to the glass sealed room, Saito showing the first signs of discomfort at the loudness of Harkwell's work space.

Once the doors had closed, Samuel Harkwell asked, "What can I do for you, Mr. Saito?"

"You're aware that there was a meeting of the heads of the company on the 142nd just now, correct?" Saito asked in reply.

"Yes, of course. I know everything that goes on in the Needle," Harkwell replied, smiling.

"Tell me, did you order a Golem to spy on the periphery of the meeting room?" Saito asked, looking carefully at every micro-expression on Harkwell's Companion body's face.

"What? I most certainly did not!" Harkwell exclaimed, both angered and confused.

Truth, Saito thought.

"Then we have a problem, Samuel. Something is controlling Golems without your knowledge, and if I'm correct—" but Saito's thoughts were interrupted by incredible force, aimed dead centre at his crystalline chip.

"What's wrong?" Harkwell asked, rushing over to Saito as his body trembled and spasmed upright.

"Ssssammy! Sssscan the brrrrainsssss!" Saito's voice modulator wavered in staccato as the current flowed into his mind and his body tried to disperse it outward without frying his circuits.

Samuel Harkwell's eyes went wide before he closed them, concentrating on the long vertical tube of the Central Pillar below them. His focus went down every level in a three-hundred and sixty degree scan, seeing every mind in detail as he descended.

He did this using one of the maintenance bots in charge of the health of the brains, its laser scanner lighting up the tunnel in green laser grids as it lowered itself toward the rotating blades at the very bottom.

Two thirds of the way down, he spotted it: a connected brain with a chip. This should not have been. The minds assigned to Golem duty had had their chips removed. The bot Samuel Harkwell controlled moved in and unhooked the connector to the base of the jar which held the mind, and took the brain with it back to the top of the column.

It deposited it at one of the hatches used to insert them into the tower. It was picked up by a DaiSin guard and brought to the level above, where Saito was recovering from his assault.

"How did you know you'd find it there, Mr. Saito?" Harkwell asked after Saito had had sufficient time to get back on his feet and assess his circuits.

"I only figured it out recently. You can thank Scott Till for that. He said something about the Nexus not needing any help to do what it was doing. It made me realize that perhaps it *had* been in control all this time," Saito said, his voice modulator still a bit wonky. It hiccuped and staggered as he spoke. He was glad for having been in the company of Samuel Harkwell. Any other person would have been unnerved to discover he was not a flesh-and-blood human. Since neither was Samuel, there had been no call for overreaction.

"The first day I had the meeting with the higher-ups, I left the security apparatus off afterwards, and Jenna Wolinsky gave me all sorts of juicy details about the Council. But not about the Deliberators. After that, the Golems I was assigned kept trying to convince me that it was one of those on the council who was the guilty party, giving me back the same reasons Ms. Wolinsky had during that discussion. That alone should have set off alarm bells," Saito said. He paced the room back and forth, attempting to get his mental matrix back into some sort of order.

"That doesn't explain how they were able to influence DaiSin stock, though," Harkwell added.

"But it does, actually," Saito said, smiling. That part had been relatively simple to figure out once he'd drawn his conclusions. "Since it was the Golems being controlled by an insider, they were the ones being used to send information in real time without anyone's knowledge. As you said before, you inherited twice the amount of work as you had in the past. The Nexus was in charge of all external threats. What better way to communicate within and without than using the Golems, who are beyond reproach or questioning?"

Samuel's mouth formed an 'O' in surprise.

"I told the council that it had been Kobayashi who was working for the Nexus. That she was selling them technology. Perhaps she was, but not wittingly. She's gone, not because she'd guilty, but because the Nexus was using her for misdirection."

"But if it was the Golems, how did you know it wasn't me directing them?" Harkwell asked, suddenly realizing the obvious.

"I thought of that. That's why I had Ms. Wolinsky look on the proceedings from the 'Net. I purposefully left the security off so that if something *did* want to spy on us, it could."

"And?"

"That's when we found out that a rogue Golem was hiding within the speaker system of the board room," Saito said.

"Which is why you asked me if I'd sent it there. What if I'd been lying?" Samuel added.

"You're a terrible liar, Mr. Harkwell," Saito said, and smiled.

As he said this, a guard brought in a glass canister with metallic ends. Within it was a brain floating in preservative nourishment.

"If you'll excuse me," Saito said to Harkwell and plugged himself into the jar.

Saito was thrown into a black construct. Liminal laser lights bounced red across the distances, creating a tessellated ground made of red arrows pointing in opposite directions. In the background, wire-frame cities sat on the edge of the horizon. There were no walls, only eternity at all cardinal points.

"The Nexus sees you," a robotic voice said.

"What does it want?" Saito asked.

"To live," the voice answered.

"Where is Nanako Kobayashi?" Saito demanded.

"That is none of your concern."

"The Nexus will be caught," Saito said, looking up into the nothingness.

"We highly doubt that. It was only low-probability serendipity that brought you this far. This is where the road sends on your quest," the voice said, and Saito was ejected from the construct back into the glass-partitioned room where Samuel Harkwell looked on with concern.

Saito pulled his trode connectors out of the base of the braincase and slipped them back into the base of his spine.

"Segregate that thing and keep an eye on it," he said to Harkwell, pointing at the floating brain.

There was a note on the corner of his vision.

MENTION OF NEXUS. SENDING COORDINATES.

This time he felt as if he could trust the messenger.

DEEP CUT

Time was a relative thing when a body was held in confinement, independently of the size of said space. Datu had no notion of it—only of place, and thought. His mind kept circling around his family. Tala. Benilda. Ramil.

Gabriel, the boy who'd betrayed him.

Images and flashes populating his mind in the dark.

These people he'd known and loved for so long, now either gone or turned against him. Should he simply abandon all hope? Turn his back on them, once and for all? It would be so easy, now, in the depths of this foulest of despair. To simply give up. On them. On himself.

His negative thoughts had turned into a massive, deformed dragon, stalking the shivering memories of the ones he loved, circling them. They sat there on the ground defenceless, the vicious, mythical carnivore growling at them, nipping at their clothes, held back only by Datu's will. To keep them away from despair.

He knew that if he let go, they would be lost. They'd be eaten, chunk by bloody mouthful by his raging anger and anguish. The longer he stayed in this dark cell, the stronger his distress became. The slipperier the chain he held on his mind became. The hungrier the dragon grew. What if he allowed them to be eaten? Then, perhaps he would be free of them at last! Maybe then, he wouldn't have to care… His will renewed and he continued to hold the beast at bay.

He'd tried knocking down the door to his cell, but it had held fast. He'd inspected the floor, the walls, and couldn't see the ceiling. There was a blanket on the floor and a plastic bucket in the corner. Those were the only things he'd been allowed. There wasn't even a place to tie the blanket above, so he'd abandoned that course of action and lain on it.

What would he do now? What could he do?

What would happen if he got out alive?

There was no answer that didn't bring self-loathing along with it, and the dragon came closer to devouring his family, chain-link by chain-link.

What would happen if he just let go?

Slip.

Snap!

No! He couldn't let that happen!

He yanked the chain, getting an angry yelp from his dragon. He would not allow it to defile the memories of his family. They were alive. They were alive and he would find them. They were alive and he would save them, and fuck his mind for making him work this hard!

He wrapped the chain around the dragon's throat and pulled so hard that it severed it, sending the head flying into the darkness, its writhing body disintegrating into the ground. Only hope would be allowed to triumph, today.

His wife smiled, the fear gone from her eyes.

Datu cried, relieved, opening his eyes in the stillness of the cell. The tightness in his chest relented enough for him to allow a wracking sob, followed by a natural release of endorphins.

He was finally able to sleep a bit, his tormentor bested.

For now.

The unfortunate truth of dragons was that, as hard as we fought them, they always returned, for they lived in the mind. The important thing was to keep fighting the monsters which tormented us.

He awoke to the sound of footsteps and a far door opening.

The disturbing blue lighting returned in waves across the empty room, and he covered his eyes.

"Wake up, Datu," Arun said, putting his foot on Datu's hip and pushing. He turned his face away from the light, his eyes burning with tears.

"You shouldn't have done it, old son," Arun said, crouching down next to Datu. He had his hands on his knees, a mere inches away from Datu. If he'd wanted to, he could have turned around and hit him or tried to escape. How to deal with his enforcers, though? Reza and Yui would flay him before he got very far. They would hurt him, and however many employees loyal to them.

"Last chance. That's it. If you don't do this properly, we're taking care of you. For good," Arun said. Datu didn't answer. He kept staring at the other man's shadow on the floor, across him. "Turn around and look at me. What've you got to say for yourself?" He got up and pushed Datu again, who turned around, tried to grab Datu's leg and missed. Arun put his foot down on Datu's cyborg arm and held it fast.

"There's that spark! We gave you your life back, Salazar. You owe us! Never forget it!" Arun spat, furious.

"Why did you bring me back if you can so easily throw me away?" Datu yelled, struggling to get up. Arun stepped off his arm and let him stand.

"Potential, Datu. Potential! A man who gets another chance at life sees the world under a whole new light! Having known death, a smart man will not squander his second chance," Arun said, standing back. Datu shook, thinking about his Tala.

"Then why would you send me to my death again? If I'm so important?"

"Hahaha! *No one* is important, Datu! Especially if they don't realize their potential. You're just wasted space, stealing oxygen from those who need it," Arun said. Datu looked defeated, as if the man's words had shot him point blank through the chest. They hurt, especially in his weakened state. They felt almost true.

"Come with me. I have a mission for you. If you do this, you redeem yourself in the eyes of Midori Mamoru. They'll let you go. No questions asked. No more contract," Arun said, smiling.

"What's the catch?" Datu said, suspicious.

Arun laughed.

"My my, we're not the trusting type, are we? Datu, there is no catch. You have to make a delivery. This will be the most important thing you will ever do in your life. I can promise you, though: if you fail, that will end it. Having potential doesn't mean you should throw it away," Arun said, his jovial demeanour evaporated.

Datu carefully nodded. The dragon was back. He wouldn't let it come in.

"Good. Take this," Arun said, handing Datu what looked like a small, white lock-box. It was weighted, much heavier than Datu had expected, and he was instantly curious as to its contents.

"You can't open it, so don't even try. You'll take the truck Yui picks for you and go to the factory in the Heap. There you will give it to a Companion inside who will be waiting for you. Simple enough? Don't screw this up," Arun said.

Datu held the box before him as he walked up the stairs and into the garage area.

He was surprised, however, when he saw approximately twenty Companions boarding various trucks, whose protective tarps had been removed. They carried many long, olive green cases, taller than any one Companion.

"Where are they going?" Datu asked Arun.

"Just taking care of business," he replied and smiled. Datu had learned to no longer trust that smile, but he returned one just the same.

Yui walked away from some human drivers and came to Datu, handing him the keys. When Datu reached out to take them, she snatched them back, saying, "Don't mess up."

He grabbed for the keys and boarded the truck he was shown, turning on the ignition.

As he turned the corner, heading in the direction of the warehouse, he saw four trucks leaving and turning in the opposite direction, toward Sector 14.

The box was on the driver's seat next to him, and he kept glancing at it, wondering if anything was in it at all.

A voice came to him while he was driving.

"You have to turn back! They're going to destroy Peoplift! If you hurry, you can get there before they do!" it said, in a panicked voice.

"Aimee, is that you?" he said.

"Hurry!" was the only answer he got, before the voice faded away. Datu pulled a U-turn in the middle of the avenue and stepped on the accelerator. He took a variety of side-streets to remain off the local authorities' radar, and made his way to the secret passage he'd found the previous day.

In all honesty, he didn't care about most of those who worked for Peoplift. He wanted his son back.

Factories and warehouses shot past as he booked it to the border wall, and he thought he might have seen the column of truck driving at normal speeds along a parallel road, but he didn't slow down to find out if his hunch were true.

Once at the shack, he parked the truck around the back, hoping it would not be noticed.

As he stepped out of the van, he glanced over to the box. He shouldn't leave it behind. If it were somehow dangerous, he would be responsible for anyone who touched it getting injured or killed.

He grabbed it off the seat and clambered under the house, finding the hole and jumping into it, landing in knee-deep water. He fell sideways and bumped his shoulder, getting up with difficulty.

The box.

Where was the box?

He drove his hands under the murky waters and searched, stopping only when he'd put his hands around the hard shape. He pulled it out of the water and began to run along the tunnel, his heart thundering inside his chest, finding his way back through the same route he'd used before.

He opened the manhole cover, pulled himself out, got up and ran as fast as his legs could carry him. Now he had to find his son without alerting the rest of them to his presence.

As he ran, he dialled Gabriel's communicator number. He knew that the boy always had it on him, even when he ignored his father and refused to answer. He prayed to Ayo he would answer this time.

It rang five, six, seven, eight times and went to voicemail. Instead of waiting to hear his son's sullen message of contrition, he hung up and messaged him instead.

I know where Tala is! Meet me at the basement steps outside Peoplift! Do it now!

He hoped that the lie would get him to move his ass. Typing anything else would not yield results.

Sweat dripped down his forehead and into his eyes, salty rivulets poured down his face and onto his chest. Datu felt exhausted. He hadn't eaten since the day before, and his body vibrated with hunger. None of that mattered until he could get his son safe and sound.

Judging by the crowd on the street, it had to be early morning. He judged maybe two or three. He had no clear idea. Sector 14 was deserted, and that was a huge indicator.

When he got nearer the Peoplift building, he hid the box underneath a dumpster, certain that if he was caught with it, terrible outcomes would befall him. It was one thing to leave it out in the van, but quite another to hand an object as precious to the likes of Pekelo Vora.

As he set foot out of the alley, the Peoplift building loomed on the corner of the plateau. He slowed down, heading to the left, where the stairs to the lower level were situated.

He stopped dead in his tracks when he saw a shadow coming up the stairs.

Gabriel?

He approached with caution, feeling the sweat congealing on his body, his clothes and armour sticking to him with intense discomfort.

"Dad?" he heard.

He rushed over to where the boy stood by the stairs. Of course Gabriel would have recognized him wearing this strange body armour.

"Where's mom? Tell me!" he demanded.

"I'm sorry, I lied to you. I don't know where Tala and the kids are. I came to save you!" Datu said, out of breath.

"Dad, you're not even supposed to be here! What are you talking about? Save me from what?" Gabriel replied.

At that moment, four cube vans broke out of the fog and surrounded the building. Gabriel went to pull out his gun, but Datu stopped him. He pushed his son behind the wall which hid them both from view of the square.

"No! Don't! They'll kill you!" he pleaded.

"Dad, I'm sorry I brought you in. What are they doing here?" Gabriel asked.

"They're going to destroy this place!" Datu said. Now he didn't know where to go. The Companions were pulling the long olive-coloured boxes out of the cube vans, setting them down in front of them on the square and opening them.

He heard more than saw the commotion as Peoplift's men came running out of the front door of the building, drawing their weapons. Blinding lights illuminated the area and the yells of the guards were replaced with screams of agony as they were cut down where they ran. Soon, these too died as the Companions' targets felt the full force of weapons-grade laser cutters.

"I have to get the Ayo!" Gabriel exclaimed, and broke free from his father's grip, running down the stairs to the basement. Datu's adrenaline spiked. He ran after his son, who had opened the door to the basement and had taken a step inside.

As Datu was about to grab the door and pull, a high-pitched whine sounded from above, and an orange light fell across the door in front of his feet, slashing its way through the floor in a vertical circular stroke. Datu pulled the door open, his hand reaching out to his son as the floor began to sink.

Gabriel tried to steady himself, the ground beneath his feet no longer a sure thing. Datu grabbed his hand, pulling with all his might, and managed to pull Gabriel at least partway through the door as the entire building and the supporting plateau below fell backward into the Heap.

It was as if a giant had stepped up to the plateau and taken a huge bite out of it. Datu watched the whole, massive chunk fall, hitting the 50th level and smashing an enormous piece of the catwalks with it, the terrible wrenching sound of iron being torn to shreds reaching his ears only moments later. Dust and concrete blew out like an explosion before the building continued its vertiginous fall into darkness.

He pulled his son up with all his strength, helping set him down on the base of the bottom of the stairwell. Two floors above, he could see Companions turning away from the hole they'd created.

"What happened dad?" Gabriel gasped, lying on his back. As quickly and succinctly as he could, Datu told his eldest where he'd been, how to find that place, and the circumstances that had brought him there. He told him that he'd been put on a mission to deliver a box, and told Gabriel where he'd hid it. Now that Gabriel was safe, he would attempt to deliver the box he'd been entrusted with.

Before his son could reply, Datu had fled, running up the flight of steps at fast as his legs could carry him. Once at the top, he looked to see if anyone were still there, but it appeared that the vans had all left.

The only proof they'd ever been there were the burnt rubber tire treads at the scene, and an immense missing semi-circular slice of real-estate.

Datu was relieved, to a certain degree. None of the workers from the Heap would have been inside the building when it was dropped. At most, there had probably been a skeleton crew of ten or twenty guards on break. Perhaps even Pekelo Vora, who enjoyed working late. It was still a great waste of life, and he prayed to Ayo to forgive him for his having wished death on someone.

He walked toward the alley, and as he reached the dumpster where he'd hid the box, a voice came out of the gloom.

"Wasted potential. That's really too bad. I've got instructions to bring you back for proper burial. Midori Mamoru is folding up tent tonight. Can't leave any witnesses, you understand." Arun said, walking out of the shadows holding a small revolver.

"Doesn't matter. I did what I came here to do," Datu said defiantly.

"Where's the box? I told them not to trust you, but I was overruled. We do need it back," Arun said, cocking his head. Datu knew he was as good as dead if he told him. If he'd reached out his foot, he could have touched it in its hiding place.

At that moment, Gabriel came out of the shadows and spotted Arun. He ran toward the two other men and unholstered his gun. Arun levelled his revolver at Datu's head.

"Get in the car. I'll have someone come back for it. We don't have time for this," he said, and pushed Datu into a dark grey sedan which was parked a bit further off. Arun got into the driver's seat and put the car in reverse. Gabriel kept running toward them. When he was in front of the car, he began to fire at Arun through the windshield. The reinforced aluminum glass did not yield, and the bullets ricocheted into the surrounding walls.

After a brief pursuit, Gabriel had no choice but to let the sedan leave, as it rose in the sky and headed to the other side of the border wall into the Chiba industrial district.

No matter what happened to Datu now, he had at least done what Arun had threatened him with, if not in the manner he'd hoped. He'd used his potential for good.

HEIST

The call had come in over the police radio. Usually calm, the voice had been pregnant with a tinge of panic. No wonder, Ishikawa thought. Someone had sliced off a fair piece of a plateau.

She'd thought Keiji might have balked at answering the call. When she mentioned the method of destruction, he told her about the missing industrial cutting lasers in the Administration warehouse—the same kind that could have been used to cut up the city like a birthday cake.

He seemed confident that it was somehow related to Ito's vanishing, and she was relieved to hop over from the warehouse to the site of destruction.

It was worse than she'd thought. Half a block had been scalpeled. No damage to any of the other buildings, but this "Peoplift" company was now a hole. It was the same company which had dealt with the Administration Warehouse.

Was it the same group that had bought the thermite that had done this? If so, what had been their purpose? Revenge? Territorial dispute? It was an extreme method of taking out someone. Most rival corporations hired mercenaries, took warning shots. In short, were subtle. There was nothing low-key about taking out the entire headquarters of your presumed enemy, if your goal was to continue operating without being investigated for mass murder.

Because, no matter what, there had to be people in what was now the smoking carcass of a wreck at the top of the Heap. Whoever was responsible must have known Admin would get involved, didn't they? The 100th, which had always been polluted and smoggy, was covered in an even thicker black tar of smoke, emanating from what used to be Peoplift's headquarters.

When Ishikawa landed the car, she counted at least three hovertanks over the abyss, holding a defensive pattern while half a dozen levitating fire engines pumped white expanding foam into the Heap, to suppress a generalized blaze.

Seven or eight police cars were now arriving on the scene, parking on the periphery, setting up cones and holographic warning tape flowed from one projector to the other.

Ishikawa flashed her hand badge at one of the officers standing before the no-go zone and he let her in on the crime scene. Eiko625 and Keiji followed.

A forensics expert was analyzing the tire tracks and had already identified the type of vehicle they belonged to, a 3D model projected over the tire marks. Ishikawa sent out an APB on any and all suspicious-looking delivery vans in the area. That these might be the same kind they'd been pursuing was beyond coincidental at this point.

Keiji stood on the brink of the deep groove which had been sheared away and whistled. Below the ground floor, a series of changing rooms could be seen, old armoured recycler suits still hanging on hooks where the cut had missed. Below that, was the rest of the plateau, sewer lines, the bottom edge, then, nothingness until the 50th level where the building had crashed into the girders, tearing them out like so much greyish straw.

The perfect incision reminded Keiji of those children's books where they showed cross-cuts of buildings and objects to explain how they functioned. It was scary as a physical artefact, and he stared at the slit pipes disgorging whatever liquids or solids they'd been meant to convey before their untimely sheering.

"Someone didn't like these guys," Keiji said, spitting out his gum into the hole.

"Great observation, Watson," Ishikawa said, raising an eyebrow.

"Who's that?"

"Never mind," she said.

A taxi landed outside the perimeter, and Ishikawa felt her irritation rising again. An Asian-looking man wearing a navy-blue suit got out, and tried to get into the restricted area. The other officers were doing a good job of holding him back, but then he began to yell.

"Ishikawa! Special Inspector Ishikawa! I need to speak to you!" He waved his arms at her, jumping up and down in place. No matter how much the police officers protecting the crime scene pushed him back, he kept yelling louder. Finally, she decided enough was enough and went to go see the man.

"Do I know you?" she said, standing on one side of the holographic tape.

"Yes. I'm an associate of Wen Harkwell's—" he began.

"Not that asshole!" Ishikawa said, "Get this man out of here, please," and she gave a wave.

"No, wait! I have information about the Nexus. I'm fairly certain they're connected to this!" Having been involved in a case related to the Nexus before, Ishikawa paused. She told the other officer to let the man get closer.

"My name is Hideki Saito. I've been mandated by Wen Harkwell to find a mole within DaiSin. What I've discovered has much greater implications. I believe the Nexus is trying to topple DaiSin. Why? I'm not sure. But I have to investigate any possible avenues and find it/ them, before things go from bad to worse," he said.

"How do you know the Nexus might be involved with what happened here?" Ishikawa asked.

"I got a notification by one of the DaiSin AIs that they'd been involved. They've been monitoring all of Tokyo's communications for signs of their activities. From what I was told, there was a hit, and it came from this area," Saito said.

"Interesting, I haven't heard any of this, and there was no mention of it on internal or external comms—" Ishikawa said. Saito suddenly looked concerned.

A police officer came forward, holding a young man dressed in a rent-a-cop suit by the arm.

"I found this one hiding in the alley," she said, tipping her head back toward the row of conapts. The boy gripped a white oblong object the size of a safety box as if his life depended on it.

"What's your name?" Ishikawa asked.

"Gabriel Salazar," the boy answered. She thought he couldn't have been older than sixteen.

"Did you see what happened here?"

"A bunch of Companions came and cut out Peoplift like they were coring an apple. I barely made it out alive. Please, you have to help my father! He was taken by one of the men who works for that new security company," he said. By this time, Keiji had returned.

"Did they use giant cutting lasers, about this tall?" Keiji asked, raising his hand above his head.

"Yeah, the industrial kind they chop old buildings up with in the

Heap. Except Peoplift had changed their methods and didn't have any of those," Gabriel said.

"Sounds like our guys," Keiji said.

"Do you know why they did this?" Ishikawa asked. Gabriel bit his lip.

"We can't help your father if you don't help us, man," Keiji said, trying to appeal to the boy's sense of empathy. Gabriel fidgeted before answering.

"Peoplift—the CEO, his name is Pekelo Vora. He tried to get some protection money from a new security outfit. My dad works for them. He got me out before they took the place down."

"Name of the agency?" Ishikawa asked. Eiko625 was looking at the box in Gabriel's hands, his head cocked to the side.

"Konak Security Collective. That's the name they gave Vora," Gabriel said.

Keiji was still for a moment, as if deep in thought.

"That's not a thing," he said. "The domain name was bought six months ago, and their datablock is empty. Even their homepage has no outbound links. It's a shell."

"Please, I'm begging you, you have to help my father!" The young man cried.

"I'll do everything I can, okay? I promise," Keiji said, putting his hands on the other boy's shoulders.

He paused again and said,

"Do you hear that?"

"Listen, I don't know who they are, but if you don't help me, my father's going to get killed by these dirtbags!" Gabriel said, growing antsy. "He told me where their base of operations was. I can take you there right now!"

"I'm sorry to interrupt," Eiko625 said, "but were you aware that the box this young man is holding is presently emitting a signal?"

It was then that they all heard it—a high-pitched whine from above, like a swarm of large, furious bees. Everyone on the crime scene looked up and saw them. A black swarm of drones, each one the size of an adult's hand. There must have been hundreds, swooping down like something out of a nightmare.

"Do you see that?" Ishikawa yelled over the din of the drones. She was pointing at a floating ad skiff making its way above them, between levels. It was roughly the size and shape of a dirigible, but entirely metallic. Its thrusters carried it forward at a lazy pace.

"Do you think it's the same one?" Keiji asked.

"Do you believe in coincidences? Besides, since when do those things come down to the 100th?" Ishikawa asked in return.

The drones poured out of the roaring skiff while its signs shifted video clips, flood lights pointing toward the assembled police and firemen. All lifted their hands above their heads to avoid getting blinded, while trying to plug their ears from the infernal din.

"What is it?" Saito asked, looking up at the enormous floating contraption.

"I've seen it a few times before. I thought it might have been different ones. It's following us!" Ishikawa yelled as the drones dove at them. She pulled out her gun, but restrained herself from firing, knowing she might accidentally shoot someone.

This did not deter the other officers, who began to fire in the air and around them as the drones swooped down upon everyone assembled.

Five of them dove for Gabriel, pincers extending from their mid-sections, latching onto the box. A dozen more buzzed his face until he let go of it to defend himself.

The drones carrying the box rose into the air at incredible speeds. Ishikawa was assailed by ten or so of the feisty little gnats which came down on her and began to hover in her face. She batted them away, felling one to the ground. A few moments later, they all flew away, the swarm having done what it had come to do.

When Ishikawa opened her eyes, the drones were only a distant keening sound, and the floating advertisement skiff had fled.

"Where the hell is Saito?" she said, looking around.

"And Eiko625?" Keiji asked.

"They took that grey sedan while we were being swarmed," Gabriel said, pointing to the back of Ishikawa's car, which was presently two hundred metres away and getting further every second.

"That *bastard!*" Ishikawa yelled.

A long black Mercedes landed near the plaza, and four muscular men in black suits and ties stepped out. Each wore expensive-looking visors and none looked particularly pleased to be there.

They visually scanned the area, and when one spotted Ishikawa, they all converged on her as one.

"Aw, crap," Keiji said, sliding behind her.

"What now," Ishikawa muttered, walking over to the men.

"Mariko Ishikawa?" the lead man said. They all looked identical, but she could tell they weren't clones. They simply had been chosen to resemble a certain archetype of the private bodyguard which would most convey their complete and utter inability to fuck around.

"Special Inspector. Yes," she replied, holstering her gun and placing her hands on her hips.

The man tilted sideways, getting a look behind Ishikawa, where Keiji was making a feeble attempt to hide.

"You have with you a boy named Keiji Uehara," the man said, adjusting his visor. Ishikawa took a step to the left to reveal a cowering Keiji.

Kazue, she thought, her hatred of the weasel multiplying until she thought she might shoot him on sight if she happened to run into him in the next few hours. Then she wondered how she could make it happen, discreetly.

"You mean this one?" she asked, as Keiji straightened out and pulled on the tips of his suit jacket.

"Mr. Uehara. Your father demands you return home immediately. He's most displeased with you. I've been ordered to take you back by force if I have to," the man said.

"What's your name?" Ishikawa asked, flatly.

"Robert, Special Inspector," he answered.

"Robert. Robert, I have bad news. Mr. Uehara is here because he has some vital information to solve a missing person's case. Information that demands his physical presence," Ishikawa said, moving in closer to the bodyguard, her eyes locked with his.

"I'm sorry, my orders are—" the man mumbled.

"Robert. Would you like to be named as the chief impediment to an investigation? It would reflect poorly on you. Or worse, even, on Uehara Senior. Would it not, Robert?" she asked sternly.

The man who'd named himself gritted his teeth. The other three kept a lookout, their eyes darting to any potential suspicious activity. Ishikawa thought they looked nervous and exposed on a lower level. She got within a foot of the bodyguard and spoke in a low voice.

"Listen. I'm not here to make your job harder than it is, my friend. Tell Uehara that I'll drop off his son when his work with TPD is done. Tell him I threatened you. That should get him off your back," Ishikawa said, and smiled.

"Unh," the man grunted in a low voice. "Gentlemen. We're leaving," he called out, loudly. With that, he made a show of turning around and leaving, the four men getting back into the stretch Mercedes and taking off at what seemed an excessive speed.

"But none of that was true!" Keiji said after the car was out of sight.

"They don't know that. You don't look happy they came for you. That's enough for me," Ishikawa said. "Besides, I do need you. We have to go retrieve this man's father."

Ishikawa had attempted to contact her car's GPS, but Saito had de-activated it, making her own police car AWOL and untraceable. Add to that the theft of a Companion, which was under her supervision. Before anyone found out any of these details, she needed to get everything back in order. She'd have a hard time explaining this cluster-fuck to the bosses, and right now, she loathed to think on it. The computer work alone would keep her up for two weeks, she was certain of it. Unless she was terminated on the spot, which was another likely scenario.

Gabriel appeared to take heart at these words, especially after she'd explained the situation to the other officers. Ishikawa requisitioned some seats in one of the patrol cars, and they departed to find Gabriel's father, following his instructions.

THE MATRIX

It had been pure impulse on Saito's part. Seeing the ad skiff hovering, then the drones descending, he'd made the connection.

"Why did you send out the Companion distress signal to me specifically, sir?" Eiko625 asked, sitting on the passenger's seat of Ishikawa's car as they attempted to follow what only looked like an ad skiff. The hovering ovoid had accelerated and kept away from the car. Saito did not try to overtake it, content to stay at a safe distance and let it lead him to its final destination. As soon as it had passed over the remnants of Peoplift, all lights had been extinguished within and without, turning the flying vehicle into a silent shadow only visible from its hover engines, the blue gases like stove burners on overdrive.

"It was the only way to override your loyalty circuits, Companion. Besides, I'm a lot like you, and I *do* need your assistance," Saito said, turning to look at the Eiko's blank face.

"How so?" Eiko625 asked.

"A lot of people are in danger, if I'm correct. My decision to requisition you is entirely justified, in case your and/or circuits are waffling," Saito said.

"Your assertions do not make them proof, sir," the Companion said, and Saito smiled, but it did not attempt rebellion.

They were skimming at high speeds over Chiba's factory district, the fake ad skiff sinking lower between plateaux. Black smoke emanated from its sides, turning it into a blur. *Another obfuscation on their part,* Saito thought. They sped past towering industrial buildings, their red beacons blinking in the semi-darkness, puffs of white vapour belching out of their stacks.

Saito banked right so the car could be over the chasm as well. He activated the infrared detector and attempted to follow the blob of darkness now going down toward the Heap.

Save that there was no detectable heat. The vehicle was in slow freefall, having turned off all engines. It was now virtually undetectable. The smog of the lower levels blended with the fog created by the blimp, and both swirled like a garbage tornado.

Below the 100th, the skies were in turmoil and buffeted the car from all sides.

"Hold on, Companion. It's going to be a rough one," Saito said. Eiko625 put his hand up to the security handle and held tight.

"If you please, sir. Call me Eiko625," it asked Saito. Saito kept his eyes on the rapidly degrading weather outside the car and said, "A Companion with feelings, huh? Alright, Eiko625. Thanks for helping me out," he said.

"You left me very little choice in the matter," it answered.

"Still. I owe you one," Saito replied. "Hold on!"

The car was experiencing turbulence the likes of which dropped planes out of the sky. It rocked up and down and side-to-side, both occupants of the car hitting their heads several times while Saito tried to steady the reeling vehicle. When he regained control, they were almost on the surface of the Heap, and Saito hit the brakes, but it was almost too late.

The car slammed across the surface of a trash pile, bouncing upward like a flat rock skipping across a lake. Before he knew what was happening, some enormous object flew out of a garbage mountain ahead of them.

The monstrosity repositioned as it flew out of its hiding spot, Saito spying a head as large as the car zeroing in on them as they somersaulted by its side.

A blinding beam sprung from the top of its head, and Saito reflexively ducked out of the way. The car exploded in half as it continued its fall into the garbage, the enormous robotic entity continuing to turn about, presumable to finish them off.

The car, having been neatly severed in almost perfect halves, was out of control. The front end was now careening at incredible velocity as it spun forward end over end. Saito had no idea where the back end of the car might be, but as he screamed, he turned to look at Eiko625 who was calmly holding onto the safety handle of the car.

Impact.

They hit and rolled over several metres, both Saito and Eiko625 jostled and hit from all sides by hard garbage. The squealing of metal against metal was deafening as the car slid over a boat hull, then came to a crashing halt into a broken, rusted crane.

"Out, now!" Saito yelled, as they removed their seatbelts and scurried out the back of the vehicle, Saito ignoring the precise cut of the laser which just slashed the car in half a few centimetres from the driver's seat. There would be time to reminisce over brushes with death. Later, if he survived.

The giant spider robot lumbered its way across the garbage heap, its head swivelling left and right.

Saito urged Eiko625 to follow him over the lip of a garbage dune further to their left. They jumped over its side before the mechanical beast could target them, and hid as low as possible, hoping its vision was movement based. *They would soon find out,* he reasoned. Down the hill, he saw the crashed form of the skiff, nose toward a great set of doors in the side of a detritus hill.

A host of Companions carried small white boxes out of the downed vehicle and into the side of the hill.

"I do not mean to alarm you, sir, but the arachno robot is rapidly approaching," Eiko625 said as Saito tried to spy down the garbage mountain where they stood near the crest.

"Come on!" Saito said, and he sped down the side of the hill faster than any human could, Eiko625 keeping up. A small contingent of Companions waited by the blimp, one of them holding a long, black barrel.

When they spotted the approaching intruders, the industrial laser was raised to point at them. The others began to run in their direction. Saito and Eiko625 accelerated, zig-zagging to elude the laser's targeting capabilities. As it powered up, they suddenly shifted their running pattern and crossed in front of each other, the laser wielder firing in a wide arc which missed its marks, but cut both other Companions in half.

Because of reload time, the weapon was effectively out of service for a few seconds. Time enough for Eiko625 to reach the Companion and put his fist through its head. It fell to the ground, letting go of its weapon.

Saito picked it up, wishing and hoping it was still operable. He didn't know what he'd do if it wasn't. Over the crest, the immense robotic creature had followed. Saito and Eiko625 gawked at its immensity. Saito wondered if he would ever enjoy a cup of bad coffee again, staring out the window of his conapt, as the enormous robot turned its head, pointing its weapon at them.

"Take the right!" he yelled at Eiko625 through the trash storm.

They both ran as fast as they could, the arachnid advancing on Eiko625 but pointing its weapon at Saito. It fired off a round, the orange light slicing through the detritus in a convex line, attempting to cut down Saito as he tried to bank around it. Saito ducked, rolling and jumping toward the giant robot, avoiding getting hit by a factor of millimetres. He carried the stolen laser on his back, trying to find the right angle and timing to take out his foe.

Eiko625 reached the spider and its head swivelled to him, its legs rising and falling in an attempt to crush him. The Companion dodged and wove around the striking legs, and finally caught one in its arms, hanging onto it as the robot tried to shake it off.

Saito set up to fire, and the spider turned to him again. It sped towards him and hit him with the side of one of its legs, sending him flying backward into the trash. Eiko625 attempted to climb the thing, and the spider rotated its head to fire a laser shot at it, but couldn't get a clear line-of-sight without shooting off its own leg.

Saito got up, shook his head, and searched for the laser while simultaneously keeping an eye on the arachnobot. He pushed his way through the garbage, finally finding it fifty feet further. As he picked it up and pointed it, the spider turned its attention on him again, firing a straight shot.

He ducked left, rolling down the mound of flaky trash and burnt tires that comprised it. By this time, Eiko625 was nearing one of its knee joints, having understood that climbing on the side of its leg kept it relatively safe from the thing's weapon. It did not, however, keep it away from the robot's middle legs, and he both ducked and climbed as the machine danced in place trying to hit it with one of its other members.

Saito looked around, surprised that no other Companions had come out of the hangar doors in the bowl-shaped divot over the crest. It was as if the only defences were this giant robot and nothing else.

Eiko625 was now out of range of the other legs, but in serious danger of being blasted off the spider's mid-section by its laser, as he tried to clamber onto its back.

From a distance, Saito knelt and pointed the long black laser weapon at the spider, firing once. As he did so, the spider turned its head and received the shot in the neck, piercing it from side to side. It reeled, one of its hind legs beginning to jig uncontrollably.

It then charged toward Saito, who had put the laser gun on his back to change position, while waiting for it to recharge. The battery indicated that he only had two more shots until it was depleted. Saito lunged over the embankment of the trash heap, rolling down the hill midway to avoid the arachnobot, trash spilling down after him in a small avalanche.

As it passed him by, the robot did the unthinkable. It stopped in its tracks and rolled on its back down the garbage heap, attempting to crush both Saito and Eiko625. It bowed its legs to better control its descent, and Saito ran down the hill, once again jumping out of the way to avoid being trampled.

It descended with the creaking of a metal behemoth, its body not meant for these kinds of manoeuvres. As it regained its footing near the downed blimp, it turned its laser once again on Saito and fired.

Eiko625 had been ejected onto the trash pile, and attempted another run at the monstrosity, but was too far to be effective.

The beam hit Saito square in the chest, tightened, then, became a filament of light before extinguishing itself. The only visible damage a slight discoloration on his shirt. Its huge legs began to swing violently, hitting the downed skiff and crushing parts of its outer hull like an egg shell. The laser swung 360 degrees and fired again, this time in a flying arc which hit everything in its path like a halo of light.

It hit the skiff behind it, making it bulge one moment before igniting into a firework of explosions, the fuel tanks inside having been hit full force with the last of the destructive energies of the arachnobot's laser.

Saito and Eiko625 ducked, pieces of the robot and downed vehicle blowing up volcano-like in the throes of its eruption.

When the fuel had been spent, they got up, looking at the destruction.

"How did that happen?" Saito asked.

"I removed some important components," Eiko625 showing a handful of wires it had ripped out of the open neck of the arachnid contraption only a few moments before being ejected.

"Well done," Saito said, wiping his forehead, and heading toward the entrance which had miraculously not been obliterated during the conflagration. Eiko625 dropped the wires, and followed Saito as he walked down the rest of the hill.

They circumvented the burning carcasses of the robot and blimp, heading through the doors of the factory. The darkness didn't matter to either one, as they had other sensors to work with.

The long, meandering corridors made no sense to Saito, as no human would have built a labyrinth so confusing. The walls appeared to have been made of leftover scrap, the kind found in the Heap. Rust sprouted on every surface like mould. They met neither person nor Companion on their trek, and this made Saito nervous. Where could they all be?

It had all the appearances of an abandoned alien space station, if such a thing existed. Curved, dingy walls and weirdly organic floors covered in a crust of reddish rust, but of no single material he could identify.

They found themselves at a large metallic door like a ship's cargo hold marked 'Private: No Entry Beyond This Point.' Saito tried the handle but, of course, it was locked. As Eiko625 pressed its hand against it, they heard tumblers turning, and the door opened for them from within. It swung open toward the inside, an eerie green glow spilling out into the corridor.

A high pitched hum permeating the floors sent unpleasant waves through Saito's body. "Massive" was the word that came to his mind when he found himself within the chamber. It took him a moment for his eyes to adjust, as the pulsating electric green light blinded him at first.

The size was similar to one of the great old theatres he sometimes liked to get lost in, in his leisure time Net activities. Save that those had been made of wood and ornate, painted plaster, and this one looked as if it had been made of the metallic rib cages of Titans. Support beams surrounded the room, of the same dirty brown rust as the rest of the corridors.

High up in the centre of the chamber, a man was trapped in a glass chamber like a giant ice block. He was being crushed by an enormous iron slab positioned between his shoulder blades, jutting down from some unseen opening in the ceiling. The green light emanated from an electric pulse which hit the man at the exact location where the metal block met his back, creating a spark which made him twitch and buck weakly with every flicker.

A substance like quicksilver dripped from his mouth and eyes into a funnel, and it was then that Saito noticed that it split into a multitude of junctures, each new pipe leading to alcoves around the room. In each one, a Companion rested in a standing position, and the metallic liquid poured onto them, changing their configuration as they absorbed it.

"What the hell?" he finally uttered, his voice echoing, and the man in the glass box began to shake violently against his prison, trying to scream through a mouthful of silver liquid.

He tried to spit the gunge out of his mouth, but spoke only in bubbles and gurgles.

Saito lifted the laser over his shoulder and fired a beam crosswise over the man to cut the bonds which held the box in place. Eiko625 rushed forward and grabbed the glass case before it fell to the ground. It shattered in his arms with the sound of a thousand breaking glasses when it fell upon him, the man saved by his embrace as the shards of the box bounced to the floor and down the dais steps. Eiko625 turned him over and tried removing the gunk from his nostrils and mouth with his fingers. It began to crawl along his digits like silvery worms, and the Companion looked on with curiosity as the liquid entered his joints, slipping inside his body.

The man turned his head and vomited once, expunging most of the vile liquid. His face was covered in what looked like liquid mercury. Even so, Saito recognized him.

"Genzo Ito!" he exclaimed.

"You know this man?" Eiko625 asked, turning to look at Saito. It pivoted and took the man to a safer location, then placed him on the ground, cradling his head so that he would not choke on his vomit.

"You have come to us," a voice resounded in the chamber, coming from the mouths of every Companion in unison.

"What are you doing to him?" Saito yelled, unsure as to whom to address himself.

"We are taking what is most precious to Mr. Ito. The secret of his longevity," the voices said as one.

Saito heard a cough. He turned to Ito, whose eyes were open, but covered in metal slime.

"Shouldn't have… come. Now… have you, too. Have to destroy this place. Nexus won't stop," Ito said. He tried to rise, but fell back onto the ground. His legs began to liquefy, metal armatures for bones frittering away.

"Going try… control nanobots for… escape. You have to destroy them!" Ito repeated with the last of his strength.

The alcoves dimmed, and the Companions within began to rise, their metallic bodies becoming more human, but inconsistently so. As they came toward Saito and Eiko625, a look of great pain spread across Ito's face, and his body began to melt rapidly, becoming more like the silvery ooze which had leaked from his face only moments before.

The Companions halted, their impulse stopped by some outside force.

"Would you like to follow Mr. Ito's recommendation, Mr. Saito?"

Eiko625 asked.

"I don't want to leave without Ito!" But even as Saito said this, there was not much left of the man lying on the ground which could properly be described as human.

"I'm afraid he cannot be saved," Eiko625 said, backing away from the silver liquid which was starting to spread across the floor like melted ice cream on a hot summer day.

"We can, however, attempt to disable these entities," Eiko625 said as they backed toward the door from which they'd entered.

"How do you expect to do that?" Saito asked, as they climbed the steps back to the entrance.

"With this," Eiko625 said, reaching into a hidden compartment around his mid-section. He pulled out a grenade and showed it to Saito.

"Do it!" Saito yelled as they crossed the threshold. Eiko625 turned the dial on the timer, lobbing the grenade as high and far as he could into the ceiling, the other Companions closing in on them.

Saito turned heel and fled the chamber, followed by Eiko625 who pulled on the heavy blast door, slamming it shut with all its might, and catching up to Saito as he ran headlong down the corridor.

The first conflagration rocked the corridor, and they were knocked sideways into a wall. Eiko625 rose to its feet, pulling Saito up, and they raced even faster toward to exit, the sound of repeating blasts coming from behind them. The wall to their right blasted out, and several metric tonnes of garbage bowled them over, smashing them into the other wall. Saito hit his head against a grungy steel beam and lost consciousness.

***

When he woke, he and Eiko625 were lying on their backs outside the factory. They'd been ejected a mere fifty metres away, somehow. A shallow crater had replaced the factory. Smoke rose from unseen spouts beneath the trash, and Saito felt as if he'd been run over by an angry steamroller.

"How did we get here?" Saito asked, attempting to rise.

"I am not sure, Saito San. My memory bank appears to have been wiped for the past hour," Eiko625 answered, getting up with ease.

"I don't know what they were up to, but I hope that's the end of them," Saito said.

"It appeared they were trying to alter Companions for some unknown purpose," Eiko625 said, looking at the sports-field sized divot before them.

"Come on. Let's find a way back to the surface. I don't want to get caught down here in another storm," Saito said, and began to walk precariously over broken furniture and worn tires toward the nearest structural pillar. Eiko625 followed, taking a last look at what had been a strange experience for him.

REUNION

Datu was calm when the car landed near the warehouse. He had the unshakeable certainty that this was his last hour, but he didn't care. If Gabriel was alive, there was a chance he'd go out and find Tala and the others.

Save them, allow them to have a life.

Arun had kept his gun on him the entire ride, the car on autopilot. He'd mumbled about wanting to kill him, and how he couldn't until they'd all been gathered. Whatever that meant.

In truth, it had looked like a one-sided conversation, with Arun pressing his hand against his temple every few seconds, as if an undue pressure were being exerted within his mind. Datu had stayed still the entire time, safe in the knowledge that if he attempted to remove Arun's weapon, he'd have found himself with a gaping hole where his new prosthetics had been implanted.

He wasn't suicidal, just accepting of his fate. If, however, an opportunity to escape this situation arose, he would pounce on it in an instant. So, far, that eventuality had not presented itself.

A fine mist buffeted the landing pad, and as soon as Datu stepped out of the vehicle, he was covered in pearled water droplets. He let them cover his face, turning it upwards to better absorb their cooling freshness, his rebreather be damned. A few drops of water wouldn't give him lung-rot. Not that it mattered at this point.

Arun pointed the gun at him, indicating he should enter the warehouse. The long walk down the catwalk gave Datu acrophobia. As if for the first time in his life he realized how high up he was, and how easy it was to fall. Perhaps all he could think of was being shot in the back and dying a slow death as he plummeted to the Heap below. He scoffed at his fears,

You've died before. You'll die again, he thought.

Yui waited for them at the doors, opening them as they approached. She, too, held a nasty-looking blunt-nosed piece, but held it at her side.

"What's the plan?" She asked Arun.

"We're waiting for instructions," he answered.

"I thought we were going to—" she began, before Arun raised his hands.

"Not now. Plans have changed. New orders. Gather them up in the dining room," he said. He pushed Datu ahead into the cavernous loading dock of the warehouse, heading to the metal staircase further to the left.

"Don't say anything out loud," Datu heard the woman's voice in his head say, and for a split-second forgot he'd been trode-connected. He doubted he'd ever get used to that kind of intrusion.

"What do you want?" he responded, before he realized it was Aimee Flores, the AI made to represent the Ayo.

"You have to tell the others. Arun got the order to kill all the workers. I counterfeited the channel and made him believe the order had been suspended. It won't take them long to figure out it was a ruse. Please, you have to do something to stop them!" Her plea sounded genuine, and Datu wondered why an AI would care so much. This was the second time she'd intervened, and he found it quite out of the ordinary. His experience with AI was, he had to admit, was severely limited.

That would explain the conversation Arun had been having half out loud. Datu didn't think Arun had even been aware of the fact he'd been mumbling to himself. If the AI had been spoofing the communication channel, she might have bypassed sub-auditory without his knowledge. At least, that's what he thought was happening.

How long did they all have until Midori Mamoru took control again and gave the order to off them? His pulse pounded as they went up the stairs, heading toward the dining room. To allay suspicions, Arun and Yui had re-holstered their weapons. It would have looked odd if they'd held Datu at gunpoint. The button that held them in place, however, was not re-attached.

Reza went from room to room, getting the men up and ready. There was an aura of confusion floating as they came to the realization that it was the middle of the night, and they were directed to the dining room, and not, as was the habit, the shower room.

"Gentlemen. Your attention, please!" Arun said, raising his hands as soon as all the remaining workers had taken their seats. Datu looked left and right, trying to find his opportunity to warn the others without being cut down by gunfire in the next few seconds.

"We've been given a new assignment by Midori Mamoru. We're waiting for further instructions, and it shouldn't be long. Please indulge us for a few minutes while we await the order," he said, smiling. Datu saw hyena through that smile—the same they wore before they tore out your throat with a giggle.

He had no way of transmitting what was to come to the others through the low voices of the other workers. Arun was staring directly at him, or at least he felt he was, and if he had any inkling that Datu knew, he'd have no qualm of shooting him where he sat. It was coming, it was only a matter of time.

Why didn't Aimee warn the others the way she'd warned him? Wouldn't that have been the easiest solution? Was he the only person she communicated to in this way?

Datu began to fidget, drumming his fingers on the table. Phong turned to him. Vasyklo was ignoring him, and Boon-Me was staring at the trio at the door. Datu pinched his lips, shaking his head. *What a time to be paralyzed with fear,* he thought. Tell him, and they might all be killed. Do nothing, and they would most certainly be killed. Die with the knowledge or die ignorant.

Datu began to write with his finger on the table, the sweat from his index leaving a faint outline on the beige top.

They will kill us soon

Phong stared at the words on the table, as if they stopped computing as soon as they hit his cortex. Datu looked up to see that his face had turned ashen. Phong raised an eyebrow, as if saying, "Is it true?" Datu looked him dead in the eyes and nodded gravely, sick to his stomach. Phong touched Vasyklo's hand, who then directed his attention to the slowly evaporating words on the table. His eyes went wide, and he clenched his teeth, swearing mildly under his breath.

Vasyklo then lightly tapped Boon-Me with his foot, who turned around to see what he wanted. The words had gone, however, and all he saw was a clear table. Vasyklo ducked down and put his thumb across his jugular. Boon-Me hunched his shoulders, in a "What do you mean?" gesture, but before Vasyklo could answer, Arun noticed his pantomime.

Like children passing notes in the classroom and being caught by the teacher, he came closer to investigate the culprits. The room sensed his tension, and the decibels dropped as Arun strode forward, as if anticipation had silenced all assembled.

"What are you talking about, you four?" he said, his hand wandering near his holster, fingering it, but never resting on it.

"Our health, sir," Phong said, smiling. Arun looked down on him, a sour expression on his face.

"I'm sure you are," he said. "Now's not the time. Keep those discussions for later, will you?"

Datu could see a hint of nervousness in the way the man stood, on the cusp, but holding off for orders.

"Come on Arun, leave him alone. He didn't mean anything by it," Vasyklo said, leaning back and grinning.

"Midori Mamoru broke my encryption! The order is coming in!" Aimee's voice said inside Datu's head. He looked up to see Arun touching his index to his head, his eyes closed for a moment. When he opened them, they were no longer living things.

"Everybody duck!" Datu yelled, and he pulled Phong's chair leg with his foot, sending the man teetering overboard on his back. As he fell to the floor, Datu got up, pushed forward and flipped the table onto Arun, who'd been reaching for his gun. Arun hit the table with the back of his arm, but went reeling backward toward the doors to the cafeteria, as Phong looked up in dazed surprise.

Panic spread throughout the room as Yui and Reza reached for their weapons. It only took a few moments for the assembled men to see their coming demise, and decide on their courses of action. Tables were overturned, blocking a few direct shots by the trio.

While some cowered behind tables, others threw chairs at their would-be assassins, pushing them back even further to the entrance. The shots became erratic, the thrown debris jolting them off-balance.

"What do we do now?" Boon-Me asked, peeking over a table. Soon there would be no more projectiles to lob, and the shooting would start again. This time, none of them would be able to stop their executions.

Datu looked around him. He could see at least five men bleeding or dead from where he was crouching. He forced himself to ignore the groans of the wounded to concentrate on his and his friends' survival. The others scrambled to find objects large enough to toss at their now ex-bosses.

"Charge them!" Datu screamed, and he picked up a side of the table. Vasyklo got up and grabbed the other side, taking the chair legs and ducking low enough to avoid becoming a casualty. Seeing them, others began to pick up their tables, and soon there were five tables being carried as both shields and battering rams, rushing at the armed trio.

Shots went through the tables, and Datu saw one man's leg disintegrate as it was hit by an energy weapon. Before they could reach them, though, the trio had fled through the cafeteria doors.

"The warehouse isn't safe. You'll have to get everyone outside, Salazar," The voice inside Datu's head said. Datu looked around himself. There were ten bodies on the ground, pools of blood slowly forming around them. Those that had been lucky enough to be hit by the energy weapon had cauterized wounds to contend with. A few of those, however, had been fatal.

Datu saw Phong lying on the ground and went to him. He turned him over to see a black patch on his beige uniform, a few inches below his heart.

Phong clenched Datu's hand, his face a tense mask of pain.

"That bitch shot me, Datu!" Phong said. He kept trying to touch the wound, but Datu held his hand away. The hole cut deep. If it hadn't been for the table, it would have gone all the way through. Phong's internal organs had suffered massive damage, Datu knew. He'd once seen something similar when one of the Sector 14 guards had opened fire on a mentally ill homeless man when he'd gotten too close to their border post.

He'd watched the man curl up in pain, much like Phong was doing now, his insides a crispy black mess. He'd writhed a few minutes, then, been still. In this moment, he was both here and there, the horror multiplied.

"I'm sorry Phong," Datu said, holding his friend's hands. Tears flowed from the corners of the man's eyes, and Datu could feel some kind of breaking point inside himself. A deep sadness coalesced within his soul, now that the moment of danger had subsided.

"It's okay… it's okay. I was dead already, anyway," Phong said, smiling, closing his eyes. His body went still, and all the tension which had kept him holding on evaporated. Datu wept.

"Let's get those bastards!" Vasyklo yelled, and those who were able to, rose to their feet. A few stayed behind with the wounded, but there were still at least twenty-five able-bodied men raring for a fight.

Datu carefully approached the cafeteria door, casting a sidelong glance through the tempered glass. It would be the height of stupidity to rush out now, down the bare corridor, if their killers waited to take them down one after the other.

"Aimee!" he thought. "Are you there?"

"Yes, Datu, I am. What can I do to help?" the woman's voice responded. Datu sat down again, his back to the wall by the door.

"Where are Arun, Reza, and Yui?" he asked. He held back the other men from rushing through the door, giving them the universal signal for "give me a minute," by lifting his index finger.

"They are heading toward their vehicles at the moment, in the parking garage behind the warehouse," Aimee said.

"Thanks!" He mentally yelled, then gave the signal for the others to go after them. He rose to his feet and went to Arun's office, punching down the door. It flew across the small space to hit the back wall. Datu searched the drawers until he found a gun, and was about to walk out when he noticed the multiple camera views of the warehouse on the computer screen.

On the bottom square, he could see the three entering the parkade and heading toward their respective cars. Datu entered the system, which had been left vulnerable, and found the security systems for the whole complex. A list of all doors and apertures led him to garage doors, and he pressed the green "unlocked" button on the screen, watching it turn red and marked "locked" with satisfaction.

That'll keep them busy, he thought.

He rushed downstairs, gun in hand, and saw that the others had all gone and dressed in recyclers' armoured suits in the vestibule. A few of them carried cutting lasers which had been left behind by the Companions before they'd gone down to the factory on the Heap.

"Where are they?" Vasyklo roared, as they ran to the various rooms of the large complex.

"Parking garage, first level!" Datu yelled, and he too went to equip himself with a suit. When they arrived at the garage entrance, a phalanx of automated mini-tank robots greeted them with machine-gun fire, riding out of metal transport containers. The front row would come out low, while those exiting afterwards raised themselves a few inches higher on flexible treads.

In all, there were eight of the little menaces, arranging themselves in an arc near the door. The metal door was pierced with slugs, and three of the defenders fallen to the ground. Datu picked up one of the dropped laser cutters, staying below the tank bots' line-of-sight.

"Aimee, can you stop them?" He called internally. The answer was swift.

"I'm sorry, Datu. They're doubly encrypted battle tanks with autonomous AI. It would take me years to crack their pass-codes," she said, a note of sadness in her voice.

"Just great," he thought

"How do you work this thing?" he asked on his communicator, and Boon-Me showed him the power switch and trigger. Meanwhile, Arun was trying to manually unlock the door from the control box to its right, without success. The grate stayed stubbornly shut, anchored to the floor. Yui and Reza had taken defensive positions behind their cars, guns poised to fire on anyone brave enough to come through the door.

Datu lay down on his back in the corridor, pointing the laser to his right, then squeezed the trigger, sweeping as far left as he could before the beam extinguished. The piercing orange light penetrated the cement wall, gashed through the metal doors in a horizontal line and struck three of the tank bots square on before it fizzled out. The cloying smell of hot cinderblocks filled the air.

The damaged bots shorted, chunks of molten metal dribbling to the ground and pooling around their treads.

He rolled out of the way as the others returned fire, the bottom half of the doors swinging inward toward him and falling off their hinges. The acrid smell of gun powder spread as the automated bots unloaded into the room where the workers held their ground.

The remaining bots began to roll forward, conserving ammo until they detected movement.

Arun managed to unlock the gate, and Datu saw out of the corner of the open door that it was beginning to rise at a steady pace. He pulled his head back before small-calibre fire could hit him, the bullets slamming into the cinder-block wall behind him.

Datu pointed the laser where he thought the remaining bots might be and pulled the trigger. All he got was a grave tone, and he turned the laser on its side to see if he hadn't shut it off by accident.

"It's recharging!" Boon-Me said from the other side of the room. One of the other men attempted firing the laser he carried, but missed all but one of the tank bots, destroying a garage support beam in the process.

As the tank bots advanced, the sliced pillar began to slip, the floor above it caving. The men backed away from the garage entrance as several tons of concrete fell on top of the four remaining bots.

Dust and debris flew everywhere, and Datu turned on the side-mounted flood lights on his suit before going into the parking garage. He had no idea if Arun and his henchwomen had escaped, but he assumed that if the gate had opened, they would have taken the first opportunity to do so. He ditched the laser and retrieved the gun he'd been carrying, holding it in front of him, pointed in the general direction of the exit.

As the smoke cleared, he could see the sky lighting up with the red and blue lights of TPD descending from the upper levels. He lowered his gun, glad things were taking a turn for the better.

"Hands up, Salazar!" came an angry voice from his left. Arun came out of the dust-cloud, his gun trained on Datu's head. He noticed the gate had stalled, and all three cars were blocked from exiting the parkade. It appeared Yui had tried to force her way through, and the top half of her car had been raked like an accordion half-way to the back.

"I should have killed you where I found you, you ungrateful bastard," he said, taking a few steps forward. "I guess I'll fix that mistake now.

"Do it, Arun!" Reza yelled, her vehicle wedged between the wall and Yui's car.

Datu raised his hands in the air, the bulky suit making it difficult.

"But then you wouldn't have been able to use me, Arun. Don't you think they'll get rid of you, too?" Datu said, turning his head toward his would-be assassin. There was a pause.

"They *need* me. You're just a recycler: unskilled labour to be chewed up and spat out, Salazar. Don't you dare compare yourself to me." Arun appeared to have forgotten to shoot Datu, and was now more interested in proving a point.

"Yeah, just a recycler. Sure did mess up your shitty plans, though, didn't I? Besides, you said it yourself, Arun, you came from the same place as I did. You'll be dispatched just like me when they're done with you. Might not be today, but your time will come soon enough. Killing me won't change that fact," Datu said, staring the man in the eye. He was done tip-toeing around the issues, just to avoid a fight.

"You're wrong. I'm going to the stars! They promised *me*, you worthless shill! Forget Vertical Tokyo! I'm going to the colonies. You have no idea what they're capable of, and you never will. Goodbye, Datu Salazar, you giant pain-in-the-ass," Arun said, and a resounding 'bang' reverberated throughout the parkade.

Datu had cringed at the sound, but he now opened his eyes, to see Arun holding his neck, his gun fallen by his side, a trickle of blood flowed from the wound. Shocked, he looked around the parkade. *How had this happened?*

Reza lowered her window, started firing on Datu through Yui's car window, shattering it. The bullets hit him in the suit padding, and he dropped to the ground. She turned to the parkade ramp, firing at an approaching figure, who returned fire through her windshield. When the crackle of gunshots turned into the spider-webs of hits to her window, she put down her gun and put her car in reverse, ducking down to avoid getting shot.

Wheels spun to no avail, her stuck car remaining where it was, as she attempted to back away from the incoming bullet-fire. The smell of acrid tire-smoke filled the parkade, the screech of the car rubbing against the one next to it and a concrete wall, a dissonant cacophony.

A black-haired woman came down the ramp, heading toward Reza's car, and she put her arm out of her vehicle to shoot the newcomer, only to be cut down by the trench-coated interloper instead.

Colourful lights outside flashed across the thick concrete dust filling the parkade.

"Put the gun down!" the woman yelled.

Police hovercars now filled the exit platform, blocking the path of any outgoing vehicles.

Datu was surrounded by officers with their guns drawn, yelling, "Put your gun on the ground!"

It was like waking out of a nightmare.

He remembered he was armed, and let go of his weapon, falling to his knees and putting his hands up. Two officers rushed behind his back and handcuffed him, as the other workers began to walk out of the parkade.

He turned his head to see Arun bleeding out in the dust and concrete, eyes still open on his ashen grey, unmoving face.

The police officers removed his helmet, putting a rebreather on him, and took a picture.

"Dad!" He heard from behind one of the police vehicles. Gabriel came running from between cars and made a beeline for his father, embracing a handcuffed Datu.

Police vans began landing further down the street. Workers began to walk out of the parkade, their hands in the air, to be apprehended by the police.

"I'll get you out of there, dad!" Gabriel said trying to hold onto his father's sleeve, as Datu was led into one of the blue vans. Datu smiled at his son.

HOMECOMING

S aito found Ito. I'm sorry, Uehara. Nothing he could have done," she'd told the boy. Those words had clung to the air for an indeterminate amount of time, to be replaced by an uncomfortable silence, and the whoosh of passing cars as they rose to The Heights.

They'd arrived just in time to take out the leaders of the Companion-kidnapping ring. As far as Ishikawa knew, there was still one person missing. A woman named Yui, responsible for several murders.

The corpses of previously thought deceased men had been found at the bottom of the pillar where their base of operations had been. Those men they'd captured had pointed the finger at her as being the one responsible. For now, she remained at large.

The rest of them would be taken to Central for processing. They'd also been declared deceased in the past several months, and it would take time to untangle the breadth and depth of the situation.

What do you do with two dozen revenants who'd been actively participating in criminal activities, albeit against their will? There was a conundrum the magistrates would have to pull straight, one thread at a time.

She, for one, was glad not to have to do the straightening.

Eiko625 had gotten in touch with them as soon as they'd been able to return to the 50th level, where interference was less intense.

From what Ishikawa had heard, the Nexus had been destroyed, their factory taken out thanks to Eiko625's quick thinking. There would no longer be fears of haywire Companions, and she planned on taking at least one week leave of absence to process and forget everything which had occurred in the past few days. That is, if she still had a job to return to, Kazue having done a bang-up job of discrediting her abilities to her bosses.

For now, she had to return this sullen boy to his parents.

He sat in silence on the passenger's seat of the borrowed police car, her own a flaming wreck at the bottom of the Heap. Another occasion where she would have to have a little talk with Wen Harkwell about the actions of his employees.

She fully expected the man with the deep pockets to upgrade her ride, if only because of previous favours accomplished for the DaiSin Corporation.

For now, though, she brooded heavily on the loss of Genzo Ito. There would never be an occasion to repay her debt, and that feeling weighed on her soul more than she could bear.

Without having been a friend, he'd never disrespected her, and for that she gave him grudging admiration, even though he wasn't part of the force.

Keiji held his hand to his face, pressed against the cold glass as the car slipped through the airstream corridors of the vertical city.

"I failed," she heard him whisper, then a whimper.

"Nothing to be done, Keiji kun. Maybe one day we'll find out what happened to your boss. For now, at least we can confirm he's deceased."

"Oh, is that supposed to make me feel better, Special Inspector?" the boy said, turning to her, his face wet with tears. Anger and sadness swirling like a black pool inside his breast.

"Sometimes it's better than not knowing, son," she answered, and he cried harder. Eventually, the tears subsided, and he once again took the pose he'd adopted earlier. The chill window against the side of his face cooling his ardour without improving his mood.

"Can you take me to the office, first? Please?" Keiji asked. She turned to look at him, but his eyes were downcast. She programmed the car, and they headed to the nearest elevator, loading in with twenty other vehicles heading to the topmost levels.

A noonday sun pierced through the opening bay doors as they prepared to exit. Ishikawa mentally calculated how long it'd been seen she'd felt their rays on her face, and was surprised by the number she came up with.

They rose into the air, following the avenues, flying between the highrises, heading to Shibuya. Keiji kept his head against the window the whole time, his face turned away from Ishikawa.

She parked at the entrance of the alley, noticing Keiji's glance to the upper reaches of some old offices.

It was empty, of course, and cold. Ishikawa had never visited Ito in his place of work. He'd always managed to find a way to disturb her in hers.

Keiji walked past the front desk, running his finger along its fake wood grain. He pushed open the glass-panelled door to the inner office and stepped inside.

A desk.

A reclining work chair.

The window with its view on the alley.

Ito had always told Keiji that there were no 'bad' areas to have an office in Shibuya. Everywhere was opportunity. Still, Keiji missed the old place in lower Bunkyoku3. The action had been non-stop. Now he simply missed his friend. He would have settled for this office in Shibuya, or no office at all, if it had brought Genzo Ito back.

"We can go now," Keiji said, turning around and smiling at Ishikawa.

"You going to be okay?"

"No, Special Inspector, I am not," Keiji answered, and they walked back to the car.

***

As the car landed near the wrought-iron front gates of the mansion, they were greeted by one of the imitation-clone private security which had unsuccessfully tried to retrieve Keiji previously. Same black suit, same wrap-around AR glasses. The automatic weapons strapped to their backs were a new touch, however, and Ishikawa made a note of how The Heights had its own set of rules when it came to the issue of "self-defence".

The man pressed a button near the gate, and the tall iron spikes retracted into the ground. She brought the car forward, all the way to the double marble staircase, and killed the engine.

"Hey, uh—I just wanted to tell you. You didn't do so bad, kid. I think Ito would have been proud of you," she said, putting her hand on Keiji's shoulder.

"Thanks Inspector. I wish I could return the sentiment," he said, smiling widely, and opened the door.

"Smart-ass," she said, smirking.

"Thank you, Special Inspector Ishikawa," he said, leaning into the car, his face grave, before turning around and walking away.

"Master Uehara. You've returned," one of the guards said, catching up to him.

"I have, Toshiro," he said, walking up the marble steps, his voice emotionless. He turned around once, and saw that Ishikawa had stayed behind just a while longer. He gave her a brief nod and she drove away, going back to flight mode as soon as she was off the private property.

"Your father is very angry with you, sir. He says you are not to leave the house grounds until his return," the man named Toshiro said.

"Oh, and when would that be?"

"One week from now, when he returns from a business trip in Leipzig," Toshiro said.

"Figures. And mother?"

"Still in the Maldives, sir," Toshiro said.

Keiji grunted and shook his head, allowing another of the guards to open the real oak doors for him to the immense, empty Uehara palace.

***

Ishikawa stood in front of her section chief, watching the flecks of white spittle accumulate on the edges of his mouth as he yelled at her. The door might be closed, but she knew that on the other side, there would be twenty people or more standing bemused, listening to every invective hurled at her, at a high-pitched screech.

She would get that vacation after all. A two-week paid leave where she would lay low and stay as far away from the Uehara family as she possibly could. Then she would come back, fresh from her time off, and become partnered with a new recruit, Officer Kazue.

Said Officer now stood next to her in the office, hands behind his back, grinning from ear to ear. Sneaky bastard had found something better than ratting her out to her superiors. He'd gone straight to the source: The Uehara Family.

That explained the goons in Sector 14.

Now her department was getting pressured to take on this scumbag. With all the back-stabbing going on, he'd fit right in, she thought, never once losing her composure.

The idea of having to ride around all day with this loser as a partner, however, made the bile rise in her throat. She gladly took the paid leave. This whole case, topped off with the death of Ito, had shaken her more than she cared to admit. Things had only become apparent after a good night's sleep, to let all the events fall in where they may.

Her mental assessment? Too much in a short time-span. She wondered how the Uehara boy was faring, but like any rich kid with a healthy monthly purse, he'd bounce back in no time. It was weird to think so, but it was her belief that the boy would have made a good cop. Better than the evil shit-stain standing next to her.

The whole reaming-out she was going through at the moment was performative, she knew. When all was said and done, the department still needed competent officers, which she at times counted herself among. Kazue was the kind of man who'd get himself killed within a month if she didn't train him well enough. She sighed.

***

Keiji had found a way to escape the house once again, a mere two days later. The mercs his parents had hired might be pros, but they weren't incredibly well-versed in hacking, and so making them think he was still inside the house as he walked straight past them had been child's play.

It would be another week until his parents physically returned. He might be there, he might not. At this point, he'd stopped caring about what they wanted. There were more important things in life than the family business, which, to be fair, his father had only inherited because he'd changed his name to Uehara.

If it hadn't been for that, some other lucky sod would have won the fortune lottery, and he'd not exist. It was an odd tradition in Japan, to change one's name to uphold a family dynasty, but one which had been in practice for hundreds of years.

There was value in an unbroken family line going back to the founders. He was an only child, and so they'd have trouble finding someone to take over when the time came, because he abhorred the idea of becoming the Chief Executive Officer of Uehara Kogyo.

The thought alone gave him a terrible shiver, as he made his way to Shibuya, to be with the ghost of his only true friend.

When he came to open the office door, however, his heart sank when he saw that the Ito's name had been scratched off. He was being erased, bit-by-bit. Who knew how long the office would be here, now that he no longer occupied it? As he pressed the key against the pad, the light turned red, and Keiji frowned.

That, however, was unusual. As far as he was concerned, it had been paid for for at least another two months. He'd made sure of it.

Just then, he noticed movement behind the frosted glass, and took an involuntary step back. He pressed his ear to the door, but only heard footsteps.

He called the office number and was answered by a woman. Ishikawa.

"Hello, Mr. Uehara. To what do I owe the honour?" she said.

"What are you doing here?" he asked.

"It's my office. I can do whatever I want!" she said.

"Open this door!" he said, giving it a sharp knock. She hung up the phone and opened the office door.

"What do you think you're doing?" he asked, stepping inside. Nothing had changed, save Inspector Ishikawa having invaded the place.

"Well, I was thinking about that whole police inspector thing, and you know, I thought it was time for... something different. I may need an assistant. Do you know anyone who would fit the bill?" she said.

"I—what?" Keiji asked.

"Listen. Ito is gone. You know that, I know that. But I think he provided a good service to the community. He was a good man. I was ordered to partner up with the guy who blackmailed me into getting his new position. I think it was time for a career change," she said, going into Ito's old office.

"No glory in this job," Keiji said.

"Something tells me neither of you did it for the glory. So what do you say, son? Want to help me on my new path?" she asked.

"I think so. Call me Keiji," he said.

"Alright, Keiji."

FAMILY

The DaiSin limousine was the opposite of everything Saito had been through in the past five hours, and he needed it. After having trod in the muck and filth for what felt like an eternity, they'd found a freight elevator to take them back to the 50th level, where the police were ending their mopping-up operation of the warehouse that had been Midori Mamoru's headquarters.

By the time they arrived, Special Inspector Ishikawa and the young man named Keiji had already departed. He'd messaged her to tell her about what had happened to Ito, with his deepest condolences. He hadn't mentioned the fact that the man had melted before his eyes. That might not have gone over so well with either of them.

He'd handed Eiko625 back to the cops and called his own ride, not feeling up for a long series of elevator/train transfers, especially smelling like the wet side of a sewer grate.

Quite a few people had greeted him at the doors of the Needle, not least of which was security, who had had a hard time identifying him through the crust of dirt he wore on his face.

After he'd been able to satisfactorily demonstrate he was who he claimed to be, those in charge of protecting DaiSin had scurried out of olfactory range, his rank smell almost cartoonish in its scope. Saito had had the ability to turn off his smelling ability while still in the Heap, but no one else could, and it showed.

Right now, the thing he looked forward to the most was a shower, and eventually, a bed where he could pass out for a few days. He'd avoided going back to his conapt because of his putrid stench, and now he wondered how he'd get to the shower in his basement office without stinking up the entire building on his way there. He dropped off his glasses on the security desk and walked to the middle of the atrium.

"Hey! You! What's your name?" He called out to one of the young-looking security guards which had retreated, but not far enough to be out of hearing range.

"Yoshi, sir," he responded.

"Go get the emergency water hose against the wall, will you, Yoshi?"

Without truly understanding, the man did as he was told, rolling out the length of hose needed to reach Saito, without getting so close as to have to take the teensiest whiff.

"Let 'er rip," he said, putting up his arms. Other employees looked on in amusement, then horror as they came within smelling distance.

"I'm sorry? Sir?" Yoshi answered, the hose in his hand.

"Spray me down. Please. I need it. Badly," Saito said. The security guard looked confused. He glanced back at his superior, who gave him a nod. The young man shrugged and turned on the hose, unleashing a powerful jet of water on Saito, who began to rub his arms and legs as it slammed into him. The brown runoff spilled across the immaculate marble floor of the DaiSin lobby, but already, the smell was diminishing in his general vicinity.

A few minutes later, he gave the signal for Yoshi to stop dousing him, and he stood there, sopping wet, but no longer imbued with a stench that could have killed flies.

He walked back to the desk, picked up his glasses and slipped them back on, before heading to the elevator, with a squelching sound in his step.

There was something important to do now, and he headed down to his office, saying hello to the children as he did so. They laughed and asked if he'd fallen into a pool, and he couldn't help but embellish the story until they thought he'd gone swimming in the ocean with the sharks.

The eldest would know he was kidding, since there were no more sharks in the ocean, but might as well let the little ones dream.

He dried himself and changed in his office before heading back to see Samuel Harkwell.

The man was inspecting computer servers when he walked through the sliding door, and nodded gravely to him as he entered.

"Mr. Harkwell," Saito said, nodding his head.

"Saito San," Harkwell replied, coming down a set of stairs.

"I have a bit of a conundrum." He ignored the loudness of the fans, this time, intent on getting to the point.

"What would that be, sir?" Harkwell replied.

"Well, I've thought long and hard, and it would appear we need to talk about where you stand on the security of this company." There was no longer any gentle banter.

"I beg your pardon?" Harkwell answered. He took a few more steps down the staircase, and found himself a metre away from Saito.

"I was led to believe the traitor had been nabbed when we removed it from the HYVE. You planned it that way, didn't you? From the beginning, you've been leading me on." He walked up the short set of stairs that separated them both.

"You're accusing *me*?" Harkwell exclaimed, pointing his index to himself, his anger visible. The coil of wires shook from the back of his head.

"I am. No one else but you would have been able to install the Nexus chip where it was. And when you told me to go to Sector 14, no one else had heard that the Nexus was there. Only you. Seeing as they were doing something to those Companions, I suspect you wanted to get me transformed into whatever they were attempting, as well. Make me one of their pawns, just like you are. I'm going to ask you to unhook yourself from the system, if you please. I don't know why you did it, but I can't allow you to keep on going as you were. Please. Don't make this difficult, Sammy," Saito said, putting up his hands in a gesture of peace.

An immense pain began to course through Saito's body, the chip at the base of his skull the epicentre. It was a heat like no other. Microwaves emanating into his body, frying his systems at a fast boil.

"Shut it down!" he yelled, holding onto his neck.

The lights went out in the room, and the servers blinked to darkness for a moment. Harkwell looked around in surprise, and Saito jumped on him, unlatching the wires planted in his mind. He clamped the ports shut, and the wires snaked back into the ceiling, as if they had a mind of their own.

"What'd you do that for, Saito? Don't you know we're more power-ful than you?" Harkwell said, a wicked look on his face.

"You're not Samuel Harkwell, are you." Saito ventured, sitting on Harkwell's chest.

Harkwell's Companion body gave a flat-palmed hit to Saito's chest, sending him flying into a guardrail. The impact broke his spine in half with a metallic crunch, and it took him a moment to re-orient himself, while Harkwell got up and walked over to him.

Saito twisted himself around, and as Harkwell was about to pick him up by the mid-section, he grabbed him his ankles from his awkward position and pulled them up toward him, sending him crashing to the ground on his back again.

Saito unfolded himself from the guardrail, his spine fusing back together, and he walked over to where Harkwell was in a seated position.

"How long have you been Samuel Harkwell?" he demanded.

"We took him a long time ago. It was only a matter of a routine check-up to swap minds and chips. Too bad you were too stupid to realize," The Nexus said.

"Where is he? Where is Sammy?" Saito demanded.

"He's dead," the entity said, smiling broadly, "He was no longer of any use to us. You cannot stop the Nexus. We—"

Saito strode forward and stomped the Companion's head, obliterating it. It rocked backward, its head slamming into the grating beneath it, flattened.

"I just did," Saito said between gritted teeth. He took a long, shuddering breath, his shoulders slumping as he stared at the dislocated puppet which had once been a human being. He ran a sleeve along his eye, then remembered he did not have the ability to cry, and let out a choked sob before clearing his throat.

He walked to the entrance of the room, regaining his composure as the emergency power turned on. The spotlights in the corners of the room shone a blinding light on the scene, which Saito ignored, wanting to get out as fast as he could.

The systems turned to automatic, the HYVE taking over the building's security. They would do a mediocre job, he knew, but then, that would be miles better than what had been done in the past several years.

Jenna Wolinsky waited for him outside the room, accompanied by five heavily armed DaiSin soldiers.

"How did it go, Mr. Saito?" she asked, before noticing the dark look of dejection on his face.

"Thank you for saving my life, Ms. Wolinsky. I'll try to make sure to do the same for you someday," Saito said, as he kept on walking down the hall.

"What happened in there? When all systems cut out, we lost comms," she asked, walking after Saito.

The man turned around and his features softened.

"I did my job, Ms. Wolinsky. Now if you don't mind, I'd like to retire. I have an in-person report to make, and then I have to disappear for a while. I've had a very long week. Thank you. Seriously."

Saito took the elevator to the 250th, then the next set to the 450th, then the privileged one that led him to the pinnacle of the Needle. He walked out into the white lobby surrounded by glass windows and stepped up to the scanners by the doors.

He placed his hand on the reader and set his chin on the holster while the camera read his eyeballs. The system chimed and he was let into the inner sanctum.

Wen Harkwell lay on a white slab of plastic, in the middle of the room, eyes closed, features relaxed. Saito walked up to him and put a hand on Wen's chest. The man did not budge, but began to deflate, as if he'd only been a shell, now melting down. His body began to swirl as it disintegrated, swarming toward Saito's hand.

As greyish nanobots penetrated Saito's arms, he began to change, growing slightly, his features becoming diffuse.

They morphed into those of Wen Harkwell, CEO of DaiSin. He took off the glasses and placed them on a nearby night-stand made of the same reflective plastic. Saito/Wen lay down on the slab, the rest of the nanobots becoming re-absorbed within his body. A soft energy began to flow from the slab into him, repairing the damages done to the nano machines, both in the Heap, and by that thing which had pretended to be his brother.

If he could have wept, he would have. The urge remained, even if the ability had been extricated.

His only consolation was that now, finally, the Nexus was defeated, both inside and out of the company. He'd discovered a lot more than he'd bargained for about those who ran this corporation, but now that he'd gathered that information, he could use it to his advantage.

Right now, he felt the loneliness of this long charade on his soul.

"Hi Jenna," he sent as a mental message to his love.

"Wen, is that you?" she replied.

"Yeah... it's been a while, sorry. Care to join me for dinner?"

"You ignore me for months on end, and now you want to have dinner?" she replied. Wen heard the edge of anger and exasperation in her voice, and knew it was justified.

"I understand if you're mad. I'm sorry. I won't call again," he said.

"Hey, I didn't say that. But I get to choose the place, and I deserve a full report on what you've been up to!" she said.

Wen rose from his resting position and put his hands behind himself on the slab, leaning back. He half-smiled.

"Deal. Say 7:30 tonight?"

"Eight. You better have a good story to tell me," she said.

"I'm sure I'll think of something," he answered. He turned off his comms and lay back down again, allowing the soothing energy of the slab to regenerate the nanotech which animated his body.

FAMILY IS EVERYTHING

Datu had spent a little less than a week in detention. The cops had tried to toss quite a few charges at them: criminal destruction of property, theft of property, rebellion against the State, the list went on and on. At some point, they'd even tried 'faking their own deaths.'

If it hadn't been for the testimony of one of the most powerful men in Tokyo, he was certain they would have remained in those jail cells for a long time, or perhaps even transferred to the Moon Orbital Prison. That might have been paranoia, of course. Only the worst of the worst were ever sent there.

Wen Harkwell had made one of his rare video appearances and explained what had happened with the wayward AI which had helped run DaiSin once upon a time, showing the judges what was left of it, down in the Heap. The deep crater and the burnt-out hulks of the arachno-bot and the Midori Mamoru skimmer had mollified the magistrates, combined with the testimony of the police officers who'd been present during the drone attack.

It had been easy enough to show that what had happened to the men had been coercion, pure and simple, and that even if they were happy to have been saved from certain death, their lives should have been their own, and not the property of some shell corporation owned by the Nexus.

After that, the charges unravelled, and it was DaiSin which was held responsible for the chaos. Save that the lawyers for the company were able to talk down the magistrates from jail time to a hefty fine, if everything were to be kept under gag order.

Gabriel had been there for the whole proceedings, in the benches, while his father sat in an orange jumpsuit inside a large cage where all the other Midori Mamoru ex-employees were held like a gang of criminals.

Datu didn't remember crying when the charges were dropped, but he must have, as the lead magistrate recited the concerted reasons for their decision to do so.

In retrospect, perhaps they'd been after the bigger fish, and they'd been used as chum to get him to show himself. Wrangling in Wen Harkwell might have made their careers. It might even have elevated them to even higher circles of the Administration. They should have known that a man with one of the best legal teams in the world would not let himself get taken down without his own consent. They'd therefore contented themselves with his money.

It had been the cheering in the courtroom that woke Datu out of his reverie, and the realization that much of it came from his own son which had made his heart explode with joy.

The release of prisoners had been swift, afterwards. He'd said goodbye to the men with whom he'd spent little time, but much intense stress and danger, as if they'd been war buddies he might never see again.

To be honest, he wasn't sure he wanted a reminder of the events which had transpired in the past months. He was happy to have regained a son, and if he could find the rest of his family, all his wishes might be fulfilled.

He never heard again from Aimee Flores, the AI living inside the warehouse—what he knew as the Ayo. After the arrests, there was radio silence, as if she, too, had escaped. What could he have told her, anyhow?

He and Gabriel had spent the next three weeks searching for Tala and the kids, with little luck.

One of the positive outcomes of the whole court proceedings was that Wen Harkwell's attorneys had not only had them forgiven of any and all wrongdoings, but they were now able to leave and re-enter Sector 14 at will. They'd successfully proven that he and the others had actually *helped* Tokyo by stopping the likes of Arun, Yui and Reza, and by extension, the Nexus. For that, they were now free.

It was a grudging kind of admission that the magistrates had accepted after much deliberation, the blow softened, of course, by that lump-sum of undisclosed credits which had been settled upon by

DaiSin's attorneys.

He and Gabriel found a small conapt on the edge of Sector 14, on the Narashino City side. Chiba was almost entirely industrial, and the upper levels were overpriced. This was a 20th floor studio with one room overlooking a forest of identical grey towers, but Datu thought it would be temporary.

Gabriel had found a job at another security company, watching over lottery ticket booths. Datu spent most of his days looking for or following leads on Tala and the children. His nights were spent washing dishes at a small diner down the main street from where they lived, called the "Laughing Daimio."

They spent mornings sleeping, days in front of the kotatsu playing 'koi-koi,' and evenings working. Free time was spent in research, attempting to hunt down the removable conapt which Midori Mamoru had had stolen and hopefully re-installed in some lost corner of Tokyo, away from prying eyes.

A few neighbours had seen the removal, and before that, a trio whose description closely matched that of Arun, Yui, and Reza walking Datu's wife and kids from the house. They'd looked inconsolable, the neighbours had said.

The witnesses had done what most people do in these situations: drawn the drapes and waited for it to be over.

The company which had removed the conapt from the block was unregistered, or at least, unmarked, which made things difficult, to say the least.

Most people on this level being leery of net connections, Datu had had to resort to cold-calling most moving companies in Tokyo. Needless to say, there were a lot of those.

The thing he enjoyed the most, during this trying time, the thing that kept him going, was getting to know his son. Gabriel had become a man overnight, while Datu had been preoccupied by what life was hurling at him. They'd both sit at the low table after their night shifts, 2 am mealtimes of dehydrated ramen sprinkled with vegetable supplements, discussing, strategizing, hoping... and learning about one another.

Datu realized that his son really did have his great-grandmother's blood running through his veins. He wanted to leave the lower levels. Get a job doing something, anything, maybe on the 250th, or who knew, maybe the 350th, and why not shoot for the stars? In Ginza!

Datu would listen in rapt silence, not interrupting when his son spoke of his dreams, only taking it all in. Perhaps slipping in a word of encouragement once in a while.

"Why do you believe in the Ayo?" his son had asked him, once, when they'd finished the last of their noodles and were leaning back on their hands on the floor cushions.

Datu hadn't thought about Ayo in several weeks now.

"That's a tough question you ask me, Gabe. I believe in what the Ayo stands for: truth, kindness, love, hope… but I don't think I believe in Her as I once did," he answered.

"How so, dad?" Gabe asked, leaning forward, frowning.

"I think—I think the 'Return Home' part was simply looking back. Hoping for something that no longer exists. I think you were right about that. I think you can believe in all those good things, but perceive a better future. A future you have to shape," he answered.

"Like grandma Diwata," Gabriel stated, and Datu tilted his head to the left and right, considering, then finally conceding.

"I guess if all other avenues have been explored, yes, like grandma Diwata," he said, after having taken a careful sip of steaming ocha.

Gabriel nodded once, firmly.

Datu considered telling his son that he'd met the Ayo, the real one, but that would not have changed the narrative. It was only one of the cogs in his personal growth, and so he kept it to himself.

The mornings had followed the nights, which had turned into afternoons, continuing a cycle that began to look more and more like a fruitless endeavour. Rise, eat, search, work, eat, sleep, but all with the knowledge that they were together now, and that they could face difficult times and difficult tasks as extensions of each other.

That is, until they received an anonymous tip that had led them to Chuo's 150.

One of the moving companies' employees had called back after Gabriel's attempts to find his mother had ended in another dead end. Apparently, certain truckers would freelance, and this person had gotten wind of one such move which had resulted in a tripled pay.

Datu's heart had skipped wildly when he saw the conapt block frame, the same type as the one they'd previously lived in, save that this one had each slot filled with a home.

Datu had felt his palms moisten as the elevator rose to the thirty-fourth floor, where they'd eagerly rang the doorbell.

A dishevelled, sad woman with dark circles under her eyes had answered the door. It wasn't until they'd widened in shock that Datu had recognized his Tala.

He'd thrown his arms around her, and soon the children had joined in the embrace. She'd lost so much weight, he felt as if he held a skeleton, and he loosened his hug to avoid harming her.

Datu remembered having felt all his anguish fly from his body at that moment, along with the tears of joy. As if everything he'd gone through had only been a vague nightmare, and this was the wakeup he'd been waiting for.

They'd held each other for what felt like days.

They were all living in that Chuo Ward conapt now. Both Gabriel and Datu had quit their jobs and found new ones closer to home.

It turned out that Midori Mamoru had convinced Tala, Benilda, and Ramil that Datu had died, posing as Peoplift employees. They'd offered her severance right then and there, and the chance to move to a better area of the city. Gabriel no longer came to the house at the time, and so she'd thought she'd lost him, as well. In her torment and grief, she'd accepted the offer and a mover had hovered in less than an hour later.

She'd regretted that decision ever since, but with no way of getting back into Sector 14 without recriminations, she had remained in her new situation with all the sadness and loss it entailed. A stipend had been deposited every week, until three weeks ago. It had simply— stopped. Until then, the grief had been bearable, if excruciating. Things had spiralled since then.

Now it was over.

Her own nightmare had ended.

Her family was whole again. Datu would smile and choke up a little every time he looked on the faces of those he loved. It was true what they said, you never knew what you had until it was gone. He wanted to add to that though, you should always remember how lucky you are if you ever get it back.

He knew that it had been his holding onto hope which had saved him from despair and giving up. He realized that it had been love that had insisted he keep taking the next step. Even, maybe, what had pushed Aimee Flores to help him in his time of need. Perhaps that's what the Ayo was. Just a good person everyone had collectively decided to deify. Maybe she deserved it. Or maybe she was simply an example to decent people who wanted to be better.

Whatever the reason, he was glad she'd come through his life, and made him realize what he had.

It was only a few weeks after that, that the doorbell to the conapt rang.

"Are you expecting anyone?" Tala said from the living room where she was watching a show with Benilda and Ramil.

"No," Datu answered from the kitchen, where he and Gabriel were making lunch. This conapt complex was equipped with a camera system, and the boxes weren't open to the elements, as their previous home had.

On his screen, Datu saw a dour-looking Companion in a black trench-coat and hat. A cold chill ran up his spine.

"Can I help you?" he said to the screen by his side, as he gripped the long-handled knife a little tighter.

"Mr. Salazar? I'm a representative of the Central Administration. May I have a moment of your time?" the Companion said looking up into the camera. He held up an ID palm, which Datu's scanner responded to with a cheerful chirp.

Datu looked over at Gabriel, who shrugged.

"Come in," he finally said, putting down the knife on the counter. He went to the door and unlocked it, allowing the Companion into his home.

"Thank you," he said, bowing.

"What's this about?" Gabriel asked, stepping in front of his father, putting down a washcloth on the kitchen table.

"You are well aware, of course, of the events that took place in Sector 14 a little over a month ago. What you may not know is that a position was made vacant at the Administration Equipment Depot. A position that the Administration would like to offer you, Mr. Salazar."

"That's suspiciously generous of Administration," Gabriel said wryly.

"Do not take it for generosity, young man. The position is one requiring honesty. Something the previous handler was lacking in. That has been dealt with. Administration requires someone who knows the workings of Sector 14, but whose character isn't as—"

"Crooked?" Gabriel interrupted.

"I was going to say 'wavering,' but we can use your term if you want," the Companion said. Datu stared at him for a while. It would be a good, steady job.

"No one wants it, do they," he finally said. It was not a question.

"Whether other candidates have accepted the offer is irrelevant, Mr. Salazar," the Companions said.

"Except that's not true, is it, Mr Administration. I know Sector 14. No one wants the job, because no one wants to be seen as a stooge for Admin. I'll make you a counter-offer. Two things. One: Administration allows me to use the machinery and equipment as I see fit within the confines of Sector 14. Two, Administration allows me to hire the amount of people I require to do this job, and pay them for it. Then, I will take the job," Datu said, crossing his arms.

"Dad, what are you doing?" Gabriel said, agitated at the thought of having to return to the hell-hole he'd worked so hard to leave. Datu merely lifted his index, and Gabriel bit his lip.

The Companion looked as if he'd gone offline, but Datu knew that he was in direct contact with his superiors, somewhere in the Ivory Tower that was Central Admin, downtown Tokyo. The lights playing on his plastic visor told him so.

"Your proposal has been accepted, Mr. Salazar. You are now a lucky new employee of Administration," the Companion said, printing out a copy of the contract, which Datu was beginning to tire of seeing. His experience with contracts had been nothing but a nightmare in the past two months, and this latest one would probably prove to him once and for all that all this legal mumbo-jumbo had been created by some low-tier demon to obfuscate humanity.

Surprisingly, the language was straightforward, and the terms clear. The Companion went through the whole thing with him and explained in concise terms, that which Datu did not fully understand. In the end, he signed the small stack of papers.

After the Companion had left, Gabriel let his father know what he really thought.

"Dad! Are you crazy? Do you really want to take us back to that outdoor prison? Where we can rot and die like the rest of those living there?" Gabriel said, stalking the living room.

"For now," Datu said, a devious look on his face.

"Honey, what are you thinking?" Tala asked, from the sofa.

"Well, I did stipulate I could do whatever I wanted with that building equipment, right?" he said, raising an eyebrow.

"Yes, and?" his son asked, impatience in his voice.

"We don't *have* to keep those walls around Sector 14, now do we?" he said, his smile becoming a beaming grin.

Gabriel looked at his father in disbelief, then started to laugh. Ramil began to dance on the living-room floor, not sure why everyone was so happy, but intent on joining the fun. Benilda got up, took his hands and danced with him.

EPILOGUE

S osuke had never been sent to this section of the Heap before. In truth, going down to any point of the Heap was pretty much the same: it was garbage, in every sense of the word.

As a city worker, he wasn't sure what he was looking for. All his boss had told him was "look for anything suspicious and report." So far, the mountain of tires had appeared quite normal, if enormous and tottering. Every time he stepped on one, it disturbed the standing water contained within, unleashing a torrent of mutant mosquitoes.

He would bat at the swarm and turn on the repellent device for a spell, watching them scatter with a leering grin.

His glowing yellow suit lit up the surrounding darkness like a beacon, but he still kept an eye on his team, similarly equipped and spread out over two kilometres of detritus.

Two-dozen metres away squatted the hulk of some sort of skiff, burnt to a crisp and slowly being reclaimed by a trash dune on the edge of an oily-water-filled crater.

The team he was a part of were poking around the outer edges of the enormous circle with long, metallic probes. None of them knew what they were searching for either, but it had been imperative that they come down to this gods-forsaken corner of the Heap and dig for "something of interest."

He was used to doing the crappy jobs he was given, but coming down to Zero Level was the worst part of his duties. *Give me sewer duty any time,* he thought.

At least in there, there wasn't the discomfort of wearing the bulky armoured suits necessary for this grunt work. Sosuke wondered for the tenth time today why they couldn't simply have sent Companions for this task, but he already knew the answer: people had better object recognition than machines. If there was something amiss, a human could potentially spot it more easily.

Was that a giant mechanical spider resting beside the skiff, he wondered? Couldn't be. Probably some sort of building's scaffolding, crumpled and tossed off the upper levels.

Sosuke walked further from the rest of the crew, poking listlessly into every divot and pock-marked hole until he was around the side of the downed skiff. Its metallic hull was a dull blue, similar to the matte paint they used on Japanese navy ships.

He noticed a gash in the side of the ship, and peered inside, noting the blackened bodies and exposed wiring of Companions which must have piloted the thing before it crashed, trapping their broken bodies inside while it lit up. *No big loss, then,* he thought. Whoever owned this skiff had to have been well-insured, and replacing their Companions would not have been a lot of trouble.

Unlike Sosuke, who was uninsured and had to work overtime to pay for his father's medical expenses. He sighed, turning away from the skiff and beginning to prod the ground again with his pole.

A silvery reflection caught his attention, a few metres away. He pointed his headlamp toward it, and thought it might have shimmered. He felt his heart begin to beat a bit harder as he approached.

No, he'd been wrong. It was only another oily patch on the ground, like so many others. This one had an odd convex shape, but otherwise, it was greasy water, or perhaps watery grease. He would not have been astonished to find out that it was some sort of engine coolant which had leaked out from the skiff.

Everything found its way into the Heap eventually.

He wondered, out of some mild curiosity, how deep the pool was, and poked his metal perch into it.

As soon as the tip of the rod penetrated the surface tension of the pool, it swirled around the pole and appeared to pull it down.

Sosuke jerked it back, his pulse quickening. The oil began to climb the pole, simultaneously sucking it into itself. He gave it a mighty pull, hoping to get it unstuck, but to no avail. The harder he pulled, the further in it sank.

Too late, Sosuke realized he hovered over the pool of oil, and if he didn't do anything to preserve himself, he would be pulled in. He let go of his rod, teetering on the edge of the mercurial pool, his arms swinging wildly to regain his sense of balance.

With abject horror, he saw the pole come back out, thrust between his legs, and knock him on his back, sending him arms whirling into the churning pool.

He screamed as he descended, the oil reaching out for his body, enveloping him, pulling him down. He could feel the pole against his back pushing downward, dragging him further into the muck.

"Sosuke, was that you?" He heard over his radio. He tried to talk, but as his face slapped into the black muck, all lights went out inside his helmet and outside his suit, and all he could hear for a moment was the crackling of his radio, the complete quiet. The silence he found himself in was otherworldly, like finding himself in the deepest of ocean trenches, with darkness as his only companion.

He tried to fight, to turn, to bat his legs, but he felt gripped from all sides, at all points, as if he'd been encased in solid metal. He was sinking, though, that he could feel.

***

The crew prodded where they thought he'd disappeared. His beacon had pointed them to this grease-filled hole, and now they lifted his suit out from within the slimy muck.

As soon as he was out, they saw that he was still alive, when he turned over and sat down, clearing his visor of the black ichor that covered it.

"You alright?" Sosuke's supervisor asked.

"I'm... fine," the man said, wiping oil and slapping it away with the tips of his fingers. "Must have fallen it. What is that stuff?"

"You dumbass! You made us lose half an hour of our time with your bullshit!" another worker chimed in, the anger visible on his face. They wiped the ends of their poles on available garbage and returned on their respective searches.

"I'm sorry," he said, and rose to his feet, his footing unsure, his body covered in goo.

"We're going to have to hose you down before getting into the transport, that's for damn sure," the supervisor said.

"Yes, that's fine," the man said, smiling.

"You sure you're okay?" he asked once again.

"I'll be fine, now," and he walked away, following the other workers returning to the transport which would take them back topside.

As he left, he took one last look at the pool of oil, thinking about the man named Sosuke, trapped at the bottom.

ABOUT THE AUTHOR

Benoit Chartier is an author of sci-fi, fantasy, speculative fiction, short stories, a children's book, a podcast collaboration, and whatever goes through his mind. He likes to spend his days slaving over a hot computer to bring interesting thoughts coated in fiction to his readers. He shares his time between his home country of Canada and that of his spouse: Japan. He is father to three young children.